BIG CHICAS DON'T CRY

BIG CHICAS DON'T CRY

ANNETTE CHAVEZ MACIAS

This is a work of fiction. Names, characters, organizations, places, events, and incidents are either products of the author's imagination or are used fictitiously. Any resemblance to actual persons, living or dead, or actual events is purely coincidental.

Published by Montlake, Seattle

www.apub.com

ISBN-13: 9781542039291
ISBN-10: 1542039290

Cover design by Caroline Teagle Johnson

Printed in the United States of America

For Welita and Grandma Chayo.
Que Dios las bendiga.

Chapter One
ERICA

Fifteen Years Earlier

"I'm running away."

I stopped flipping through the CD cases and glanced over at my cousin Mari.

"Yeah, okay. Don't forget to write." I turned to look at my other cousins, Gracie and Selena, and the three of us rolled our eyes and snickered.

We were sitting in a circle underneath the big lemon tree in our grandparents' backyard, passing around the saltshaker and eating the lemons we'd picked off the ground. The tree's full branches hung low and shaded us from the hot July sun as we looked for something to listen to on our abuelo's old CD player.

Mari sighed loudly and stood up. "I'm serious, you guys," she insisted as she brushed grass off the back of her denim shorts. "I'm going to leave tomorrow, or maybe even tonight."

We ignored her because we knew better. Mari was a mentirosa and a major drama queen. She threatened to run away as often as I called my younger brother a pinche cabrón behind my parents' backs.

And that was a lot.

"Whatever you say, *Ma-ri-sol*," I answered, exaggerating the roll of the *r* in her full name because I knew it irritated her.

"How about Kelly Clarkson?" Gracie asked, oblivious to Mari's death stare.

"Nah. Erica, where's your Green Day?" asked Selena, who had now gone from eating a lemon to rubbing one back and forth across her right knee. She'd already explained to us last week that she'd read in one of her fashion magazines that the acid in lemons lightened up dark skin. She had also started squeezing lemon juice onto her wavy brown hair while lying out in the sun since my tía refused to take her to my mom's salon to get highlights.

Gracie's chubby face scrunched up at her sister. "Selena, you know I don't like them. How about Mariah Carey?"

"My parents are getting a divorce!"

Mari's scream shut us up. This time we all looked up at her. Her greenish eyes brimmed with tears, and her bottom lip trembled. "My mom is moving to Whittier, and I don't want to go with her. So I'm going to run away."

Then she let out the most awful cry and crumpled to the ground. She slapped her hand over her mouth as if to stop the torrent of sobs and gulps that now filled the afternoon air around us. But we could still hear her pain. Feel it even.

Pure sadness made my heart quicken in anxious beats, and my mouth went dry.

Gracie scrambled over to her and cradled her in her arms as she tried to soothe her crying with soft words. Selena went to her, too, and brushed Mari's golden-brown bangs away and gently bent down to kiss her forehead.

The highlights that Selena searched for in the drops of lemon juice came naturally to Mari. She was also blessed with a perfectly flat stomach—the kind Gracie might have had, too, if she didn't eat so much pan dulce. And the big chiches I kept praying would magically appear on my chest one morning had set up shop on Mari's instead.

We all had our reasons to be a little jealous of Mari. But I knew none of us wanted to be her at that moment.

"What happened?" It was all I could think of to say.

Gracie let Mari go so she could sit up and wipe her face. In between hiccups, she told us everything.

Mari's dad had lost his job a few months ago, and that had triggered all sorts of problems between her parents. The fights were always the same—Mari's dad yelled at her mom for spending too much, and her mom yelled at her dad for drinking too much.

"They sat me down last night and told me. My dad is going to move in here with Abuela and Abuelo, and I have to go live with my mom in Whittier—wherever the hell that is!"

All of us had lived in the same city since we were born. I could walk to Mari's apartment if I really wanted to (I never did, but in my defense, I never walked anywhere). And something told me Whittier was a lot farther than that.

"What about the rest of our summer?" Selena cried. "Remember, we were going to make up more dance routines and go see that new road trip movie. Why can't you live here with your dad? That way we'd see you every day like always."

Mari shook her head and started wailing again. "I don't know. I asked my dad if I could live with him, and he just told me I had to go with my mom. Maybe he doesn't want me?"

"There, there," Gracie whispered as she patted Mari on her shoulder. At fourteen, Gracie liked to think she knew better than the rest of us.

She didn't.

"I'm sure your dad wants you to live with him," Gracie soothed. "But you're a girl. You need your mom. Remember how he freaked out when you started your period?"

Even though we were all still very sad, I knew I wasn't the only one smiling at that memory. Tío Ricardo had walked into Mari's room to wake her up for school that morning. But then he ran right out, yelling at Tía Vangie to call 911 because he thought someone had attacked Mari in the middle of the night and left her to bleed to death in her own bed.

A tiny snicker escaped from Selena. But Gracie shot her a look that shut her up fast. She told Mari that everything would go back to normal once her dad started working again. But Mari wasn't convinced.

An amazing idea popped into my head, and I stood up to announce it. "Mari, if you want to run away, then we'll all run away with you," I declared.

Gracie spun her head around to look at me, arching her bushy eyebrows to the sky. "We will?"

"Yep. It's Monday. That means Abuelo is going to take Abuela to the market in a little while. We'll just ask to stay with Welita and sneak out while she's watching her telenovela."

Welita was our abuela's mother. She was seventy-six years old and had lived with our grandparents for as long as I could remember. We called her Welita because it was short for *Abuelita*. I had no idea what her real name was.

That meant she would be the one to tell our parents that we were gone. She might even cry. Shame and sadness washed over me.

Welita was always saying how family was the most important thing in this world. And we were doing this to stay together.

She'll understand. Eventually.

So there, under the lemon tree, we hatched our plan to run away to the beach. I was in charge of picking our favorite CDs while Mari filled up her backpack with lemons and whatever else she could find in our abuela's pantry. Gracie took the bus schedule from Welita's dresser and said she would figure out the best route to the beach. Selena pulled down all the sheets and towels that had been drying on the backyard clothesline and stuffed them into a trash bag. Between the four of us, we had almost twenty-five dollars.

We were about three blocks away when Gracie stopped in her tracks. "Selena, who's going to feed Gidget?"

Selena didn't even look at her sister and kept on walking. "Mom, I guess? They're not going to let the cat die just because you're not there to take care of her."

"And what about Joanna's pool party on Saturday?" Gracie continued. "She's your best friend. Don't you think you should call her and let her know you're not going to be there?"

That made Selena stop. She told us we needed to go back so she could call Joanna.

We stood there arguing for a good ten minutes about it before Mari finally threw up her hands. "Forget it! Just forget it! You three go back, and I'll go by myself."

Mari spun on her heel and marched away. I had to stop her before it was too late.

"Wait, Mari. I'll still go with you!" I yelled. Mari turned and ran back and practically tackled me with a big hug.

"Mari, if you still want to go to the beach, then we'll all go with you," Selena interrupted. "But I think maybe you should wait a few days, or even a few weeks, and see what happens. Like Gracie said, you never know—they could still work things out."

It took a little more convincing, but Mari eventually agreed to stay. We turned around and walked hand in hand back toward our grandparents' house. But once we turned the corner onto their street, we froze.

There, standing on the sidewalk, was Welita. She wore a gray sweatshirt over her flowered housecoat and brown chanclas. And ay caray, did she look pinche mad.

By the time she'd corralled us into the kitchen, I thought she looked less mad and more relieved. But she was mumbling in Spanish, and I couldn't make out if she was saying that she was going to spank us or feed us. Turned out it was neither. Instead, she asked us in Spanish where we had gone, and—"¡Madre de Dios!"—why had we taken all her sheets and towels?

Since I was the only one who knew enough Spanish to answer her, I explained it all. Then I translated what Welita said back to everyone else. She knew about the divorce, but running away wasn't the answer.

"Pero, we'll never see her again," I cried in my usual Spanglish.

"No llores. Big girls no cry," she told me. When she had to, Welita used the small vocabulary of English she'd learned thanks to '60s American music and '80s sitcoms.

Welita continued.

"She says it's time we learned that family is forever and that won't change," I told my cousins. "But it's going to be up to us to stay close."

Later, when our parents came to take us home, she never said a word about our failed beach adventure. Instead, as we each headed out the door, she kissed us on the forehead and whispered, "Que Dios te bendiga."

It was the blessing she always gave us whenever we would leave her. She once told me it was better than goodbye because she knew that she would see us again soon.

So a few weeks later, when we gathered together underneath the lemon tree, we told Mari, "Que Dios te bendiga." We swore to each other that we would always be close and be a part of each other's lives . . . no matter what. One by one, we took turns etching our initials into the trunk of the tree. And underneath, I carved the letters *BCF*.

"What does that mean?" Gracie asked.

"It stands for Best Cousins Forever," I explained.

"But that's silly," Selena said. "Of course we're going to be cousins forever. We're related. Duh."

I traced the rough lines with my thumb. "I know we'll always be cousins. But this way we'll always remember that we promised to be Best Cousins, okay?"

The other girls nodded, and we crashed into each other for a hug.

How could I know at that moment that the lemon tree and the promise we'd just made would only survive a few more summers?

Chapter Two
ERICA

Present Day

"Who the hell breaks up with his girlfriend two days before Christmas?"

It was a rhetorical question, of course. I knew the answer. They knew the answer. I just asked it because I still couldn't quite believe it.

The answer was my boyfriend . . . scratch that . . . my ex-boyfriend. That was who.

"Ugh. I hate that pinche asshole," I yelled and slapped my steering wheel. Instant pain burned my palm, and I cursed again.

"Maybe you should pull over. It's not safe for you to be driving when you're so, um, ragey," Gracie said through the speaker of my cell phone attached to the dashboard.

"Rage is good. She needs to get it all out now." Selena's voice cut through next. "Besides, angry driving is better than weepy driving. Crying will just give her premature wrinkles, and no one wants that. Right?"

Despite my anger, a smile tugged at my lips. While one cousin worried about my safety, her sister fretted about my appearance. It was classic Gracie and Selena. And it comforted me, like always.

That's why I had texted them 911 as soon as I crawled out of bed about thirty minutes ago. I needed to yell and scream and call Greg all kinds of names—in both English and Spanish. I needed to make some sense of how a man who had told me he loved me could simply walk away after two years together with barely an explanation.

My world had fallen apart last night, and I needed my primas to help me put it back together.

A familiar twinge of sadness pinched my chest. There should've been three voices on the other end of the speaker. But I hadn't even bothered texting Mari this time. Why should I? I was done holding out hope for replies that came days later—if at all.

No, the only cousins I needed to talk to at the moment were the ones on the line.

"I still can't believe he first tried to break up with you over the phone," Selena said, her disgust palpable even through the speaker.

I nodded as I glanced out my window at the passing storefronts. "Right? Only reason he finally came over was because I threatened to sell the video games and clothes he kept at my place. He could barely look at me even then, the pinche cabrón."

"I'm sorry."

The crack in Gracie's voice knotted my own throat. Dear Lord, if she started crying, then I was going to lose it too.

I blinked away the wetness behind my eyes. "Knock it off, chillona. You can't be sorry or sad right now either."

"I just hate seeing you get hurt . . . again."

"Me too," I admitted on a long sigh.

"All right, that's it. No more feely feelings," Selena ordered. "Welcome to the single ladies' club, Erica. You're going to love it here. There's lots of tequila and sex and all-around fabulosity."

"That's not even a word, Selena."

The younger Lopez sister groaned. "God, Gracie. Do you always have to be the teacher? I happen to use that word all the time. You're just irritated because I'm talking about s-e-x again."

"No I'm not. I don't know why you think I'm such a prude."

"Um, because you're almost thirty and still a virgin?"

"I'm not almost thirty, Selena."

"Your birthday is only five months away, Gracie."

Uh-oh. Here we go. I held my breath for what was coming next.

"Just because I don't talk about sex all the time like you do doesn't mean I've never had it," Gracie huffed. "Besides, not all virgins are prudes."

"And you would know this because?"

The sisters bickered more, and the heaviness in my heart lightened. And for the first time that morning, I believed I could get through this day.

"Ya cállate," I said, trying to get them to shut up. "I'm here."

"We just parked behind you," Selena answered.

I glanced in my rearview mirror and watched as my cousins climbed out of Gracie's beat-up Nissan Maxima. Then my swollen and bloodshot eyes came into focus.

Shit. How was I going to explain *those?*

With a heavy sigh, I stepped out of my own car and met Selena on the sidewalk in front of our grandparents' house. I immediately laughed when I saw her full makeup, perfectly curled hair, stylish outfit, and knee-high brown leather boots.

"Selena, it's fucking five thirty in the morning, and we're about to go make tamales, not enjoy a few cocktails," I scoffed before a thought hit me. "Wait, is this what you wore out last night? Have you even been to bed?"

Gracie finally joined us. "She got to the house around one in the morning and then was up at four," she said, then let out a big yawn.

"Four?" I said and shook my head. I couldn't imagine ever getting up that early just to put makeup on. My family was lucky I remembered to brush my teeth before heading out the door.

Selena put her hands on her hips. "Beauty means sacrifice. I keep telling you guys that. I like looking my best, no matter who's going to see me."

I rolled my eyes and was about to say something sarcastic when she unexpectedly pulled me in for a hug and whispered, "You're going to get through this. I promise."

Two more arms wrapped around my shoulders, and Gracie squeezed me tight.

Tears threatened to make my eyes even puffier, so I gently pushed them away and shook my head.

"Thanks, guys. Guess we might as well go inside."

All of us turned to look at the beige-and-brown single-story house behind the white wrought-iron gate. The lawn was neat. The plants and bushes expertly trimmed. I couldn't help smiling at the juxtaposition of such a tidy exterior with the chaos that I knew was waiting for us on the inside.

"Is it too late to spend Christmas in Italy?" Selena groaned as Gracie grabbed her hand and dragged her toward the driveway. I followed behind and pulled the hood of my sweatshirt over my head as far as it would go. Too bad the sun wasn't up yet. Sunglasses would have come in handy right about now.

Gracie pushed open the door of the enclosed outside patio, and a familiar Christmas carol that was way too cheery for five thirty in the morning greeted us. Different conversations bounced around the room. It was chaotic and noisy, and it hurt my ears. And even though it still felt like a vise was squeezing the sides of my skull into my brain, I smiled.

Christmas Eve morning had officially arrived.

As my cousins abandoned me to greet the rest of our family's female members, I snuck into the house. I wasn't ready to receive kisses on the cheeks—or worse, worried looks because of my appearance.

Frankie Valli and the Four Seasons crooned "I Saw Mommy Kissing Santa Claus" from the small CD player on the counter as Welita stood at the stove stirring something in a big silver pot.

"Siéntate, mija," she told me after I stopped to give her a kiss on the cheek. Wafts of cinnamon, chile, and Ponds face cream danced across my nose. Almost immediately, the pain in my head lightened.

After taking a seat, I watched as she pulled bowls from the cupboard and then moved back to the stove. Her long white hair was twisted into its usual thick braid, and she wore a white-and-yellow flowered housecoat with a red Christmas tree apron over it. I knew she'd already been up for hours getting everything ready for the tamales. Even though she was almost ninety-two, she was just as sprightly and active as ever.

Gracie and Selena joined me at the long kitchen table a few minutes later.

"I'm in desperate need of coffee," I said as I reached for one of the empty Christmas mugs arranged next to the coffee carafe in the middle of the table.

"How much did you drink last night anyway?" Gracie asked. She tried to cover it, but her judgy tone came through loud and clear.

I spooned some sugar into my coffee and began to stir. "Let's see. I started with a couple of beers after that very fun phone call with Greg. And then I hit some tequila shots after the ass"—I glanced at my welita, who was grabbing spoons from a drawer—"jerk left. I might have had a few glasses of wine right before going to bed also."

"Jesus, Erica." Selena laughed, but I could feel the judgment from her as well. She was one to raise eyebrows. The woman could put away her liquor with the best of them, and I'd held her hair more times than I could count when her fancy martinis came back with a vengeance.

"Anyway, I'm done with alcohol . . . and men," I said firmly. "This is it. No más."

Gracie rolled her eyes, and Selena chuckled. I was about to call them some not very nice names when Welita placed a bowl of menudo in front of me, bent down, and whispered in my ear, "No más."

A smile formed on my lips. She understood in more ways than one.

Gracie also got a bowl of menudo from her, while Selena was served her usual cereal. She never touched the traditional Mexican soup made with hominy and tripe. In fact, she couldn't even look at it and focused on her cornflakes way too intently.

"Listen, Erica," she said after swallowing her first bite. "I know you're sad right now. But you really have to think of this as an opportunity to focus on yourself. You're twenty-eight. This is when you're supposed to be figuring out who you are and who you want to be. But you can't do that if you always stick to what—or who—is comfortable and safe. Do things you've never done before. Experiment a little. Take charge of your life. Be a . . . um. What's the word you use? Chicharona?"

I almost fell out of my chair. "Are you trying to say *chingona*?" I finally said after laughing so hard.

Gracie hissed, "Shhh. Don't cuss. Welita is right there, remember?"

"It's not a bad word anymore, Gracie," I said. "It's like calling yourself a badass bitch. It's empowering."

"Exactly!" Selena agreed. "Be empowered, Erica. Be the chingona of your own life."

I could always count on Selena for a good pep talk. She was right. I needed to take this time to focus on me and what I wanted to do with my life.

But I wasn't going to figure that out today. At least not before ten a.m.

"Can we change the subject now?" I asked after taking a sip of my menudo. The hot spicy broth instantly warmed my chilled skin and comforted my broken heart.

"Well, I just want to say that you are both going to love what I made you this year," Gracie said with a huge smile. My cousin was the queen of hobbies, which meant our Christmas gifts usually reflected whatever activity she'd taken up that year. Last year we got pretty earrings made with colorful beads. The year before that it was hand-painted ceramic mugs. I knew she was getting pretty good at crocheting and had a feeling that a new scarf or beanie was in my future.

"I don't know how you have the time to make so many gifts every year. I'm just warning you all that I took the easy road and got everyone gift cards," I admitted.

Selena clapped. Shopping was her favorite—and only—hobby. Always had been. Even as a teenager, she was always into the latest styles. The only difference now was that at twenty-seven, Selena could finally afford to feed her addiction.

"I can't wait to give you my gifts too," she added. "Although, now that I'm thinking about it, the vibrator I got for Gracie might get better use for you, Erica, since you're single again."

Gracie spit out the menudo she'd just slurped and began coughing up a storm. From the kitchen, Welita called out to ask if she was okay.

I slapped Gracie on the back and told our great-grandmother in Spanish that a piece of hominy had just gone down the wrong pipe. That satisfied her, and Welita walked out of the kitchen and into the patio, her arms full of boxes of raisins for the sweet tamales.

As soon as the door closed, Gracie reached over and pulled on her sister's ear. "You're awful, Selena. Please tell me you're just joking and that you didn't really buy that," she begged.

Selena threw up her arms. "Of course I am. Oh my God, could you imagine the look on Dad's face if you ever whipped one of those things out?"

That made her roar with laughter, and I couldn't help but join in. Although she fought it for a few more minutes, eventually even Gracie cracked a smile. When the giggles died down, I looked at an empty chair across the table and sighed.

"Anyone know if she's coming this morning?" I asked, then immediately regretted it. I hadn't had enough coffee yet to bring up the sore subject that Mari had become.

Gracie shook her head. "I don't think so."

Selena shrugged hopefully. "Maybe she'll show up tonight for dinner?"

"Yeah, right," I said with a bitter laugh. "I'm sure there's a perfectly good excuse that she'll text us . . . eventually. Shall we take bets now on what it is?"

"Erica . . . ," Gracie warned. But I ignored her.

Starting with the one made under the lemon tree all those years ago, Mari had broken so many promises that I had begun making a list.

"Let's see. Is she flying to Hawaii? Oh no, that was last Easter. I bet she got a last-minute appointment with that Beverly Hills stylist. Nope, wait, that was on Abuela's birthday. Hmm, maybe she pulled a muscle doing yoga and needs to stay off her feet. Oh, wrong again. That was on my fucking twenty-first birthday."

The waves inside my stomach thrashed wildly again at the thought of that memory. I'd never been so pissed and so hurt. We all were—even if Gracie had acted like it hadn't been a big deal. A sour taste invaded my mouth, and it wasn't just because of the hangover. I pushed away the bowl of menudo and my coffee.

"Okay, Erica. You don't have to remind us," said Gracie, in her usual don't-make-a-scene tone. "You're not the only one who's upset about how she's been lately."

"Lately? Lately? Gracie, she's been ditching us—ditching this family—since she was sixteen. I don't understand why everyone is still so afraid to call her out on it. She's not a little girl anymore. Jesus Christ, she's not going to break if someone actually gets upset with her!"

I yelled that last sentence, surprising all of us. Even Gracie, who would normally scold me for the JC comment, seemed shocked into silence.

Our eyes turned to the kitchen door in expectation that someone—our abuela or one of our tías—would come running through it to find out what was going on. When no one came after a few seconds, I let out a big sigh. "I shouldn't have yelled. I'm just on edge. You guys aren't the ones I'm mad at. I'm sorry, mis amores."

They mumbled back that they loved me, too, and went back to eating while I rubbed my stomach. It still wasn't right. Maybe it had to do with the new heaviness in the air. I hated it. This was Christmas Eve. We were all supposed to be jolly, for Christ's sake.

Literally.

"So guess who's coming to LA in January?" Selena teased in an obvious attempt to lighten the mood.

"Adele?" Gracie asked. My cousin was obsessed with Adele. Anytime we mentioned we had big news of any sort, she immediately assumed it had something to do with the singer. I mean, I loved Adele as much as anyone. But there were other things in life to get excited about.

Things like . . .

"Nathan!" I squealed.

Selena smiled, and I could've sworn an unnatural shade of pink colored her cheeks. Nathan Tennant was a professional recruiter from New York. They'd met last year at a conference in Denver and hooked up every time he was in town for client meetings. Unlike me, my cousin believed the only kinds of relationships she needed with men were the ones that came without strings. She'd told me they had a sex-only arrangement, and it worked so well because he happened to live on the other side of the country.

"Yep," she answered. "He's only going to be here for three days, so don't expect me to be around those three nights."

"Don't you ever want more than three days here or a weekend there?" Gracie asked for the millionth time. She still couldn't grasp the concept of a fuck buddy.

Selena rolled her eyes. "No."

"I don't believe you."

"You don't need to believe it," she explained. "I believe it, and that's all that matters."

"But that's the thing, Selena. I don't believe that you believe it."

"Then that's *your* problem."

"Nope. I think it's yours."

They both stared at each other over their coffee cups in a showdown of wills and last words. It was something they'd been doing since we were little girls. Depending on how stubborn one of them was feeling, they could stay like that for several minutes. At least they didn't pull each other's hair anymore while doing it.

"Girls!" my mom barked from the kitchen door, and we all jumped. "What are you doing in here? It's time to get to work. Clean up your dishes, and go wash your hands. Dale! Dale! We're already behind."

The orders were enough to make Selena and Gracie call a truce, and we did as we were told.

A few minutes later, we walked into the patio. It was time to make the tamales.

"Merry Kismas!" a little voice squeaked from below as I felt a tug on my sweats. I looked down, and it was my six-year-old cousin, Araceli. She was still wearing pink fleece pajamas—the kind with the feet—and her light-brown hair was tousled all around her sweet, pudgy face.

"Merry Christmas, baby," I said, managing a half smile.

"I'm not a baby!" Araceli huffed and then stomped off in the other direction.

"Celi, behave!" my tía Espy yelled after her daughter and then came up to me and gave me a kiss on the cheek. "Merry Christ . . . ay, mija, you don't look so good." She stepped closer and studied my face. Her eyes narrowed. "You're not pregnant, are you?" she asked me.

Tía Olivia, Gracie's and Selena's mom, happened to be walking by at that moment carrying a large metal bowl filled with shredded chicken. Hearing the word *pregnant,* she quickly turned back around and stared her sister-in-law down.

"Espy, how many times have we told you—it is *impossible* for you to be pregnant? You just gained a few pounds, that's all."

Last year, Tía Espy was convinced she was pregnant again, even though she had just turned forty-eight years old. Araceli had been her miracle baby, and even after that difficult pregnancy, Espy had wanted to have one more. She refused to believe that the crying jags and ice cream cravings were because of menopause—not a baby. Espy wouldn't even believe her own doctor until he did an ultrasound and showed her an empty uterus. We let her grieve for a couple of days, and then Selena and I showed up at her house with a bottle of tequila and a gallon of mint chocolate chip ice cream and told her to get over it.

My abuela appeared from the kitchen doorway with unopened bags of corn husks. In Spanish, she told Espy that if her cheeks and butt were getting fatter, then she should cut down on the frijoles and guacamole.

"Ay, Mama Garcia, I'm not fat! And I didn't say I was pregnant," Espy yelled. "I asked Erica if she was!"

Chapter Three
SELENA

As soon as she said it, I knew she regretted it. Tía Espy's big brown eyes grew even bigger, and she covered her mouth with her hand.

And Erica's face went white. Which was quite something to see since she was normally darker than Gracie.

Suddenly, everyone in the patio stopped talking. My abuela's mouth opened a little, and the bag of husks dropped to the floor. Erica's mother stood up from behind one of the tables and then quickly fell back into her chair again. Araceli and my other younger cousins continued singing "Rudolph the Red-Nosed Reindeer" with Burl Ives, unaware of the potential scandal unfolding right before them. I heard someone clear her throat, and another whispered, "Ay, Dios mío."

I knew someone had to put a stop to the madness before my teenage cousins announced it on Facebook—or rather "El Chisme Book," as my mother called it.

"Erica's not pregnant!" I finally yelled. "She's just *severely* hungover."

The color returned to my abuela's face as she picked up the bag of husks and walked away muttering in Spanish that "hangovers are God's punishment for drunks." Chattering filled the patio once again as everyone returned to what they were doing before they heard the words

Erica and *pregnant* in the same breath. Tía Espy weakly smiled at my cousin and mouthed, "Sorry."

"Don't worry, Espy, I don't think you're a gordita," I could hear my mom say from the corner of the room. "It's not your fault God gave you too much junk in your trunk."

That made everyone laugh, and the scandal for the day had been discarded as easily as my Louis Vuitton purse from last season.

"Okay, Abuela, I'm ready to count," I announced as I pulled an apron over my head.

"Selena, we haven't even started filling the tamales yet," my mom said as she passed me carrying a stack of plates.

I looked around the patio and put my hands on my hips. "Well, I guess you ladies better get to work then."

A dish towel hit me in the middle of my face, and cackles of laughter followed.

"Seriously, Erica?" I couldn't help but laugh, too, especially when I threw the towel back at my cousin, but it hit Tía Espy's head instead.

"Sorry, Tía," Erica yelled. "But that's what you get for making everyone think I was pregnant."

The chatter continued as everyone took their seats along the tamale assembly line. We'd had the same places for as long as I could remember. As the family grew, more tables and fold-up chairs were added. But the process remained the same.

Abuela and Welita were at the head of one folding table mixing salt and lard into the tamale masa. They used their bare hands and seemed to be the only ones who knew when the consistency was just right. My tías, Mom, and Gracie were responsible for spreading the masa onto the corn husks, softened by overnight soaking.

After getting a layer of masa, the husks were then passed on to Erica, who filled them with a mixture of shredded pork and red chile. Later, she would switch to shredded chicken, green chile, and jack cheese. Then we'd make a dozen of cheese only just for me to take home since I didn't do spicy or chile or salsa. If there was any masa left, Welita would prepare sweet tamales made with raisins, nuts, and pineapple.

My fourteen-year-old sister, Rachel, and two other younger cousins were stationed at another table with me. They wrapped each tamale in a square sheet of white parchment paper, and I arranged them in large silver pots. I also counted the tamales, marking every dozen on a notepad. My abuelo—the only man in the house for the tamale making—then took away the heavy pots to prepare them for steaming on the kitchen stove.

Later that evening, the entire family—tíos, husbands, kids, teenagers—would come back to my grandparents' home to eat the cooked tamales and open presents.

That was our tradition. As much as I whined about getting up before the sun, I really didn't want to be anywhere else.

"Selena, how's your job going?" Erica's mom asked as other conversations took place around us. Tía Marta was married to my tío Luis, the oldest of my abuela's five children, and liked to know everyone's business. As the family's go-to hairdresser, she was used to people spilling their guts while she trimmed and dyed. No wonder Erica ended up becoming a newspaper reporter.

I shrugged. "It's fine. Can't complain, I guess."

Truth was, I had plenty to complain regarding the Umbridge & Umbridge public relations firm, where I'd worked for the past five years. But I didn't feel like talking about the place on my day off.

"She hates her boss," Erica offered, even though no one asked her.

When I shot her a dirty look, she frowned and wrinkled her forehead.

"*Hate* is such a strong word." My mom, the second oldest, joined in. "My girls don't hate people. Right, girls?"

I thought about the last email I'd gotten yesterday from Kat, and my mom was right. *Hate* wasn't the word that came to mind. *Loathe* and *detest* were closer to the truth.

"She's very demanding," I explained since everyone was now looking at me. "Sometimes she's hard to please."

My mom shrugged. "Maybe you just need to work harder? You don't always want to be an assistant, no?"

Familiar annoyance tightened my shoulders. "I'm not *her* assistant, Mom. I'm an assistant account manager. There's a difference. Maybe if you would listen when I talked about my job more instead of worrying about who I'm dating, you'd know that."

There was a definite bite to my voice. I hadn't meant to sound so bitchy. I hadn't meant to replace the lightness of Christmas Eve morning with our usual debate. Guilt sank my heart as I watched my mom's lips form a thin line. I knew I'd pushed a button.

"Greg broke up with me last night," Erica announced.

Gasps broke out across the room, and, just like that, the tension began to dissolve.

I caught my cousin's eye, and she mouthed that she was sorry. Even though she'd started the conversation, it hadn't been her fault for the way it had turned. But I was grateful anyway for her basically throwing herself on her sword.

Because, as expected, the mama bears came out swinging.

I never liked him anyway.

You could do so much better, mija.

I know a very nice doctor I could introduce you to.

Even my mom joined in on the chatter. Meanwhile, poor Erica slumped farther into her seat with every well-meaning piece of advice. I made a note to myself to pull her aside later and check in to see how she was doing.

"What about you, Gracie? Any potential novios?" Tía Marta asked after the Greg bashing had finally come to an end.

"Marta, Gracie is very busy with her job. She doesn't have a lot of time right now to be dating," my mom answered instead.

"Pues, you never know. She could meet some nice man at her job."

Erica shuddered. "Yeah, right. I've met all of the male teachers at St. Christopher's. They're either priests, over sixty-five, or married. Muy gross."

"Well, she doesn't have to date another teacher. I'm sure one or two of her first graders have some cute single dads she could—"

"Marta!"

My abuela's admonishment silenced my tía, and we all tried to stifle our own chuckles. I then noticed Gracie's red face, and my amusement quickly faded. I'm sure she hated that her nonexistent dating life tended to be a topic of conversation when we all got together. I had tried to help by dragging her with me on double dates or to parties where I knew there'd be lots of single men. Once I even made her a profile on a dating website. She was angry about that and said she was perfectly capable of getting dates on her own but just hadn't found anyone worth dating.

My mom had already told me more than once to stop pressing the issue and even commented that perhaps I should follow Gracie's example and be more "selective" when it came to dating.

And that was the day I stopped talking to my mom—or any of the tías—about my love life.

My mind then drifted to Nathan, and the one thing I hadn't told my cousins. The moment I had seen his text that morning, my stomach had done some serious gymnastics. I'd seen him last month for two glorious nights and could usually go at least two more months before I needed another fix. But never had his texts made me feel so . . . giddy. What on earth was that about?

Gracie's words from earlier came back.

Don't you ever want more than three days here or a weekend there?

I hadn't lied. I honestly didn't want more. Because more meant hope. More meant risk. And I couldn't let either of those happen again.

Quickly, I dismissed my reaction to his text as basic lust. He was fantastic in bed, and my body remembered. That was it. I needed to forget about Nathan for today. God forbid I accidentally drop his name in front of my mom or tías. I didn't want to be the target for another Garcia women inquisition.

I loved my family, but I loved them even more in small doses. At least I lived far enough away that sometimes, if I truly needed a break, I could use work or traffic as an excuse not to come home every weekend.

And then it hit me.

Did that make me just like Mari?

Disturbed by the thought, I stood up to stretch. The pace was slowing down, which meant I could take a short break. I pulled my chair next to Erica and Gracie at the other table and checked my phone.

"You know what sucks the most about Mari not coming to Christmas dinner?" Erica asked after a few minutes.

It was totally scary how she knew exactly what I was thinking sometimes.

"What?" I asked and put my phone down, preparing for another Erica rant.

"No buñuelos," she said with defeat.

I smiled.

Mari's homemade fried tortillas sprinkled with sugar and cinnamon were Erica's red-light food—she could never have just one. I scrunched up my nose. "Eh, I never liked them. Too much sugar. And, like, what are those little seeds called again? They have this bitter taste, like black licorice."

"I think they're called anise," Gracie explained from across the table.

"Well, whatever they are, they're gross. You know what we should have instead for dessert tonight? Crème brûlée!"

Erica laughed as she picked up another husk layered with masa. "And where exactly are you going to get crème brûlée on Christmas Eve? Because I know for sure that you are not going to be sifting and mixing later. God, do you even know how to turn on an oven?"

Now Gracie was laughing, too, and I gave them both a very mean look since I couldn't flip them off with my mother and abuela in the same room. It was true that I didn't cook or bake or even use my kitchen that much. But what I lacked in culinary skills I made up for in other useful ways. Ways that would send my sister straight to church to pray for my perverted soul.

In fact, I was just about to tell them that I happened to be very close friends with a sexy baker who owed me a special favor when Erica held up a husk and yelled, "Who's spreading the masa on the wrong side of the leaves again?"

"Espy!" everyone yelled back.

Laughs filled the room, and eventually I went back to counting. Fortunately, there were no more tense conversations for the rest of the morning. Topics ranged from menopause remedies to labor horror stories to who still had Christmas shopping to do. The usual stuff that came up when a group of adult women got together.

And although nobody ever said her name again, I knew I wasn't the only one trying to forget that one of us was missing from the table.

Chapter Four
MARI

"Merry Christmas, cariño," Esteban said as he leaned over to kiss me on the lips. With a weird grin on his face, he then showed me a small white box wrapped with a delicate green ribbon. Although it was already after nine in the morning, we were still lying in bed. I was feeling lazy, and if it were up to me I'd spend my entire Christmas Day right here buried underneath my warm sheets and down comforter.

But it was never up to me.

I sat up and took the box from Esteban and gingerly lifted the lid. It was an exquisite diamond heart pendant on a yellow-gold chain. "It's lovely," I said. "It will match my earrings."

He nodded. "Exactamente. That's why I got them for you," he said. He took it out of the box, and I sat up with my back to him. I lifted my hair so he could put the necklace on me. "You are so beautiful, Marisol, and you deserve beautiful things," he whispered in my ear as his hand slipped under my silk camisole.

"Let's make a baby," he whispered as he kissed my neck.

"Esteban, we already agreed we'd wait until next year."

He stopped kissing me and moved so he could meet my eyes. "Next year is only seven days away. We can start a little early."

"It doesn't work like that. I need to be off my birth control for at least a month. My appointment with the doctor is in a few weeks. I'll find out for sure when we can start trying."

That seemed to satisfy him because he went back to nuzzling my neck.

A drop of guilt needled at me for the lie I had just told him. There was no doctor's appointment. Between my charity commitments and the round of holiday parties I had either hosted or attended, I simply hadn't got around to scheduling one. Not that it mattered. Esteban was going to start a new trial the first week of January. It would be a miracle if I even had dinner with him during the week. I told myself he'd forget about it eventually. Just like he had all the other times.

Honestly, I just wasn't ready. I was only twenty-eight. Couldn't I have at least two more years enjoying my kid-free life?

Esteban rolled on top of me and pushed my panties to the side. My thoughts drifted back to the earrings he had given me last Christmas. I had worn them that day as he had asked me to, but that evening I had put them back in their white box and . . . oh, yes. That's right. I had put them in the bottom of my lingerie drawer. Satisfied that I would be able to find them after all, I closed my eyes and tried to enjoy myself.

God, that sounded so bad.

Of course I was going to enjoy my gorgeous husband being inside me. Especially since it had been days since the last time we'd made love.

Technically it had really been a quickie in the shower. And—technically—we never, uh, finished because his leg cramped up and he had to drop me back on my own two feet in order to massage it with searing hot water.

"Yes. Uh-huh. I'm. Going. To."

Wait, wait, wait for me, I screamed silently.

But it was too late. With one final thrust, I knew I wasn't going to be getting an orgasm for Christmas.

Later, while Esteban showered, I sat on the edge of my California king bed and lazily lifted my right index finger to brush the pendant. It really was lovely. It just wasn't exactly what I was hoping for. As soon as I saw that little box, I knew that there was no way there was the latest iPad stuffed inside it. It wasn't like I hadn't dropped enough hints. Esteban got me what Esteban wanted to get me. And that always meant jewelry.

I should have been grateful, I guess. When I was growing up, how many times had I wished for a man who would shower me with diamonds? Especially when the electricity would get turned off in our small apartment because Daddy hadn't sent a check that month. I decided back then as I tried to do my homework with a flashlight that I would marry a rich man—not someone like my father who would rather spend his money on beer than his family. When I met Esteban, I thought my wish had come true. He was ten years older but as handsome as the movie stars he defended in court, he was ridiculously successful and rich, and he adored me.

Still, I made a mental note to order the iPad myself later. It was my own damn fault for hoping that Esteban would get me something I actually wanted.

I touched the pendant again. It really was a beautiful and thoughtful gift.

Stop being ridiculous and start being happy. It's Christmas.

"Esteban! Your breakfast is getting cold. Please come downstairs, mijo," my suegra yelled from the kitchen downstairs. Blanca Delgado stood at only four feet, eleven inches, but she had a voice that could set off car alarms—especially when she was telling her son what to do. "Esteban!" she screeched again. "It's Christmas, and you need to be spending it with your family. Come downstairs now!"

"He's in the shower!" I yelled back and then collapsed backward onto the bed.

Your family.

Warm, familiar memories of helping Welita get the tamale supplies ready the day before Christmas Eve played like a movie in my head. I watched as the girl I used to be excitedly unwrapped presents in front of a brightly lit tree in Abuela's living room and then stuffed her face with candy canes and See's chocolates. The magic of Christmas waned when I was a teenager, as it usually did for most—even though I had other reasons for not being as impressed with the holiday as before. And even though I had tried hard every year as a wife to re-create that feeling of wonder and joy in my own home, my efforts were always overshadowed once Blanca arrived. Whether it was being personally offended by the height of the tree in the foyer or secretly replacing the animals in my nacimiento display, my suegra always let me know she could do better for Esteban because *she* was his family.

When would that woman finally admit that I was Esteban's family too?

It was an hour later when I finally made my appearance downstairs. I had taken my sweet time to straighten my hair, put on my makeup, and dress in a cream-colored turtleneck sweater, black leggings, and caramel leather riding boots. Esteban and his mother had already eaten without me, of course. So I made myself a cup of coffee, sat down at the breakfast table in the kitchen, and nibbled on one of the buñuelos I had baked the day before.

"I think those are the best you've ever made."

A smile tugged at my lips before I even met the soft brown eyes belonging to the familiar deep voice.

Chris Ramos, my husband's oldest friend and firm partner, stood in the entryway leading to our dining room.

"I guess that means you've already helped yourself to some . . . as usual. It's a wonder that you left any for me."

He laughed and then shrugged. "What can I say? Esteban offered me a cup of coffee after I arrived, and they were just sitting there on the counter. You know I'm no good at saying no to temptation."

Even from a few feet away, I could see the way his smile faltered for the briefest of seconds. My stomach twisted. And although I wasn't quite sure why, I felt guilty about it.

"I'm glad you like them—the buñuelos, I mean. And eat as many as you want. Take some home too. I think I made way too much this year."

"¡Basta! There's no such thing as too many buñuelos. Especially yours." Chris leaned against the doorway and crossed his arms over his chest. His usual three-piece suit was replaced today by a deep-red collared shirt, pullover black sweater, and dark-colored jeans. Jeans that fit so perfectly it was hard not to notice. So hard.

Twist. Knot. Flip.

"Well, I guess we better go join everyone else before they start opening gifts without us," I said and got to my feet.

Ever since Chris's divorce three years ago, he'd joined us on Christmas morning for brunch and presents. Truth be told, I was happier than usual to have him this year. He was a good buffer between me and Blanca. And I desperately needed it after last night. We'd hosted a Christmas Eve dinner for about forty of Esteban's coworkers, clients, and their spouses. Letty, our cook/housekeeper, and I had made all the food and had done all the setup. Blanca, who'd arrived from Sacramento two days ago, didn't lift one finger to help the entire time.

I don't even know why I expected her to. She was used to being waited on hand and foot. The only time she ever cooked was for her precious Esteban.

She adored Chris too. And although she only saw him on Christmas, she considered him like a second son. Which meant she was usually too busy fawning over her two favorite men to worry about what I was doing. Or rather, what I was doing wrong.

As if reading my mind, Chris stopped me just before I walked past him. "Don't worry," he whispered as he squeezed my hand. "I'm not going to let her ruin your Christmas."

Unexpected tears wet my eyes. I laughed them away, embarrassed at how much his words meant to me and how disappointed I was that Esteban hadn't told me the same thing this morning. "Ah, Chris," I whispered back. "We need to find you a wife. You are too good of a man to be all alone."

He smiled softly and then reached out and pushed a strand of my hair behind my ear. "But I'm not alone. I'm here with you . . . and Esteban." He paused, took a deep breath, and said, "Merry Christmas, Marisol."

And before I could stop him, or even decide if I should stop him, Chris leaned down and brushed a light kiss near the corner of my lips. My heart beat wildly as I met his determined eyes. He seemed to search mine for a response, but I didn't dare give away the tumbling routine going on in my gut.

Chris was my friend. He was my husband's *best* friend. He had no right to stir up these kinds of feelings inside me.

So what if I occasionally allowed myself to wonder what would've happened if I'd met Chris first at their firm's dinner party five years ago? And what harm was there in sometimes wishing that Esteban was more thoughtful and more attentive like Chris?

They were just thoughts. Innocent what-ifs. I never expected anything to come from them.

Maybe nothing had.

That's when I remembered. I looked up, and relief washed over me when I saw the spray of green leaves and red berries still hanging from the doorway. I poked Chris in the chest. "You know, it's not really a rule that you *have* to kiss someone under the mistletoe."

If I had expected him to sheepishly laugh or turn red with embarrassment, I would have been wrong. Instead, he shrugged and said matter-of-factly, "What mistletoe?"

He walked away then, leaving me too shaken to move just yet. And even though I knew she was sixty miles away, I could hear Welita's voice in Spanish telling me one more time, "Be careful what you wish for."

Chapter Five
GRACIE

Dear God, thank you for all of your blessings on this beautiful Christmas Day. Thank you for giving us the opportunity to spend this morning together at home so we could open our gifts to each other and then come here to Mass as a family again. Please forgive me for any trespasses, including wishing that Erica's ex-boyfriend would break his leg or get the stomach flu. I'm also sorry for wanting to take back the jacket I got for my little sister Rachel after she told me that my hair wasn't its usual crazy mess. I realize now that she was just trying to be nice . . . in her own bratty kind of way. And please continue to keep . . .

An elbow to my side interrupted my after-Communion prayer. I looked over to Selena, who was kneeling next to me on my left. She was trying not to laugh as she slyly motioned to the little boy in the pew in front of us. He looked to be about two years old, and he was wearing the cutest reindeer sweater and red knit cap. He also kept lifting his mother's skirt up and down, causing her to flash her flowered underwear at Selena.

I wanted to laugh, too, but then remembered I wasn't finished praying.

Please continue to keep our family safe and healthy. Amen.

Oh, and happy birthday, Jesus.

"That poor woman. I'd probably never show my face in this church again," Selena declared after Mass was over.

"Her name is Mrs. Hardwick. She has four kids who go to the school, so I'm pretty sure she's coming back," I explained as we waited for our parents near the church entrance. They had wandered off to greet some friends and hand over a container of tamales for Father Emilio.

As Selena and Rachel busied themselves on their phones, I waved to familiar faces. They were mostly parents and students in my first-grade class here at St. Christopher's. Others were teachers and staff whom I hadn't seen since Christmas break started four days ago. It was definitely a close-knit school and church community—one I'd been a part of ever since I was a little girl.

People often asked me if I felt strange teaching in the same classroom where I had once been a first grader too. If anything, I felt more comfortable there than I did anywhere else. My teacher back then had been Sister Sheila. She was Irish and had the prettiest skin and kindest green eyes. Back in those days, most of the nuns and priests at St. Christopher's had come from Ireland—a fact that made a seven-year-old me believe the country must have been a very holy place indeed.

So much so, I had once asked Sister Sheila if I could still be a nun even though I was Mexican. That had made her green eyes sparkle.

"Of course you can, my child. God doesn't care what country you're from or whether your skin is white, brown, black, or green. He calls people to serve based only on what's inside their heart."

That's when I decided that I wanted to be a nun and a teacher. Years later I learned Sister Sheila had left the convent, moved to Idaho, and married a dentist. I don't think that in itself changed my mind, but by the time I started college, whatever call I thought I'd received to become a nun had disappeared. But I had still wanted to teach.

"Gracie! Gracie!"

Instinctively, I took a deep breath and turned toward the voice. "Hello, Sister Catherine. Merry Christmas."

Sister Catherine was the principal of St. Christopher's. If her five-foot-ten-inch frame wasn't intimidating enough, her loud and stern tone could make even the most seasoned teacher quake in her sensible shoes.

She offered me a curt nod before responding. "Merry Christmas to you, too, Gracie. I wanted to let you know that we were able to hire a substitute PE teacher a few days ago."

"That's wonderful," I said with a careful smile.

"Yes, it is. He's also going to coach our basketball teams. Which brings me to the reason why I came over here. You're going to need to use your classroom for the after-school homework-help sessions. The small multipurpose room by the basketball courts is going to become the new coach's office."

My heart dropped. "But, but, the older kids don't fit into the first graders' desks. That's why we moved into the multipurpose room in the first place."

"I know, dear. But that's not an option anymore, as I just explained. You'll just have to get some folding chairs from the auditorium. Now, if you'll excuse me, I really must go talk to the Dennisons."

"Great," I muttered under my breath as she walked away.

Selena moved to stand next to me. "If she had been my principal back then, I probably would've been expelled in the fourth grade."

"You and me both. Well, okay, maybe just you. I can't believe she's making me move out of that multipurpose room. Do you know it wouldn't even be a multipurpose room in the first place if I hadn't spent the summer cleaning it out, painting the walls, and asking the PTA for money to buy bookcases and tables? It's not fair."

I hated that I was whining like a little girl. I also hated that I hadn't stood up for myself—and my students.

Selena shook her head. "Seriously, Gracie, if I had to work with that woman, I'd find a new career. I don't know how . . . or why you do it."

I shrugged and tried to calm down, especially since I didn't want to make a scene. There were too many parents from the school still milling about. The gossip patrol would have a field day.

But Selena wasn't done. "Why don't you go find another job that will pay you what you deserve? That way you can finally move out and get your own place."

"I swear, as soon as I can afford it I'm gonna move out like you, Selena," Rachel suddenly chimed in from out of nowhere. "I'm gonna buy a condo, too, just like you."

Rachel adored Selena. They shared the same taste in music, clothes, and apparently condo ownership. As for me? Well, we didn't exactly share makeup tips.

"You know, Rachel, before you can buy that condo, you'll have to graduate college and get a good job. But first, you have to finish high school," I told her. She rolled her eyes like she always did when I brought up school. She wasn't the best student, and her grades were starting to reflect it.

"Yes, I know. You've only told me that about a million times. I'm going to go wait by the car," Rachel said.

I must have made a face because Selena put her arm around me. "Don't take it personally. She's fourteen. Remember fourteen? Adults were the enemy." She laughed.

"She doesn't treat you like the enemy."

"That's because I buy her stuff, and you nag her like Mom," Selena explained.

I almost argued about her characterization, but then let it go. Rachel was the least of my worries. Moving out of the multipurpose room was not something I was looking forward to doing once I got back from the break.

Why couldn't the new PE teacher set up a desk somewhere else? I knew for a fact that there was an empty storage room in the auditorium that could be turned into a perfectly good office. Why did it seem like I was always the one who had to compromise or give up something?

Guilt snaked itself around my heart.

I sighed and closed my eyes.

Dear God, I know I'm being selfish. Please grant me the patience to deal with this change. And I swear to you that I will go out of my way to welcome this new teacher with open arms.

Whatever it takes.

Amen.

Chapter Six
ERICA

I pulled into the parking garage located underneath the five-story building that housed the offices of the *Inland Valley News-Press*. God, how I wished I could turn around and drive the eight miles back home to my apartment. But there was a mandatory staff meeting in less than ten minutes. It was the only reason I hadn't called in sick.

Two days into the New Year and I was already a fucking mess.

I blamed the jacket.

It had shown up at my door just as I was leaving to go to a New Year's Eve party at a nightclub with Selena. I'd cursed Amazon when it had sent me an email three days before Christmas explaining that Greg's gift would be delayed after all.

And I cursed Amazon again for finally delivering it. I wasn't emotionally prepared to open the box and see the black leather jacket I'd purchased when I still thought my boyfriend loved me.

So instead of going to the club with Selena, I'd ended up at Greg's apartment with the stupid jacket and a bottle of his favorite whiskey. And then we'd ended up in his bed.

Of course, the pinche asshole had acted just like a pinche asshole as soon as it was over.

I'd spent New Year's Day both miserable and disgusted with myself. I couldn't even admit to my cousins what had happened until this morning.

"Okay, guys, I'm about to park," I said. "Thanks for letting me vent. Again."

"Anytime, sweetie," Selena sang through my phone's speaker. "And please stop beating yourself up. Having sex with your ex is part of the breaking-up process. We've all done it. Well, except for, you know."

"Whatever, Selena," Gracie said, annoyed as usual. "Erica, good luck meeting your new boss."

I blew out a big breath. "I'll need it. Did I tell you he's a Pulitzer Prize winner *and* a *New York Times* bestselling author?"

"You did," Selena droned. "Many, many, many times."

I grimaced. Before the breakup, Adrian Mendes had been the regular subject of my venting—and cursing. Our staff had found out two weeks ago that he was going to be the paper's new city editor. Tom, our publisher, couldn't contain his giddiness as he told us that our new boss, Adrian Mendes, was *the* Adrian Mendes—the *Washington Journal* reporter whose investigative articles had uncovered a major bribery scandal involving two senators and a highly respected fund-raising organization. Although I had absolutely no idea who the man was, at the time I had pretended to be as impressed as everyone else. Apparently, this Mendes guy had left his newspaper after landing a big book deal, and his first novel, about a political scandal and murder, had topped all kinds of bestseller lists. Five years ago, he was the hottest new thriller writer.

And now he was joining the staff of the *News-Press*.

None of it made any sense. So, of course, it freaked me the fuck out. Actually, it was freaking the fuck out of everyone in the newsroom. What was a guy like Adrian Mendes doing in Inland Valley—a suburb forty miles east of Los Angeles? We weren't a small town, but we weren't exactly a bustling hub of political intrigue either. I mean, the last national news story to come out of the city was when a plane carrying a Hawaiian congressman had to make an emergency landing at the local airport after one of his aides suffered a heart attack in midflight (the aide survived!).

Brian, our fact-checking guru, wasted no time in trying to google as much information as he could about our new boss. And except for a few magazine interviews and links to his old articles, not much could be found about him. He barely had a social media presence, and his website was super out of date. As for pictures, Brian could only find one that seemed to be his author photo. It wasn't a close-up, though. You couldn't even see any distinguishable features except for the semiscowl across his clean-shaven face.

Basically, the man was a mystery.

So conspiracy theories about why he was joining the staff ran the gamut from him being a spy from the paper's parent organization sent to evaluate operations ahead of a major layoff, to him being a spy from the paper's biggest competitor sent to evaluate operations ahead of a major takeover.

Whatever the reason he was here, I hoped it wouldn't make my job harder. Especially now that my personal life was absolute basura. No, worse. Like the trash you forgot to pull out to the curb on trash day and now had to wait another week before it got taken away.

"It will be fine, Erica," Gracie said. "You'll see."

Gracie's last words to me still hung in the air as I stepped inside the coffee shop located within the building's lobby. Maybe she was talking about my job. Maybe she wasn't. Either way, I couldn't shake the nagging feeling that things were going to be far from fine.

I checked the time on my phone. I had exactly seven minutes to get a mocha latte and a raspberry streusel bar—my go-to stress relievers. With one guy ahead of me in line, there was no reason I couldn't make the meeting on time.

"I'll take a cortado," I heard the dark-haired man tell the girl at the counter.

"What is that?" she asked.

"It's like a cappuccino, but cooler."

"Oh. Then, no, we don't have that."

"Okay. What about a chaider?"

Even I could see the girl's blank expression from where I stood behind him.

"It's a combo of hot apple cider and chai tea," he said, answering her unasked question with a hint of contempt.

She shook her head.

He sighed and pointed at the menu above her head. "Fine. Just give me a black coffee. I'm assuming you have that, right? And I'll take one of those raspberry-streusel-bar things too."

The girl smiled, but I highly doubted it was genuine. "Yes, we do have regular coffee. And, you're in luck. We only have one bar left."

"No!"

Ay, carajo. Had I really just yelled that out loud?

The man spun to look at me, and embarrassment enflamed my cheeks.

Arched eyebrows hovered over dark-rimmed glasses. The brown eyes behind the lenses squinted in confusion. "Excuse me?" he asked, disdain dripping from every syllable that seemed to have been torn from what I imagined to be a very pursed mouth hidden underneath a dark, unruly beard. Maybe on another day, I'd think this guy was good looking in a cool, nerdy kind of way. But as soon as he opened his mouth with those words, his handsome features contorted into just another pendejo-face. And whatever embarrassment I'd felt after my outburst quickly dissolved into full-fledged annoyance.

I'd hated it when Greg would use that kind of tone with me whenever he thought I was being unreasonable or silly. He used it again when I'd asked him the night we broke up if there was another woman.

"Don't be ridiculous, Erica," he'd scoffed, as if the reason we were breaking up could be so trite. He then proceeded to explain that there really wasn't any one reason why he had come to the conclusion things weren't working out. But it all came down to the fact that he could never see himself marrying me anyway, and it was better to end things now before wasting any more of each other's time. And so he'd gathered his things, told me to have a good life, and walked out my door, not caring in the slightest that he'd just stolen my trust and heart.

I wasn't about to let another guy steal anything else. Even if it was only a piece of pastry that I probably shouldn't have been eating anyway.

The surly man's eyebrows arched even higher as I took a step closer. "Look, there's plenty of cheese danishes still in the case. Or how about a nice bran muffin?"

I didn't care if I sounded or looked crazy. It had become a matter of principle at that point.

"Are you *actually* being serious right now?" he asked.

There was that tone again. My pissed-off meter was dinging off the charts. It had been hovering in the red zone ever since the breakup, and honestly, I was so goddamn tired of trying to hold it together. Even as Greg was ripping my heart to shreds, I'd forced myself to be reasonable and rational so we could continue our conversation until I could understand what in the hell was happening. Because if I had started crying and screaming, he would've just shut down. "I don't speak hysterical," he'd once told me.

Well, fuck that shit now. I was about to be fluent in hysterical.

"I am . . . *actually*," I said, stepping closer to the stranger and trying to sound as sarcastic as him. "Let me put it in simpler words for you since I don't have time to explain it again. I want that last raspberry streusel bar. No, I *deserve* that last raspberry streusel bar. So, pick something else, and move on with the rest of your day."

Something flashed across his face, and he looked like he wanted to say something to me. Instead, he shook his head and told the girl (who, by the way, was secretly giving me a high-five with her eyes) that he'd just take the coffee.

Two minutes later, I bit into the pastry and nearly cried. It was the most satisfying and sweetest bar I'd ever eaten. I savored every last crumb. The sugar and confidence high carried me all the way to the *News-Press* conference room. The anger was gone. So was the anxiety. I was feeling pretty damn good.

That is, until after just a few minutes into the staff meeting, Tom asked my new boss, Adrian Mendes, to stand and say a few words to everyone, and the mean stranger who tried to steal the last raspberry streusel bar from me stood instead.

Ay, Dios mío.

Of course it would be *him*. This New Year was really starting off like shit. First, I make a fool of myself by sleeping with Greg. Then I make an even bigger fool of myself in front of my new boss. If I'd run into this guy anywhere else, I would've found the nearest bush and hid behind it. But since there was no shrubbery inside the *News-Press* office, once the meeting ended I pulled on my big girl chonies and walked right over to where Adrian Mendes was talking with Charlie, our newly promoted managing editor.

"And here's Erica Garcia, our education reporter," an oblivious Charlie announced proudly to the man standing next to him. "Erica, this is Adrian."

The recognition was instantaneous. His initial polite smile thinned, and his complexion darkened one more shade.

I smiled the biggest smile I had ever smiled in my life. "We've already met," I explained to Charlie. "Um, can I talk to Adrian privately?"

Before becoming the managing editor, Charlie had been a reporter for twenty years. He could still smell a story a mile away. A look passed between us, and I knew I'd have to give him the full details later. "Of course. I'm going to go check the wire feed."

As soon as he was out of earshot, I started. "So I want to apologize for my attitude earlier. Obviously, I had no idea who you were. And if it makes a difference, I've had a crappy couple of days. But that's no excuse. I shouldn't have taken it out on you. I am sorry, and I just want you to know that I plan to be nothing but professional from here on out."

"Okay," he said with a curt nod and walked out of the conference room.

Wait. What? That was it?

No, it couldn't be. I caught up to him in the middle of the hallway, just outside the copy room.

"What do you mean, okay?" I asked as I stepped in front of him.

He raised those eyebrows again. "Okay means okay. I don't know what else you expect me to say?"

"I don't know," I answered with a shrug. "I guess I expected something more."

Adrian fixed his glasses before answering. "Well, there's not. So is that it? Can I go set up my desk now?"

I didn't answer and instead moved out of his way. I watched him walk toward the newsroom, and for one tiny second, relief washed over me. But then my new boss stopped, turned around, and gave me more of a sneer than a smile.

"*Actually*, there was something else. I forgot to ask. So how was that raspberry streusel bar?"

There was no disdain or contempt this time in his tone. In fact, there was no emotion at all. And just like that, my anxiety from before came rushing back. "Um, it was good. Why?" My voice was quieter than I wanted it to be, but at least it didn't shake.

He nodded. "Just wanted to make sure it was worth it. See you inside, Ms. Garcia."

I stood there for a few minutes trying to comprehend what he had meant. Was he really the kind of guy who would use something like that against me? Fine, maybe I had made a scene in the coffee shop. What did it matter? No one from the paper had been around to see it. And, technically, it had all happened before nine in the morning and before he was officially my boss. Besides, I was a fucking great reporter and Charlie and Tom both loved me. If he gave me any shit, I'd go straight to them and was pretty sure they'd have my back.

So what if he had a Pulitzer or a publishing deal? I knew this town and this paper like the back of my hand, and no one, especially not some condescending transplant from Washington, DC, was going to change that.

Ms. Garcia, huh?

I could give people names too. For example, Adrian Mendes had officially become Pinche Asshole Number Two.

Chapter Seven
SELENA

"Selena, what do you think?"

Wait. Did Alan Umbridge, principal of the Umbridge & Umbridge Company, just ask for my opinion about something?

Shit.

Every one of the firm's nine staff members was seated around the oval table inside the office's main conference room. I had been doodling flowers and butterflies on my legal pad and daydreaming of that new Marc Jacobs wallet I had been eyeing for the past week at Neiman Marcus. Hearing my name startled me, to say the least.

I cleared my throat and pushed my glasses up. "Well, I think we should definitely incorporate some type of direct mail and frequent-user campaign. Even some type of rewards-card idea and . . ."

"No, no," Alan interrupted. "I was asking about how many times a year do you think a person might book a round-trip bus ticket to Mexico."

"Oh. Well, I'm not sure. I guess we could ask the company for some data from the past few years."

"Well, of course we could ask for data, Selena. I just thought you might know off the top of your head. For example, how many times do your relatives do it?"

Now I understood what Alan Umbridge was asking. "Actually, Alan, I don't know of any relatives that have booked a bus trip to Mexico in the past several years."

"Really? Does that mean they don't ever go back to visit their country?" he asked.

"This *is* their country," I said very slowly and carefully.

"Of course. Well, when they do go back to visit Mexico, how do they get there?" he asked.

"Um, an airplane?" I tried not to sound sarcastic. It didn't work. He raised his eyebrows, shrugged his shoulders, and proceeded to talk to Vera from Creative about the direct mail piece.

After the meeting I went back to my cubicle, wishing once again I had an office so I could close the door and vent all my frustration by throwing something. But I had been at Umbridge & Umbridge for five years, and I figured it would take another five before I got that office and the respect that came with it.

Instead, I was an assistant account manager hired because the company wanted to bring in more Latino clients.

They *literally* told me that during my interview.

Every once in a while I'd be brought in to a meeting if an existing client wanted to expand their advertising into the Spanish language media. I'd be asked what newspapers my family read or what TV shows my family watched.

One time, I even got asked what kind of food my family ate on Thanksgiving (a local pie shop wanted to know if it was worth their dollars to run a spot on a Spanish radio station advertising their Thanksgiving specials). When I responded, "Uh, turkey" in the same sarcastic tone I had used today, Henry Umbridge (Alan's brother) actually asked, "Turkey tacos?" I almost spit out my caffè macchiato that time.

Grabbing my cell phone, I headed to the parking lot and called Erica.

But instead of encouraging my indignation, she just laughed her ass off when I told her what I'd said to Umbridge.

"You suck," I told her.

"Come on, Selena. Think about it. They want you to be the expert on every kind of Latino from Cubans to Puerto Ricans to Mexicans. Like all of the Latinidad in the world can be limited to one language and one culture. Meanwhile, they have no idea that you're just making up shit as you go along," she said.

I sighed. "Because Seth was right. I am a 'whitina.'"

My ex's name had slipped out of my mouth before I could stop it. I winced in preparation for Erica's reaction. We'd all sworn never ever to mention him again.

Seth and I had dated for almost all of my senior year in college. I was head over heels in love with him, and I did anything he wanted me to do—even if it meant dropping a class because he wanted me to always have lunch with him or cutting down on visiting my parents and Gracie on weekends because he wanted us to hang out with his fraternity friends. I honestly thought we were going to get married. That is, until I met his parents.

They'd come into town for his birthday, and we all went to dinner at a very expensive restaurant in Beverly Hills. Within the first thirty minutes, I knew they were racists. Later that night I had a full-on meltdown and asked Seth if he was with me because he knew his parents would be pissed that he was dating a Latina.

But it was so much worse than that.

"Of course not," he'd said with a laugh. "Besides, you're not *Latina* Latina. You're, I don't know, a toned-down Latina. That's different."

I'd been so gutted that it took everything I had not to cry in front of him. Not just because I realized how blind I'd been, but because he was an awful person, and I had wanted so hard to be just like him and his friends. I thought of my welita and how she had once told us how a woman in the grocery store had laughed at her broken English. Welita had said that if she'd cried in front of her, then the woman would have known the power she'd had over her. She'd always told us that people who hurt us don't deserve our tears.

So instead of crying, I broke up with Seth right then and there. And I swore I'd never give a man the power to hurt me.

"No! Not at all!" Erica insisted. "Fuck that guy and his fucking racist nicknames. All I meant is that it's not your fault they wanted you to be their token Latina at the agency. That's on them. You have every right to call out their prejudiced assumptions because they deserve it."

I almost admitted to Erica that I wasn't always so brave.

Not because I wasn't proud of my Mexican heritage. Sometimes I was just too tired to defend it. Even in the first grade, I learned it was much easier if you didn't talk with an accent and didn't bring egg burritos to school for lunch.

Then, in college, I suffered a whole new identity crisis. I was constantly scolded by strangers who would look at my brown skin and not understand why my Spanish was limited. It didn't matter to them that we spoke English at home because my dad was trying to learn the language. Instead, they told me in English, "Your parents should be ashamed of themselves."

I couldn't win either way.

As a kid, I was ashamed about not being white enough. But as an adult, I was ashamed for not being Mexican enough. In fact, I was so *not* Mexican that a privileged white racist asshole felt comfortable enough to date me.

Old hurt made my eyes water. Not what I wanted at all. I wasn't about to let anyone at Umbridge & Umbridge see tears. I cleared my throat and changed the subject.

"I hate my job," I told Erica.

She sighed. "No, you don't, Selena. You just hate your boss. Just like I do."

I winced, remembering Erica's story of her awkward first day with her new editor.

"Fine. I don't totally hate this place. But something is going to have to change soon, or else I'm going to start looking elsewhere."

Erica was right. The joke was on them. They had no idea I was making it up as I went. As long as they paid me a nice salary, mileage, and a Christmas bonus, I could put up with their bullshit for a little longer.

At least I was going to try.

Chapter Eight
MARI

I had just started to make myself a sandwich when the rumble of the garage door opening stopped me. Letty and I looked at each other in confusion.

Of course, it had to be Esteban. But he usually never came home in the middle of the day. So, just in case, I wrapped my fingers around the butter knife I'd been using to spread mayo on a piece of sourdough bread.

"Esteban, you're home," I said with some relief as he appeared and then let go of what would've been a very useless weapon.

"I forgot some files here," he said as he walked toward his home office. I followed behind.

"You should've called. I could have brought them to you so you didn't have to make the trip," I told him.

He walked inside the office and grabbed some manila folders sitting on his desk. Esteban kissed me on the cheek before heading out the door. "It's fine. I know you're busy. Don't you have your homeless coalition meeting today?"

"No, that's next Friday."

"Oh. Well, I'm sure you have more important things to do than drop off files at the courthouse."

I don't. I have absolutely nothing important going on because you decided I didn't need to work so I could devote my time to you, your career, your friends, and this house. The highlight of my week is going to be making that damn turkey sandwich with my homemade sourdough bread.

"It's no trouble," I told him with a smile. "You know I don't mind helping you."

He kissed me again. "I know. That's why I love you so much. Speaking of, I went ahead and told Alicia that she could count on you again to chair the firm's charity gala this year."

My body stiffened. "You did? I was really hoping to take a back seat this year."

Esteban was already walking away. "It'll be fine," he said over his shoulder. "You can take off next year."

That's what you said last year.

Then he was gone.

As I went back to making my sandwich, I chided myself for not putting my foot down about the charity gala. It wasn't that I didn't want to help. It was just that being chair meant being the ultimate hostess that evening. My only job at the event was to smile, look beautiful, and charm everyone into spending tons of money on the auction items. I'd grown to hate being on display like that. That's why for the past two years I'd told Esteban to find someone else to do it and I would take on something more hands on. Like usual, he'd either forgotten or chosen to ignore what I wanted. Why hadn't I made him listen to me this time?

Because you always give him what he wants.

It started the first night we met.

I was working part-time for the company that catered his first firm's holiday party at a Pasadena hotel. I had a business degree but had just been laid off from my job and needed the money. Plus, I'd always wanted to open a catering business of my own, and I figured I could get the experience—and clients—I needed by schlepping for this company. I was one of the servers who walked around the guests holding up silver trays covered in bacon-wrapped shrimp and cream cheese wontons. Esteban kept calling me over throughout the evening, and by the sixth or seventh wonton, I knew he was interested.

We flirted back and forth for a while, and then he disappeared toward the end of the party. Disappointed, I changed out of my uniform inside the hotel lobby's restroom and figured I'd spend the rest of that Saturday night at home on my couch—alone. But when I walked out, he was there waiting for me. He slipped an envelope into my hand and said, "Here's a little something for your great service tonight." Then he walked back inside the ballroom.

Inside the envelope was a hotel key card and a note scribbled on hotel stationery: "Meet me upstairs in Room 305 so we can continue getting to know one another. Or if I've misread you, then call me tomorrow so I can apologize."

Obviously, there was no need to call him.

Within one month, we were living together in his LA high-rise apartment. Within three months, we were engaged. I quit my job, and he promised to help me start my business once we were married. Looking back, I could see that I started to lose my voice during the wedding planning. I'd wanted a small, simple ceremony at the beach; he'd insisted on a traditional Catholic church wedding, complete with ten bridesmaids and groomsmen. We fought a lot, and one night I gave him back the diamond engagement ring and told him the wedding was off. But instead of walking out on him, I ended up letting him convince me to elope that weekend in Las Vegas.

At first, I enjoyed my new life. Then Esteban and Chris branched out and started their own firm. I was a founding partner's wife and needed to look and dress the part. That meant spa and nail appointments in the morning, followed by shopping excursions in the afternoon. Whenever I'd mention the catering business, he'd beg me to postpone it a few more months. There was always a client dinner party that needed hosting or a home remodeling project he suddenly wanted to complete. Eventually, I stopped bringing it up. Instead, I filled my appointment book with social lunches with other firm wives and joined boards for the homeless coalition and the children's hospital foundation so I wouldn't feel so . . . shallow.

Perhaps I wouldn't have been so bitter if Esteban didn't work so much. And since he had a new trial starting that afternoon, dinners for one were on the menu for the next couple of weeks.

That also meant that the only pounding that would be taking place in our house would be in the kitchen. With dough.

The sound of the doorbell interrupted my thoughts, and I focused back on my sandwich. The bread had turned out amazing. It would be a shame to let it go to waste.

But I nearly choked on the first bite when Letty returned to the kitchen followed by Chris.

He was back in his suit today. This one was dark gray with a dark-blue shirt and patterned tie. Like everything else he wore, it fit him like a glove.

Wait. When did I start noticing his clothes?

"Hope you don't mind me stopping by? I came to return this."

Chris put an empty plastic container on the counter next to me. It was the one I had sent home with him with buñuelos inside. He leaned down, and I offered my cheek for his usual greeting kiss. My eyes darted to Letty, but she was busy emptying the dishwasher. The kiss was quick and innocent. Yet, my nerves were on heightened alert as I remembered the one he'd given me on Christmas morning.

"It's disposable, Chris. You didn't have to bring it back." I picked up the container and placed it in the sink. I'd probably just throw it away after he left, but I needed an excuse to get some distance between us.

"It is? Oh, well. And I even washed it too," he said with a pout, and I couldn't help but smile back.

"You just missed Esteban," I offered.

"I know. I just got off the phone with him."

That meant he knew Esteban wasn't here. "Oh. So, are you on your way to court too?"

Like Esteban's, most of Chris's hearings took place at the Pasadena Courthouse. Their bigger trials were held in downtown Los Angeles. They were criminal defense attorneys and had represented some of the most famous and powerful people in Hollywood. It wasn't unusual for them to even team up on some of the higher profile cases, a.k.a. the ones that the tabloids cared about.

"I'm not second chair on Esteban's case this time. And I'm already done, actually. I only had a few motions, so no more court for me today. Who knows? I may not even go in to the office."

I shrugged. "Well, you are the boss. I guess you can do whatever you want." Although I couldn't remember the last time Esteban had taken a day or even an afternoon off.

He was about to say something when his eyes fell on the loaf of sourdough bread. After bending down to take a quick whiff, he looked at me. "Marisol, did you bake this?"

I nodded. "Last night," I said as I walked over to the counter to cut him a slice.

"She never sleeps, so she bakes," Letty offered.

It was true that my chronic insomnia had turned me into a pretty good baker. Still, I didn't like the disapproving looks I was getting from both of them.

"I sleep enough," I told them.

Letty rolled her eyes and then announced she was going upstairs to fold laundry.

"Oh my God," he raved after a couple of bites. "This is amazing. It's even better than the loaves I usually get in San Francisco."

"Really?"

"Really. Marisol, you should sell this."

I ignored him. "Hey, since you're here, do you want to check out the backyard? They finally put in the fountain a few days ago."

He tilted his chin up and narrowed his eyes, trying to figure out why I was changing the subject. But he only said, "Sure. I'd love to see it."

The relandscaping of the backyard was another one of Esteban's busy projects for me. One rare summer afternoon, he'd come out of his home office and announced that we should have dinner on our patio. He'd even barbecued salmon fillets and corn on the cob. We'd talked and laughed and enjoyed a couple of glasses of sangria with our meal. I remember being so content. So at peace.

And just when I thought it couldn't get any better, Esteban announced we should redo the backyard. "Remember when we bought the house, you mentioned how nice it would be to have a fountain and a garden with a pergola? I think it's time for us to finally do it," he'd said at the time.

I'd known then that *us* meant *me*.

So I was the one to meet with the contractors and pick out the plants and stones. But when it came down to picking a fountain, Esteban decided he knew what was best. He chose the most expensive one, a huge structure made from beautiful Italian black marble. *Only the best for you, cariño,* Esteban had said after he vetoed my choice for a simple cobblestone structure. It sat in the center of our sprawling lawn and was surrounded by an assortment of blossoms and plants.

"It's nice," Chris said after examining it from different angles.

"It's not the one I initially chose," I admitted.

"Like I've always said, Esteban has good taste." He turned to look at me. A slight breeze swept past us, and Chris asked if I was cold.

Not in the slightest.

He didn't say a word after I told him I wasn't and instead slid his fingers across the smooth marble.

"I still think a cobblestone one would have fit this garden better," I continued, surveying the greenery. "The one I wanted was simple, but it was well built and beautiful in its own way. It would have brought out the beauty of the flowers even more. This marble fountain is rich and flashy. I think it's almost too much for this garden. The flowers are overshadowed, even lost, because of it."

The sadness in my voice surprised me.

"You could still change it, you know," he said, turning to face me again.

I sighed. "No, it's too late. We've already invested so much time and money into this one. It would be a waste to just get something else."

"But if it's what you want, Marisol—if it's what's going to make you happy—then how can that be a waste?" His tone, soft and low, brought back the same butterflies from Christmas morning.

I didn't fully understand why at that moment, but I needed him to know I wasn't the kind of person to make such a drastic change on a whim.

"It's not as simple as it sounds. There's a lot involved in undoing something as big as this. Who knows? Maybe I just need to give it a chance? Maybe I'll realize that I can live with it."

"Ay, Marisol. When will you learn that living with something you don't love is not living at all?"

When I didn't answer, he shook his head and sighed. Then he said he had to leave and walked out through the backyard gate, leaving me alone to wonder if he had been talking about the fountain at all.

Chapter Nine
GRACIE

I sat in the cafeteria of St. Christopher's Academy desperately wishing I could die.

Dear God, I take that back. Of course I don't want to die. But could there be a small earthquake or a random fire drill at least? Amen.

Wishing for small disasters normally wasn't on my to-do list. In fact, I'd woken up that morning fully intending to have a pretty good Friday. Then I walked into our weekly staff meeting and everything changed.

Perhaps an act of God wasn't necessary. At this point, I would've settled for a nosebleed or emergency phone call. Anything to get me out of having to stand up in the next five minutes or so and introduce myself—or rather reintroduce myself—to Tony Bautista.

"Hi, Tony. I'm Kevin Donald, and I teach seventh grade. Welcome," Kevin said.

He still looked the same. His dark wavy hair was cut shorter, and there were fine lines now in the corners of his eyes, but everything else was the same. His light eyes, the dimple on his chin, and his beautiful, beautiful smile. He had aged well.

"Hi, Tony. I'm Linda Johnson, and I'm the choir director, and I also teach sixth grade. Welcome," Linda said.

Tony Bautista was the prince of St. Christopher's back in the day. And every girl had wanted to be his princess—including me. From the first day he'd transferred into Mrs. Warren's fourth-grade class, Tony Bautista was my secret crush.

"Hiya, Tony. I'm Randy Richards, and I teach eighth grade. So glad you're joining us. Welcome," Randy said.

And he was responsible for the best and worst day of my life.

I could still see the striped shirt and black jeans he wore that day in the eighth grade when he walked over to my desk and grabbed my hand to lead me to a table in the back of the classroom to work. We'd been randomly paired up to do some type of project that I'd long since forgotten. Tony, however, was unforgettable. He was charming, funny, and nice. At the end of the period, he told me how much he was looking forward to working with me, and maybe we could even get together after school at McDonald's to brainstorm. I was on cloud nine that entire morning. And then the lunch bell rang.

"Hello, Tony. I'm Mrs. Gosling, and I'm the art instructor for the seventh and eighth graders," Mrs. Gosling said.

I had been in one of the stalls in the girls' restroom when Tracy Kellogg and Luz de la Torre walked in. They were giggling. "So, he really asked you out?" squealed Luz. "Yep," Tracy responded. "I mean, I figured he would eventually, but I have to admit I was kinda worried once I saw how he was acting with that Gracie." I froze at the mention of my name. Slowly, I placed my ear against the stall's door. Tracy continued, "So I told him that if he wanted to ask out Gracie, then that was totally cool because Brian wants to ask me out. You should have seen the look of absolute horror on his face! He went on and on about how he was just being nice to her so he could sweet-talk her into doing the project all on her own . . ."

"Hello, Tony. I'm Sister Claire, and I teach fifth grade. Welcome," Sister Claire said.

I ended up staying in the restroom way past lunch and then went to the nurse's office and told her I had a stomachache—which was true. I didn't go back to school for the rest of the week (I was so sick with embarrassment my mom really thought I had some type of flu). By the following Monday, the teacher had paired up Tony with another group, and I ended up doing a make-up project all on my own anyway. I managed to stay away from him—and Tracy—for the rest of the school year.

"Hello, Mr. Bautista. I am Sister Patricia, and I teach computer science and the fourth grade. Welcome, sir," Sister Patricia said.

Still, I kept tabs on him throughout high school, even though I attended St. Francine's all-girls school and he went to Trinity—the all-boys school across town. He was Trinity's star baseball player, so it was easy to hear about what he was up to. He ended up getting a full scholarship to one of the UC schools, but then he tore some type of muscle in his leg, and his college career was over. I lost track of him after that.

"Hello, Tony. My name is Sister Elizabeth, and I teach the second grade. Welcome!" Sister Elizabeth said.

And now I'd found him. He was right here at St. Christopher's, standing by Sister Catherine. She had just made the announcement that Tony Bautista was joining the faculty as the substitute PE teacher and basketball coach. The rest of the staff had just finished introducing themselves. Now it was my turn.

I slowly stood up from my chair. My cheeks burned, and my legs shook underneath my long flowered skirt. I gripped the edge of the table so I wouldn't lose my balance.

"Hi, Tony. My name is Gracie Lopez, and I'm in the first grade—er, I mean I teach the first grade. Welcome," I said.

He smiled just as he had smiled at everyone else he'd just met for the first time.

A wave of relief traveled down my body. I didn't want him to remember me, or rather, the girl I had been. I immediately began thinking of ways I could become invisible and avoid him the rest of the school year.

My plans flew out the window, probably along with my composure, when Sister Catherine opened up her big mouth.

"Tony, did you know that Gracie is an alumnus just like yourself? In fact, I think you two must have graduated the same year. Isn't that right, Gracie?"

Dear God, I'm going to faint. Please don't let me faint. Amen.

My cheeks, along with the rest of my face, caught fire as I slowly raised my eyes to meet his. I could tell he was trying to place me. His brow furrowed. His eyes squinted. And then, suddenly, there it was: recognition. I was no longer Gracie Lopez, first-grade teacher. I was Gracie Lopez, the chubby, drab, awkward brown-haired girl he had known, but never really known, for four years.

"Oh yeah." He smiled. "Gracie. Now I remember. Wow—I almost didn't recognize you. You, you look better, er, I mean different."

After a couple of snickers from the female faculty members, Sister Catherine went back to our in-service meeting. And I went back to wishing I could disintegrate right there on the spot.

Tony Bautista was now responsible for two of the most embarrassing days of my life.

Chapter Ten
ERICA

"You buried the lede again, Ms. Garcia," Adrian's voice bellowed from the other side of my cubicle. My fingers froze on the keyboard of my computer, and I willed myself to not let out the exasperated sigh rolling in my throat. For the umpteenth time I cursed Charlie for giving Adrian the desk directly opposite mine. So what if it was also right outside his office and convenient for the two of them to talk back and forth? It sure as hell wasn't convenient for me.

It had been two weeks since Adrian had joined the paper. Coincidentally, it had also been the hardest two weeks for me on the job. The man liked to criticize every sentence, every word choice. He did it with everyone, but because I happened to be the cabrona sitting within earshot of him, he seemed to voice his criticism with my reporting even more.

I took a breath and rolled my chair a few inches to the left so I could meet the glare I knew was waiting for me just above our shared partition wall. "Excuse me?" I asked as evenly as I could.

Adrian pointed to his computer screen. "I thought this story was supposed to be about how the board is going to vote next week on whether to implement later start times in the fall for the high school?"

"Yes, that's exactly what the story is about."

"Then why do you start it off describing this woman's morning routine?"

My fists balled on my lap. "Because it shows how she has to drop off her four kids at three different schools before 7:50 a.m. in order to make it to her job on time and that any changes to the current school schedule will affect that. It shows that this vote isn't just about start times. It gives the story a human perspective."

Fortunately, I succeeded in not adding the word *asshole* to the end of my sentence.

Even without the insult, Adrian still shook his head disapprovingly. "I understand why you interviewed her. What I don't get is why you start the story with her. You need to start it with the facts—what the board is voting on, when it's voting, why they're voting, et cetera, et cetera. After you set up the facts, then you can go into your interviews with the parents who support it and the ones who don't."

Obviously, I knew the facts needed to be shared early on. But I wanted to draw the reader in. I wanted the reader to care about the vote even if they had no stake in it. Maybe I should've told Adrian that. Maybe I should've challenged him a little more.

Instead, I said, "Fine. Send it back to me and I'll rewrite it next week. The vote isn't until Wednesday, so it can run in Tuesday's edition."

"It's still running Sunday as scheduled," he said, looking directly at me. "You need to finish rewriting it today."

This time I didn't hold back. "That's impossible," I argued, my voice an octave higher than before. "I'm already on deadline for three other stories. And two of them I haven't even started because one of my phone interviews isn't for another hour."

"Not my problem. Just get it done, Ms. Garcia," he ordered before focusing back on his computer.

And just like that, Adrian had dismissed me.

Impulsively, I picked up a pen off my desk and gripped it tight. If Charlie hadn't walked out of his office at that exact moment and smiled at me, my Bic pen would have taken flight over the partition headed for a direct collision with Adrian's temple.

The realization of what I'd almost done shook me. I needed to get out of there. I needed caffeine and lots of sugar.

"I'm going to grab a coffee from downstairs."

He barely nodded, but I took it as a sign of permission that I could leave and walked as fast as I could to the lobby elevator. The doors opened. That's when I realized I'd forgotten my wallet.

"Dammit," I whispered and made a U-turn back into the newsroom. Good thing Adrian wasn't at his desk. I didn't think I could take one more example of how I'd messed up the article. Why did he enjoy picking apart my work so much?

Ugh. He was such an arrogant prick.

I yanked my wallet too quickly out of my purse, causing it to fall off my desk, and everything inside spilled in various directions all over the floor.

Of course.

Dropping to my hands and knees, I searched for my things so I could collect them. My favorite lipstick had rolled underneath my desk, so I crawled over to it. Thank God I'd picked slacks instead of a skirt that morning. I reached for the lipstick but froze when I heard Adrian's voice from above.

"I'm telling you, Charlie. It's like she's pushing me on purpose. Ledes are Journalism 101. Read this, and then explain to me how I'm supposed to think of her as one of my star reporters."

My gut knew he was talking about me. Then Charlie confirmed it.

"Look, Adrian. I've known Erica for two years and she's a professional. There's no way she's purposefully doing anything to make your job harder. Maybe we three need to have a sit-down and figure out how you two can make this work."

My blood boiled. Perhaps not literally. But the heat emanating from every nerve in my body convinced me that anger was burning me from the inside out.

"Fine," Adrian grumped. "We'll do it your way and talk it out. But if things don't improve, then we'll have to take this to Tom. You both brought me here to make the *News-Press* into an award-winning newspaper. And I can't do that if you insist on keeping someone so . . . mediocre."

I bit my lip to keep from screaming. Fortunately, someone called Adrian's name, and I heard them both walk away. When I was sure they hadn't moved to the front of my desk, I carefully crawled out and stood up. Hot tears wet my eyes, and I grabbed my purse and headed to the women's restroom. I stared at the floor as I walked inside. No way did I want to meet anyone's eyes. It was empty, so I locked myself into the last stall, buried my face in my hands, and allowed myself to cry like I had been wanting to cry ever since Greg walked out of my condo.

Sure, I'd shed a few tears since then. But a part of me had held back the real grief. Partly because my cousins hadn't let me wallow and partly because I didn't want to give Greg that kind of power over me.

Maybe I hadn't been the most perfect girlfriend, but I'd worked hard to keep the relationship going. And what did I get in return? An ex-boyfriend.

Now, Adrian was basically treating me the same way. In all my adult life, I'd never been accused of being unprofessional. In fact, I prided myself on a strong work ethic and being a team player, goddammit. What I lacked in talent, I more than made up for in dedication.

So how fucking dare he call my best efforts "mediocre."

Eventually, the tears stopped and the frustration morphed into indignation. Charlie had defended me, and that counted for something. I had proven myself to both him and Tom, and deep down I knew that they weren't going to let Adrian get rid of me without a fight.

Perhaps I needed to look at the situation in a different way. I had been trying to give the jerk the benefit of the doubt because of his experience and his Pulitzer. But screw that. I knew I wasn't the only reporter who had issues with how Adrian ran the newsroom. It was time to play offense.

By the time my phone rang from inside my purse, I had a plan to put Adrian in his place before he could put me out.

"I need a drink," I said as soon as I answered. The ringtone had already told me it was my friend Deanna on the other end.

"Just tell me when and where, and I'll tell Mr. Dawson in the other room that we need to reschedule his emergency appendectomy," she said with a laugh.

Deanna was a surgical resident at the county hospital, and we both knew she'd never ditch a patient to go day drinking. "No, that's okay. Go save Mr. Dawson's life. We'll just drink after Sunday's game." I didn't add that I also planned to do some solo drinking tonight.

"That's actually why I called. I wanted to make sure you were coming. I didn't know if you'd be feeling soccer after . . . you know."

I did, but I didn't want talk about it. Instead, I forced a smile Deanna couldn't see and answered, "I'll be there."

A group of us had been meeting up on Sunday mornings to play pick-up soccer games at a local park. It was a coed team, and Deanna was our goalie, her boyfriend Mark was our lead scorer, and I played defense. I'd missed last weekend's game because I'd had to work and was itching to get back on the field.

Soccer was a big part of my life—had been ever since my dad put me on a team when I was just six. Since then, I'd played in countless youth organizations and traveling club tournaments and on my high school varsity team. But dreams of playing professionally ended my first year of college, when I tore my ACL in my second game.

Even after surgery and months of rehab, I still wasn't at the same level I had been and knew I would need a plan B for life after college.

Hello, journalism.

"We're playing at ten now, and it's your turn to bring the waters," Deanna said.

"Too bad we're not playing tomorrow," I mumbled as I leaned my head against the restroom stall door. "I have a lot of anger that I need to let out on some soccer balls."

"The Pinche Asshole again?" My friends and cousins also now referred to Adrian by his nickname.

"Yep."

"Sorry, Erica. Well, try not to let him get you down too much."

"I know. At least I'm off for the next three days. I'm going to sleep, drink, and binge-watch everything on Netflix."

"Sounds awesome. Just be ready to kick some ass on Sunday. All right, I really better go see if Mr. Dawson is ready to be appendix-less. Love ya. Text me later."

"Will do. Bye, babe."

If Deanna hadn't had a patient on the table, I probably would've told her everything I'd overheard. It was better that I didn't, though. Adrian's words—especially that one in particular—still stung, and I needed to focus on the four stories I had to write.

Somehow, I managed to do just that.

I hit send on the revised school board vote story just after nine p.m. Exhaustion had set in, and all I wanted to do was go home, take a shower, and collapse onto my bed. The only people left in the newsroom besides Adrian and me were two photographers and our copyeditor, Steve.

Adrian barely spoke to me as he edited all my stories. That suited me just fine, and so I busied myself by catching up on Twitter and Facebook. I'd shut him out so much that it startled me when he finally said, "You can go."

"Okay," I answered. He didn't need to tell me twice. I turned off my computer and grabbed my purse and sweater. With one last wave to Steve across the room, I stood up to leave.

"The lede still needed some work, but it was an improvement over your first attempt. I'm glad you took my constructive criticism to heart."

Wait. What?

"Constructive?" I could hear the snarl in my voice, but I was out of fucks to give.

"Yes, that's my job as your editor. To teach you how to make a story better. Anything I tell you, I'm only offering it as constructive criticism."

"Oh, so *now* I'm teachable?"

Adrian narrowed his eyes. "I don't know what you mean. Everyone is teachable."

"Even if they're—oh, I don't know—say, a mediocre reporter?"

Confusion crossed his face, and then the realization hit him. I should've been more satisfied by the way he kind of squirmed in his chair. But, again. Zero fucks.

"Listen, Erica, I—"

So I was Erica now? Hell to the nope. He'd been a complete ass to me all day, and he didn't get to justify or try to explain it. I'd had enough.

I took a long, deep breath and willed myself to stay calm. "Look, Adrian. I'm sorry, but I'm really tired. Can we *not* do this right now?"

He opened his mouth as if to say something but then seemed to change his mind. He only nodded.

And that was all I needed to walk away.

He was my editor. One of my bosses. I had to make this work if I wanted to stay at the paper.

That's when a thought hit me from out of the blue.

Do I want to stay at the News-Press*?*

Chapter Eleven
SELENA

My orgasm blindsided me.

It came so suddenly, so forcefully, that all I could do was mutter four-letter curse words and then curl into a shaking ball of tremors.

Totally amazing.

"I guess that was good for you, yes?"

Nathan rolled back onto the bed behind me and kissed my shoulder. I could feel the smug smirk on his face. The bastard.

"Obviously, you already know the answer," I said between pants and smiled into my pillow.

Sex with Nathan had always been pretty fantastic. Duh? I wouldn't have kept taking his phone calls if it hadn't. But I couldn't deny how next level this time had been. We'd started making out on the couch in his hotel suite as soon as we got back from dinner. And, honestly, if it hadn't been for my growling stomach, I probably would've jumped him right there in the airport parking lot. It wasn't that I'd missed him or anything like that. It was just that I'd abstained from any, um, self-satisfying activities since I'd found out he was coming back into town.

It was the longest two weeks of my life.

I was convinced that was the reason why I'd been extra responsive. It had nothing to do with missing him.

Nothing at all.

When my breathing returned to normal, I turned over to face him. "Can you tell that I've been waiting for this?"

He reached out and stroked my cheek. "I've been waiting for this, too, Selena. We shouldn't go so long in between visits next time."

"Hey, don't blame me. Not my fault you're slacking in racking up the LA clients," I teased and playfully pushed his shoulder.

Nathan was in charge of West Coast recruitment for his agency, and Los Angeles was his number one region. When we'd met at the conference in San Diego last year, he wouldn't leave my side once I told him that I lived in the city. But by the second day, he'd forgotten all about trying to lure me away to a new job and set his sights on trying to lure me into his bed. No wonder he was so good at his job. The man could be very convincing when he wanted to be.

"Ouch," he said, feigning hurt. "Besides, last I checked, New York is only a plane ride away. When was the last time you visited?"

I laughed. "Um, I don't think Umbridge & Umbridge would approve of me expensing a coast-to-coast booty call."

Nathan laughed, too, and pulled me closer to him. "Maybe you should just get a job in New York then," he said and kissed me.

I wanted to get lost in his kiss and his touch. But the budding apprehension in my chest kept me tethered to reality.

Stop it, Selena. He's not Seth.

It was true. Nathan was tall and thick with wavy brown hair. Seth was my height, skinny as a rail, and a ginger. In addition to their physical differences, Seth came from a wealthy and well-connected family in New Hampshire, and Nathan was raised by a single mother in the South Side of Chicago. Seth was all about appearances and making money. Nathan couldn't have cared less about either.

Seth had hurt me. Deeply.

Even though I knew in my heart that Nathan would never dare, it was better for both of us to keep things casual. I opened my mouth to let him know I was ready to get back to the reason—*the only reason*—I was here.

Afterward, we put on some clothes and raided the mini-bar water bottles and snacks.

"You know, I was serious about the whole job in New York thing," he said once we'd settled back on the bed. "There's a position open at this agency, and I know I could get you an interview."

"Which agency?" I asked after popping a chocolate-covered almond into my mouth.

"Kane Media."

I stopped chewing. Kane Media was one of the biggest and most respected of the New York agencies. It had swept the Clio Awards last year thanks to some pretty innovative campaigns. In the advertising world, winning a Clio was like winning an Oscar, Tony, and Emmy all on the same night. That's how good Kane Media was. It was the kind of agency I could only ever dream of working for—in about five years.

"There's no way," I told him. "I don't have enough experience."

"But you do, Selena. Plus you can really turn on the charm when you want. I'll get you in the door, and you just be your normal fantastic self."

Okay, for that comment, I had to kiss him. And keep kissing him.

"So, is that a yes?" he said after a few more kisses.

I pulled away to look him in the eyes. Nathan wasn't the type to lead me on, but I still needed to be sure.

"You can really make this happen?"

His expression was sincere. "I can really make this happen. Come on, Selena. I know Umbridge doesn't realize what you're capable of. You've put in enough years and sacrifices there, and it hasn't gotten you any closer to a promotion. A position with Kane can be a life changer."

No kidding.

But it was also a huge risk. What if I got the job and then was a complete failure at it? Umbridge was small potatoes compared to Kane. There was no way I'd worked on enough accounts to keep up with the New York industry. If that happened, I wouldn't just embarrass myself; I'd embarrass Nathan.

"Well?" he asked.

"I'm not sure. Let me think about it, okay?"

He sighed and kissed me softly. "Okay."

And then we headed into round three.

Chapter Twelve
MARI

The offices of Delgado & Ramos were located on Colorado Boulevard in the heart of Old Town Pasadena. Because it was surrounded by trendy eateries and the Paseo Colorado mall, I usually only visited Esteban's firm when I had other appointments nearby.

Today, however, the only item on my agenda was to surprise my husband and take him to lunch.

The idea had come to me in the shower when, for no reason at all, I started to cry.

All right. I had a reason.

Esteban had left before the sun, or I, was even up. He hadn't even woken me to say goodbye. My brain told me he was just in trial mode. I should've been used to it by now. He didn't mean anything by it. He never did.

Still, it had upset me. And when I was done with my shower pity party, I decided to take matters into my own hands and go see him.

He had mentioned last night as he was crawling into bed that he only had court in the morning and planned to work the rest of the day in the office to catch up on paperwork. It was a perfect opportunity to stop by and steal him away for an hour or two.

As I headed up the elevator to the third floor, my stomach dipped. Why was I so nervous?

The doors opened, and I waved to Carla, his assistant, as I passed her desk.

"Oh, Mrs. Delgado. He's not back from court yet," she called to me.

"That's okay," I sang over my shoulder. "I'll just wait in his office. He should be back soon."

And wait I did.

An hour and four unanswered texts later, I gave up.

"I know he'll be sorry he missed you," Carla said as I walked out of his office.

I couldn't even answer her. Rage and embarrassment tightened my throat. So I offered her a quick smile instead and then made a beeline for the elevator. And just when I thought my day couldn't get any worse, Chris stepped out.

"Marisol! What a nice surprise. What are you—" His expression changed from delighted to concerned. "What's wrong? Did something happen to Esteban?"

Shaking my head, I walked around him and stepped into the elevator. He followed me.

"I know something is wrong. Please tell me so I can help you," he said as the doors closed. Chris touched my shoulder, and I squeezed my eyes shut to keep the tears at bay.

"It's nothing. I promise. It's actually kind of stupid." The waver in my voice evidently didn't convince him since he put his other hand on my other shoulder.

"If it was nothing, you would look at me."

Slowly, I opened my eyes and attempted a smile. "I wanted to surprise Esteban by taking him to lunch, but he never came back from court. It's not his fault, really. He didn't know I would be here waiting."

"Did you call or text him?"

"I did and so did Carla. Wherever he is, I guess he's too busy to look at his phone."

"I'm sure there's a reasonable explanation," he offered.

Maybe it was just my emotional state, but he didn't sound too convincing.

The doors opened on the bottom floor, and we both stepped out. "It's fine," I said. "Please don't worry about me."

"Look. I haven't eaten, and I know you haven't eaten, so let's walk down the block to that bistro you like and grab something. I know I'm not Esteban, but I can be a pretty decent lunch date."

The nagging feeling in my stomach returned, along with the whispers of a thousand reasons why I should say no.

But I didn't listen.

"Sure. Let's go."

We walked in a comfortable silence to the restaurant. By now the lunch rush was thinning out, and we were seated right away. The waitress recognized Chris and came right over so we could order—a cheeseburger for me and a prime rib dip for him. After she came back with our iced teas, he broached the elephant that seemed to always be in the room with us lately.

"So, I know it's none of my business, but is everything okay between you and Esteban?"

My body tensed. "Why? Has he said something?"

"No. It's just something I've been sensing. Honestly, Marisol, you just don't seem happy."

The tears threatened to spill again, so I took a sip of my tea and willed them to go away.

"If you need to talk, I'm right here. I might have been Esteban's friend first, but you also mean a lot to me. I hate to see you hurting."

And although I tried my best to hold it back, one tear escaped and slid a slow, sad trail down my cheek. Before I could do it myself, Chris reached across the table and wiped it away.

His touch did something to me then. It was the contact I'd been craving all day. The reassurance I'd needed to prove somehow that I mattered to someone. Even if that someone wasn't my husband.

His touch gave me permission to finally tell him everything.

He let me talk all through lunch. It was as if he'd pierced my dam of emotions that had been building up over the past year. I told him about Esteban working too much, about how he wanted a baby, but I didn't, about my catering business dream, and about how I felt like I'd never do anything important with my life.

"What do you mean?" he interrupted. "You volunteer with the homeless and at the children's hospital."

I shook my head. "Correction. I volunteer on boards that make decisions that are supposed to help the homeless and the children's hospital. It's not like I'm doing something to make a difference. Not like the people who actually work there day in and day out. What they do is important. What they do matters."

"It sounds to me like you're looking for some purpose in your life, right? So go find it."

"How?"

"Well, why don't you do something with your baking? You obviously love it, and, until you open your business, think of a way that you can use that talent to make a difference."

Everything he was saying made sense. Still, I couldn't help but feel guilty about complaining about my life and my first world problems. And deep down I knew that Esteban only wanted to make sure I had everything I needed. It wasn't his fault if I wasn't telling him that. I wasn't the same girl he'd married, the girl who only cared about designer shopping trips and making appearances at all the hot ticket events. Back then I thought it was his responsibility to make me happy.

I knew different now.

"You must think I'm such a whiner. Poor little rich girl and all that."

He shook his head. "I know money doesn't buy happiness. Look at our clients. They are living lives envied by millions. Then something happens, and whatever buried secrets they've been hiding are exposed for everyone to judge. I learned a long time ago not to believe everything I see."

I offered him a genuine smile. "Thank you, Chris. For lunch and for listening to me. It seems like forever since I just sat down and talked to someone about things like this."

"Really? I would think you would have a bunch of girlfriends that you could confide in."

I shook my head. "I've always been the kind of person who had lots of friends to do stuff with, but there's no one I'm really close to."

"What about your family?"

Whatever my face said, Chris knew he'd hit a sore subject. "Sorry. I forgot you don't really like talking about your mom."

My mom. My dad. My cousins.

"No, it's fine. My mom and I talk now and then. But she's busy with her own life in Arizona, so I don't like to bother her with my drama." Especially when she used every phone call as an opportunity to ask for money. I'd sent her a check for $500 at the beginning of the year and figured I wouldn't be due for another chat until spring.

"And your dad?"

"We're not close. He and the rest of my family live in Inland Valley. It's a suburb about forty miles east of here."

"I know where it is."

"Right. Anyway, he's remarried and has a kid. I hardly see him. I try to go visit my abuelita and grandparents when I can. But it's been a while."

"Do you think you and your dad can ever have a real relationship?"

I shrugged. "I don't know. He tries now and then to reach out. So does his wife. But I'm not ready."

Guilt twisted my stomach so much that I placed one palm on top of it. The years hadn't dulled that pain, no matter how hard I tried to convince myself that I had valid reasons for staying away from Inland Valley.

"I used to be close with my three cousins when I was younger," I said, surprising myself with the admission.

"Used to be?"

"We were more like sisters, actually. But then things changed."

"What happened?" he asked softly.

I shrugged. "I'm not sure. I moved away with my mom, and it wasn't the same anymore. They weren't the same."

The lump in my throat wouldn't let me say anything else. Not that I could ever find the right words anyway to explain how betrayed I'd felt all those years ago. My dad basically abandoning me was bad enough. But it was so much worse when I realized that Selena, Gracie, and even Erica had broken their promises to always be there for me.

"I'm sorry if I'm pushing too much," Chris said after a few minutes of silence. "Like I said, I want to help any way I can because I can't stand seeing you so sad all the time."

His words surprised me. "I'm not sad all the time. Am I?"

"Well, maybe *sad* is the wrong word. I just know that your smile has been missing lately. Don't get me wrong. You're still as beautiful as ever. But when you smile, I mean really smile, then you're stunning."

I didn't respond right away. How could I? When I finally found my voice, all I could manage was "Chris."

With the mention of his name, he covered my hands, which had been busy tearing the straw wrapper into shreds. "I need to tell you something, and I don't want you to say anything until I'm done. Okay?"

No problem, since my voice had vanished again. His dark eyes flashed with emotion, and his jawline clenched. His gaze was so intense that I couldn't have looked away if I'd tried.

"You know Esteban is like a brother to me, right? I owe him a lot. And the only reason I haven't said this sooner is because of how much he means to me. But I can't hold it in anymore. Especially not after everything you told me. What I've been wanting to say, what I'm trying to say, is that I think I'm in love with you, Marisol."

The words still hung in the air between us when my phone vibrated and sang. I didn't have to look to know who it was.

"Don't answer it," he whispered.

"I . . . I have to." I pulled my hands from underneath his and picked up the phone.

"Hello?" I said, hoping my voice didn't sound as shaky as I felt.

"Marisol!" Esteban's voice was so loud that I winced. "I just got back to the office. I dropped my phone in the courthouse parking lot, and the screen shattered. First, I tried to get it repaired at one of those kiosks at the mall, but they told me I'd damaged the home button as well. I've been at the Verizon store for the past hour or so getting a new phone. I didn't get your texts at all, and Clara just told me how long you waited for me. What's wrong? Did something happen?"

Chris met my eyes. I knew he'd heard most of Esteban's story. Especially the last part. I lowered my head. "Nothing is wrong. I just thought it would be nice to have lunch together, that's all."

"Marisol, you know how busy I am. I can't always drop everything just because you want me to."

I bristled at his comment but tried hard to control my expressions and tone in front of Chris. "I know. It's my fault. I should've asked you this morning if it was okay if I stopped by. I'm sorry."

"Are you home now?"

"No. Actually, I ran into Chris when I was leaving, and he offered to take me to lunch. We're just down the street at the bistro."

"Perfect. Come back to the office."

"Really?" The irritation from earlier softened.

"Yes. You can bring me a sandwich. I haven't had a chance to eat and only have about twenty minutes before I have to jump on a conference call."

Disappointment deflated me, and I sank into my seat. "Of course. I'll be there in a few minutes," I said and braved a glance at Chris. He wasn't staring at me anymore.

After I'd flagged down the waitress and ordered Esteban a club sandwich to go, I excused myself and headed to the ladies' restroom. The annoyance was back, and it had brought its friend—embarrassment. As usual, Esteban had scolded me like a child, and I hadn't defended myself. But this time, Chris had heard it. I must have sounded so pathetic.

About five minutes later, I walked back to the table. I hoped Chris would've been long gone so I could pretend his love confession never happened.

But like I said, I never get what I want.

He stood up when he saw me and handed me the white plastic bag that had been sitting on the table. "Esteban's sandwich," he said.

"Thank you. I'll just pay for it up front."

"I just had her add it to the bill. It's been taken care of."

"Chris, you didn't need—"

He shrugged. "It's fine. Let's go."

Chris was quiet as we made our way back to the office. Which was fine with me. Then, just before we were going to turn the corner onto the firm's street, he grabbed my hand and pulled me into a covered alcove of an empty storefront.

"What are you doing, Chris?" I said as he held me by the shoulders.

"I want to make sure that you heard me back at the restaurant. I don't want you to have any doubt about what I said before Esteban called." His face grew close, and I could hear every breath he took in and expelled. Deep. Frantic.

"I heard you. But I can't—"

He put a finger to my lips. "Don't say anything else. Just know that I meant it. You deserve to be happy, Marisol. And I want to be the one who makes you happy. I know you're not ready to hear that. That's okay. Just know that when you *are* ready, I'll be here."

Chris didn't move right away. I wasn't sure if he expected me to move either. I didn't even know if I could.

Then, as quickly as he'd pulled me into the alcove, he was pulling me back out onto the sidewalk. When we arrived in front of the building, he told me to tell Esteban that he'd be out for the rest of the day and that he'd call him later.

Then he continued walking down the block.

It took me a few minutes to compose myself. By the time I made it to Esteban's office, I was doing my best to shake off what Chris had told me.

Of course he loved me. I was his friend. He just needed to realize that he wasn't really *in love* with me.

He just couldn't be.

And I'd do everything in my power to convince him of that before he decided to do something stupid.

Chapter Thirteen
GRACIE

The school day was only half over, and I already had a migraine.

Dear God, I know he's just a little boy, but give me the patience I need to deal with little Arnold Carter.

In the morning, he'd insisted that he'd swallowed a bug and wouldn't stop dry heaving all through our counting songs. Then, with ten minutes to go until the lunch bell, he refused to stop pinching his nose.

"It stinks in here," he whined. "I think Mr. Bubbles is dead!"

Then his next announcement, that our classroom goldfish was definitely on his way to heaven, elicited tears around the room. Even after I had them all gather around Mr. Bubbles's tank to watch him swim, Arnold wouldn't stop.

"Then there's another dead fish in here somewhere. I think it's in your desk!"

The realization that he might have been right made me freeze. I took a long, deep whiff and smelled dead fish.

Oh no.

"Ms. Reed?" I called over to my parent volunteer. "Can you help me open some windows so we can air out the classroom during lunch?"

Then I asked her to take the kids a few minutes early to the cafeteria. Once they were all gone, I walked over to the windowsill closest to my desk and grabbed the paper bag sitting on top of it.

Slowly, I brought it up to my nose and then smelled it.

Yep. Arnold was right. The bag definitely smelled like dead fish.

I took the bag holding my tuna sandwich outside to throw it away. Far away.

The bell rang, and a chorus of kids laughing and yelling filled the courtyard. My head throbbed instantly.

Thank God I wasn't a cafeteria monitor today.

Still, I needed to find something to eat so I could take some aspirin.

I looked at the closed door of the teachers' lounge and debated about whether to walk inside. I'd been eating lunch in my classroom for almost a week now—trying to bring foods that didn't require refrigeration. This morning, though, tired of peanut butter and jelly, I'd decided on a tuna sandwich. I couldn't find my dad's blue cooler bag that he sometimes used for lunch, so I had to stick with my usual paper sack. Now everything had turned into a stinky, soggy mess.

It was a self-inflicted seclusion. I had banished myself to the confines of my classroom for lunch—away from the staff refrigerator, away from conversations that didn't revolve around "boogers" or "potty," and, most importantly, away from any risk of having to sit next to or across from Tony.

So far I had been successful in keeping my distance. It wasn't too difficult most of the time. I saw him during staff meetings, of course, but there was no chance of any interaction or talking since Sister Catherine demanded full attention all the time. I also made sure we were never on the same schedule for recess watch, dare he try to chat with me as we made rounds. So all that left was lunchtime.

My stomach grumbled. There was usually fruit on the lounge's counter and extra sodas in the fridge. Then I remembered today was

Mrs. Gosling's birthday. That meant there would be cake, maybe even cupcakes. I took a deep breath and decided it was worth the risk.

The heavenly scent of buttercream frosting met my arrival inside the teachers' lounge. Everyone was already eating their piece of cake.

"Gracie! I was just going to take you over a piece," Mrs. Gosling said. "Poor thing. You must be so busy, spending your lunch break inside the classroom so much."

She walked over and handed me a slice, and I wished her a happy birthday. Then I made my way to one of the sofas in the corner and sat down. It was a white cake with fresh strawberry filling. I took a bite and stifled a moan. It was so delicious and buttery. I was enjoying my cake so much that I didn't notice for a few seconds that I had sat down right next to Tony.

"It's really good, isn't it?" I heard him ask.

I almost choked on a piece of strawberry. Actually, I did choke but was able to cough it up before it lodged in my throat. Tony patted my back and asked me if I wanted some water. All I could do was nod.

Dear God, please don't let me die of embarrassment. I don't really think it's possible, but just in case it is, please don't let that happen. Amen.

He came back a few seconds later with a bottle of water and held my cake as I took a few gulps. When I could finally talk, I thanked him as he handed me back my plate.

"It went down the wrong way," I managed to explain. "Guess that's what happens when you inhale instead of chew." In the corner of my eye, I thought I saw him smile. Before I could say something else, the lunch bell rang, and he stood up and left.

◆ ◆ ◆

The next morning during recess I was summoned to Sister Catherine's office. I walked inside and was surprised to see Tony sitting there talking with her and laughing. When he saw me, he stood up and waved hi.

I nodded and smiled and then sat next to him in the other chair. I looked at Sister Catherine and tried to read her expression. I had no idea whatsoever what she would have to tell us together.

"Thank you both for coming. As you know, the committee has been hard at work getting ready for the fall fiesta," she began.

The fall fiesta was St. Christopher's biggest fundraiser of the year. It was a three-day event with carnival games, a couple of rides, and lots of food booths. It was exactly the same as when I was a student at St. Christopher's. And maybe that was the problem. Over the last couple of years, the profit margin had been getting smaller and smaller. I'd heard rumors that some members of the committee had already quit because the school board was thinking of canceling the whole thing if the next fiesta didn't make more money.

"Well, we've had some people leave the committee due to scheduling conflicts, and I've been asked to fill those spots with teachers."

Uh-oh. It was starting to dawn on me why I was sitting in this chair.

"Because both of you are very familiar with the fiesta—having been students—and because you are the youngest members of the faculty, I think you two could offer some fresh insight into the planning and perhaps get our fiesta back to the level of popularity it was when you went to St. Christopher's."

Sister Catherine had a huge smile on her face, and she actually looked excited (although it was hard to tell since I had never really seen her get excited about anything).

Tony spoke first. "Well, I'm honored, of course, Sister, that you would think of me. But I have basketball practice after school, and there are a few games on Saturdays too. I just don't know if I would have the time for the meetings."

Silly Tony. He didn't realize that Sister Catherine wasn't *asking* us to do it.

“The committee is willing to work around both of your schedules. I think Friday evenings around six would be fine, yes? The first meeting is in a few weeks,” she said with a tone of finality.

Realizing we’d been dismissed, we both stood up and walked toward the door.

“Oh, and the committee is expecting you to come with lots of ideas, so be ready,” she called out.

Back outside, Tony shrugged. “I guess we’re on the fiesta committee.”

“Yes. I guess so,” I answered and tried to smile.

Really? You couldn’t think of anything more clever to say?

“Okay, then. Guess I’ll see you later.”

I was halfway to my classroom when the realization hit.

See you later.

I was going to be on a committee with Tony—that meant seeing him outside of usual school stuff. And, he looked far from thrilled about it. It was like the eighth grade all over again.

Only this time, I couldn’t pretend to be sick and stay home for a week.

Chapter Fourteen
ERICA

I should've known the day was going to go to shit.

First, I couldn't find my favorite water bottle, the one I always took with me to the games. I remembered I'd last had it when I'd gone with Selena to the movies the day after Christmas. So I called her to see if she had it.

"Oh yeah. I was going to tell you that you left it in my car, but I kept forgetting. Sorry. I can bring it over later."

"No, that's okay. I wanted it for the game, but I need to leave in a few minutes," I said as I headed to the kitchen to find another one. "Just give it to me the next time we go out, okay?"

"Sure thing. Hey, what are you wearing to Rachel's quince? I can't find anything, and it's two weeks away."

My younger cousin's quinceañera would be the social event of the year for my family. It seemed everyone had been getting ready for it for months now.

"Two weeks already? Damn. I thought I had more time. I'll probably just wear something I already have."

Selena scoffed. "Seriously? Don't say such horrifying things to me so early in the morning."

I rolled my eyes as I packed my sports bag with my cleats and extra hand towels. "Whatever, Ms. I-work-at-a-fancy-advertising-agency-and-make-the-buku-bucks. Some of us can't always afford to buy a new outfit for every occasion."

"Can't or won't? You could always find a better-paying job, or do what Mari did and marry rich."

So many sore subjects were in that sentence. "Not funny, Selena," I said.

"Speaking of Mari, my mom says she RSVP'd for two for the quince."

It was my turn to scoff. "Yeah, well, I'll believe it when I see it. I gotta go or else I'll be late."

As I drove to the soccer field, I tried to shake the simmering annoyance at the thought that Mari might go to the party. I should've been happy that she was finally going to show up to a family function. Instead, I was angry. Now, my cousins and my tía and tío and everyone else had hope they might see her. But I knew better.

If I'd pushed down any of that irritation during the drive, it came roaring back with a vengeance when I got a text from Charlie just as I pulled into the parking lot in front of the soccer field. He wanted to meet with me and Adrian first thing the next morning.

Well, fuck.

That meant the Pinche Asshole had told him about what happened on Thursday.

I yanked my bag from the passenger seat and got out of the car. As I walked to the field, I called Adrian every bad word I could think of. In fact, I was still cursing his name when I thought I saw a guy who looked like him, in *my* team's uniform, kicking a ball around with Mark.

It couldn't be him. There was no way.

You're just seeing things because you're so mad at him right now.

But the closer I got, the more it looked like him. And then the sinking realization hit me.

It *was* him.

Deanna ran up to me just as I dropped my bag in shock.

"I swear I didn't know," she cried. "I swear on my life."

I just kept shaking my head. "What? How? What the fuck?"

"Apparently, he lives in those new town houses on the other side of the field, and he stopped by to watch the game last Sunday. Remember, I didn't come last week either? Anyway, Mark told me that he'd recruited a new player, but I swear I didn't know it was him until we got here and he introduced himself."

How could this be happening?

"Does he know I'm on the team?"

She nodded furiously. "He does now. As soon as Mark heard him tell me that he worked at the *News-Press*, he told him about you. Mark had no idea, either, that he was *your* Adrian, you know, Pinche Asshole Adrian."

"He's not *my* Adrian. Shit. I didn't tell you everything that happened last Thursday. It's gotten way worse between us, Deanna. How can I be on the same team as him?"

She hugged me and whispered, "Please. I know this sucks. But we need you. Plus, who knows? Maybe it won't be that bad."

It was.

The Pinche Asshole barely acknowledged me with a nod when I finally got the nerve to join the rest of the team on the sidelines. I mumbled a quick "hey" before heading out to the field to practice some goal kicks. But just knowing he was nearby, probably watching me and judging me, threw me off my game. It was as if I hadn't kicked a ball in my entire life.

And once the actual game started, it didn't get much better.

Adrian was our new forward. He ran fast, but he was a complete ball hog. Poor Mark and our other forward, Saul, might as well have sat out the first quarter. By halftime, I couldn't keep my mouth shut any longer.

After taking two long gulps of my water, I walked over to Adrian, who had sat down on a nearby bleacher.

"So can I talk to you?" I asked after he finally looked up at me with squinted eyes.

"Sure. What's up?"

Oh, nothing much, except you're making me hate a game that I've been playing since I was a kid.

"This isn't the newsroom. You do realize that you're not the boss of everyone on the field, right?"

He shrugged. "I don't know what you mean."

"I mean, you're not the only forward we got. This is a team. You don't need to try to score every single goal. Pass the ball once in a while, for Christ's sake."

Adrian stood up. "If I have the best shot, I'm going to take it. I won't apologize for trying to win."

"But see, that's the point. You don't always have the best shot. Be man enough to accept that and give it to someone who does. Or else we won't win. Simple as that."

I didn't wait for him to respond. I didn't trust myself, because I was too angry.

And I only got angrier.

It was as if he hadn't heard me at all. He continued trying to score every time he touched the ball. Not only that, but the other team regrouped and was getting closer to our goal with every possession. They kept putting the pressure on me and the other defenders, and with only a few minutes left, they were given a corner kick. I took position near the goal and yelled at Adrian and Mark to move up.

The ball landed right in front of me, and just as one of the players on the other team ran up to kick it, I swung my right foot and sent it flying toward Adrian. But it missed his foot by about twenty-four inches. Another player stopped it and then kicked the ball straight into our goal.

The score tied up at 1–1.

Son of a bitch.

"Don't worry about it," I yelled to Deanna, who was visibly frustrated at the miss. I wanted to say something to Adrian, but he was already taking position at the midfield line.

During the next play, Mark and Adrian volleyed the ball back and forth a few times. But just when I thought they'd do one more pass, Adrian sent the ball flying and was able to tuck a low shot into a corner of the net.

We won the game.

By the time we came off the field, I was sweating, achy, and still royally pissed. I thought better of confronting Adrian again. So when Deanna asked if I still wanted to come with them to the bar to celebrate our win, I told her I wasn't up to it.

I expected her to argue, but she knew exactly why I wasn't in the mood to celebrate.

After peeling off my cleats and socks, I threw my stuff back into my bag and slipped on my sandals. I said my goodbyes and headed to my car.

I should've known my escape wouldn't be that easy.

"I just wanted to tell you that you played a good game," he said after stopping me.

"Thanks." I continued walking.

He caught up to me again. "You're good at stealing the ball. But I think you could work on your long-distance kicks."

That stopped me. "Excuse me?"

"It's not a bad thing. It's just if you practiced more, you could improve your aim."

"My aim is fine, thank you very much."

"Then what was with that pass after the corner kick?"

"Nothing. It was perfect," I insisted. Who in the hell did he think he was anyway?

"Yeah, so perfect that it missed me by a mile."

I lost it. "Hold up. That was a solid pass. If you missed it, then that's on you. Maybe your pretentious wannabe-hipster beard is starting to impair your depth perception? Just because you think you know all there is about reporting and editing doesn't mean you know everything about soccer too. What is wrong with you anyway? Do you need to be the best at everything so bad that you enjoy pointing out what's wrong with everyone else? Yes, we all saw that you can play. So what? That doesn't mean that the rest of us can't."

I threw my bag over my shoulder and walked faster to the parking lot. Within seconds, there was a sound of cleats clacking on the pavement behind me.

"Is this about the game or about what you overheard on Thursday?"

My hands clenched into fists at my side and I spun around. "It's both. You obviously don't trust me as a reporter, and I don't need that kind of questioning or judgment on the field."

"I was only trying to help."

"How? By being my own personal soccer editor?"

He threw up his hands. "Fine. If you really can't be a grownup and separate your feelings about me as an editor and me as a teammate, then I don't need to come back next Sunday. Problem solved," he said.

"There's no problem because I'm going to quit."

He dragged his hand down his face. "Jesus. Why do you have to be such a martyr?"

"What are you talking about?"

"I'm trying to be chivalrous and let you stay on the team."

That sent me into a tailspin.

"Let me? Let me? Let's get a few things straight, Mr. Mendes. First of all, I don't need your goddamn chivalry. Second, I don't need your permission to do anything outside of the newsroom. If I want to quit the fucking team, then I'll quit."

He shrugged and shook his head. "Fine. Do whatever you want. But when are you going to realize that you don't need to play defense all the time? Especially in the newsroom."

"Oh, I don't? So why then did I get a text from Charlie this morning saying he wants me and you to meet with him first thing tomorrow morning?"

"What?" To his credit, he did look surprised.

Liar.

"If it seems like I'm on the defensive all the time, it's because I'm trying to save my goddamn job. Not all of us can get a book deal or a Pulitzer. This is the only job I've got, and I need it. So excuse me if I feel like you've made it your personal mission ever since you got here to prove to everyone that I don't deserve it."

That shut him up long enough for me to jump in my car and speed away.

◆ ◆ ◆

The next morning, I walked into the *News-Press* office prepared for a fight.

I knew I'd crossed a line after the game. I was in a bad mood as soon as I stepped on the field, and I took it out on Adrian. But I couldn't change what I'd said, and now I'd have to face the consequences of having a big mouth. On the drive over, I'd practiced what to say in case I needed to convince Charlie why he shouldn't suspend me or make me clean out my desk.

He and Adrian were already in the conference room when I got there. I took the seat on the opposite side of the table from them both. Then I nearly fell out of it when I saw Adrian's face.

He'd shaved.

And the asshole looked even sexier.

That bastard.

"All right," Charlie began. "Thanks for meeting me this morning, guys. I didn't want to do this in my office because, with the glass walls and doors, it's kinda like being inside a fishbowl. Plus, reporters are nosy, so I figured meeting in here would give us some privacy."

We both nodded.

"I heard from a third party that there was, um, a very loud disagreement between you two Thursday evening. I know there's been some tension building, and I think we should talk about it and figure out how we can move forward."

I opened my mouth to defend myself, but Adrian beat me to it. "Yes, it's true. There was a slight disagreement over the direction of a story, but it was nothing. In fact, I spoke to Erica over the weekend, and I can see now that my, uh, management style could be better in terms of team building. I hope she'll understand that I'm still learning, too, when it comes to being a city editor."

Did I walk into the wrong conference room? Was Adrian Mendes actually admitting that he wasn't perfect at something?

Perhaps I wasn't the only one who'd done some thinking last night? Either way, I had wanted a chance to fix things, and he was giving it to me.

"And I realize now," I quickly interrupted before he could go on, "that I don't need to be so defensive when it comes to Adrian editing my stories. I feel confident that we'll be able to put our issues behind us and work together as a team from here on out."

He met my eyes that time. I couldn't say for sure, but I think he kind of smiled.

Charlie exhaled a huge breath. "Well, that's good. I guess we didn't need to meet after all. Now, if you'll excuse me. I haven't had my coffee yet."

We all stood up to leave. I was about to follow Charlie out the door when Adrian called out, "Erica, can I talk to you for a minute?"

I nodded and walked toward him.

"Did you mean what you said?" he asked. "You know, about us working together?"

I let out a long sigh. "I did. Look, I thought about what you said about me being defensive all the time, and it wasn't all lies. I didn't see your edits as wanting to help. Instead, I saw it more like you wanting to point out how much I sucked."

"You did? I apologize then. Like I said, I need to work on how I approach things . . . and people. How about we start over?"

I smiled and nodded. "Sounds good to me."

"And what about the team? You're really talented, Erica. I can tell how much you love playing. Please don't quit on my account."

"I'll think about it. And . . . thanks." Then, before I could stop myself, I blurted, "I'm sorry about what I said about your beard. But you really do look better without it."

Adrian blushed. He honest to goodness blushed. My heart stopped at the cuteness of it.

No, no, no. You absolutely cannot think about your boss like this.

So I did the only thing I could think of to get my heart beating again.

I ran out of the conference room.

Chapter Fifteen
SELENA

I checked my new Apple Watch for the third time. Even after a few days, the giddiness of seeing how amazing it looked on my wrist still hadn't waned.

But even if it had been my old Swatch watch from the third grade, I still would've known that Kat had taken a two-hour lunch.

Katherine "Kat" Martin was the senior vice president of marketing at Umbridge & Umbridge. She was beautiful, smart, fashionable, and my boss. She was also one mean, cold-ass bitch.

Kat was actually hired only a few months before me, but you would think by her superior attitude and air of self-importance that she was the mother-effin' CEO. I did my best to stay out of her way and do my work without much direction. For the most part, Kat communicated with me via email, even though my cubicle was directly outside her door. And the door was usually open. She wrote all her emails in CAPITAL LETTERS and never once said the words *thank you*, *please*, or *good job*. Some days, it would seriously cross my mind that she purposefully withheld information from me in order to make me look bad.

It wasn't my job to keep tabs on her. And I honestly enjoyed the time when she was out of the office. Something she'd been doing more and more of lately. I couldn't have cared less about where she was or what she was doing.

Unless it was now, when *her* boss was asking me if I knew.

Alan had walked to my desk at exactly 11:30 a.m. after realizing she wasn't in her office. I told him what I always told him: "I think I saw her heading toward the copy room."

I never knew where Kat disappeared to because she never told me. Still, I knew enough to know that I would look bad if I said as much. So I always lied.

Today, though, Alan wasn't giving up.

When he called to ask me again if I'd seen her, I checked my watch and realized she'd been gone for over thirty minutes by then. I said I thought she'd gone to lunch.

But now it was 1:30 p.m., and he was standing in front of me and asking again. As awesome and high tech as my new watch was, it couldn't tell me where Katherine had gone.

I was about to fess up and tell him I had absolutely no idea when I saw her quickly walk into her office and shut the door. But not before I noticed that her blouse was untucked from her skirt and her bun from this morning was long gone.

"She just got back," I said and pointed behind him.

He spun around and headed straight for her office. Relieved I was off the hook, I went back to answering emails. My reprieve didn't last long.

Less than ten minutes later, I was summoned by Kat.

Her door was open, and I wondered when Alan had left. She glared at me from behind her desk.

"Why didn't you text me that Alan was looking for me?" she said as soon as I sat down.

I shrugged. "I didn't know you were going to be gone so long."

Her eyes narrowed. "What's that supposed to mean?"

"I thought you were still in the building. I figured you'd be back eventually."

"Next time, text me. Don't assume anything, all right?"

"Okay," I answered. Part of me wanted to ask where she'd been. But I knew better. "Is that it?"

She handed me a folder before turning to her computer screen. "Alan wants you to look at these stock photos of couples and pick the ones you think we could pass off as Hispanic."

I opened the folder and noticed two pages filled with images. "Are you seriously asking me to choose an image based on the color of the people's skin?"

Kat turned back to look at me. "That's exactly what I'm asking. What's the big deal?"

Any other day, I would've kept my mouth shut. But I didn't appreciate having to lie to Umbridge on her behalf.

"Not all Latinos are brown, you know. I think the graphics department should go back to the drawing board and find images that specifically used Latino models."

I braced myself for her usual sarcasm. Instead, she crossed her arms in front of her chest and leaned back into her chair.

"Come to the conference room in five minutes. You're going to sit in on this new client meeting."

Kat rarely invited me to new client meetings. My instincts told me something was up. Dread swirled around my gut, and I instantly regretted my lunch choices.

I had checked her calendar when Alan was looking for her, so I knew she was meeting with someone named Scott Anderson from a company called Cup of Sugar. The company sounded vaguely familiar to me, but I didn't have enough time to do a quick internet search. I left her office and stopped at my desk to grab a notepad, a pen, and my iPhone. Then I speed walked to the conference room.

Kat was already there, seated at the head of the conference table, and to her right was a man I assumed to be Mr. Anderson. He was younger than I'd pictured, maybe late thirties or early forties. To her left was Henry Umbridge.

"Scott, this is my associate Selena Lopez," Kat introduced me in her fake syrupy-sweet tone. "I asked Selena to join us since you mentioned over the phone that you were also interested in getting some ideas for social media strategies. I figured we could discuss those today as well."

Mr. Anderson stood up and shook my hand. His palm was cool and his grip strong. I noticed his eyes were hazel and that his smile was warm and easygoing. "Thanks for being here, Selena. I can't wait to hear all of your ideas."

Oh crap! So that's what the bitch was up to. Pull me in at the last minute so I wouldn't be prepared and then profusely apologize to the client for my incompetency. That way Kat could blame our lack of social media strategy on me, rather than her, since it was one area where she was not an expert. And I was. Or I was as close to an expert as Umbridge & Umbridge could offer.

As Kat went through her cookie-cutter PowerPoint presentation on advertising, public relations, and marketing plans, I remembered where I had heard the name of the company before. It was the company Nathan had met with last month.

Cup of Sugar was a start-up app that allowed neighbors to rent or sell things to people who lived nearby. Nathan told me the company was getting ready to expand, and he was brought in to help find people for some key positions. He had been really impressed by the company's grassroots beginnings and their plans for the future.

And, fortunately for me, I had actually listened to every word.

"As you can see, Scott, we at Umbridge & Umbridge are really a full-service agency that can deliver award-winning and effective strategies that will take your company's brand up to the next level," purred Kat as she concluded her PowerPoint.

Scott nodded and smiled at Kat and then turned to look at me. Umbridge did, too, and so did Kat with her evil Cheshire grin.

I cleared my throat and smiled back.

"Forgive me, Mr. Anderson, but I don't have a PowerPoint presentation like Kat," I began. I could tell the Wicked Witch was about to feign surprise, so I quickly continued. "But based on your company's roots, I figured you'd appreciate a more organic approach."

For the next twenty minutes, I talked about creating a social media strategy that would elevate the brand's awareness while also keeping its casual and homegrown appeal.

"Wow, I'm really impressed, Selena," Mr. Anderson said after I finished my impromptu pitch. "I'll definitely be in touch in a few days about next steps."

Pride welled up inside me. Along with a little smugness. Okay, a lot of smugness. Especially when I glanced over at Kat. Her thin lips and crossed arms told me I'd done a better job than I'd even thought. It was an amazing feeling. And the fact that it also made Kat stew in her jealous juices was a bonus.

I stayed sitting as everyone else stood up to leave. Kat always expected me to put away the laptop and display boards and clean up the coffee cups and croissant trays after all client meetings. So I gathered the papers on the table and started to power down the laptop. That's when I noticed that she'd left behind her cell phone. I grabbed it and was just about to run out the door after her when she appeared.

"I knew I forgot something," she said.

"I was just about to go find you," I explained, handing her the phone.

Of course, she didn't thank me. "Did you look at my texts?"

"What? Of course not."

She scrolled through her phone, smiled, and then stuffed it into her pants pocket. Her smile disappeared. "I was going to meet with you later about this, but I have to run out for an errand and might not be back for the rest of the day," she said. "I've decided to bring in Rebecca to handle the social media strategy for this account."

My heart dropped. "I don't understand. I think I proved that I—"

"You did fine today, but I'm not convinced your approach is what Cup of Sugar needs."

"Mr. Anderson seemed to like my approach."

I couldn't help but add the dig.

Her eyes narrowed even more. "Yes, well, Mr. Anderson isn't your boss. Besides, you're not going to have the time to devote to an account of this magnitude. We have some new campaigns starting up, and you're going to be up to your eyeballs in status reports."

As soon as Kat left the room, I collapsed into a chair. What the hell had just happened? I'd totally given a damn good presentation. Especially since I'd had absolutely no advance preparation—and she knew that. How could she take me off the account? It wasn't fair.

But I refused to cry about it. That wasn't my style.

Instead, I picked up my phone from the table and texted Nathan.

Guess I was going to plan a visit to New York after all.

Chapter Sixteen
MARI

The warm water felt good. It was a quiet Sunday, and I took advantage of it by going for a quick dip in my heated backyard pool.

I was always a pretty good swimmer. It was the one good thing I inherited from my dad. Supposedly, he'd won lots of high school swim meets back in the day (according to my welita). So before I could even walk, my dad put me in our apartment complex's pool and taught me to tread water. Also, according to Welita, he used to call me his "pescadito." Something I also don't remember.

What I do remember is that every summer until we were eleven or twelve, my cousins and I took swimming lessons at the local public pool. While they stayed in the basics class in the shallow end, I quickly moved into the advanced group on the deep side. My abuelo would drive us there and then sit in the car listening to the radio while we had our lesson. He'd always make a big deal about us getting his car seats wet, so we'd sit on our towels and shiver the whole ride home.

I ended up making the swim team in high school, but dropped out halfway through my first season. My dad had made a big deal of wanting to come to the meets, so rather than tell him I didn't want him there, I just quit.

I was just coming up for air on my tenth lap when I noticed a pair of expensive men's dress shoes standing at the edge of the pool. I rubbed the water out of my eyes, slicked back my hair, and saw my husband looking down at me.

"I love watching you swim," he told me. Even with a chlorine haze, I could see the desire in his eyes.

It turned me on immediately. "I know. Why don't you take off your shirt and jump in? I could teach you a few strokes."

"As tempting as that sounds, I just came out to let you know I was home, but I'm leaving again." He bent down just as I'd propped myself up on the edge of the pool with my elbows. "Finish your swim."

I wasn't going to let him off the hook that easy. Especially since it had been days since we'd made love. "No, that's okay. I was done anyway. Wait there, and I'll get out and walk with you back to the house."

Pushing myself away from the edge, I gave him a sly smile. Then I turned to dive underneath the water. I knew I was showing off my swimming skills, but I actually had another type of show in mind. I wanted him to watch me walk out of the pool. I was wearing one of my sexiest bikinis—it was white with silver loop trimming—and I was grateful to be able to model it in front of him.

Once I arrived at the shallow end, I slowly stood and walked up the three steps so he could take a good long look. The cool air ignited goose bumps along my skin, and I shivered. Esteban grabbed my striped towel from one of the loungers and wrapped it around my shoulders.

I raised my head to kiss him, but he pulled away.

"You're going to get me wet," he whispered.

"That's the idea," I whispered back with a smile.

"We can't."

"Sure we could. I'm already half-naked."

"Chris is inside waiting for me."

At the mention of Chris's name, I took a step back. "Chris? Why?"

"We're headed to Santa Monica to meet a new client for dinner. I told you about it last night."

Bits and pieces of the conversation began to come back. The one we'd had while he was in the shower and I was brushing my hair before bed. That's what constituted quality catching-up time during trial mode.

"Yes, you did. Guess I forgot."

He gave me a look that said he knew I was pouting. "I'll try to come home early."

I returned his promise with a quick smile, even though I knew it was a hollow one. Client dinners always ran late. I knew better than to expect anything that night other than a date with my vibrator.

He gave me a kiss on the forehead and told me to hurry up and get inside before I caught a cold. But I waited a good fifteen minutes before following his instructions.

There was no way I was going to risk seeing Chris when I felt so exposed.

And I wasn't just talking about my skimpy bathing suit.

Later that night, I awoke to soft kisses on my neck. My hand reached out in the darkness to touch Esteban's cheek.

"You're home," I whispered.

"I'm sorry. I thought if I made it home by eleven, you'd still be awake."

Heavy fingers found my right breast, and I sighed. "I'm awake now."

"Yes, I can feel that," he said as he pinched my nipple until it hardened.

Warmth pooled between my legs, and I pulled him toward me until our lips met in the single ray of moonlight coming from the window above our bed.

Our breaths grew ragged, and we pulled clothing away until there was nothing left to keep our hot bodies from touching each other.

"I've missed you," he rasped.

"I'm right here," I told him and guided his hand to my sex.

He pushed a finger inside me, and we both groaned. "I've been thinking about doing this all night. I could barely listen to my client through dinner because images of you in that sexy swimsuit kept racing through my head."

We kissed until I shuddered hard against his hand. Then he moved between my legs and finally gave us both what we needed.

Later, when he held me against his chest, it felt like before. The before when we were connected and on the same page. Maybe that was why I decided to say something.

"Guess who called me today?"

Esteban kissed the top of my head and asked, "Who?"

"Julissa from down the street. She's throwing a baby shower for her daughter in a few weeks and asked if I'd make some of my lemon scones for the party. She even wants to pay me."

I'd been so excited after I'd hung up the phone that I'd almost called him right then. But telling him now, like this, was so much better.

I was wrong.

Esteban pulled away from me. "Pay you? You're not some caterer for hire. Who in the hell does she think she is?"

Although I could barely see his face, his anger was unmistakable.

I sat up and pulled the sheet against my nakedness. "Why are you so upset? I thought you'd be proud of me. Julissa goes all out for her parties and only hires the best. That means she thinks my scones are the best. I want to do it."

"Absolutely not. The women who will be at the baby shower are the same women you see at the club or on your committees. You don't think they'll use this opportunity to treat you differently? Don't you remember how hard it was for you when we first got married? You finally feel like you belong. Why would you want to risk that?"

He wasn't wrong. How many times had I come home crying after some stuck-up snob had made a snide comment about me being a gold digger? Or pretending to be nice to my face, only to make fun of me behind my back?

Since when had I gone from hating these women to becoming one of them?

That made me want the job even more. "But Esteban, I . . . I need . . . something for myself."

He wasn't backing down. "I thought we agreed that when we got married, you were going to give up any notions about a catering business."

A different kind of heat ran through my body. "I didn't agree to that. And you know it. I said I'd wait, and now I'm done waiting. You promised me."

Esteban got off the bed and walked to his closet on the other side of the bedroom. But before he went inside, he said, "And you promised me a baby."

So much for being on the same page.

Chapter Seventeen
GRACIE

"What do you think of the new PE teacher?"

I had just come back from escorting students and parents across the parking lot, and Sister Patricia's question nearly made me stumble over the curb. It was after school, and we were on traffic duty.

I thought carefully about my response before answering. "The students seem to like him okay."

It was the truth. My own students sang his praises every Wednesday after they returned from whatever activity he'd had them complete.

Sister Patricia waved the line of cars forward. "Yes, I suppose. Still, there's something about him that doesn't sit quite well with me."

"Really?" My voice sounded more interested than I wanted it to seem.

"You must feel it too. That's why you never talk to him, right?"

My head jerked up to face her. "I talk to him."

She shrugged and waved at the cars again. "Well, you say hello. But I've never seen you have an actual conversation with the man."

I thought about the last few days. I'd seen Tony in the teachers' lounge for our weekly staff meeting and also on the playground during recess. Not exactly the best opportunities to really chat. Part of me had wondered if I should go and ask him about the fall fiesta. The committee was scheduled to meet next week, and we still hadn't brainstormed any plans. I had held back from bugging him about it. Mostly because I didn't want him to think I was making up excuses just to talk to him. But today Sister Catherine had popped her head in during tutoring and mentioned how much she was looking forward to hearing our plans and was going to earmark twenty minutes on the agenda just for us. I had no idea if Tony wanted to brainstorm with me or come up with his own ideas, and I'd convinced myself it was never the right time to approach him.

Shame weaved through my heart.

Dear God, am I purposely avoiding Tony? Is it that noticeable? Am I a horrible person for turning in the opposite direction whenever I see him walking toward me?

I realized then that God didn't have to answer. He'd sent Sister Patricia instead.

"Perhaps I should make a better effort of being friendly with him?"

She raised her chin as if to motion behind me. "Here's your chance. He's walking over here right now."

My body froze as my mind played out different scenarios in my head. Should I turn to face him? Should I wait for him to come up to me? What would I say?

Even without looking, I sensed when he was standing behind me.

"Oops," I heard him tell Sister Patricia. "Guess I got my traffic-duty day wrong again. I'm happy to stay if you need my help, though."

She glanced at me before answering. I lowered my eyes. "We're fine. Thank you. I believe you are on duty tomorrow."

"Okay then. Have a good rest of your afternoon, ladies."

I mumbled a quick "Thank you" before leading the next group across the busy lot.

This time I stayed on the other side of the sidewalk until enough people had gathered again at the curb. When I got back to my spot, Tony was long gone.

And Sister Patricia was as smug as ever.

An hour later, I was back outside and headed home. The sky had turned a dark gray, and the threat of rain loomed. The air smelled damp, yet the parking lot asphalt was as dry as it had been that morning.

Still, it felt like a storm was on its way.

I unlocked my trunk and dropped my backpack inside. It was already after four in the afternoon, and I still needed to get home and help my mom with dinner. She had texted me twice to remind me to stop and pick up milk for the mashed potatoes. But tutoring had run a little late, thanks to one fifth grader who'd accidentally deleted everything he'd completed on the laptop—including his homework for the next day.

The trill of a whistle and hands clapping diverted my attention from the trunk to the basketball courts on the other side of the parking lot at St. Christopher's. I knew from the schedule posted in the teachers' lounge that our eighth-grade boys' team was playing the team from the middle school down the street. That meant Tony was there.

I thought about what Sister Patricia had said earlier and the look of excitement on Sister Catherine's face.

The nuns had backed me into a corner. It was time to get it over with.

I pulled my backpack out again, slung it over my shoulder, and strolled to the basketball courts.

Dear God, please don't let me make a fool of myself in front of him again. Just once, I want him to see that I'm perfectly capable of holding a professional conversation. He's just another teacher, correct? There is no reason at all for me to be nervous. Okay? Thank you, God. Amen.

The bleachers were half-full, and I found a seat four rows up. I noticed Tony standing courtside and yelling to different players as they dribbled the ball back and forth. I pulled my folder and a pen out of the backpack. I had no interest in watching the game, so I figured that while I waited for Tony, I could get some work done.

"Hot damn. His ass looks good in those jeans today."

My head shot up to see who was talking and about whom they were talking. It was the blonde in front of me, and she was staring at Tony.

"Today? Every day," said the woman sitting next to her.

They both giggled like schoolgirls, and I rolled my eyes.

The blonde leaned over to her friend and said in a low, but not low enough, voice, "I've been trying to get him to come by on a Saturday to run some drills with Sean, but he's been busy."

"He does that?"

"Yep. He went over to Monica's after school one day last week to practice with Timothy. Then after she invited him to stay for dinner, he said he already had plans with his girlfriend."

I couldn't help but lean forward a little. Tony had a girlfriend?

"He has a girlfriend?" Apparently, the friend was just as surprised as I was.

"That's what he said, but I think he just said that so he wouldn't hurt Monica's feelings. I mean, come on. You've seen the way he flirts with all of us. And if he really does have a girlfriend, then he's obviously not happy with her."

I hated that I was eavesdropping like this. It was wrong. It wasn't my business to know if Tony had a girlfriend or if he was going to cheat on her with one of the moms from the team.

I also hated how bothered I felt about it all.

A whistle blew, and the game was over. So was any urge I'd had to talk to him about the committee meeting. I would come up with my own ideas and bring those to Sister Catherine. Tony could do whatever he wanted.

The moms who had been sitting in front of me headed down to the court. The blonde gave a high-five to one of the boys, and I assumed he must have been her son. Then she and her friend joined the circle of parents—mainly moms, I noticed—surrounding Tony.

That was enough for me. I shoved everything into my backpack and climbed down. Without even a glance in their direction, I walked quickly past the fan club gathering.

"Gracie! Hey, Gracie! Wait up!"

I didn't wait, though. Tony's calls just made me walk faster. But he had longer legs and caught up to me. "Hey there!"

"Oh. Hey," I said when I turned around to face him.

"Were you watching the game?"

"Just the last few minutes. Congratulations on the win. See you tomorrow."

I had taken a few more steps when he jumped in front of me. "You got a hot date or something?"

What? Why would he say that?

"Excuse me?"

"You seem to be in a rush, that's all. I was hoping we could talk about the fiesta committee."

"Yeah, now is not a good time. I have to get home."

"Okay. How about we get together some day after school to talk about some ideas? Sister Catherine pulled me aside right before the game and basically warned me that we needed to impress the committee."

Ah, so Sister Catherine was applying the pressure on him as well. Of course. He was probably panicking because he had forgotten all about it. And just like in the eighth grade, he expected me to save the day.

"I'll let you know. I'm pretty busy this week," I told him and started walking again.

But Tony wouldn't let me go. "Then next week," he said after catching up to me again. This time he just kept walking beside me.

"I'll check my schedule and get back to you."

"Did I do something to piss you off?" he asked.

We'd reached my car, so I stopped and turned to face him. "Why do you say that?"

He shrugged. "Because you seem to have no problem chatting or being friendly with the rest of the teachers in this school. But all I get when you see me is a polite 'hello' or 'see you tomorrow.' And now I'm trying to reach out so we both don't look like idiots at the committee meeting, and it's like you can't even be bothered."

Guilt shamed me into looking at the ground instead of him.

He's right. You're judging the man based on the past and gossip. You know better.

I met his gaze. "I'm sorry if I've come across that way. It takes me a while to warm up to new people."

"New? You've known me since forever." He smiled, and it put me at ease.

"Um, not really. But you're right about us needing to be prepared for the meeting. How about we meet up on Monday? I don't have tutoring on Mondays."

"That works. But can it be later, like around six? I have practice."

I thought about his possible girlfriend.

"Are you sure? I don't want to impose on your personal life."

"I'm sure. Monday is perfect. All right, I better get back in case any of the parents still need to talk to me."

"Okay."

I was about to open my car door when Tony called out again. "Oh, and Gracie? See you tomorrow."

Chapter Eighteen
ERICA

My beer bottle was empty and I needed to do something about it.

I wandered through the sea of bodies that had crammed into Deanna and Mark's small living room, determined not to stop until I'd reached the assortment of beer choices chilling in buckets outside.

I was debating whether I'd do another hefeweizen or move to Coronas for the rest of the night when a plaid-covered chest appeared out of nowhere and blocked my path.

The red-and-gray pattern was instantly recognizable. After all, I'd seen it practically the entire day. I looked up to meet Adrian's bespectacled face.

After our talk in the conference room, our working relationship had improved. Somewhat. He was still an arrogant know-it-all. But now he actually seemed to be trying to be more—human. He made sure to tell everyone "good morning" when he came into the newsroom and every so often would release a "good job" to one of us reporters.

I didn't quit the team after all. I was big enough to admit (only to myself) that he was a pretty good soccer player. We'd won every game since he'd joined, so who was I to ruin something if it was working? I'd decided I could live with seeing him every Sunday outside of work.

And, I guess, a Friday night here and there too.

"Hey there. Guess you were able to make it after all," I told him.

"Hi, Erica. And yes. Steve only needed to copyedit one more story, so I figured it would be okay for me to leave," he answered as he surveyed the crowd. "I didn't expect this many people."

The urge to snicker was strong. It was a party, for God's sake. What the hell did he expect? A candlelit dinner for four? But I tried to contain the sarcasm for both of our sakes.

"Deanna likes to go all out when she throws parties. She even invites their neighbors so they don't complain about the noise."

He nodded as if he was the kind of person who went around judging other people's entertaining decisions. "Smart. But why do it on a Friday night?"

Guess he *was* that kind of person. "Deanna is on call tomorrow," I explained, growing impatient that he was still standing between me and a very good buzz. "She didn't want to chance having to leave in the middle of her boyfriend's thirtieth birthday party."

"Oh."

When he didn't move out of my way or continue the conversation further, I offered, "If you want a drink, they're outside."

Without waiting for an answer, I walked around him and headed for the backyard. It didn't take him too long to follow me.

"What are you drinking?" he asked just as I was pulling another hefeweizen from one of the buckets.

I showed him the bottle and grabbed an opener from a nearby table. He nodded his approval and grabbed the same.

"The food is in the kitchen," I said after taking my first drink. "They have a sandwich tray, chips, and pizza. I know Deanna got a cake, too, but she hasn't brought it out yet."

"Okay. I'll probably get something in a little bit. Did you already eat?"

"Yep. The sandwiches are pretty good. I'll probably go back for seconds later. I need something to absorb all of the alcohol I plan to drink."

I laughed, but he barely cracked a smile.

All righty, then.

It was time for me to ditch my boss and go find people who would appreciate my self-deprecating sense of humor.

But when I went back inside in search of my friends, Adrian was right behind me. He stayed with me as I chatted with two of Mark's coworkers from the dealership, offering his unsolicited opinions on foreign-made cars. Then he tagged along when I found a seat on the sofa next to a couple who used to play on the team but were taking a break after just adopting twin toddler girls from China.

"Where's Greg?" Kyle asked me after giving me a hug.

The mention of his name stopped me cold. Of course Kyle couldn't have known what had happened since it had barely been a month since our breakup. While I was getting better about talking about Greg, I didn't feel like going into the gory details at that moment. So I shook my head and scrunched up my face. "It's a long story. Besides, I want to see the babies!"

Kyle shot a look at his partner, Devon, who offered me a sympathetic smile. They understood perfectly.

"They're beautiful," I cooed as Kyle scrolled through photos on his phone of the two girls with chubby cheeks and adorable smiles.

"My mother insists that they look like me when I was a baby," Devon said, and we all laughed.

Well, almost all of us.

"But they're adopted, right?" Adrian asked in a confused tone.

"They are. That's why it's funny," I explained.

He nodded, but I still didn't think he understood.

Jesus Christ, this guy was going to kill me.

Still, something kept me from telling him to go away, and he stuck with me for the rest of the night. And after we'd joined in on the happy birthday singing to Mark, we took our pieces of cake and walked back outside. I held our plates as Adrian opened two more hefeweizens for us and motioned for me to take a seat on Deanna's back porch swing. Then he sat down next to me.

We ate and drank in silence for a few minutes before I couldn't take it anymore. "Am I crazy, or does this beer go perfectly with this cake?"

"It's the cream cheese filling," he said matter-of-factly.

"For real?"

"Yes, Erica. For real. Wheat beers complement the lighter cheeses."

"Wow, Mr. Mendes. You continue to impress me with your random knowledge."

"Guess that will be my go-to party trick then. I'm not good at chitchat, in case you haven't noticed."

"Just a little bit," I said honestly and tried not to grin.

"Erica, I'm sorry if I offended your friend earlier."

"Who? Devon? Don't even worry about it. He didn't punch you in the face, so he obviously didn't care."

He nodded and smiled. "That's good."

We took more drinks and more bites.

"So, uh, who's Greg?"

The fork holding a glob of frosting stilled in front of my mouth. I couldn't think of a reason not to answer, so I put the fork down.

"He's my ex. We broke up just before Christmas."

"Who breaks up right before Christmas? Seems to me that's more like a January first thing to do."

"January first?"

"Yeah. That way you still have a date for New Year's Eve."

"True. Does it count if you sleep with your ex on New Year's Eve, even though you broke up before Christmas?" It was out before I could stop myself from saying it. I winced, bracing myself for his judgment. Or worse, disappointment.

Instead, he seemed to nod in understanding. "So how long were you together?" he asked.

"Almost two years. I actually thought I was going to marry him. He, on the other hand, didn't think I was the marrying type, I guess."

"I almost got married," he announced.

The admission took me by surprise. "When?"

"A long time ago. She and I dated in college, and I proposed to her the Christmas after our graduation. But then I got the job in Washington, and she didn't want to move with me. She still lives here. Well, in Los Angeles. You know I'm from here, right?"

I didn't know, but I still nodded.

"Anyway, it all worked out. We were too young to make that kind of commitment."

"Have you seen her since you've been back?"

"Nope. Her parents and my parents are really good friends, so I get updates all the time about how she's doing. I don't even know if she would want to see me. And that's okay. She made a life for herself after I left. I don't need to be a part of it if she doesn't want me to."

It was weird hearing Adrian talk about something so personal. And yet, it wasn't weird at all. It felt comfortable. Natural.

"What about your parents?" I asked, suddenly wanting to know more about him and his life outside of work. "Do you get to visit them often?"

Even in the low light, I could see his jawline tic. "No."

"Why not?" I was a reporter. Of course I wasn't going to let it go.

"Well, my dad wasn't too thrilled that I took the job with the *News-Press*. He wanted me to go work with him at the family business."

The alcohol or sugar high made me brave. "Adrian, can I ask you a question?"

"Shoot," he said as he took our empty plates and threw them in the nearby trash can.

"Why *did* you take the job? Didn't you have a big book deal or something? Just seems like such a big . . . change."

He sat back down. "My second book tanked."

"You wrote a second book?"

He laughed. "Exactly. I had spent up my advance—buying an apartment in DC will do that quickly—and with the sales so low, there was no way the publisher was going to give me another contract at that level again. I couldn't think of a way to reinvent myself or the books I wanted to write, so I had to look for a job. I already knew there was no way I was going to go work for my dad, so I called up a few contacts, and my old editor told me about the opening here. It was what I was looking for at the time, I guess. My dad has been pissed at me ever since. I call my mother every week, but I'm not ready to face him just yet."

"That's too bad. I talk to my family every day and see them every weekend. Of course, they only live about five minutes away from my place."

"Do you have a big family?"

I couldn't help but smile. "Massive. I'm pretty blessed because my grandparents are still around. So is my great-grandmother. We call her Welita."

"Short for abuelita, right?"

"Yep. She's a real firecracker, and she makes the best tamales in the world. Well, technically, we make the tamales and she supervises to make sure we get her masa recipe right."

"I haven't had homemade tamales in years. You need to bring some to work sometime."

I shook my head. "Sorry. Our family's tamales are only made on Christmas Eve morning. Maybe if you're still around in December, I might be able to sneak you a couple."

"I'm going to remember you said that," he said with a laugh.

Although I'd been annoyed earlier that Adrian had latched on to me, he was turning out to be not such a bad guy.

"For what it's worth, you're way cooler than I've given you credit for."

"Thanks. And, for what it's worth, you deserve more than a guy who breaks up with you right before Christmas."

And to my surprise, it turned out that it was worth quite a lot.

Chapter Nineteen
SELENA

I didn't mind the whispers so much as I minded the looks.

First, there was genuine surprise. Followed by obvious curiosity. And then, finally, delightful approval.

All because a very handsome stranger had shown up with pizza and beer to the Inland Valley Civic Center. A stranger who was now helping my family get ready for Rachel's quinceañera the next day.

I looked over at Nathan, who was über focused on wrapping a plastic fork and knife together with a teal paper napkin. "Selena, does the fork go on top of the knife or vice versa?" he asked out loud.

"On top," Gracie and Erica answered in unison.

We were all sitting together with Rachel at a round table inside one of the civic center's banquet rooms. Our group was in charge of wrapping 150 sets of forks and knives. My mom and tías were busy in the opposite corner assembling centerpieces. I could feel their stares burning a hole in the back of my head.

It was going to be such a long night.

Nathan had called me a few hours earlier to let me know he'd wrapped up his meetings early and wanted to meet for dinner. But when I told him I couldn't because I had to help get things ready for the party, he asked if we needed another set of hands.

I only gave him the address because I honestly thought he had been joking.

"So, Nathan. Is this the most exciting Friday night you've ever had or what?" Erica teased.

He looked at me and winked. "Second most exciting."

"What was the first?" Rachel asked innocently.

I coughed up the swig of beer I'd just taken. Erica laughed her ass off. And poor Gracie turned a shade of red I'd never seen before.

I was sure my complexion was probably in the same Pantone family. It didn't help that Nathan looked pretty pleased with himself. That is, until I kicked him under the table.

He made a face at me before answering Rachel. "My most exciting Friday night had to be the night . . . I went to my very first Cubs game. I was eleven years old."

We all looked at Rachel, and she seemed satisfied with his answer and went back to tying the bundles we'd created with strips of white ribbon. Then she made me choke on my beer again when she asked Nathan if he wanted to come to her quince.

"Rachel, that's very sweet of you, but Nathan is flying back to New York tomorrow afternoon," I managed to say.

I looked over in his direction, fully expecting him to politely decline. Instead, he surprised me for the second time that night and said, "Well, I could switch my flight to Sunday. If there's room, I'd love to come."

Rachel jumped up and clapped. "Yay! I'm going to go tell my mom right now."

Before I could yank my sister's sweater to stop her, she was already screaming the news from the top of her lungs.

Great. That was really going to sound the alarm for the busybody squad in the corner.

"You made her day, Nathan," Gracie said. Was she swooning?

"I can't wait until tomorrow," Erica added, looking directly at me with a sly smile.

◆ ◆ ◆

"So, who are the kids sitting in the pews in the front again?" Nathan whispered as the Mass began.

"That's her court of honor," Erica, who was sitting on his left side, whispered back.

"Court? Like a royal court? Is that why she has a tiara on?"

I just shook my head. He'd started asking questions last night and learned pretty quickly that I was not his best source for information. I had passed on having a quince myself, opting for a sweet sixteen party instead. Gracie had also declined, mainly because she hated the idea of having to ask boys from school to be in her court since all our male cousins at the time were under the age of six.

Our sister, however, loved being in the spotlight. And if there was any opportunity to dress up in a fancy dress and dance with a boy, she was going to take it.

Up until today, Erica was the only one of our cousins to have one.

"So when does she change her shoes?" Nathan asked a few minutes later, and I was impressed that he remembered her explanation last night of some of the traditions.

"That happens at the party, not here at the Mass."

He nodded as if all these unfamiliar rituals made perfect sense to him.

I couldn't help but snicker, so I looked away. And straight into the amused glance of Tía Espy, who was sitting in the pew across the aisle from us.

"He's so cute," she mouthed.

"He's just a friend," I mouthed back.

She winked at me, and I rolled my eyes.

Because I didn't want her or anyone else to know that my heart was going a mile a minute. I told myself it wasn't a big deal that Nathan had wanted to meet my family. He was a friend, after all. I told myself this weird feeling in the pit of my stomach was only because Nathan had surprised me.

Seth always had an excuse when I'd invited him to family parties and dinners, so nobody except Gracie and Erica had ever met him. Small favors, I guess.

Later at the civic center, I made my cousins swear that when they were asked about Nathan (because they would be), they'd explain he was only a friend from out of town. It still didn't stop Erica's mom from peppering him with twenty questions as we waited in the buffet line.

"So what do you do?"

"Sounds like you travel a lot. Don't you ever just want to settle down?"

"How often do you come to California?"

"Do you like barbacoa? Or are you one of those vegetarian vegans?"

The last question threw him, so I explained. "It's like shredded barbecue beef. My uncle makes it for all of our big family parties."

"Oh. Well, I've never had it before, but I'm willing to try." Then he added, "I like my meat."

As he moved down the line, he chatted with each relative who was serving the food. When I noticed my mom serve him two extra dinner rolls while wearing a huge dopey smile, I lingered after he moved away and told her, "Behave, please."

"What did I do?" she asked, trying to act offended. But I wasn't fooled.

"I already explained that he's not my boyfriend," I said as low as I could. "We're just friends."

Friends who sleep together.

"So what do you think?" I asked Nathan when we were back at the table and he'd taken a few bites of his barbacoa, rice, beans, and potato salad.

"It's amazing. Your relatives made all of this?"

"Yep. Even the salsa that's on all of the tables," I answered and took a drink of my punch.

"Hey, why don't you have any meat on your plate? I know for sure you aren't one of those vegetarian vegans," he teased.

"Selena doesn't like real Mexican food," Gracie said as she sat down next to me with her plate.

"Um, yes, I do. Okay, well, some of it. Hello? I've got some rice on here," I said, pointing to my nearly empty plate.

"If the party had been at our abuela's house, Selena would've ordered her own pizza," Erica said. Everyone laughed, and I couldn't be mad. It was totally true.

"Oh, believe me. I know how much Selena loves her pizza. Just another reason to go to New York," Nathan said. I kicked him under the table. But it was too late.

"When are you going to New York?" Erica and Gracie asked at the same time.

"I'm not. I mean, I don't know yet. Nathan wants me to visit, and I'm still thinking about it."

I ignored his arched eyebrows and put a fork filled with rice into my mouth. I didn't plan on offering any more fuel for the gossip train. Even the mere mention of the remote possibility of me moving to New York for a new job would make its way through the reception hall before I could say "Statue of Liberty."

"Anyone else not surprised that she's not here?" Erica announced. I was grateful she was changing the subject. I'd just wished she'd changed it to something else.

Mari and Esteban hadn't shown at the church, and part of me was hoping they'd walk through the hall doors soon. The other part of me wouldn't let me hold my breath.

I couldn't pinpoint the exact day, but sometime after she turned sixteen, Mari began to drift away. The divorce was hard on her. We all knew it. But we were young and naive to think we could make it easier somehow.

First, it started with excuses as to why she couldn't come visit on her dad's court-appointed weekend. She was sick. She had a school project to do. She wanted to spend the night at a friend's.

So we stayed in touch by writing letters and talking on the phone. But by college, even those became fewer and farther between. I couldn't remember the last time she'd come for Easter or someone's birthday party. And then she'd missed this last Christmas.

"The party's not over. She and her husband might still show up," Gracie offered.

"Who is *she*?" Nathan leaned over and asked me.

"Mari, my cousin."

Satisfied with the answer, he went back to eating.

Erica shook her head. "I don't understand why everyone keeps hoping she'll change."

"Selena, you forgot to introduce your friend to somebody."

We all looked up to see Erica's mom standing next to our table with Welita. I wondered how much they'd heard. I nudged Nathan and we both stood up. Welita shook his hand as I made the introductions. She told him, in Spanish, that she hoped he was having a good time. And, to my amazement, he answered.

That impressed her, too, since she looked at me, pointed at him, and gave a thumbs-up.

Before my tía guided her back to another table, Welita said something to Erica in Spanish. She nodded sheepishly.

"What did she tell you?" I asked after they'd left.

Nathan answered before Erica could even open her mouth. "She said that you're never supposed to give up on family."

That meant that Welita had heard us talking about Mari.

We all stayed quiet after that and focused on finishing our food. Eventually, Nathan started asking questions again about the quinceañera traditions, and before too long we were laughing and Mari's absence had been pushed to the backs of everyone's minds.

Later, the lights in the hall dimmed, and the deejay announced my sister and her court. She looked so beautiful in her dress, and I could tell that she was deliriously happy. As I watched her and her court perform their carefully choreographed waltz, part of me *almost* regretted not having had a quinceañera of my own.

The waltz ended, and we all stood to applaud the performance. A popular song blasted over the speakers next, and Erica screamed in excitement. She grabbed my hand and dragged me to the dance floor. So I dragged Nathan.

The three of us danced to the next two songs before Nathan and I begged for a break and sat back down at our table.

"Since when do you speak Spanish?" I asked him as I watched my cousin and sister walk over to talk with my mom and Welita.

"Our next-door neighbor used to watch me at her house after school. I picked up words here and there by watching telenovelas."

That made me laugh hard. "What other talents do you have that I don't know of?"

He leaned over and whispered in my ear, "I have lots. Maybe if you behave yourself, I'll show you some new ones later tonight."

My heart sped up, and goose bumps erupted across my neck and down both arms. Since when could this man turn me on with just a few words? And although I'd been irritated by my family's reaction, I had to admit that I was enjoying having Nathan at my side. And not just because of what we'd do once we got back to my place. He made me laugh and genuinely seemed to like my family.

What did all of it mean?

Then I remembered he'd be gone in a few days, and it would be a month or two before I saw him again.

So, in reality, it didn't mean a thing. Nathan was a friend, and we liked to have sex. That was all.

And I was perfectly fine with that.

I really was.

Chapter Twenty
MARI

When Esteban walked through our bedroom door, I had just pulled out the last of the pins.

My scalp and the roots of my hair hurt after having been stretched by an updo that had taken forty-five minutes at the salon to create. I still wore my blue cocktail dress, though. Not because I was comfortable in it, but because I wanted him to see it.

He did.

"Why are you dressed up?" he said as he walked into his closet to hang up his suit coat and tie.

"Because for some silly reason I thought we were going to my cousin's quinceañera today."

"I thought that was next week," he called out.

I didn't answer right away. Instead, I walked up to him and shoved the invitation I'd been gripping for nearly two hours into his chest. "Nope. It was today. At three p.m."

He followed me out of the closet. "Shit. I'm sorry, cariño. I totally forgot. Why didn't you text me?"

I turned around and threw up my hands. "Because I'm tired of chasing you down and asking when you're going to be home. It's Saturday, Esteban. Did you really need to be in the office this late?"

He tried to pull me toward him, but I wouldn't budge. "You know this trial is a big deal. When I'm not in court, I need to be getting ready for court. I'm sorry I forgot. Besides, I didn't think you really wanted to go."

I hadn't at first. But then I had called Welita a few weeks ago to ask what kind of bread she used in her capirotada recipe. She kept telling me how excited she was about the party and that she couldn't wait to see me. Even after all these years, Welita still knew how to lay on the guilt. So, I had changed my mind.

Getting Esteban to agree to go had been easier than expected. I knew he was feeling his own guilt for making me say no to Julissa, and he'd been bringing me home presents every day since our big fight.

A sour realization struck me then. Had he only said yes to the party because he never had intended on going?

I accused him of exactly that.

"Of course not!" he insisted. "I really did forget. Besides, you could've gone without me."

I threw up my hands. "Ugh. That's not the point. I told you I needed you there to help me face my dad. You said you would go with me."

This time he was able to wrap his arms around my waist and hug me. "I'm sorry. Let me make it up to you. We'll spend tomorrow afternoon together, and I'll take you shopping and then to dinner. Anything you want, anywhere you want to go."

Esteban kissed me, but I didn't kiss him back.

I wanted to tell him that he couldn't buy or kiss his way out of everything. I wanted to tell him that I felt like I didn't exist anymore in this marriage. I wanted to tell him that if he wasn't careful, his best friend could steal me away.

"Really? You're really going to be mad at me because you missed a party you probably didn't even want to go to?"

I pulled away and took a deep breath. "It's not just about the party. Sometimes I feel like I'm not a priority to you."

"What are you talking about? You are my world. You are my only priority."

"You know that's not true. At least not anymore."

He looked as if I'd slapped him. "Marisol, everything I do is for you."

"I know. I know. But sometimes it would be nice if instead of doing everything, you were just here with me."

"Is this about the trial? You know it's not going to last forever. Things will go back to normal."

I didn't want normal. Not anymore.

But I knew I couldn't make him understand. At least not tonight. So I headed for the door.

"Where are you going?" he asked.

"To bake."

"Wearing that?"

I looked down at my dress. "No, silly. I'll put an apron on."

But when I got to the kitchen and pulled the apron out of the drawer, I put it right back in.

Suddenly, I didn't care about my dress. Or the apron.

I eyed my phone, which I'd placed on the counter. The urge to text Erica overwhelmed me. Then I remembered that she was probably at the party. Selena and Gracie would be there too. And although I'd convinced myself that I was ready to see them, I wasn't so sure anymore if I was ready to talk to them.

I thought about calling Chris. I hadn't seen or spoken to him since the day we went to lunch. It had almost been a relief that he hadn't dropped by again. But the longer I went without talking to him, the more I wished that he'd at least send a text.

And then what?

No, there was no one I could call. So I opened my recipe box and pulled out the card for a spinach-and-bacon quiche. If I couldn't sleep, then I'd make sure I'd have something to eat when the sun came up.

Chapter Twenty-One
GRACIE

It turned out that Tony and I were both busier than we'd thought.

So instead of getting together on Monday, we had to do our brainstorming right before the committee meeting on Friday. He suggested we go to the Denny's diner down the street from the school, and I agreed.

I rushed home after school to change into a pair of jeans and a red peasant blouse that I knew hid the parts of my body I was self-conscious about. I "borrowed" some mascara and lipstick from Rachel's makeup bag and tried to do something with my hair but couldn't figure out how to work her hot rollers. After fifteen minutes of getting ready, I looked at myself in the mirror. My sweaty forehead, ruddy cheeks, and frizzy hair made me want to cry.

"You can't lose fifty pounds or make yourself over in thirty minutes," I muttered to my reflection.

So I washed my face, put my hair in a ponytail, and drove to Denny's. I wasn't going to kill myself trying to impress Tony. I wouldn't let him have that control over me again.

At 4:33 p.m. I walked into the restaurant and looked for Tony. I didn't see him, so I got a table and sat down and waited.

Dear God, please don't let me have a panic attack. Amen.

But with every minute he was late, my anxiety climbed. And the more it seemed possible that he'd stood me up. I was such an idiot.

I finished my coffee, left a couple of dollars on the table, and grabbed my keys out of my purse.

"Hey, sorry I'm late!" Tony slid into the booth across from me. "I wanted to take a shower and change, but then I got a call, and it took me longer than I expected. Sorry for making you wait here for me."

I smiled and put my keys back into my purse. "Oh, it's fine. No problem."

The waitress appeared, and Tony ordered a burger and fries and a Coke. I ordered a salad and a glass of water. I pulled out the notebook I'd brought, and we started talking about the fiesta.

"I remember that the fiesta was like *the* place to be when we went to school there," Tony said. "I would beg my parents to take me all three days, and I would just hang out there with my friends."

As he reminisced, I just nodded and interjected a few words here and there. He updated me on what some of our old classmates were up to, since he still kept in touch with the same group of friends. Justin Silva was a lawyer in Miami, Lacey Buenavista was a divorcée with three kids in Seattle, and Tracy Kellogg was now Tracy Johnson—a real estate agent in Houston. Apparently she and Tony had dated off and on throughout high school, but then went their separate ways during college.

"I always figured you two would end up together," I said matter-of-factly.

"Me too, I guess. But then I hurt my knee, and when her future of becoming the trophy wife of a major league baseball player disappeared, then so did she," Tony said, a hint of bitterness in his tone. "It's a good thing too. I don't think she would have ever wanted to come back here to Inland Valley and St. Christopher's."

"And what about you? Why did you come back?" I asked, surprised by my own braveness to carry on a deep conversation with him.

He took a big bite of his burger and shrugged. "Honestly, it's the only place that would have me. After my knee surgery, I had to leave school since I was there on a scholarship. I stayed in Texas, though, and found a few trainer gigs at a couple of high schools. I even got my bachelor's degree in kinesiology after a few years. My dream has been to get a trainer job with either a university or even a pro team, but I could never get my foot in the door. Earlier this year, I applied for a position with the baseball team at Arizona College, but I got an email back that they were on a hiring freeze because of the budget. The same day I got another email from Jerry Patterson—remember him? His kids go to St. Christopher's, and he's on the PTA. He said he was recommending me for the PE instructor position, and two weeks later I'm on a plane back to California and back to Inland Valley."

He ate his last french fry and asked what happened to me after high school. I told him the very nonexciting truth. I went to the state university in Los Angeles, got my teaching credentials, and got a job at St. Christopher's—my first and only.

"What about marriage? Or kids?" he asked. I willed myself not to blush, but I could feel the warmth on my cheeks already.

"No—well, not yet anyway," I said, looking down at my salad. I could feel his stare, so I forced myself to look up and met his eyes. "What about you? Any future Mrs. Bautistas out there?"

"Right now? No. But, yeah, I'd like to settle down one day."

"You should . . . um, well, what I mean is, that you are good with kids. You'd probably be a good dad."

"Thanks. You know, Gracie, that first day in the lounge, I didn't mean to embarrass you," he said. I could feel my cheeks on fire now. "It's just that you, well, I guess I was surprised to see you there. I mean it had been such a long time. Anyway, I just wanted to say it was nice to see a familiar face, and I hope, you know, we can be friends again."

Again? Did I miss the part where we were friends before?

"Sure, of course. Besides, we are the two youngest on faculty. We kids got to stick together," I tried to joke.

He smiled and then started asking me if I had any ideas about the fiesta. I had the usual stuff—more rides and more games. I also told him about my idea for a chili cook-off. He liked everything on my list, but he had some ideas of his own.

"We really need something to draw in a bigger crowd," he started. "You know, like, maybe live music."

"Well, the church choir performs on Sunday, and the rest of the weekend there's a deejay—I think it's a parent who volunteers his time," I told him.

"No, I mean like real bands and singers. I'm sure there are some local acts who would jump at the chance to perform in front of a live audience."

He looked so cute, getting all worked up about how to make the fiesta a destination event. He started throwing out names of bars and clubs he could visit to track down possible performers.

Later that night during the committee meeting, Tony pitched our ideas, and every single one of them was a hit. Besides the local bands, he even said he was going to call up a friend and see if we could get one or two bands or singers who'd had records in the '80s or '90s and find out how much they would charge to perform. Even Sister Catherine was fired up and afterward came up to us and gave us both a hug.

"You two make a great team," she gushed. When she walked away, Tony winked at me and said, "We do make a great team."

I smiled and floated all the way to my car.

Chapter Twenty-Two
ERICA

I have many outstanding qualities. But winning graciously has never been one of them.

Whether it was a game of tic-tac-toe with my little cousin or a tournament match against another coed soccer team from across town, I tended to go overboard on the celebrating.

That's why I was still dancing like an idiot an hour after our hard-fought victory on the field.

"There's not even any music playing," Adrian explained, as if that would stop me.

"There will be," I said. "I'm just getting warmed up."

We were with the rest of the team at our usual after-game hangout—the Scoreboard. I should've been exhausted after playing three games that day. Instead, I'd gone home to take a quick shower, changed, and took a Lyft to the sports bar. By the time I'd walked through the double doors, I was reenergized and ready to celebrate with adult beverages and dancing. Lots of dancing.

Adrian rolled his eyes and shook his head. "You're ridiculous sometimes, you know that?"

I nodded and smiled, then took a sip of his beer. "Hey, I was drinking that," he complained, but I knew he didn't really mind. Well, not anymore anyway.

If anyone had told me two months ago that I'd be sharing a beer with Adrian Mendes in a bar, I probably would have punched them out for spreading lies. Who could've ever guessed that we would become such good friends?

He could still be an asshole when he wanted to, especially if he thought you were being lazy in your reporting and writing. The rest of the time he was funny and generous, and I didn't even mind his random vomiting of facts and stories. Well, not that much.

Mark and Deanna walked over, so I decided to take a break from my one-woman shimmy-and-shake show and sat back in my chair. The rest of the players and their families and friends were scattered at different high-top tables and booths surrounding the bar's only pool table.

"Don't tell me you were doing your victory dance again," Deanna groaned as she took a seat.

"She was," Adrian answered. "And I was embarrassed for her."

I socked his right shoulder. "Oh, stop. You know you loved it. You were even going to bust out some moves of your own before they came over."

"You're such a liar. I have never, nor will I ever, bust a move. What does that even mean, by the way?"

It was my turn to groan. "Oh my God, please do not start a whole discussion on the origins of various urban slang phrases."

"Fine. At least not right now I won't," he said.

"Ah, you're the bestest," I teased. And because we won our game and because I was in an extremely good mood, and mostly because I'd already had two beers, I put my arms around his shoulders and hugged him. Almost immediately, he straightened his back, and his body tensed beside mine. I let go.

"Okay, who's up for another round?" he asked, getting to his feet.

We all raised our hands, and he and Mark headed to the bar. He turned and asked if I also wanted to share nachos, and I agreed.

It didn't take but three seconds after he walked away for Deanna to pounce. "Did you really just hug him?"

I was as surprised as my friend at what I'd done but played it off. "So what?"

"So what? I feel like I'm missing something. The hugging, the flirting? What happened to Mr. Pinche Asshole?"

I put out my hand in a stopping motion. "Whoa! Hold the fuck up. First, there's no flirting going on here. And second, he is most certainly still Mr. Pinche Asshole. Well, sometimes."

"If there was no flirting, then what do you call that little dance you were doing in front of him and agreeing to share a plate of nachos?"

"Um, excuse me? I'll share nachos with anyone. You know that."

Deanna pursed her lips and muttered, "Mm-hmm. Whatever you say."

"I say we're friends. And that's all. Okay?"

"Okay." She still didn't look like she believed me.

For the next hour or so, because of Deanna's accusations, I was hyperaware of what I said or did around Adrian. Did I stand too close? Did I accidentally brush his arm with my arm? Did I stare too long or smile too big?

If I'd made him uncomfortable with the hug, he didn't show it again. Still, I didn't want to give him—or anyone else—the wrong impression. He was my boss and my friend, and I sure as shit didn't want him to think I was coming on to him in any way, shape, or form. So when another guy, someone not on our team, came up and asked me to dance, I jumped at the chance.

The song was fast, and at first I wondered if I could keep up. He twirled me around, and my buzz kicked in. With his hands on my hips, he moved my body in unison with his. I placed my arms around his neck and relaxed my body so he could manipulate it like a rag doll. It was like he was dancing for both of us.

"You move pretty good," my dance partner yelled in my ear. "You smell good too."

I looked up at him and smiled. He was cute, but not my type. No specific reason why. He just wasn't. And that meant he wouldn't get a second dance.

After another minute, he tried to tell me something, but the music was too loud for me to make out every word. "What?"

He leaned in close again to my ear. "I said, 'Do you wanna get some air?'" The song ended and this time I heard every word—and the intention of getting me alone with him—loud and clear.

"Actually, I'm going to sit the next one out. Thanks, though."

He walked me back to the table and then left in search of another partner. Deanna and Mark had wandered off to go talk with some of the other players, so it was just Adrian at the table. I took a sip of my beer but didn't sit down.

"Did you finally get all that dancing out of your system?" he asked.

"Maybe. Or maybe I'm going to dance with every single guy in this place." Then I hastily added, "Well, you know, except for you, since you don't dance."

"Who said I didn't dance? All I said was that I wasn't going to bust a move."

I laughed out loud and took another drink. Then almost spit it out when Adrian stood and grabbed my hand. He led me to the dance floor just as a slower number was starting up.

"Okay, okay. I believe you. You don't need to prove anything," I said, trying to pull my hand out of his grasp. I looked around, not wanting others to see us for some reason, but Deanna and Mark were still on the other side of the bar.

"Jesus Christ, Erica. Stop talking," he ordered as he put one arm around my waist and pulled me against him. I drew in a sharp breath when our bodies made contact. His arms were strong, his chest and stomach hard. Why hadn't I ever realized how fit he was? And before I could wonder if he was thinking the exact opposite of me, we started to move.

I should've known he'd be a good dancer, given the fancy footwork he did to manipulate and dribble a soccer ball. What I didn't expect was how serious he was taking our dance. No jokes, no teasing. He just swayed me back and forth, and soon I couldn't help but rest the side of my head against his chest.

If he'd been any other guy, in any other bar, I would have pushed my body closer. That's how good it felt to be in his arms.

"Did you just shiver? Are you cold?" he asked.

"No, not cold."

"Okay, then."

We danced without speaking, and it was easy to close my eyes and get lost in the music. His cologne tingled my nose—a light woodsy scent tangled with some type of citrus. Maybe lemon? I greedily inhaled the smell of him.

I could do this all night.

The song ended, of course. Regretfully, I slid my arms from his neck. But he didn't let me go right away. Or maybe it just felt like that.

"Thanks for the dance," he mumbled and walked back toward the table.

Deanna and Mark were waiting for us. "Wow, Adrian. I didn't know you had those kind of moves," she said. "Hey, Erica, did you know he could move like that?"

I ignored her sly grin. "I had absolutely no idea," I answered.

"I guess I'm full of surprises tonight," he said. "In fact, I got one more—next round is on me."

But another drink didn't sound so good. I couldn't stop rocking back and forth, and not because I couldn't stop dancing, but because I felt light headed. I pressed my hand to my forehead and cheeks. I was also burning up.

"I'll be right back," I told everyone. "I need to get some air."

I walked out of the bar and leaned against a nearby wall to steady myself. A few minutes later Adrian found me.

"Are you okay?" The concern in his voice touched me.

"Yeah, sure. I'm fine. I probably should slow down on the beers, though."

"Good. I'll stay out here with you, then."

I shook my head and closed my eyes. The world continued to spin. "You don't have to do that. Go back inside. Buy everyone their drinks."

"I gave Mark my wallet. Probably not the best idea now that I'm thinking about it. But I'm not going to leave you alone, especially when you're not feeling well."

I looked at him. "We're not in the newsroom, Adrian. You don't have to feel responsible for me."

He shook his head. "This has nothing to do with that. We're friends, right? And friends don't let their friends hang outside bars by themselves. However, I feel like I need to warn you that if you start throwing up, I'm outa here."

That made me laugh. "Good to know. I didn't realize you were one of *those* people."

"Yes, I am. Like now, even though we're just talking about it, I want to gag. For some reason, I'm okay with seeing blood, though."

The weirdness of our conversation helped center me. I began to feel normal again. "So if I ever need to go donate blood, you'd come with me?"

"Not only would I come with you, but I'd even hold your hand."

Although I'd never donated blood in my life, the thought of having Adrian by my side if I ever had to did something to my insides.

And I knew I couldn't blame that on the alcohol.

Chapter Twenty-Three
SELENA

I arrived at New York's LaGuardia Airport just after eleven at night on a Thursday. Nathan was waiting for me, holding a sign that read, "Sexy lady from Los Angeles."

He kissed me, and I smiled against his lips.

"What were you going to do if I wasn't the only sexy lady from Los Angeles arriving tonight?"

"Oh, you weren't. Two other women came up to me before you did. Let's just say it's been an awkward night."

That made me laugh hard. I was so happy to be in New York.

And with Nathan.

Something had definitely changed between us the last couple of months.

When we'd first hooked up, I'd told him it was a onetime thing. He'd agreed. Then he'd found me on LinkedIn and messaged me that he would be back in town in a few weeks and asked me to dinner. I declined dinner but offered to meet him at his hotel. And that was basically how things had been for the past year. Then a few months ago, he began texting me even when he wasn't in town. Texting turned into weekly calls, and most of the time we didn't even have phone sex. But

I still didn't consider us dating. Much to my family's disappointment. He was the topic of every conversation now.

How's Nathan?

When is he coming to visit again?

Why don't you bring him over for dinner?

Why do you not want to be happy?

Do you want to be alone forever?

Et cetera. Et cetera. Et cetera.

The truth was, I didn't know what I wanted from Nathan. And I didn't know what he wanted from me. Besides, I had enough on my mind with the account manager job interview with Kane. I couldn't think about relationship stuff too.

Even still, I didn't argue when he suggested I stay at his apartment rather than get a hotel room. It made sense since I was arriving late and only planned to stay until Saturday night.

It worked out perfectly too. We stopped to pick up takeout—I had no idea so many food places in New York stayed open so late. After dinner, we had sex (of course), and then I passed out from exhaustion.

By the time I arrived for my interview the next day, I was well rested and ready to make an impression on Kane's search team.

The team included the company's HR director, the director of client services, and the director of the marketing department. Their questions were tough, but I was prepared.

What I wasn't prepared for was when they told me to wait in the room for my second interview.

Second interview?

Apparently, because I was an out-of-town candidate, they decided to do the next round in the same day. This time, my interview would be with Leo Markham, vice president of marketing, communications, and public relations.

His size alone was intimidating.

When he entered the room, it was as if everything shrank. Including me.

He was well over six feet—that much I knew. His large hand swallowed mine, and his deep voice reverberated even in the large space.

Where the search team was easygoing and warm with their questions, Leo was stiff and arrogant.

"Based on your résumé, I honestly don't know why I'm interviewing you today," he said matter-of-factly from across the table.

It took me a few seconds to digest what he'd said. "Excuse me?" I asked, trying to figure out if I'd heard what I'd heard.

He let out a long, bored sigh. "On paper, you're not qualified, Ms. Lopez. So, tell me why I should continue with this interview."

I tried to channel my sister's patience and my mother's constant advice about not saying anything if you can't say anything nice. "Well, isn't that the point of an interview—so I can let you know what's not on that paper?"

"Fine. Go right ahead."

I cleared my throat and then gave him the spiel I'd been practicing all morning. I talked about the accounts I'd worked on and the awards I'd helped Umbridge & Umbridge win over the past few years.

But the more I talked, the more I clenched my fists under the table. Markham still looked bored. He didn't even bother to stop checking his phone. Except for when I started to go over my daily responsibilities. That's when he held up his hand.

"That's all fine and good for your little agency. But Kane is a player in a whole different world. Our clients have the highest of expectations, and I just don't see how someone with your limited experience can meet those expectations."

And that's when I decided I'd had enough.

"You know, just because I may not work at a big agency right now doesn't mean I wouldn't be an asset to Kane. In fact, I think I'd be a pretty fantastic addition to your team. Yes, I'm used to a smaller office and fewer people, but guess what? Less people means less hands to help. Here you have a person to focus just on advertising, someone else to take care of social media, and another one to focus on PR. I have to do everything at my agency. That means I can look at accounts from all perspectives and understand the strategies behind them. Also, some clients need to have their hand held. They don't want to feel like they're just another contract. They want personalized service and to feel like their project isn't getting lost in the shuffle. That's my specialty. Why? Because I make time to answer their calls and their emails. And they love me for it. I think your clients would love that kind of personalized attention, too, especially since you are so *big*. But it sounds like you've already made your decision about me, so I don't want to waste any more of your valuable time. I'm sure you have better things to do in this big, giant agency of yours."

My heart was beating like crazy. And I held my breath as I waited for Leo to say something.

His eyebrows arched, and his eyes widened in surprise. For a second, I thought he'd start yelling. Instead, he put down his pen and said, "Well, I guess there's nothing left to say."

I stood up, smoothed down my skirt, and grabbed my portfolio off the table. I picked up my purse and pulled my sunglasses down over my eyes. "Thank you for your time."

I walked out of his office with trembling knees, but my head held high. I cursed at myself for losing control the entire elevator ride down and in the taxi ride back to Nathan's apartment. Fortunately, he had meetings the rest of the day and had given me his key. I didn't want to face him just yet.

Of course, Nathan texted soon after to ask how everything had gone. I'd just responded: Fine.

The rest of the afternoon, I tried to read and watch television. But my mind was racing a mile a minute, so I filled the bathtub and tried to soak away my anxiety.

And when Nathan called later to ask me to dinner, I prepared myself for the worst. Nathan had recommended me for the job. He might be pretty angry that I'd just thrown it away, along with his reputation and commission. So angry that he might want to put me on a plane himself.

I packed all my clothes back into my suitcase and even got on the airline's website to see if I could catch a red-eye home that night.

So, thinking I had only hours left in the city that never sleeps, I sipped two very strong rum and Cokes and headed to the restaurant to meet him. He was already at the table when I arrived, drinking a Stella Artois.

He seemed relaxed, even happy. All that meant was that Kane's people hadn't told him yet.

I studied the menu, ordered the sixty-dollar steak, and enjoyed every morsel of it. In between we made small talk about our childhoods, our families, and what we loved about New York. Then when the waiter asked if we were ready for dessert, I told him to come back in five minutes.

"All right, Nathan. I want to enjoy my raspberry cheesecake, but I can't until you know the truth."

He set down his napkin. "What do you mean?"

"I might have torpedoed the interviews today. I didn't mean to, but that Leo guy is kind of a jerk, and tomorrow you're going to hear that I was a total bitch and that they would never ever offer me a job in a million years."

Nathan almost spit out his ice water and started laughing.

"I actually don't think there's anything funny about this," I said rather sternly.

"I'm sorry, Selena, but I do think this is quite funny." He laughed. "What makes you think all of that? Their HR guy called me right before I called you to meet me for dinner."

I must have looked rather shocked because he cracked up laughing one more time.

"And what did he say?" I asked slowly.

"They loved you. I knew they would. Leo is very selfish when it comes to handing out compliments, but he had nothing but good things to say about you."

This time it was me who almost spit out my ice water. Leo said "good things" about me? Now I was totally confused. Nathan must have seen the confusion spelled out on my face.

"Selena, you did great. They're going to interview a few more candidates, but you're at the top of the list right now. I'm pretty sure the job will be yours if you want it. What do you say?"

At that moment the waiter came back to our table.

"I say, I'll take the raspberry cheesecake," I announced.

I couldn't ignore the heaviness that suddenly weighed on my shoulders.

When I didn't think there was a possibility I'd get the job, I'd wanted it more than anything I'd ever wanted before. But now that it could be mine?

I wasn't so sure.

Was I really ready to leave LA behind? I was definitely ready to say goodbye to Umbridge & Umbridge, but did I really have to go all the way to the opposite coast? I thought of my sister, Erica, and the rest of my family. What would they think about me moving away? This was way more than just getting a new job. It was more like getting a brand-new life.

The next morning, I left Nathan's apartment and told him I needed to go think.

And I always did my best thinking with a couple of shopping bags on each arm.

Within an hour, I was standing inside the only New York landmark I was interested in visiting: Bergdorf Goodman on Fifth Avenue.

I strolled the aisles in both adoration and awe. This was definitely my happy place. If I took the job, I'd probably spend a good chunk of every paycheck right here.

That was both a pro and a con.

Excitement tingled every nerve as I spotted the handbag department. Then I nearly squealed when my eyes fell on the most beautiful thing I'd ever seen.

I fingered the light-pink Prada handbag and pictured a few outfits it would match. Then I bent down to inhale the luxurious aroma of the leather. The sales clerk at the nearby counter didn't even blink. Like a sommelier of fine wine, she understood exactly what I was doing.

"It just came in this week. You'll be one of the first to buy this style," she teased. The lady sure did know a sucker when she saw one.

"I might be getting a new job," I announced. As if I needed to explain to a stranger why I was considering spending a couple grand on a purse.

"Congratulations. Sounds like you definitely deserve to treat yourself."

I nodded and smiled. I did deserve it.

"You always did have great taste." A once-familiar voice tore me away from worshipping the purse.

My cousin Mari stood next to me at the counter.

I shook my head in disbelief. "Oh my God! You're here in New York!" I said as I gave her a hug and quick peck on the cheek.

"You too," she answered with a smile. "Esteban is in town to meet with a potential new client, and I tagged along. New York is one of my favorite cities."

"That's nice. I'm in town visiting a friend."

Although I wasn't sure if Mari talked to anyone in the family on a weekly basis, I still didn't feel right telling her about my interview and not Gracie or Erica.

"While Esteban is in meetings, I thought I'd do a little shopping. Is that new?" That last question was for the sales clerk.

"It is. Just came in this week." I shot the girl an evil glare. She didn't see it.

"Ooh, it's so lovely. I'll take it." Mari whipped out her credit card and handed it to the clerk. I noticed that she didn't even ask the price or whether I planned on buying it first.

Although I was a little irked, I couldn't help but hear Gracie's voice telling me to make an effort to catch up with Mari.

After Mari took the shopping bag holding the precious purse inside, I stepped closer. "So, I'm going home tomorrow, but I'm free tonight if you want to grab dinner," I said.

Her eyes widened, and her face softened. For a second, I thought she would take me up on my offer. But then her smile fell.

"Oh, I wish I could. I really do. But I'm meeting Esteban for dinner. It's kind of a date night," she said sheepishly.

A wave of unexpected relief washed over me. "Oh, of course. I totally understand. No worries."

Mari smiled again and gave me a hug. "Well, it was great seeing you, cousin. Maybe we could grab dinner once we're back in California?"

"Sure," I said, already knowing it would never happen.

Then she was gone.

"Miss, did you want to get one too?" The clerk suddenly seemed to remember me.

I shook my head. "No thanks. It's not really what I was looking for."

With that, I turned around and walked out of Bergdorf Goodman. I didn't know what made me sadder: the fact that I didn't have a new purse or that I had been a little relieved that I didn't have to make awkward conversation with Mari over a glass of wine tonight.

I suddenly understood what Erica was always so angry about. It didn't matter whose fault it was: the fact remained that our relationship with Mari wasn't the same anymore. How much I wished we could all be like we were before.

Suddenly, I couldn't wait to get home.

Chapter Twenty-Four
MARI

My cousin Selena was in New York.

As I dressed to meet Esteban for dinner, the thought continued to pop into my head.

So did the memory of how awkward it had been between us.

It had been months since the last time I'd seen her or any of my cousins. I'd received updates now and then when I did go visit my grandparents and Welita. I knew she still worked for a boutique PR agency in LA and, as of my last visit, didn't have a steady boyfriend. She'd mentioned she was here visiting a friend, but I got the vibe that there was more to the story.

A wisp of regret swirled within me. I should've asked her to grab a coffee instead when I declined her dinner invite. But, then again, she didn't seem too eager to chat any more than we had already.

Maybe it was because I'd bought that purse she'd been eyeing?

I looked over at the handbag sitting on the hotel bed and sighed. Why had I done such a stupid thing? Was I really so petty that I bought an expensive purse just to show my cousin that I could?

Yes, you are.

Memories of when I'd visit my dad after the divorce spilled over. I always felt so out of place, even though my grandparents' house had been my second home growing up. My cousins were far from wealthy, but their parents bought them pretty much whatever they wanted. I remembered one day we went to the mall because Gracie had gotten $100 for her birthday. Selena and Erica had some money of their own, too, and I had to watch from the sidelines as they shopped at places I could never afford. They had no idea that the outfit I was wearing that day had come from a thrift store.

When Erica noticed I wasn't buying anything, she offered to get me a shirt I'd been eyeing. Then Gracie tried to buy me some earrings. Instead of being grateful, I got mad and embarrassed and stormed out of the store.

Looking back now, I knew they'd only wanted to make me happy. And as usual, I took it completely the wrong way.

Part of me wanted to text Selena and ask her if she still wanted the handbag as an early birthday present. But I knew she'd never accept it. She didn't want my leftovers.

Why had I been such a bitch?

Rather than answer my own question, I focused on getting ready for my date with my husband.

He'd told me two days ago that he was traveling to New York for the weekend to meet with the director Tuck Hunter, who was in the city scouting locations for his next movie. Tuck had fired his lawyer last month and was looking for someone new to represent him during proceedings on drunk driving charges back in Los Angeles. Since Esteban was going alone, I pleaded for him to take me. I loved New York. I loved the shopping, the restaurants, and even the crowds. San Marino was so quiet. Stifling even. I much preferred the chaos of NYC. But besides wanting to visit the city, I figured a weekend away could help us reconnect and get back on track. We needed to finally have that long conversation. I needed to make him understand why I wasn't happy.

Although he'd warned me that he'd be busy with meetings most of the time we were here, he had promised to take me out tonight. I had hoped we'd also make a Broadway show, but he'd texted that the meetings were running late and asked me to meet him at the restaurant at eight p.m.

And so I'd gone back out shopping and picked up a red fitted dress just for the occasion. It was the perfect outfit to seduce him with.

Esteban was waiting for me outside the restaurant when I arrived, and he took care of the cabbie as I got out.

"You look beautiful as always, cariño," he said before he kissed me on the mouth. And it wasn't a quick peck either. He lingered on my lips, tasting and teasing. My heart fluttered, and I wrapped my arms around his neck.

"You know, we could just go back to the hotel and order room service," I said when he pulled away.

He grinned and brought my hands to his chest. "I know you've been cooped up in that hotel room, and I'm so sorry that I couldn't get away earlier. Tuck is a busy man, and we basically met in the back seat of a car as he was driven around town to all of the location sites. As much as I would love nothing more than to take you back to our room and ravage you, you are dressed for a night out, and a night out is what I'm going to give you. Besides, they're already expecting us."

"They?" I asked as he pulled me toward the restaurant.

"Yes. We're having dinner with Tuck, his manager, his personal assistant, and, of course, Chris."

I stopped walking. "Chris?"

He turned to explain. "Oh, that's right—I didn't tell you. I called him this morning and asked him to fly out after all. He arrived a few hours ago and is going to stay through Monday in case we don't get through everything tomorrow. Now, come on. We already have a table."

The restaurant was busy, and we had to squeeze through the crowd waiting near the hostess stand. I'd looked it up during the cab ride over and was excited about eating there. Although the Korean steak house had only been open for about a year, its rave reviews and celebrity clientele had made it quite the hot spot.

But when we finally cleared the crowd and arrived at our table, the last thing on my mind was food.

Esteban introduced me to Tuck and to Luca, his manager, and Darcy, his assistant. Chris stood, and I held my breath as he walked over to me. "It's nice to see you, Marisol," he said as he kissed my cheek. Then he pulled out the chair next to him and motioned for me to sit down. Esteban took the chair on the other side of me.

Grateful that someone had already poured me a glass of wine, I grabbed it and took a huge gulp.

Why hadn't I stayed at home?

I did my best to join in the conversation during dinner, mainly answering questions about my thoughts on New York and my work with the homeless coalition.

"Yes, my Marisol is a busy woman. I don't know how she does it all," Esteban boasted after I'd told them about the firm's charity gala in the fall.

My cheeks burned hot. "He exaggerates."

"And she's quite the baker too," Chris chimed in. "I keep telling her she needs to open up her own catering business."

I jerked my head to look at him. What on earth was he doing?

"Oh really?" Tuck said. "You know movie sets are always in need of good caterers. If you ever do decide to take the plunge, let me know, and I can give you some contacts."

I'm sure my eyes must have popped out of my head. "Thank you so much, Tuck. That's very nice of you."

Esteban wrapped one arm across my shoulders. "Yes, thank you. It's still a ways down the road, though. Marisol has some other priorities right now, don't you, my love?"

I didn't nod, but I didn't argue either. And soon the conversation drifted to other things.

As I sat there pretending to listen, my stomach churned with unease. Why hadn't I said anything?

Because it wouldn't have made a difference. He might have pretended to be on board in front of these people, but you know his tune would change back home, and he'd find some way to convince you to put it off once again.

My heart pounded in my ears, and my throat became dry. If I didn't get it together soon, I was going to have a full-blown panic attack. I mumbled an "Excuse me" and went in search of the ladies' room. Fortunately, it was empty, and I began to pace back and forth. This trip had sounded like such a good idea, but it had definitely been a mistake. I couldn't distract myself with baking here. I'd have to ride out my anxiety with deep breaths and a wet paper towel against my forehead. It took me a few minutes to calm down.

Finally composed, I walked out of the restroom and right into a waiting Chris.

"Are you okay?" he said.

"I'm fine, thank you. I need to get back." I moved past him, but he held my elbow.

"Why didn't you say anything else? Why didn't you tell Esteban that the catering business is a priority?"

"Because it's not and because this isn't the place or the time to have that conversation."

He shook his head and let out an exasperated sigh. "If you were my wife, I'd—"

"But I'm not," I said and took his hand off my elbow. "Please, don't start."

Chris moved even closer, his face only inches away from mine. "I care about you, Marisol." His voice was rough and deep, and his eyes raked through me like fire.

I couldn't look away. And for a second, I wondered what would happen if I turned ever so slightly and lifted my lips.

Footsteps broke our trance, and an elderly woman entered the hallway. We broke apart to let her pass. It was the pause I needed to let sanity take hold and cool me down.

"Nothing can ever happen between us, Chris. You know that deep down. It's better for both of us if you start to accept that."

I hated the pained look that crossed his face before he reined it in. He didn't say anything else and disappeared into the men's restroom. I took a breath and walked back to my table.

I was worried he'd say or do something when he returned a few minutes later. But he didn't. In fact, he barely looked at me or talked to me the rest of the night. Darcy, the pretty redhead assistant sitting next to him, became the center of his attention instead. I told myself it was better this way. He'd needed to hear what I'd said because I'd never reciprocate his feelings. I was married.

And, the next morning, when Esteban texted me that he'd run into Darcy coming out of Chris's hotel room, I rolled my eyes, laughed, and ignored the queasy feeling in the pit of my stomach.

Because it was better that way.

Chapter Twenty-Five
GRACIE

It was my third date with Tony. Okay, technically it wasn't really a date, but it was the third time we were going out together. We were doing "research" for the fiesta by checking out local bands that might be interested in playing.

Tonight we were headed to a bar in Riverside to see Come On, Jolene perform hits from the eighties.

"Eighties cover bands are always a big crowd draw," Tony explained as he drove along the freeway. "Do you know some of those songs are now getting played on classic rock stations?"

"I feel so old." I laughed. It wasn't true really. Sitting here in the truck next to Tony, I actually felt young—like I was back in the eighth grade.

Dear God, I want to thank you in advance for such a great night. I know it's just starting, but I didn't want to forget. Amen.

"Well, if it makes you feel any better, you don't look old. You look great. You really do." He kept staring ahead, and I was glad because I knew my face was turning beet red. I wanted to say something witty or give him a compliment, too, but I couldn't open my mouth.

"So, have you ever been to this bar before?" he said after a few moments of silence.

"Me? Um, no. Bars aren't really my thing."

"What is, then? What do you like to do for fun?"

"I don't know. The usual stuff, I guess. Read, watch television, tutor after school, and volunteer at the animal shelter."

"You realize that's not really the usual stuff, right?" he said with a laugh.

Why didn't I like more things that were fun?

"I also like to spend time with my family," I added. "I have a pretty big one, so it seems as if there's something to do every weekend. They keep me pretty busy actually."

"That's cool. My parents moved to Florida a few years ago, so I don't get to see them as much."

For some reason, I didn't think I should mention that I still lived with my parents.

"Everyone on my mom's side of the family lives in Inland Valley. It's nice having them so close, especially my great-grandmother."

"Wow. That's awesome."

"It is. And she's still such an active lady. She helps my abuela in the garden or cooks breakfast for everyone. She likes staying busy. My sister wants us all to pitch in and buy her one of those electric scooters; that way she can zoom down to the corner store whenever she wants."

Tony laughed, and I felt more at ease. So I kept talking. I told him stories about all the things Welita let us do when she babysat us—from building forts out of my abuela's blankets to trying on her jewelry and high-heeled shoes.

I hadn't realized how much or how long I had been talking until we pulled into the parking lot of the bar. I hadn't even noticed until then that we'd gotten off the freeway.

"I'm sorry. I've just been blabbering away," I said after Tony turned off the engine.

He turned to me. Even in the shadows, I could make out his easy smile.

"That's okay. I liked hearing your stories. In fact, I would be perfectly happy just sitting here all night listening to you talk."

My heart thumped wildly underneath my floral print blouse and baby-blue cardigan. "You're easy to talk to," I finally said. It was the truth. Other than with my family and some coworkers, I struggled with how to hold conversations with others. I never knew what to say. So, I preferred listening and observing.

Until Tony.

He considered my words for a moment. "You're the first person to tell me that," he said eventually.

"Really?"

"Really. I guess you just bring out the best in me, Gracie."

Tony gave me another smile before turning back around. As he got out of the truck, I unbuckled my seat belt in a daze. Did he really mean that, or was he just being polite?

We didn't talk again until after we had been in the club for about half an hour. The band actually turned out to be pretty good. The music, combined with a couple of beers, had loosened Tony up, and he started talking to me again. We were sitting next to each other in a small booth. I was still sipping my first piña colada, and he was working on his second beer. Every time he wanted to tell me something, he had to lean in close to my ear because of the loud music. Every once in a while our knees touched or his arm found its way across the seat behind me.

And when Come On, Jolene started playing their version of "Careless Whisper," Tony grabbed my hand and told me it was time to dance.

I didn't have time to say yes or no. We joined the couples on the floor, and Tony wrapped his arms around me and pulled me close. I tried not to stiffen up. I had danced with a boy before, but it was all the way back in high school. It was during a distant cousin's quinceañera in Mexico.

I was almost seventeen and the boy was nineteen. He first asked my sister, but she told him no because she had set her sights on someone else. He didn't technically ask me with words, just simply held out his hand and motioned to the dance floor with the other. I think it was known that we were from California and that our Spanish was limited. I looked around, hoping that someone would intervene, but instead I just saw my mom staring at me with a dopey-looking smile. Figuring it was better than sitting there with my younger cousins, I took the boy's hand and let him lead me to the floor.

We danced to a couple of fast songs and then to a slow one. After that one was over, he led me away from the crowd and into a darkened breezeway that connected the church to the hall where the reception was being held. In broken Spanish and English, he told me I danced well and then asked if he could kiss me. I said, "Sí," and instantly his mouth was on mine and his hands were on my breasts.

As he tried to shove his tongue between my teeth, all I could think was that I was finally having my first kiss. I closed my eyes and tried to enjoy the moment so I could remember it later. I kissed him back and tried to match his fervor, even though I had no idea what I was doing. I let him squeeze and pinch wherever he wanted, but when his hand started to creep up my skirt, I'd finally had enough.

I told him no and pulled his hand out. At first he laughed and started kissing me again. This time I moved my head and weakly pushed him away. I could see the change of expression as his eyes flashed with anger. He told me something in Spanish and then left me there alone in the breezeway. It was Selena who found me. She fixed my crooked skirt and rebuttoned my blouse. Then she took me to the restroom so I could redo my hair and makeup. The rest of the night she stayed by my side, turning down every boy who came to ask her to dance.

She never asked me what happened, but I'm sure she had an idea. My shame was obvious, and it took me another three years before I'd let any guy come close to kissing me. Don't get me wrong. It wasn't like I was turning them away by the dozens. But I definitely sent out the signal not to even look at me sideways.

My only other "date" was with this guy named Will from my college algebra class. We had sat next to each other for an entire semester and barely exchanged looks. Then, during the summer, I ran into him at the bookstore. We were both looking at movies and somehow ended up back at his apartment watching *The Da Vinci Code*. His roommate was out of town for the weekend, so we were alone and drinking an off-brand beer. Halfway through the movie, Will held my hand. I smiled at him, and then he leaned in to kiss me. It was a nice kiss—not hard and desperate like my dance partner's back in Mexico.

So I didn't balk when he suggested we go into the bedroom and make out. I let him take off my jeans, but not my shirt. He took off his shirt and his jeans, but left on his boxers. We kissed more, and then Will asked me to touch the bulge between his legs. I agreed, and before I knew it, he was moving my hand up and down until he came inside his boxers.

He told me he would call me, but he didn't. Finally, one day after class, he pulled me into a corner and told me how sorry he was, but he couldn't date me after all. He said what we had done in his apartment that day was a sin and if we dated then we'd probably sin again, and he was trying to be a good Christian.

I had never been so mortified. That Sunday I went to all three Masses and confession. I thought I'd never escape the feeling of dirtiness.

It took several years after that encounter to even allow myself to think about having sex with someone. I was curious, of course. But not curious enough to do anything to pursue it. I figured when I found the right person, it would happen naturally.

Dancing in Tony's arms felt that way. His hand pressed against my back, the way he breathed into my hair—all of it felt right.

"You're a good dancer," I told him.

"Thanks. So are you."

I laughed. "You're a bad liar."

"I'm not lying. See?"

He spun me around expertly, and I couldn't help but laugh out loud in delight. But when he pulled me back toward him, I noticed the space between us was smaller. His chest was hard against mine. Desire burned through me, and I ached to touch him all over.

I looked up into his eyes, and for a second I thought he was going to kiss me.

"Do you want to get another drink?" he said just as the song ended.

"I'm fine," I said back.

But I really wasn't.

By the time he parked his truck in front of my parents' house later that night, the butterflies in my stomach were out of control. I silently wondered if I'd even be able to walk to my front door, based on how mushy everything felt inside me.

"I had a nice time," Tony said before I could open my door.

I looked at him and smiled. "Me too."

"Before you go, can I ask you a question?"

"Of course," I answered, willing my voice not to sound so shaky.

Tony turned in his seat. "How come you never talked to me when we were in school?"

If I could've guessed all the questions he would ask me, that wouldn't have even been in the top one hundred.

"I talked to you."

He shrugged. "Maybe a word here and there. But, honestly, it kind of seemed like you were avoiding me."

"You noticed that?" I blurted out before I thought better of it.

Tony nodded. "I knew it. But why? Did I do something to make you hate me?"

Not even close.

But I couldn't tell him that. Instead, I took a breath and remembered what Selena and Erica had told me. If anything was ever going to happen, I needed to make the first move.

So, I told him the truth.

"Remember that time in the eighth grade when we were paired up to do that project?"

He furrowed his brow. "Kind of?"

Dear God, do I really have to do this right now?

God didn't answer, but Selena's voice did.

Tell him, Gracie.

I took a deep breath. "Well, we were. And you were nice and seemed excited to be paired up with me. But then I overheard that the only reason you were being nice to me was because you wanted me to do all the work."

Saying the words out loud seemed so silly. Why oh why had I held on to this memory for so many years? I definitely wished I could run to my bedroom and hide under the covers.

To his credit, he was obviously embarrassed.

"I wish I could say that it wasn't true," he admitted, and my heart sank. "But I know I was kind of a little asshole back then and really didn't think about anyone else's feelings. I'm so sorry. I never meant to hurt you, Gracie."

A new warmth spread over me. "I know," I answered.

"Can we start over and be friends? For real?"

I couldn't help but smile. "Yes. I would like that."

Realizing there was no way I could handle any more revelations tonight, I waved goodbye and escaped his truck as quick as possible.

Part of me wanted to text Selena as soon as I was in bed. Another part of me wanted to keep the moment to myself just a little longer.

I put my phone away and drifted to sleep with a smile on my face.

Chapter Twenty-Six
ERICA

"Feliz cumpleaños, Welita."

"Gracias, mija."

It was Welita's birthday and Easter Sunday. I handed her the bunch of lilies I had just purchased at the corner flower shop, and she put them with all the others on the kitchen table inside my abuela's house. There were about six or seven assorted flower arrangements—including more lilies.

It was almost tradition now—or maybe a running joke—that ever since she'd gushed a few years back over an orchid someone had given her, everyone now always gave Welita some type of potted flower as a gift: poinsettias for Christmas, lilies for Easter, and tulips for Mother's Day. And she never said anything remotely negative as her simulated garden of gifts grew with each visitor. One time I asked her why she didn't tell people what she actually wanted so that everyone would stop giving her so many flowers.

In Spanish, she told me, "Why? If someone wants to give me a flower, then I am happy to receive it. A gift is a gift, and you should always be grateful for anything someone gives you out of love. The day you tell someone what to give you is the day you no longer get gifts out of love, but rather obligation. Well, for me, I'd rather have the love."

I handed her my other gift, wrapped neatly in pink paper. Her wrinkled and brown-spotted hands struggled with pulling the paper free from the tape. Worry tightened my chest until she finally pulled the CD free.

She stared at it for a few seconds without saying a word. "It's the soundtrack for *Jersey Boys*!" I explained. "You know, the play about Frankie Valli and the Four Seasons."

Her confusion turned into delight. I'd told her about the Broadway production after she'd asked if there were any more Four Seasons albums or CDs I could buy her. Selena and I had already promised to take her to see the musical as soon as it came to Los Angeles.

"Put it on for me," she said in Spanish.

I walked over to her old CD player on the counter and spotted an enormous arrangement of wildflowers and daisies in a beautiful crystal vase sitting next to it.

"Welita, who gave you these flowers?"

"Marisol." She explained that my cousin had stopped by yesterday and had also brought her a pineapple upside-down cake.

For some reason this tidbit of information bothered me. While I was glad that she had at least made an effort to visit Welita, I was irritated that she'd done it the day before the family party. The arrangement was also too much, and, to me, it looked like she was showing off her money. Or rather, her husband's money.

"¿Qué te pasa, mija?"

Welita's question startled me. I guess she could read my irritation all over my face.

I told her the truth.

"I just wish Marisol would've come today," I said in Spanish. "I haven't seen her or talked to her in a long time. I guess I just wish we were all still as close as we used to be when we were little girls."

She nodded sadly, and for the first time, I saw how tired she looked. Was that why she was inside the house, instead of in the patio with the rest of the family? Was that why she still wore her usual flowered housecoat instead of her church dress? Had she even gone to church today?

The worry returned, and I asked her if she was feeling okay. She told me she thought she was getting a cold. We talked a little more until she let me know she wanted to lie down for a little. But before she walked to her room, she grabbed my hand and said, "Nunca es demasiado tarde."

I knew she was talking about Mari. I didn't want to believe it was too late for us either. But I also didn't know how to fix this. At least, not today I didn't.

So, I promised her I'd reach out to Mari, and that made her smile.

I must have still been scowling when I went back outside to the patio because my mother asked me what was wrong. When I told her, she just shrugged.

"I don't understand why you concern yourself so much with what your cousin does or doesn't do."

"Because it's not right, Mom. She hasn't been a part of this family for a long time, and I'm tired of someone not calling her on it."

"But why do we have to, as you say, 'call her on it'? You aren't little girls anymore. Your choices are your own. We can't force Mari to be part of this family if she doesn't want to be."

I wanted to say more about Mari and my worries about Welita. But it wasn't the time or the place. Instead, I made my rounds and greeted all my tíos and tías with a kiss on a cheek and a "Happy Easter."

"How's the paper, Erica?" Tío Ricardo asked after giving me a hug.

"It's pretty good," I answered. "Where's Tía Espy?"

"She's in the backyard. She's trying to get Araceli to come inside and eat."

I smiled. It touched my heart to see my tío so happy and healthy. He hadn't always been. And of everyone in the family, Mari had hurt him the most. I never understood why she hated Tío Ricardo so much.

My own dad and I butted heads every so often, but I still respected him. I still talked to him.

Mari, on the other hand, had turned her back on her dad a long time ago.

Even more irritation bubbled inside, and I didn't want my tío to see it. "Okay, well, I better go get some food before it's all gone."

Jesus, why was I in such a bad mood today?

I could've blamed it on the cloudy gray skies. But it was probably more because I was the idiot who'd started Weight Watchers and a Pilates program right before a holiday.

Gracie had practically begged me to join with her. Her sister would have joined the program, too, but we all knew there was no need for Selena to lose an ounce. So, although I was in decent shape because of soccer, it wouldn't hurt for me to tone up in certain places. Plus, I wasn't the healthiest of eaters—or drinkers.

But dumb me should've convinced her to wait until after our Easter potluck.

I longingly ogled the containers of homemade macaroni and cheese, mashed potatoes, rice, and fried chicken. Then with a very sad sigh, I served myself green salad, steamed broccoli, and two slices of ham.

After I dropped into a chair next to Gracie, I could tell she was just as miserable as I was. She kept pushing around her broccoli, probably silently willing it to turn into a cheeseburger. I smiled. I didn't want to be the only one suffering on the day of Jesus's resurrection.

"All I'm saying is that if I don't lose like fifteen pounds by next month, then I'm going to drive to East LA and eat me one of those huge burritos from El Tepeyac, and I'm not even going to regret it," I told her.

"Erica, even if you were following the program perfectly—which I know you aren't—it would be physically impossible for you to lose that much weight in just one month. Maybe, at the most, you might lose three or four pounds." She stuffed the broccoli in her mouth and crunched away.

Just like with everything else we did together, Gracie decided that she knew more about Weight Watchers than me. She was real committed, too, calling me every day to tell me what she *hadn't* eaten. I almost fell on the floor yesterday when she told me she had asked Selena to help her buy some new clothes once she hit her 20 percent goal.

Gracie wanting fashion advice from Selena? Hell had definitely frozen over. Or someone had a crush on that new PE teacher at her school.

At our first official weigh-in, Gracie had lost 6 pounds. I'd lost 1.8 (but I told my mom it was 2, because if I had peed right before, it would have been). I explained to our meeting leader that I was also doing Pilates, so I'd probably gained some muscle. Eileen—that was her name—just smiled at me and handed me back my little weight record book. During the meeting, Eileen gave Gracie a gold star for losing at least five pounds. All I got was an "I hope I see *less* of you next week, honey." Grrr.

I later told Gracie that I wanted to find a meeting with a different leader because I didn't think Eileen "got" me. The lady had lost twenty pounds twenty years ago and was as thin as a rail.

"How in the hell is that flaca going to inspire us to lose weight?" I asked.

Gracie told me we had to give it some time, and if I still didn't like her, then we could switch meeting days. I was already thinking of skipping the meetings altogether and just doing it online. I didn't need Eileen or anyone else pointing out if I'd gained a pound or two or not. That's what my abuela and mother were for.

"I'm stuffed!" proclaimed Selena, who was sitting on my left side. She pushed her plate away from her, and I fought the urge to grab it and lap up the bits and pieces she'd left behind. Easter was probably Selena's favorite food holiday because in our family it was potluck-style and most of the food was traditional American, save for the beans and salsa, made especially for my abuelo and tíos.

"I hate you," I muttered as I picked up a carrot from my plate and then dropped it right back onto it.

"What? I thought the best thing about Weight Watchers was that you could eat whatever you wanted as long as you added up the points? Don't hate me just because you'd rather use your points for rabbit food instead of deviled eggs." Selena laughed and then got up to check out what was on the dessert table.

"She's right, you know," Gracie added. "We're not supposed to deprive ourselves. If you want something else, then you should eat. Otherwise you're not going to be able to last."

"So then why aren't you eating some cake or pie? Isn't that what our weekly points allowance is for, hmm, Ms. Weight Watcher?"

"I'm not eating cake or pie because I don't want cake or pie," Gracie responded and went back to focusing on her piece of broccoli.

"Mentirosa," I told her.

Selena came back to the table with a bowlful of fruit salad and a very large piece of pineapple upside-down cake. "Are you calling her a liar because she won't admit that she has the hots for Tony the gym teacher?" she said with her mouth full.

Gracie shot her sister a dirty look. "Whatever, Selena. If anyone is a mentirosa here, it's you. Erica, did you know Selena visited Nathan in New York? She says it doesn't mean anything, but I think she's lying. I think they're starting to get serious."

Selena rolled her eyes. "For the love of God, Gracie. I already told you we aren't even dating."

I was too busy cutting into Selena's piece of cake and inhaling every crumb to even pay attention to their squabbling. It was moist and sweet and delicious and so much better than anything I'd eaten so far. I was just about to cut another inch off when Gracie grabbed my fork.

"You had a bite, now leave it alone. Don't you have anything to say about Selena and Nathan?"

I gave her my most pissed-off look. "That was just mean, Gracie. You don't take a starving chica's fork away like that." I was serious too. She had crossed the line. "Anyway, Selena lusting after some guy is not news. What I want to know is why you're trying to change the subject? Come on, Gracie, spill the tea. What's the deal with Tony?"

"Yeah, Gracie," Selena teased. "What's the deal?"

She hemmed and hawed for a few seconds and then gave in to temptation.

"Aaah, forget it." Gracie grabbed Selena's plate and dove into the cake. "Oh. My. Gosh. This is amazing. Who made it?" she said with her mouth full.

"Who do you think?"

"Mari?"

"Yeah, apparently she was here yesterday to drop off a gift for Welita too."

"Yesterday? Why didn't she come today?" Gracie asked.

"Abuela said she was hosting a brunch for Esteban's clients at their house."

"Of course she is," I muttered.

"Erica, don't be like that. At least she came by to see Welita. That counts for something, doesn't it?"

I shrugged and got up from the table and headed straight for the desserts. I was mad at myself for allowing my issues with Mari to cloud another family day. Selena and Gracie never understood why it bugged me so much. Sometimes I didn't either.

About thirty minutes later we visited Welita in her bedroom. She looked less tired, but still not herself. I watched my cousins to see if they seemed worried. They didn't, so we talked with her for a bit.

Afterward, the three of us decided to take a walk around the block so Gracie and I could work off the piece of cake we'd brought for Welita but had ended up eating ourselves.

"Gracie, I'm sorry I teased you about Tony," I said after we'd passed the neighbor's house. "My body was starved for carbs at that time, and you didn't deserve my misdirected anger."

She put her arm around me. "It's fine. I just don't want it to be like how it was when we were in school, and everyone thinks I'm following him around like a little lovesick puppy dog," Gracie admitted.

"We don't think that, we promise," Selena said. "But if you really like him, then you should ask him out. And if you don't, you could still just screw him."

I let out a surprised laugh. Gracie, on the other hand, was appalled.

"You know I don't like talking about this, Selena," she huffed.

"Why? It's perfectly normal to talk about sex. How else are you going to learn?" Selena ducked before Gracie's right fist could hit her shoulder.

"Seriously, Gracie," she continued. "I'm not saying you need to go out and get laid tomorrow. I just don't want this virginity thing to hold you back. When it's meant to happen, it will happen. But it's not going to happen if you spend every Friday and Saturday night home with Mom and Dad."

"What if it's too late for me?"

Selena and I stopped walking. Had Gracie just admitted that she actually wanted to have sex one day? I'd always assumed her choice to stay a virgin had to do with religion. But that didn't explain why she never really went out or had a real boyfriend.

"It's not too late," I offered. "You're still young, smart, beautiful, and one of the nicest people in this world. There is a man out there who's going to want you because of all that. But Selena is right. You're not going to find him without at least looking a little."

She nodded. "I know. It's scary out there."

"Ain't that the truth," I said with a snort.

Selena gave her sister a hug. "Yay! I'm so glad we talked about this. I'd make a good sex therapist, wouldn't I?"

We all laughed again and continued walking.

"So, what about you, Erica?" Selena asked. "Anything going on in your sex life that you want to talk about?"

For some reason, I thought of Adrian but quickly dismissed it.

"Actually, there is. The other night I almost had an orgasm thinking about deep-fried chocolate-covered Twinkies. What do you think that means?"

I didn't duck quick enough, and both sisters landed punches on my arms.

Chapter Twenty-Seven
SELENA

Something was going on at Umbridge & Umbridge.

After taking an informal poll around the office, I'd found out that all the senior leadership team was behind closed doors in the conference room. Everyone, that is, except for Kat.

I knew this because I'd seen her walk into Henry's office right before I saw everyone else walk into the conference room.

One of the girls in Payroll instant messaged me to ask if Kat had come out yet. I messaged her back that she hadn't and asked if she had heard anything from her friend in IT. She hadn't.

Both meetings had been going on for thirty minutes, and the longer they took, the more I wondered if either of them was about the viral Twitter campaign last week for one of our clients. It hadn't exactly gone as expected.

After the meeting with Cup of Sugar, Kat had decided she needed to oversee all social media campaigns from brainstorming to execution. And even if a client didn't want a social media component, she was going to convince them they needed it.

So she talked George & Sons—a successful real estate development company in the city—into doing a special online Q&A with the founder's son and vice president of the company as a way to promote the upcoming unveiling of their latest shopping center. On the morning of the Twitter chat, Kat and the company's VP, Darren George, set up a laptop in his office and started tweeting about the project and encouraging questions from Twitter users. About ten minutes into the chat, one Twitter user began posting questions about a pending lawsuit facing the company instead. The same user also accused Darren of bribing city officials and withholding pay from their construction workers. Although Kat said that she'd tried to take over the responses, Darren had become so enraged with the unrelenting tweets that he'd tweeted back with insults and profanities. The exchange blew up and even became the subject of an article on BuzzFeed. The company canceled the unveiling, and I'd heard that Darren was now being investigated.

The door to Henry's office opened, and Kat walked out. Although her expression was stony as usual, when our eyes met, I could've sworn hers were watery.

My phone rang, and I jumped. It was Henry. "Selena, can I see you in my office, please?"

"Yes, I'll be right there."

I grabbed my phone, and then a pen and notepad just in case, and took a seat inside his office.

"As I'm sure you are aware, the Darren George Twitter fiasco has turned into quite the blemish on our agency's reputation. In cooperating with Mr. George, we've been looking at this internally to come up with an explanation as to how something like this could've happened. Unfortunately, we were not prepared to uncover what we did. All I can tell you is that because of her role in the situation, Kat has been terminated, effective immediately."

My mouth fell open.

"The senior leadership team was called into a staff meeting for the next hour, and they will be informed at the conclusion of that meeting. Since you report directly to Kat, I felt it was necessary to let you know as soon as possible. I've given her thirty minutes to clean out her office, and she requested that you be allowed to help her. I agreed."

Wait. Kat was fired, but I still had to work for her? What kind of hell was this?

"I'd appreciate your cooperation and confidentiality during this time. We'll talk later today about her accounts and what you're comfortable taking on in the interim."

He stopped talking, and I figured it was finally my turn to say something.

"Um, okay."

Evidently satisfied with my response, lame as it was, Henry dismissed me.

As soon as I walked out, my phone vibrated with a text. It was from Kat:

Bring me 5 boxes from the mailroom.

Even in disgrace, Kat stayed true to her bitchiness. I guess I had to give her credit for that at least.

Minutes later, I walked into her office with the five boxes and extra packing tape.

"Close the door and start packing up my bookshelves."

I nodded and did as she asked. We worked in silence for the next fifteen minutes or so. She cleared off her desk except for the computer and telephone and then handed me items from her drawers to put inside a reusable shopping bag.

When we were done, she asked me to help her carry some of the boxes to her car.

The main office was still pretty empty when we walked outside. I was relieved because I didn't want to deal with any stares or looks of pity. It didn't matter that I didn't like the lady. No one should have to endure a walk of shame like that.

It took three trips, but we were able to finish by Henry's deadline.

It wasn't until she'd closed the packed trunk of her car that Kat finally talked.

"What did he tell you?" she asked before pulling out a pack of cigarettes and lighter from her purse. After all this time, I had no idea she was a smoker.

"Who? Henry? He just said you were being fired for what happened with the George Twitter thing. For what it's worth, I think that's kind of shitty. It's not your fault some rando Twitter dude decided to attack Mr. George like that."

She took a drag and blew out the smoke. "It *was* my fault. I was the rando Twitter dude."

"Um, what? How is that even possible? You were with Mr. George in his office during the tweets."

"I finally figured out how to use Hootsuite."

Kat explained that she'd set up the fake Twitter account a few weeks ago and then programmed the tweets the night before the Q&A.

"If you look at the stream of tweets, never once did the guy respond directly to anything Darren or I posted. They were all just repeated accusations."

"But, but, why?"

She laughed with a bitterness that made my blood run cold. "Revenge. Straight up. The bastard was cheating on me."

The realization of her words slapped me. "You and Darren?"

"Yep. It's been going on for a few months. I started to get suspicious because he'd cancel things at the last minute or always had an excuse why I couldn't come over. So one night I waited outside his house and saw him with this other woman. She works in his office. She's even come along to client meetings before. What a bastard, right?"

I nodded, even though I still couldn't grasp what was happening. "Wow, Kat. I don't know what to say."

"I admit I went too far. I was so blinded by my rage that I also didn't plan it out very well. Apparently, some of the things I accused him of were only known to a few people. It didn't take him long to suspect me and tell Henry about our affair. Then I guess IT found some evidence on my laptop. I fessed up as soon as he confronted me about it."

I was in shock. Never would I have ever thought Kat would do something like that.

"I'm only telling you this because I can tell you're eager, Selena. And if you keep doing what you're doing, you're going to get to the top. My only advice is, don't ever compromise your career over a man. It will never be worth it."

Kat threw her cigarette on the ground and stomped it out. She stuck out her hand, and I shook it. Then she got in her convertible BMW and drove off.

I didn't go back inside right away. I needed a few minutes to process everything.

Things were about to change at Umbridge & Umbridge.

And the longer I stayed outside, the longer I didn't have to think about whether I wanted anything to do with those changes.

Chapter Twenty-Eight
MARI

It was the third Wednesday in May. And, like every third Wednesday for the past three months, I was sitting in the conference room at Delgado & Ramos, wishing I were anywhere else.

"Oh my gosh, Marisol. Where did you buy these muffins? I absolutely must pick some up for my husband. He loves cranberries."

Alicia, the firm's manager of community partnerships, had just taken a bite of one of the dozen cranberry-orange muffins I'd baked the night before. We were waiting for our other committee members to arrive for our monthly meeting to plan the fall charity gala.

"I didn't buy them anywhere. I made them," I said as I made notes on our agenda.

"Shut up. You did not."

"She absolutely did."

A familiar deep voice made me stop writing. I looked up just as Chris was taking a seat next to me.

"What are you doing here?" I didn't care how I sounded or that there was someone else in the room. I wasn't in the mood to deal with him—or his games.

Alicia laughed. "Someone didn't read her emails this morning. Chris is the newest member of our committee. Isn't that wonderful? It sets such a good example and lets everyone in the firm know that this event is a priority. I'm sure it will help increase attendance this year."

He gave me a sly grin and a wink just as others on the committee showed up.

Don't let him distract you. Even though you don't want to be here, this is for an important cause. You have to stay focused.

"Chris, did I just hear that you're joining our little committee this year?"

My shoulders tensed at the sound of the syrupy voice.

I slowly turned around to see Dawn Beck.

Dawn was one of San Marino's busiest socialites. If there was a gala, auction, fundraiser, or charity dinner to plan, Dawn was on the committee. I'd met her when I'd joined the San Marino Ladies Lunch Auxiliary four years ago. Other members included another councilman's wife, a surgeon's wife, and other stay-at-home wives who needed to fill their days planning fundraisers and talking about other women they hated and their next vacation destination. After only six months with the group, I knew the hierarchy and how it worked. So until anyone had the cojones to stand up to her, Dawn was the president of the auxiliary and had the ultimate power. But I knew better than to give her any type of ammunition to use against me.

Something I know she hated.

Once she'd heard that I planned the firm's annual gala, she volunteered herself to join the committee. I saw it for what it was, though—a thinly veiled attempt to dig up some dirt.

"It's true," Chris told her after she'd planted a kiss on his cheek as a greeting. "I decided it was time."

She squealed like a little girl and clapped her hands. "We're going to have so much fun."

Chris laughed and looked over at me. When I didn't respond, he excused himself and said he was going to get his phone from his office and would be right back.

After he was out of earshot, Dawn grabbed my arm and pulled me close.

"Is Chris still single?"

I thought of what I'd seen back in New York. "Um, I'm not sure. I don't really keep track of his dating schedule."

Careful, Mari.

Dawn's love of gossip was almost as big as her love for her personal trainer's abs. And even though she would decapitate anyone who breathed a word of her indiscretions to her councilman husband, Dawn prided herself on being the spreader of bad and scandalous news. If I showed even a glimpse of being uncomfortable talking about Chris, she'd make sure all the other women in the San Marino Ladies Lunch Auxiliary knew it by tomorrow.

It wasn't the first comment Dawn had made about Chris. The two had met at the New Year's Eve party at our house. She was drunk and hung on him almost all night. Even Esteban was appalled by her obvious flirting. Chris, on the other hand, took it in stride but acted like a complete gentleman—even when she "accidentally" spilled her wine on his crotch and then tried to clean it up with her bare hand.

That night, I didn't really care either way if Chris slept with her. I just didn't want any potential relationship to affect my relationship with Dawn or my inclusion in the auxiliary. But Chris didn't take her bait, and she ended up going home with her oblivious husband, very drunk and very frustrated.

I pulled myself away from her and tried to focus on reading the agenda again. A few more committee members showed up, and I was relieved for the buffer.

Temporary as it was.

"I think you need to throw one of your famous cocktail parties and make sure he's there. Eye candy is the best party dessert you can have. Way more interesting than muffins," Dawn whispered in my ear just as Chris walked back into the room.

The rest of the meeting was uneventful, thank God. We discussed silent auction items and AV needs for the band. We also finalized the menu and approved the design of the save the date card. And since this year's charity was a shelter for abused women and their children, the committee decided to hire a freelance writer who could interview some of the shelter's clients and staff to include testimonials in the event's program book.

When the meeting was over, I encouraged everyone to take a muffin or two for the road. Letty had warned me not to bring back any, since I still had two dozen more at home.

"This is going to be one of the best galas ever." Alicia beamed at me from across the conference room table. "You always do such a great job, Marisol. You have no idea how happy I was when Esteban said you'd chair the committee again."

"That's very kind of you to say. But it is a committee effort."

"Marisol is very humble," Chris said. He'd taken the seat next to mine for the meeting. Luckily, I'd been too focused on my agenda to be distracted by him.

"I know," Alicia continued. "That's why we love her so much."

"Definitely," he responded.

"Well, I better let the agency know that we can move forward with printing the save the dates. We could even get them in the mail by early next week!"

Alicia left, and I began collecting my papers. I noticed Dawn get up, but she didn't leave. Instead, she took out her phone and started talking to someone.

Chris leaned closer. "Alicia's right, you know. There might be a committee planning this thing, but you are definitely the one making everything happen."

Without looking over at him, I said, "So why did you join the committee, exactly?"

"Because it's an important event for the firm."

"This is our third year doing it, and neither you nor Esteban have ever sat in on a planning meeting before. So, try again."

"Fine. I guess it's my way of apologizing to you for how I acted in New York."

My hand stilled for a second. "What do you mean?"

He rolled his chair even closer. "It was wrong of me to act like that, especially with Esteban around," he said in a low voice. "It was inappropriate, and I apologize. I also shouldn't have slept with Darcy. I was mad at you for what you said, and it was a stupid thing to do."

That made me finally look at him. "I accept your apology about acting inappropriately," I whispered. "But that's it. You don't owe me any explanation about Darcy because it's certainly none of my business who you sleep with."

I couldn't help but glance at Dawn, who had ended her phone call but was now lingering in the doorway.

"Marisol . . . ," he began.

I rolled my chair backward and stood up. "Thanks for coming today, Chris."

As I gathered the rest of my things, I heard Dawn ask Chris if he could show her his office. I waited a minute or two and then headed for the elevator. On another day, I would've stopped to see Esteban. But I didn't want to chance getting stuck in an elevator with that woman.

Later that afternoon, I couldn't shake the knot of fury rumbling in my belly. Dawn had really gotten to me. I needed something to distract me from both her and Chris.

I pulled out my box of recipes I'd handwritten on index cards. Some were from Welita and my abuela. And some were my own. When I worked at the catering company, I used to beg the chefs to let me help them prepare the dessert items. Then later, after the event was over, I'd go home and sit at my kitchen table rewriting their recipes and adding my own spices or ingredients for a twist.

As I thought about Dawn and how much she wanted to get her hands on Chris, I kneaded and punched the bread dough for my new capirotada recipe. Most of the time, I'd make the Mexican bread pudding with whatever I had in the pantry. But after talking about it with Welita, I wanted to try a new recipe that was very similar to her traditional recipe. I was excited to serve it at an auxiliary brunch next month.

I'm not sure exactly when I really learned how to bake. It might have begun with the first time Welita let me and my cousins help her make flour tortillas.

One by one, she let us pour one ingredient into her large yellow ceramic mixing bowl. Then we watched with envy as she stuck her hands into the white mixture and began combining it until it became a grainy white dough. Finally, when she was satisfied with the texture, she'd give us each a chunk of the dough so we could knead it and then roll it into a ball. We'd do it over and over again until we had about two dozen little dough balls lined up along the counter. She'd then roll them out into the shape of a tortilla and cook the flat rounds on her cast-iron comal. As she cooked, we cleaned up what we could and then sat at the kitchen table anxiously awaiting our first taste. We each got one tortilla and then promptly slathered butter on top, rolled it into a tube, and took a bite. It was my most favorite thing in the world to eat.

When I was a teenager, I started looking for recipes on my own. I'd see some in magazines or in my mom's cookbooks (she never used them anyway). If I was sad or lonely, I'd bake a cake or pie. I didn't do it because I wanted to eat them. I just liked creating something that people would enjoy. Sometimes I'd eat a piece of whatever I'd made or save one for my mom. Most of the time I gave it away—to friends, neighbors, my cousins, whoever wanted it.

Baking became my escape—something to do when I couldn't sleep or when I needed a distraction.

"Why are you upset?" Letty asked as she walked into the kitchen with two bags full of groceries.

"I'm not upset," I lied.

She set the bags on the counter. "Pues, I guess you just really, really hate that dough."

I stopped pounding it and pushed it away. "I had my gala meeting today. Dawn Beck was there."

Letty grimaced and then pulled a bag of rice out of one bag. "That mujer is a piece of work. I don't know how you can stand being around her and those huge fake chiches."

I laughed and wiped my hands on my apron so I could help put things away. "Those aren't the only fake things about her."

"What did she say this time?"

"The usual. I guess I just wasn't in the mood to deal with her today. Especially when she started talking about Chris."

Shit. Why did I bring him up?

Letty shook her head. "Why does that gringa think that Señor Ramos could ever be interested in her?"

"Because of her fake chiches," I joked.

Letty laughed. "Yes, probably. But even if she wasn't such a bruja, she's still a married woman. Señor Ramos is too good of a man to do something like that."

I had just opened the refrigerator door to put away the orange juice, grateful that she couldn't see my face and start asking questions.

"Of course," I said while moving things around on the shelves for no reason. "I know it's ridiculous to even think that Chris would even be interested in someone like Dawn."

Because apparently he's in love with me.

"And you should know better about doing things that can't be undone," she said.

Panic heated my cheeks. Had I said that out loud? I spun around to face Letty. "What did you say?"

Letty pointed at the dough still sitting on the counter. "You've been baking long enough to know that too much kneading will ruin the dough. You can't undo it once it's done, and that looks way overdone."

My knees nearly gave out from the relief.

"You're right. It does look like that. I'll start over."

And that was probably another reason why I loved baking. Correcting your mistakes was as simple as starting a new batch.

Too bad other things couldn't be as easily fixed.

Chapter Twenty-Nine
GRACIE

Summer meant a break from school, but not from the fiesta planning committee.

And although I lamented to my family about having to still go to the weekly meetings, secretly I was pleased because that meant I also continued to see Tony.

Sometimes we ate an early dinner together before the meeting, or we ate a late bite after. I never said anything to anyone. But Selena was suspicious and gave me the third degree whenever I told her I couldn't go out with her.

"Come on, Gracie. I doubt the St. Christopher Fiesta Committee would fall apart if you missed one meeting," she'd whined this past Thursday.

I told her that we were voting on some important issues, and Sister Catherine had already said that Friday's meeting was mandatory.

"Fine," she said after a while. "Then we can meet after the meeting. What time will it be over?"

The meetings never went past seven, but I didn't want to miss out on a possible dinner with Tony. Again, I told her the meeting would probably go late because of all the things we were voting on. She seemed convinced and said she'd ask Erica to go out with her.

Then this morning, she called me again.

"All right, fess up. Mom says you didn't get home until after eleven, and I know that there is no way Sister Catherine and all those old fogies on the fiesta committee would stay that late, no matter what serious decision-making had to get done. So, what's going on? Where are you sneaking off to on Friday nights?"

"I'm not sneaking off anywhere," I'd whispered into the phone. I was in the living room when I answered, and the entire family was there watching a soccer game. I walked into our backyard and tried to convince Selena that I wasn't hiding anything.

"Gracie, you are such a bad liar. That's what makes you Gracie. So give it up because you know later you're going to feel guilty and call me back and tell me anyway." Selena sighed.

"All right. All right. I really am going to those fiesta committee meetings. What I have not told you is that Tony Bautista is also on the committee, and sometimes we go together or have dinner afterward," I rushed that last part out, hoping that Selena didn't hear me. And at first I thought she really didn't because there was complete silence on the other end. Then she screamed, and I nearly dropped my phone.

"I KNEW IT! I KNEW IT! I totally knew there had to be some guy. You've been wearing mascara and skirts! I told Erica you must have some secret boyfriend!"

"He is *not* my boyfriend. We're just friends, colleagues. We happen to be on the same committee, and sometimes we have to do research, so we do it—well, not *it*—we work after or before the meetings."

"Whatever. I know you, big sister, and even though you may say you're just friends, I know you have a crush." Selena laughed.

"I do not have a crush on Tony Bautista."

"Yes, you do."

"No, I do not."

"Yes, you do."

"No, I . . . forget it. Forget I said anything. I've got to go now. Mom and I are going to Abuela's." Then I hung up on her before she could say anything else.

Turned out my mom was also suspicious.

"All I'm saying is that it's nice if you are seeing someone, but I don't understand why you are keeping it a secret," she explained after my umpteenth denial. We had come over to visit my grandparents and Welita.

"Ay, Olivia, déjala en paz," Welita told her.

"Yes, Olivia, leave Gracie alone. When she wants to tell us about her novio, then she will," my abuela added.

"But Abuela, I do not have a boyfriend. I just, I just have a friend. He's also a teacher, and we are on the committee together for the fiesta. That's all. There's nothing going on," I vowed.

"Is that all, really?" my mom asked, and I tried to ignore the sound of disappointment in her voice.

When I nodded, my abuela reached over and patted my hand. "Well, then, that is nice, too, mija."

"And, who knows, maybe one day you will be more than friends," my mom suggested, and again, I tried to ignore her tone. This time it sounded a little too hopeful.

"Please do not say that, Mom. Besides, I'm pretty sure all he wants from me is friendship," I admitted—both to myself and to my family.

"¡Basta! That's enough," my abuela said. "Gracie, you don't know the future, so don't think like that. Things never happen the way we think they are going to happen. Look at my mother and father. They met when she was just a girl. She didn't think she was meeting her husband that day. No, of course not. But that is the way life is. If God wants it to be, then it will be."

Then she asked Welita to tell me the story of the day she met my great-grandfather.

Like always, a wistful smile spread across her face, and she began talking. I had heard the story many times before, but I did not interrupt. Not just because I enjoyed hearing it but because I knew she enjoyed telling it.

She was fifteen, and a young police officer had stopped by her father's shop to repair a hem to his uniform. She offered him water, and he asked if they'd met before. My welita said they hadn't.

"Because I would have remembered him," she told me in Spanish.

A few years later, Francisco Martinez came back to the shop and asked her to be his wife. She was only seventeen. Her parents gave them their blessing, and within ten years, they had five children. My great-grandfather used to tell her that he recognized her that first day from his dreams.

Even now, it made her blush. "Qué tonto," she said after a while, wiping her eyes with a tissue. Because as much as the memory made her smile, it also made her sad. My great-grandpa was killed in the line of duty. At the age of thirty-four, she became a single mother of five kids. Eventually, she came to the United States to find work. But she never remarried.

My mom jumped from her seat and told Welita that she wanted to show her the blanket she'd been crocheting. I knew it was my mother's way of trying to distract her.

"Gracie, por favor, go to the car and get me my bag. I think I left it in the trunk."

As I walked to the car, I thought about Tony. If he left now, would I miss him? I thought that I would, and that bothered me. Love lost can be a painful thing—my welita was proof of that. I didn't like feeling vulnerable.

But I also didn't want to be alone for the rest of my life.

A high-pitched scream interrupted my self-debate, and then my mom yelled my name. I ran inside and froze at the scene before me. My mom and abuela were kneeling on the floor beside Welita. Her eyes were closed, and there was a bloody gash on her forehead. She was clutching her chest.

"Gracie! Call an ambulance! I think Welita is having a heart attack!"

Chapter Thirty
ERICA

I hated hospitals.

I couldn't stand the smell, the bright fluorescent lights, or the constant beeping of the machines that somehow kept people from death. Even after my mother gave birth to my younger brother, I had to force myself to go visit.

At least then I knew what to expect when I got there.

The elevator doors opened at the second floor. A sign above the nurses' station told me I was in the right place—Cardiac Intensive Care. I walked to the counter and waited while a woman in purple scrubs talked very fast on the phone and typed on a computer.

"Excuse me," I said. She looked at me and held her hand up so I could wait for her to get off the phone. When she finally hung up, she asked what she could help me with. I told her I was there to see Felicidad Martinez.

"There can only be two people in her room at a time, but right now the cardiologist is in there. The family waiting area is down the hall to the right." She pointed past the elevators.

I made the long walk down the hallway, reading each sign carefully to make sure I was going the right way. As I got closer, I knew again that I was in the right place. Not because of some sign, but because of the chatter. I turned right, and there was my family. My cousins, my parents, and other relatives I hadn't seen in a while. I made my rounds and greeted each one with a kiss on the cheek. They smiled, but I could see how sad everyone was.

I found a seat next to my mom and took her hand. My dad held the other.

"Where's Abuela?" I asked. My mother explained that all Welita's children—well, the ones who lived locally—were talking with the cardiologist in the room. He was going to give them his diagnosis and options for treatment—that is, if there were any.

Gracie and Selena sat across from me, and they looked as upset as I felt.

Then I noticed a woman sitting by herself on the other side of the room. It took me a moment before I realized it was Mari.

I caught Gracie's eye and motioned to Mari. Gracie shrugged.

About ten minutes passed before my abuela and her siblings appeared with the doctor. Everyone stood and gathered around him.

"I'm Dr. Jonathan Tang, and I'm the cardiologist taking care of Felicidad. Her children have given me permission to tell everyone what's going on."

We all nodded.

"Felicidad suffered a major heart attack. Preliminary tests show some damage to the main arteries. We had to place a stent, but she is stable for now and conscious. We have her on some medications through an IV and oxygen to help her breathing."

"Doctor, what is the next step?" My mother's voice was anxious.

"Well, it's hard to say. Because of her advanced age and the fact that she has other health issues, surgery is very risky. But if we don't do surgery, there *is* a chance that she could have another heart attack in the near future. It's hard to predict because of her condition. But with the stent and additional medication, there's a good chance that her heart can last for several more months, even a year or so."

Only a year?

He said it as if that was a long time. It wasn't. Not to us.

As he continued to answer questions, I made my way back to my chair. I knew deep down that it didn't really matter what else he had to say. The outlook was bad.

I wanted to cry. Hell, I wanted to fucking scream. That wouldn't do anyone any good either. So I went to see my welita.

The same nurse from before directed me to her room. But I didn't walk inside because Mari was already there. Her back was to me, but I recognized her hair and the sundress she'd been wearing when I saw her in the waiting room. She was mumbling something, and her head was bowed.

She was praying.

I drove home an hour later in a fog. A very exhausted fog.

My head throbbed, and my stomach cramped from hunger since the only thing I'd eaten all day was a bag of chips from the hospital's vending machine. I'd regretted not bringing with me the taco salad that had arrived at the table at Casa Comida just before my cell phone rang. I had run out of the restaurant as fast as I could, leaving behind my salad and my coworkers.

I pulled into my carport space and tried to summon the energy to get out of my car and climb the stairs up to my front door.

Then I noticed Adrian walking down them.

"Hey," I said when we met on the sidewalk.

"Hey," he answered and stuffed his hands into his pockets. "How are you?"

"I'm okay. What are you doing here?"

"Marion from the reception desk took up a collection and bought you a basket. I was going to deliver it, but you didn't answer your phone, and I didn't want to just leave it in front of your door."

"Oh, sorry. My phone died about an hour ago."

"No need to apologize. Do you want me to get the basket from my car?"

"Sure. Just come up, I'll leave the door unlocked."

He nodded and walked to the street. I went upstairs, unlocked my door, and collapsed on my couch.

I was taking off my shoes when Adrian came inside carrying a small basket wrapped in cellophane and topped with a bright-blue bow.

"She wanted to get you the deluxe one with caviar and stuff, but you know how broke and cheap reporters are," he explained as he placed it on my coffee table.

I smiled. "That was nice of everyone."

A shooting pain in my head made me wince.

"Are you sure you're okay?"

"I just have a killer headache. And I'm starving. But I have no food in my fridge."

He pointed to the basket. "There's stuff in there."

I changed into sweats and a T-shirt and grabbed us two water bottles. Then we devoured a box of sesame crackers, three triangles of gourmet cheddar cheese, half a stick of summer sausage, and a bag of pretzels. Adrian was still working on a can of macadamia nuts as he recounted the stories everyone had worked on that day.

He was just in the middle of telling me how Tristan, our city council reporter, had gotten the mayor's public information officer to hang up on him when another shot of pain hit. The food had helped my stomach, but not my head.

"Headache's still there?" he asked.

I nodded.

"Come over here." Adrian grabbed a nearby toss pillow and put it on his lap.

"Why?"

"Because I'm going to rub your temples. It will help, I swear."

"That's okay. I can rub my own temples."

"Erica. Stop talking and get over here."

Pain gripped my head like a vise again. Food and drugs hadn't relieved the pain, and Adrian was offering to help. I guess I didn't need to make a big deal out of it.

I stretched out across my couch and laid my head on the pillow. He placed his fingers over my temples and started massaging. His touch was gentle, and the pain eased.

My eyes closed and my thoughts drifted back to Welita.

When I was younger, I'd get migraines and sometimes would have to call my abuelo to come pick me up from school in the middle of the day because my parents were at work. When I got to the house, Welita would pour me a glass of cold milk and make me lie down in the spare bedroom. She'd bring in a ziplock bag filled with ice cubes and place it on top of my head. If the pain was still too much, she'd lie down next to me and rub my head until I fell asleep.

I didn't realize I was crying until Adrian wiped a tear from my cheek.

"Shhh," he whispered. "Everything is going to be okay. She's going to be okay, you'll see."

"I want to believe it. But you didn't see her, Adrian. She was hooked up to these machines, and her face was nearly covered by an oxygen mask. I've never seen her look so frail."

"Of course she's frail now. Her body just went through a major trauma. That doesn't mean that she can't come back from it."

"Maybe. I hope so. My entire family is a mess right now. Even my cousin Mari, whom I haven't seen or spoken to in months, was there, and she looked devastated. I don't even want to think about what will happen to us if . . ."

I couldn't even say the words.

Adrian stopped rubbing and helped me to sit up. Then he grabbed my shoulders and looked me in the eyes. "You have to believe that she'll be okay. Because when you see her again, she has to believe it too."

He was right. And even though I knew it, I still couldn't stop the rush of tears.

Panic and old instincts shook me. Would Adrian think I was some hysterical baby just like Greg did? I tried to turn away when stifling my sobs with my hand wouldn't work. I moved to get up, but Adrian wouldn't let me go. Instead, he pulled me against his chest. I gave up and let him hold me while I cried.

A thousand minutes passed. Or maybe less. But during that time, I noticed a few things. He was wearing my favorite cologne of his—the one that smelled like the woods and lemon. He had loosened his tie, rolled up the sleeves of his dress shirt, and kicked off his shoes. He was comfortable, almost like he was at home. I also noticed that even though his chest rose evenly, his heart was racing underneath.

And he was holding my hand. His grip warm, but strong.

The last thing I noticed was how all of it made me feel.

And then I couldn't un-notice it.

Holy shit. I was falling in love with Adrian Mendes.

Chapter Thirty-One
SELENA

It was late when we finally left the hospital.

There was nothing more we could do at that point, and Welita needed her rest. A few of my relatives were going to stay through the night in case anything happened, but the rest of us were sent home.

Because of the hour and because of everything else, I decided to stay at my parents' rather than make the drive back to Los Angeles.

Gracie and I shared her bed and talked until I heard soft snores in the dark. My body, however, couldn't rest. Especially since my ears were on high alert, anticipating a phone call in the middle of the night that would summon all of us back to the hospital.

Eventually, the shadows drifted away, and the sky lightened in preparation for the sun's first rays. I decided I might as well get up and start the coffee for everyone.

My mom had had the same idea.

She was seated at their kitchen table, cupping a mug and staring at nothing in particular.

"Good morning," I said as I kissed her cheek.

"Good morning. Coffee is ready," she said and took a sip.

When I finally joined her at the table, I noticed the bags under her eyes. "Guess I wasn't the only one who didn't sleep."

She shook her head. "I couldn't. Just in case, you know."

"I know." I reached over and covered her hand with mine. "She's going to be okay. She has to be."

My mom didn't say anything.

"Welita is a tough cookie—you know that. Besides, Araceli's birthday party is in a few weeks. You know nothing is going to stop her from being there. Besides, she's making the beans."

We both laughed about that for a few seconds until she covered her face with her hands and began to cry.

I wiped away my own tears and hugged her. "Oh, Mommy. It's going to be okay. You'll see."

We stayed like that for several minutes. Both of us holding on to each other and the hope that Welita would get better. When the heaving stopped, I pulled away and offered her a napkin to blow her nose.

"Thank you, Selena, for being here," she said with a small smile.

"Where else would I be?"

"I know. But it was nice to have all of my children under the same roof again. It gave me some peace, and I need that right now."

"I'm glad. Although, next time I spend the night, I'm going to use the air mattress. Gracie snores."

She laughed. "Whatever you want. It means a lot to have everyone here during something like this. I know it's selfish, but I don't even want to imagine one of you moving away so far that I could only see you on holidays."

Although I smiled, my heart sank into my stomach.

I hadn't said a word to anyone about why I had really gone to New York, so I knew her comment was an innocent one. Or maybe there really was such a thing as a mother's intuition.

My phone rang, and I told my mom I'd be back to finish my coffee.

"Hey," I told Nathan as I walked out the front door.

"Hey there. Did I wake you? I know it's still early there."

"Um, no. I actually haven't even gone to sleep. My welita had a heart attack yesterday."

He gasped. "Oh my God, Selena. I'm so sorry. How is she?"

"Not good. It's pretty much touch-and-go right now. We may know more later today."

"Well, I know the timing sucks, but I was actually calling to tell you some good news. You're one of three final candidates for the Kane position."

I stilled. "I am? Wow."

"We can go into the details later. They're hoping to make a decision by the end of the month. They could ask you to come back to New York for another interview."

"I don't know, Nathan. With everything that's going on with my welita, I just can't commit to leaving town right now."

"I know. We'll work something out if it comes to that, okay? Don't worry about it—just be there for your family."

"Thanks. You are a very good recruiter, you know that?"

"Gee, thanks."

I laughed a little. "You are also a really great guy. No wonder my family loves you." The last sentence slipped out before I could catch it. I squeezed my eyes shut and hoped he hadn't heard.

"They love me, huh? Good to know. Does that mean I get an invitation to the next family shindig?"

"Don't push your luck."

"I don't know, Selena. I'm pretty charming. I may just win your heart after all."

"Nathan—"

"What? We both know this thing between us is changing. And if you move to New York, there's no reason why we couldn't be together like a real, actual couple."

My heart was going a mile a minute. Since when did Nathan want to date me?

I stayed quiet because I wasn't ready to have that conversation.

"Are you still there?"

"I am, but my mom is calling me, so I better go."

He sighed. "Selena, don't you dare freak out on me. Please."

"Goodbye, Nathan. I'll text you later, okay?"

I hung up the phone before he could say one more word.

Chapter Thirty-Two
MARI

It's funny how you can get your mind to focus on the tiniest of details in order to block out, or ignore, the bigger picture.

I studied the pattern of the silver spoon in my hand and was amazed that I had never noticed it before. It was an infinity sign, actually a triple infinity sign. I grabbed the fork lying on the patio table and studied it as well. The same sign. I felt relieved. I don't know what I would have done if they hadn't matched.

"Marisol, I'm asking you a question." I looked up to see Esteban standing right next to me. Letty stood behind him.

"What? I'm sorry. I guess I must have been daydreaming," I told him and put the fork back down on the table. "You know I didn't get much sleep last night."

"Yes, of course, I know." His exasperation was obvious.

Esteban was still awake when I'd returned from the hospital last night. He'd held me and let me cry. At some point I couldn't tell if my tears were because of Welita or because it had felt so good to be with him like that.

And for the first night in a long time, I didn't go downstairs to bake.

It was just after five a.m. when I finally crawled out of bed. I knew he still had thirty minutes until he had to wake up, so I left him sleeping. Then I decided to have my espresso in the backyard to watch the sunrise. I had no idea what time it was now. Or why Esteban looked so irritated.

"What's wrong?" I asked, trying to read Letty's concerned face.

He sighed. "I can't leave for court until you tell me where your keys are so I can move your car to get mine out of the garage," he scolded. "And, of course, you've probably forgotten that Letty is taking the Mercedes to get a tune-up. Sometimes, Mari, I really don't know what you would do without me. Where are the keys?"

"I told you last week that I was going to take the Mercedes and that Letty didn't need to do it for me," I argued. I hated when he talked to me like he was talking to a child.

"And have you done it? No. So I asked Letty to do it today."

"But that's not her job," I insisted.

Esteban looked at his watch. "I don't have time for this. I told you I needed to stop by the office before court, and now I might not be able to do that. Please go get your keys."

He followed behind me as I climbed the stairs, still complaining that I was making him late for all the important things he had to do that day. I wanted to scream that I was important too. But I was too tired. The keys were in the pocket of my sundress that I had worn last night to the hospital. After I gave them to Esteban, he stormed out of the house, and Letty said she would be back soon. And then I was alone. My big house seemed bigger. Or did I just feel smaller? I walked back to the patio and sat back down at the table with my cold espresso and matching silverware.

And when Letty came back a few hours later, I was still sitting in my bathrobe in the same exact spot.

"The car is in the garage, and I left the keys on the table in the foyer," she said quietly as she sat down next to me.

"I'm sorry you had to do that, Letty. Esteban was wrong to ask you."

She shrugged. "It's fine. I don't mind helping if you need the help."

I rubbed my tired eyes. "I'm not a child, you know. I was actually on my way to the mechanic yesterday, but that's when I got the call about my welita."

"I don't think you are a child, Marisol," she responded and covered my hand with hers. "How is she?"

"She might not make it," I whispered, and tears stung my eyes. "And it hurts me to know that I may not see her again. I should've visited her more often. I should've called her more than I did. And now that I might lose her, I just feel so much regret."

I covered my face in my hands and cried.

"I am sorry, Marisol. I know how difficult it is to lose someone you love," she told me.

Of course Letty understood. She lost her daughter to meningitis when she was only eight years old. Her husband was killed a few years ago in a car accident. She once told me that my hiring her had saved her life. Because now she had a new family to take care of.

"Does it still hurt to think about your husband and daughter?" I asked after I'd stopped crying.

"Of course," she said softly. "Family is the most important thing in this world. Sometimes, though, you don't realize it until you don't have it anymore."

"What if your family does something to hurt you?"

She seemed to think about this for a moment. "People aren't perfect, Marisol. We all make mistakes, and the only thing we can do is hope that we are forgiven. I know you don't like to talk about your parents, and I'm not saying you should. I just think that sometimes holding on to only the bad things that happened to us leaves us too tired to enjoy the good."

And with that, she stood and let go of my hand.

"I hope your abuelita gets better, Marisol. When you're ready to eat, come back inside and I'll make you something."

I sat on the patio for a little longer, thinking about my family and how far away I felt from them in every way.

My mom was in another state—it wasn't like she was going to drop everything and be a part of my life like a real mom. And if I was being truthful about things, she had never acted like a real mom even when I was growing up.

And although I wanted to blame my dad for that, too, a part of me knew that wasn't totally his fault. But that didn't mean I needed him in my life either.

He'd tried to talk to me at the hospital, but I hadn't been in the mood. He'd followed me to the parking lot, and I jumped when he called out my name.

"I just wanted to make sure you got to your car safe. It's dark out here," he said.

"Thanks," I responded and then turned my back on him again to open my door.

"It's good that you came," he continued. I knew he was just trying to be nice, but I was too tired and too sad to care.

"Did you think I wouldn't? Unlike you, Welita always remembered that I was a part of this family."

He stepped closer, and instinctively I moved behind the door to put a barrier between us. Although my dad had never hurt me physically, I guess emotional wounds also have a memory.

"I've never forgotten that you were part of this family, part of my family," he answered. "I wish . . ."

"What do you wish, Dad? Huh? That I'd just pretend that you didn't become a drunk after the divorce and basically forgot you had a daughter?"

He shook his head. "I told you, I never forgot. I was going to say that I wish one day you'd let me explain everything. You don't know what I went through."

That was the tipping point. "What *you* went through?" I scoffed. "Wow. Okay. Well, it's late, and I'm way too tired to listen to whatever excuses you think you have. So, I'm leaving now."

He'd said my name again, and I slammed my door closed in response.

My cheeks grew warm as I thought about his words again. How dare he play the victim. How dare he want to excuse the fact that he'd basically abandoned me and my mom. My teenage years were the hardest of my life, and I'd worked my ass off to get everything I'd ever wanted.

I looked around my big backyard with the beautiful fountain and sparkling pool and smiled. Then I stopped.

Because for the first time in decades, I knew I'd trade all of it in a heartbeat if it meant Welita would get better.

Chapter Thirty-Three
GRACIE

When I arrived at Tony's house, I was all prayed out.

I didn't think it was possible to run out of prayers, but I had. I'd asked God over and over again to heal Welita and let her come home.

Six days after the heart attack, she was still in the hospital.

That doesn't mean he's not healing her. It just means it's taking time.

Slowly, we'd given ourselves permission to get back to our lives in one way or another. For me, that meant meeting with Tony to finalize our list of game booths and review the contracts for all the bands.

I'd had to cancel on him a couple of times. He was understanding about it, and I appreciated him moving forward on the things that couldn't wait. So when I rang the doorbell, I was determined to focus on the fiesta and nothing else.

When he opened the door to let me in, he greeted me with a huge smile.

Then he hugged me. "I'm so glad you could come today," he whispered in my ear. "I've missed you, Gracie."

"Me too," I said, still not quite believing I'd heard him right.

He showed me inside his studio apartment. "Do you want some water or something else to drink?"

"Water is good," I said as I sat down on his black futon couch.

Tony walked over to the kitchen area and grabbed two glasses from his cupboard.

"I like your place," I offered.

"Thanks. It's a month-to-month lease while I look for something more permanent. I still have stuff in storage but figured, why should I get it out if I'm just going to move soon anyway?"

"Are you looking anywhere in particular? My cousin Erica lives in the complex over by the new shopping center on Market Street. They're pretty nice and affordable. I can ask her to check if there are any available units if you want?"

He handed me a glass of water and sat down. "Sure. I'm willing to move wherever, really."

"Great. Now, let's look at those contracts."

"Definitely. The first one is for the mariachi trio that's going to play on Sunday. They'll also need us to send a list of specific songs. If not, they'll just do one of their usual set lists."

"Do they have some titles to choose from?" I asked.

Tony handed me a paper, and I recognized many of them.

"This looks good. I think—" Sadness squeezed my heart, and tears welled in my eyes. One of the songs on the list was a favorite of Welita's. She requested that someone sing it or play it at every party.

I tried to laugh it off despite the fact I was obviously crying. "Jeez, I'm such a wreck. I'm so sorry."

Tony took the paper away and hugged me from the side. "Hey, no need to apologize. I get it. Please don't be embarrassed."

"I bet you had no idea I was such a basket case. You probably kick yourself every day because you got stuck with me to do this."

He lifted my chin with his finger so I would look at him. "Actually, I thank Sister Catherine every time I see her for putting us on the committee."

His face was so serious. "You do? Why?"

"Because I have the perfect excuse to spend time with you, Gracie. You're not a basket case at all. And you know it. In fact, you're one of the sweetest and most caring people I've ever known. You're beautiful on the inside and out."

"I am?" I whispered, not ready to believe what I was hearing.

He moved his face closer to mine. "You are, and it's been killing me not to kiss you every single time we see each other."

"It has?"

"Is it okay if I kiss you now?" His warm breath fanned my face.

I had no words anymore. So I nodded and closed my eyes.

His kiss was soft, tentative. But when I kissed him back, he pressed his lips harder against mine. We broke away to look at each other, and the desire in his eyes was unlike anything I'd ever seen before. He didn't want me just because I was there and convenient.

Tony wanted me because of me.

This time, I kissed him. Hard.

He got the message, and in a matter of seconds, his tongue was breaking through the seam of my lips. But what happened next took us both by surprise. Somehow, some way, I knew that if I wanted something to happen between us, it had to be my move. Like with our first kiss, he needed permission. It was like he was at the edge of a cliff and was trying to figure out if I wanted to jump off with him. And I didn't let myself think about whether I was wrong. Yes, I was a virgin, but I knew enough about sex to know when it was in the air.

So I took his hands from my shoulders and brought them to my breasts. He didn't even hesitate. His kisses grew more fervent as he caressed and squeezed them through my shirt. It felt amazing to be wanted like this, and I became lost in his passion. I didn't want to think about anything anymore. I just wanted to feel.

So I stopped him. And then I moved on top of him to straddle his lap and pulled off my shirt.

He held my face in his hands and searched my eyes. "Are you sure?" he whispered.

I smiled and nodded. Then, to make sure he knew I was serious, I unclasped my bra.

He groaned as his mouth engulfed one of my breasts. I closed my eyes and cried out in pleasure when his tongue flicked one nipple while his fingers rubbed and teased the other. I'd never felt anything like this before. And I only wanted more.

So did he.

"Let's move to my bed," he said, his voice hoarse and thick with desire.

We watched each other as we undressed. I pushed away thoughts of what he might think of my naked body. I couldn't worry about that now.

Besides, I was too entranced by the perfectness of him.

He saw me staring, and my cheeks burned with a giddy embarrassment. But he didn't tease or laugh. Instead, he walked over and pulled me against him.

Our kisses started up again, hard and demanding. I couldn't get enough of his taste. Our breaths were ragged as our hands grabbed and clawed each other. Somehow, we eventually managed to get on the bed.

And then I was underneath him.

He reached into his nightstand drawer and pulled out a condom. Then he asked me one more time if I was sure.

For a few seconds, I honestly didn't know. Then it hit me. Tony was making me feel all sorts of things, but none of them were bad. I wasn't afraid. I wasn't anxious.

I felt safe with Tony.

"I'm sure," I finally answered. And to prove it, I grabbed his face and kissed him long and deep. That was all he needed.

He sheathed himself and pushed inside me. Pleasure turned to pain, and I took a sharp breath.

My eyes watered, and I turned my head so he wouldn't see the emotion I knew was written all over my face.

"You feel so good," he whispered against my jaw.

With each slow and steady thrust, Tony taught me about sex. Yes, it hurt at first, but eventually the pain turned into something different.

"I'm almost there. Are you?"

I turned to look at him again. Sweat had beaded across his forehead, and his breathing had become gasps. "What do you mean?"

"Your orgasm. Are you going to come?"

The words wouldn't leave my lips.

My nonresponse must have spoken volumes. "Let's catch you up then," he said with a wicked smile.

As he pushed and pushed into me, Tony bent down and took a nipple into his mouth. He moved one hand between us, and I gasped when his finger stroked my tight bundle of nerves. A wave of warmness overcame me, and a burst of pleasure blasted through me.

Tony reached his climax as well and collapsed onto his back. My body continued to tingle, this time from the gratification of knowing that Tony had enjoyed being with me as much as I'd enjoyed being with him. I never knew how satisfying it could be to have that kind of power to give pleasure to another person.

Unfortunately, the euphoria didn't last long.

Could he tell it was my first time? Would he kick me out now?

But all he did was kiss my shoulder and ask if I wanted to use the restroom first.

I nodded and suddenly felt self-conscious about him seeing me naked, so I hesitated.

"You can take the sheet with you if you want."

"Thanks."

So I went to the restroom to clean up, and when I got back, he had his boxers on but was lying on his side on the bed. He patted the pillow next to him.

"Come over here."

He kissed me softly when I lay next to him. "That was amazing. Thank you."

"I should be thanking you," I said with a laugh. His forehead wrinkled in confusion. But he didn't ask me to clarify.

We lay there just looking at each other for another minute or so.

"What are you staring at? The ugly pimple on my forehead?" Instinctively, I covered it with my palm.

"Stop it." Tony reached over and pulled my hand away. "I was staring at your nose. It's cute. Like a bunny's."

"It is?" I smiled.

"It is." He leaned over and kissed the tip.

I moved closer, and he turned on his back so I could snuggle in the crook of his arm. It was the happiest I'd been in days.

Maybe I should've been more conflicted about losing my virginity. Maybe if it hadn't become more like a to-do item on a checklist, then I would've been more reflective about the whole experience.

Selena, for sure, was going to be all sorts of reflective once I told her. She could analyze enough for both of us.

Satisfied, I closed my eyes and let myself enjoy my moment of no regrets.

Chapter Thirty-Four
ERICA

"How about we go a little shorter?"

I looked up from my phone and stared at my mom. She was holding a pair of scissors in midair, and I instinctively moved my head away from them.

"How about no?" I answered back.

"Ay, Erica. Don't you ever want to try something new?" She met my eyes in the reflection of her shop's mirror. At least the scissors were a safe distance away now.

"Not really. Besides, you and I both know these curls are hopeless. All I need you to do is trim the chaos every six or eight weeks."

She let out a long sigh and began combing and trimming. "I don't understand. Selena has a new haircut or color every single time I see her. What are you so afraid of? Hair grows back. Color fades."

"I'm not afraid of anything. Why change something if it works?"

So what if I was a creature of habit? There was nothing wrong with going with what you knew, what you were comfortable with. I liked what I liked. That didn't mean I was scared of anything.

"Did you go visit Welita this morning?" I asked, changing the subject before she tried to convince me again to get highlights.

My mom nodded. "I took Abuela and Abuelo. Tía Olivia was already there, so we had to take turns going into her room."

"How is she? I visited last weekend but haven't had a chance to go back. By the time I get out of work, visiting hours are over."

"She's okay," my mom said. She didn't smile, and I recognized the worry in her eyes. "She's still on oxygen. They're not happy with her blood pressure, so it will probably be a while before she can come home."

My throat knotted with dread. Every time it looked like Welita would be able to leave the hospital, she had another setback. I knew she hated not being in her own bed and not having the strength to do all the things she used to do. I hated it too. We all did.

"So, how's work?" Now it was my mom's turn to change the subject.

I shrugged. "It's all right. We had a big meeting the other day, and the publisher is making some changes. He's worried about the competition from the online news sites because they've beaten us a couple times on breaking stories. He said he wants us to work on more in-depth projects."

"Does that mean you'll get more money?"

"Chale," I scoffed.

"Then what does it mean?"

"It means they'll give us more than one day to work on these bigger articles. But we still have to put out at least two daily stories. That's why I've been working so late."

My mom started brushing off the loose hair from my shoulders and back. "So, basically, you're doing extra work, but without extra money. Maybe it's time to move on, Erica."

"And go where? The *News-Press* is the only paper in town, Mom."

"Other towns have other papers. Who says you have to stay local? Or what about getting a job at one of those news places on the internet?"

I'd never admit it to my coworkers, but I did subscribe to one of them. It was called Above the Fold. I even followed some of its reporters on Twitter. They were covering some really important topics, not just the regular old day-to-day crime blotter or city council agenda items. But I could never see myself working for such a place. I didn't have the experience . . . or the talent.

Besides, I still liked working for the *News-Press*. I knew my beat, and I had lots of established sources. Why change something if it wasn't broken, right? It might not have been a big metropolitan newspaper, but it had some good qualities.

Like being able to see Adrian almost every day.

Heat burned my cheeks at the thought of him. I glanced up to see if my mom had noticed. Luckily, she had her back turned and was talking to one of the other stylists. It didn't seem like it. God, if she kept pushing me about work, there was a good chance I'd accidentally bring up Adrian. That topic was too dangerous right now. I needed to distract her so she'd stop with the questions.

"Hey, Mom," I said when she turned around and I could see her face in the mirror again. "Today's your lucky day. How about you give me a blowout?"

I had done some really stupid shit in my life.

But falling in love with my boss really had to be the stupidest.

At least I was pretty sure that's what was happening.

That was the only explanation I had for why, a few hours later, my newly straightened hair and I were walking into the backyard of Adrian's parents' house to attend their anniversary party.

The evolution of these new feelings had happened slowly, under my usually observant radar. It started with calls to tell me about the documentary he'd just watched on Netflix. Adorable.

Then I dragged him with me to buy a new coffee table at IKEA, and he spent an entire Saturday afternoon trying to put it together. Fucking sexy.

Before long, we were eating lunch together at work almost every day and hanging out on our days off. I was officially a lost cause.

But when he invited me to his parents' house for their anniversary party, the alarm bells finally sounded. He hadn't even met my cousins, and now he wanted me to go with him to a family event? It was too much, too fast. I said no.

So, he fired from the big guns. "Come on, Erica, I already told you that me and my dad don't get along. I need you there. You have this way of calming me down, of making me see when I'm being an asshole. This is an important day for my mom, and I don't want to ruin it by fighting with him."

Well, shit. How could I argue with that?

What the asshole didn't tell me was that his parents lived on a huge estate in Holmby Hills, an affluent neighborhood in West Los Angeles. Or that they owned a multimillion-dollar Hispanic supermarket chain known as Mendes Market.

"Hold the fuck up. Your family is *that* Mendes family?" I shouted at him once I saw all the customized canopies emblazoned with the Mendes Market logo dotting the sprawling green lawn.

"Didn't I mention that?" he said as he surveyed the crowd.

"Um, no, you didn't. Wait. The family business your dad has been bugging you to take over is the supermarket business?"

"Yep."

I immediately felt out of place in my black-and-white sleeveless romper. "I wish you'd told me, Adrian. I would've dressed up."

"Why?" he asked and stopped walking to look at me. "You look nice. I like your new hair too."

Instinctively, I smoothed down one side. "Well, at least my hair is somewhat tamed. Although, I bet by the end of the day, my wild curls will be back."

"Good. Because I like those wild curls even more."

I didn't know what to say to that. Should I compliment him on his very crisply pleated slacks? Even if I wanted to, though, I couldn't. The connection between my brain and my mouth had short-circuited thanks to the way Adrian was now watching me. His expression had softened, and his dark eyes reflected something I couldn't decipher.

And just when I thought that maybe he was working up the nerve to tell me something, his eyes moved past me and the moment was gone.

"There they are." He pointed over my head.

I turned to see a very good-looking couple standing next to one of the canopies. He grabbed my hand to take me over there, and in normal circumstances it would have made my heart do silly things. But I was in too much shock to feel much of anything else.

The beautiful dark-haired woman in a lovely burgundy dress threw up her hands in joy when she spotted us. "Mijo! You made it!" Everyone around her turned to look as we walked up the pathway to meet her.

She threw her arms around Adrian's neck and planted kisses all over his face. I already loved this woman, and I hadn't even officially met her yet.

"Hello, son."

The deep baritone voice was such a contrast to the light giddiness of his mother. I nearly gasped when I looked at his father. He was the spitting image of Adrian, just twenty years older.

Adrian pulled away from his mom to shake his dad's hand. Then he turned to me. "This is my friend Erica. She works at the newspaper too."

His mom smiled, and I shook her hand and then his dad's. "It's nice to meet you both. Happy anniversary."

"Thank you, Erica. Welcome to our home," she said. "I hope you two are hungry. There's a different kind of food and drink under each canopy. I couldn't decide on a menu, so I just told the caterer to do it all."

"My wife never does anything half-assed," his dad droned.

That made me laugh, and I looked over at Adrian. For some reason, he didn't appear to think it was as funny as I did.

His mom ordered him to eat and then threatened to come find him later so he could say hello to their family and friends. We grabbed plates and settled on the tent where they were making street tacos. Then we picked up some sodas and found seats at one of the many round tables spread throughout the backyard.

"Shit. I still can't believe you're rich," I said after taking a couple of bites of my carne asada taco.

He shook his head. "I'm not rich, Erica. My parents are. I live only on what I make at the *News-Press*."

"But why?" He gave me a look. "I'm kidding. You know that. It's still kind of cool."

"In a way. It's been such a long time, though, since I've been around all of this. I feel like a stranger, almost like I don't belong."

The regret in his voice pained me. I reached out and grabbed his hand. "Don't think like that. Your mom is obviously thrilled that you're here. Even your dad. They want you here."

His gaze locked on mine. "Thanks, Erica. I'm glad you're here with me."

"Hello, Adrian."

We both turned around to see a knockout brunette standing behind us. Adrian pulled his hand away and stood. "Hello, Isela."

By their awkward hug, I figured she must have been his ex.

I wasn't a reporter for nothing.

I was impressed. She was drop-dead gorgeous, and for a moment I wanted to be her best friend. But when she barely looked at me as Adrian introduced us, she became my mortal enemy.

So it's going to be like that, huh?

"How are your parents?" he asked and invited her to take a seat with us.

"They're good. I think they're inside the house right now with your mom. I just arrived, and she told me to come outside and see you."

Yeah, right. Blame his mom.

I was taking a big bite of one of my tacos when Isela finally decided to look at me.

"So how did you two meet?" she asked, her voice sweet but also deadly terrifying.

My mouth was full of carne asada, so Adrian answered. "Oh. Oh? We're not dating. Jesus, no. Erica is a reporter for the newspaper. I'm her editor."

That made me cough up a piece of corn tortilla. When he'd introduced me to his parents, I worked *with* him. Now, I was his employee *and* a woman he was very clearly not in a relationship with.

"Oh."

Isela's eyes widened, and I watched as the light went on inside that pretty head of hers. And it burned bright with hope for a reunion now that he'd made it clear we weren't a couple.

"There you two are," Adrian's mom called from a few feet away. "We want to take a photo. Isela and Adrian, come over here, please."

She stood and headed over to the group.

"So, you almost married her, huh?"

He nodded. "How did you know? Let me guess, a woman's intuition or something like that?"

I scoffed. "God, no. But the fact that you nearly pissed yourself when you heard her voice was a very good hint."

"Was I that bad?"

He was, but he already looked embarrassed enough, so I let him off the hook. "Nah, I'm just messing with you. And your mom is giving you the evil eye, so you better get going."

He took a step and then looked back at me. "Aren't you coming?" he asked.

"Me? No, that's okay. I'm going to grab some more tacos. Go ahead, and I'll wait here."

"Sure?"

I nodded, and he took off. As I watched the group of people hug him and pat him on the back, I knew that he had nothing to worry about. He definitely belonged here.

What I didn't know anymore was whether I did.

And why in the hell did that bug me so much?

Chapter Thirty-Five
SELENA

Gracie thought I was crazy, but I believed Kat's spirit still haunted the offices of Umbridge & Umbridge.

"She's not dead, Selena. How could she be a ghost?" Gracie said over the phone.

"I didn't say she was a ghost. I said it was her spirit that I could feel sometimes."

It had been weeks since I'd seen my old boss. Yet, I couldn't help feeling like she was constantly watching me, waiting for me to mess up. This morning, for example, I'd nearly sent an email by mistake to the very client I was complaining about to our art department.

"It's your guilt."

I froze at my sister's comment. "Um, what do you mean? I didn't get her fired. She did that all on her own."

"You didn't, but there's obviously something you feel guilty about that has to do with work. That's why you're being paranoid and hypersensitive about everything."

Oh my God. Did Gracie know about the job in New York? My Zoom interview with a few more department heads was just a few days ago. It went well. At least I thought so. But I hadn't said a word to anyone but Nathan.

After a few more minutes, it became clear that Gracie was clueless about my interview. But she still might've had a point. Was I feeling guilty about a possible new job and purposefully messing up so Umbridge would fire me? That way the decision to go to New York would be out of my hands.

Stop it, Selena. They haven't even offered it to you yet.

After I hung up with Gracie, I tried to concentrate extra hard to make sure I didn't have any more close calls. I thought I'd done everything right up until it was time for me to head out.

That's when Alan Umbridge called me into his office.

Shit.

"Is everything okay?" I asked as soon as I sat down in the chair in front of his huge desk.

He sat back and crossed his arms. "Things are fine. But I believe they can be better."

Dread filled my chest, and I clenched my fists in my lap to try to stay calm. "Oh?"

"Yes. I want you to know that we've noticed how you've taken over Kat's responsibilities and clients without us even having asked you."

Now my knee was shaking on its own. "Well, yes, um. I didn't want us to fall behind. I'm sorry if I—"

Alan snorted. "What are you sorry about, Selena? You've really impressed us with your initiative and team player attitude."

"Oh? Oh! Thank you," I said, slowly unfurling my fists.

"And to show you how much we appreciate all of your work, we definitely want to make it official since you're already basically doing Kat's job. We want to give you a promotion."

Shock made my mouth drop. Was this really happening? I couldn't believe it. I had to ask to make sure. "Are you offering me the position of senior vice president of marketing?"

Alan coughed into his hand and shifted in his seat. "Well, no. Your new title would be project manager."

And just like that, my excitement bubble burst. I knew it was too good to be true. "So, I'd be doing everything Kat was doing, but without her title?"

"It would still come with a pretty good salary increase," he offered.

"But not Kat's salary."

He shifted in his seat again. I'd never seen him squirm so much. Part of me wondered if he'd been expecting me to just fall on my knees and thank him for the opportunity.

"It's definitely a step up, Selena. I really hope you'll take it."

"Do I have a choice?" I didn't mean to sound so snippy.

Whatever softness I'd seen on Alan's face minutes ago dissolved. He was back to being stern Mr. Umbridge. "Of course you have a choice, dear. But I must tell you that if you decline, we are going to post the position, and that person will be your new boss. And I can't guarantee when another opportunity to advance will come your way."

In other words, I needed to take the job.

Then I remembered I did have another choice. Kane Media was close to making a decision. I didn't have to say yes right away.

I stood up. "Thank you, Mr. Umbridge. I really do appreciate the offer. Is it okay if I take some time to think about it?"

Surprise made his bushy eyebrows arch to the top of his forehead. "Yes, if that's what you need." I smiled and nodded and turned to leave. Then he warned, "But don't take too long, Ms. Lopez. We won't wait forever."

Chapter Thirty-Six
MARI

The first thing I noticed was how much older she looked.

Had new wrinkles appeared over the past few weeks? New age spots? This wasn't the Welita I'd seen a few weeks ago.

Fear took hold of my body, and I froze several feet away from her hospital bed.

A strong, warm hand grabbed mine, startling me. For a few seconds, I'd forgotten that Esteban was at my side.

I'd overheard Letty telling him the other day that I was still very worried about my welita. She'd suggested he come with me for a visit. I didn't think much of it because I hadn't expected him to really do it. But he'd surprised me this morning and told me he would drive me to the hospital.

Now we were here. And I couldn't bring myself to get any closer.

Esteban bent down and whispered, "Cariño, she can't see you from here. Go to her."

He gently tugged my hand, and I let him lead me farther into the room.

Welita let out a small groan and turned her head. Immediately, her face brightened when she saw us.

"Marisol," she said weakly.

It was all I needed. I went to her bedside and touched her cheek. "Hola, Welita, ¿cómo te sientes?"

She sighed. "Más o menos, ¿es tu marido?"

I laughed when she pointed to Esteban. "Sí, Welita. He's my husband."

"Qué bueno. Gracias por tu visita."

We spent the next fifteen minutes talking about her favorite nurses and the awful food they were trying to feed her. I was so grateful that Esteban and Letty had made sure I kept up with my Spanish. Esteban's mom loved to correct my grammar whenever she was in town, but I didn't care. All that mattered was that Welita always understood me.

When Esteban left us alone to take a phone call, she grabbed my hand and asked me if I had talked to my cousins. I told her I'd seen Selena in New York.

"Y Erica? Graciela?"

"Not for a while," I admitted. She always knew when I was lying anyway.

"Soon?" she said.

I smiled at her English. "Yes. Soon."

"Bueno." Her bony, cold fingers curled into mine a little tighter. "Yo solo quiero que seas feliz, Marisol."

Tears stung my eyes because I wanted so much to reassure her that I was happy. I wanted her to know that my marriage was good, that my cousins and I were going to be okay, and that she didn't have to worry about me anymore.

Again, I couldn't lie to her.

So, I offered her a smile and instead said, "I know, Welita."

Later as Esteban drove us back to San Marino, I couldn't stop thinking of Welita's words.

Yo solo quiero que seas feliz, Marisol.

She used to say that to me a lot when I would visit her and my grandparents after the divorce. I was a stubborn teenager who hated my dad and hated the fact that I was forced by a judge to go see him one weekend a month, but Welita was the one who could always get me to be not so grumpy. She'd let me cook with her, and then we'd play cards or watch her novelas together at night. In between, she'd try to tell me how much my dad loved me, how much they all loved me. She would plead for me to tell her why I was always so sad. "Yo solo quiero que seas feliz, Marisol," she'd say.

But my mom always made me promise never to tell Welita or my grandparents that my dad had stopped sending us money. She said they wouldn't believe me or they'd make excuses for him. "Once you turn eighteen, you never have to see him or them again anyway," she'd say. And so I never said a word to Welita. Even though part of me wanted to. I knew that it hurt her when I'd refused to open up. I just didn't care back then.

Now, when I really wanted to tell her everything that was making me sad, I couldn't. Because I knew that would hurt her, too, and I couldn't do that to her. Not anymore.

"Why are you so quiet?"

Esteban's question pulled me from my somber thoughts.

I wiped away the tear hidden by my sunglasses before he noticed. "I'm just worried about her. She didn't look so good."

"She's been through a lot. But I'm sure the doctors are doing everything they can."

"I guess."

"What did you two talk about when I was on the phone?"

I hesitated for a few seconds before telling him. "She wanted to make sure I was happy." Then I took a breath and continued. "I didn't want to tell her that I'm not."

Esteban turned in my direction, but I looked away to stare at the car next to us on the freeway. "Qué? I don't understand?"

More tears streamed down my face. The sunglasses couldn't contain my sadness anymore. "I'm not happy, Esteban."

"Of course you're not, Marisol," he scoffed.

I whipped my head to look at him. "You know?"

"Yes, I know. It's normal to feel sad right now. You're worried about your abuelita. This will pass."

I wanted to tell him that he was wrong. I wanted to tell him that I wasn't happy in our marriage anymore. Yet, I couldn't find the words. Or rather, I didn't even want to look. I was exhausted emotionally and mentally. I didn't have it in me to have that conversation.

"You're probably right," I said and leaned my head against the window.

His hand squeezed my knee. "I know I am. Hey, I know what will cheer you up. Let's pick up some dinner from that little Italian place in South Pasadena. We can even get your favorite—tiramisu."

Tiramisu wasn't my favorite. I just always ordered it because I knew it was his.

"Actually, my favorite is their chocolate cake."

He laughed. "Since when?"

Since always? But I didn't get the chance to answer because, as usual, he'd already decided.

"It's too rich. And you'll never finish that piece all by yourself. We'll just get the tiramisu so we can share."

I didn't have the energy to fight him. Besides, I knew I wasn't going to be eating anything anyway. All I wanted to do was go home, crawl into my bed, and pray for Welita to get better.

I couldn't have cared less what Esteban wanted. That's how done I was with everything.

Chapter Thirty-Seven
GRACIE

Dear God, thank you again for making Tony Bautista my boyfriend.

As I looked across the table at the man in question, I couldn't help but offer the silent prayer of gratitude because I still couldn't believe we were together.

Well, technically, we hadn't said it out loud. Or officially. And we weren't using terms like *boyfriend* and *girlfriend* just yet. But I couldn't think of anything else to call us.

We had dinner together almost every night, either at a restaurant or at his apartment. He took me to the movies and other places on the weekends.

And we were having sex. Lots of it.

We were a couple. Weren't we?

Tony glanced up from his salad plate and caught me staring at him. "What? Do I have blue cheese dressing in my beard again?"

I laughed and shook my head. "No. I was just thinking."

"Thinking about what?"

"Just stuff," I said and took a big gulp of my iced tea. I prayed he wouldn't press me for more information. I was still working up the nerve to ask him what I wanted to ask him tonight.

He shrugged and went back to eating his salad. That let me blow out the breath I'd been holding and focus on finishing my salad too.

Once the dishes were clean and all the leftovers put away, we moved to the couch to watch an episode of our favorite series on Netflix.

Another check mark in the "Couple" column.

Tony pulled me against his side and moved his arm behind my head. When he kissed my hair, a small, satisfied sigh escaped me.

"This is nice," I told him.

"It is."

And that's how we stayed for the next thirty minutes. As the credits began to roll, Tony adjusted his position so he could press his lips against my face, then my nose, and, finally, my mouth.

Kissing Tony had become my new favorite hobby. I had no idea how that would translate into Christmas presents later on.

Holiday plans? That was definitely couples' territory.

I knew I needed to ask my question, but I couldn't concentrate with a second tongue in my mouth. I pulled away. "Could you do me a favor?"

His devilish grin gave away his naughty thoughts. I playfully slapped his arm. "Not that kind of favor. I wanted you to rub my shoulders. Cleaning the dry-erase boards gave me a kink on my right side."

"Not what I was expecting, but yes, I can definitely do that."

I turned around so my back was to him, and within seconds his strong hands were massaging away the tightness I'd been feeling since that afternoon.

Soon, I was relaxed enough to ask.

"Are you doing anything the Saturday after next?" I began.

"Not that I know of off the top of my head. Why, did you want to do something?"

"Well, it's my mom's birthday. We're having a barbecue at the house. I thought it would be nice if you could come."

The fingers that had been rubbing my shoulders stopped.

Uneasiness began to creep through me. "But I'll understand if you don't want to. My family is pretty big, and they can be intimidating. You know what? Never mind. It's not a big deal at all."

His chest heaved with a deep sigh. "Gracie, I think we need to talk." Tony turned me around to face him again. I didn't like the look in his eyes.

"What's wrong?"

"Remember when I said earlier that I might move?"

"Yes. But I thought you'd stopped looking at other apartments?"

"I did. But only because there's a possibility I might be moving back to Texas."

My throat tightened as he told me that he had been invited to interview for a trainer position with a college baseball team. I didn't recognize the name of the school, but it didn't matter. It was in Texas. "If they offer it to me, I'm going to take it. It's an amazing opportunity."

I swallowed my pain. "It is. I'm really happy for you, Tony."

He reached out and cupped my chin. It took everything I had not to pull away. "You're wonderful, Gracie. And I've loved spending time with you these past few months." He then took my hands and squeezed them. "Shit. I'm sorry. Please don't think I only wanted to get laid. I do care about you, but I can't offer you what you need right now when my life is so . . . up in the air. You're the type of girl who deserves a real boyfriend. Someone who can promise you forever. And that's not me. At least, not right now."

I didn't know what to say. My sister and Erica came to mind, and I tried to think of what they would do in this situation. Forcing all my emotions down, I attempted a smile and nodded. "I get it. I care about you too."

I have no idea if Tony believed my brave front. It probably didn't matter since he'd gotten himself off the hook of having to deal with a hysterical Gracie. I'm sure that's why he didn't try to stop me when I told him I had to get home and grade papers.

During every crisis in my life, big or small, I always turned to God for answers.

But as I drove home later, I didn't even want to talk to him about this.

Chapter Thirty-Eight
ERICA

He was nearly twenty minutes late to our meeting.

I was already pissed before, but I was raging now.

Adrian had stood me up for his ex-girlfriend.

If I'd had any doubt about Isela's intentions, they were wiped clean weeks ago. First it started with texts. Then phone calls. He told me it felt weird to be talking to her again, but it also felt nice since they'd known each other for years.

I kept my mouth shut for the most part. I didn't want to act like a jealous hag. Even though I was.

Although I accepted I had romantic feelings for him, I knew nothing could ever happen between us as long as he was my boss. He was by the book all the way. Not to mention the fact that he'd never once shown the slightest hint that he liked me that way too.

I was resigned to pushing my feelings down, as always.

But it was getting harder now that Isela was encroaching on my territory. She'd shown up at the newsroom an hour ago to take Adrian to lunch.

He'd seemed surprised, even annoyed, I thought, and I settled in my chair, ready to witness him telling her to back the fuck off. Okay, he probably would have never said that. Those were my words.

Yet, he let her convince him, and then they were headed out the door. A few minutes later he texted and said he'd be back in time for our two p.m. meeting to read over the most current draft of a big school board article I was working on. I had found out that construction had stopped on a new high school because it turned out the budget for it had been so mismanaged that the district was in the hole for millions of dollars. The board had hired a consultant months ago to review the books, and his report was explosive.

My story was almost ready. So much so that I wanted to convince him to run it that Friday. My sources at the district had mentioned that another reporter had visited the superintendent yesterday. If someone else was sniffing around, that meant something was about to break, and we needed to be the ones to break it first.

Adrian, however, wanted to get a third confirmation on the report since I'd first received it anonymously through the mail. I'd been able to verify its authenticity by two district employees. He'd insisted we needed one more.

I had planned to be reasonable and hear his side out during our meeting. But the longer it took for him to walk through the door, the less gracious I was feeling.

He finally arrived at 2:27 p.m.

"I know, I know. The food took forever." He rushed as he sat down next to me and placed a notebook and pen on the table.

I shook my head and shoved the article toward him. "We only have half an hour to go through this now. The staff meeting is at three today."

"I'm sorry. Do you want to reschedule for tomorrow?"

"No, I don't. I already told you that we should run it Friday. That means it has to go to Charlie today so he can take it to Tom tomorrow for his sign-off. The graphics team is going to need some time to pull all the stuff together."

He took a breath. "Isela thinks we should wait for the third confirmation. We need to do this right."

My head whipped around. "Isela? You talked to her about my story?"

"Yeah, over lunch. She wanted to know what I was working on and . . ."

"And you wanted to impress her," I finished for him.

"What? No, that's not it at all. We're both too close to this. Sometimes it's good to bounce things off an impartial person."

"Who the fuck is Charlie then? Jesus, Adrian. This could be a huge story. We both said we were going to keep it under wraps until the night before we publish. I haven't told a single soul, not even my cousins."

"She doesn't live in town, Erica. Who is she gonna tell?"

"You know that's so not the point."

He threw up his hands. "Fine, you're right. I shouldn't have said anything. Forget that for now and focus. Don't you find it somewhat interesting that Isela agrees we need the third source?"

"Actually, I don't because she's not a fucking journalist."

I was so mad now. The f-word was about to replace *the* in every single sentence that came out of my mouth.

"Exactly. Journalists aren't going to be the only ones reading this article. She agrees with me that it will help legitimize our sources."

"Of course she's going to agree with you. She wants to get back together with you."

He seemed to consider this. "Really?"

"Oh. My. God. I can't believe you're doing this. If we wait to confirm with a third source, we're going to get scooped by the *Times*."

"I think you're wrong."

"And I think you're being an asshole because you know I'm right."

The vein in his neck pulsed with irritation. I could tell he was pissed but was trying to choose his words carefully. His hesitation gave me a window to strike.

"Playing it safe doesn't sell newspapers anymore. If we keep getting beat by the *Times* or these other online news sites, we both are going to be looking for new jobs sooner rather than later. Or maybe you don't care and want to work for your dad after all?"

He sat back in his chair and folded his arms. "You really say everything that pops into your head, don't you?"

I shrugged.

"I think you're taking advantage of our friendship," Adrian said.

That hurt me. Deep. "Are you fucking serious right now?"

Adrian dragged his left hand down his face. "Erica, don't be difficult," he implored. "You know what I mean. You would never be like this with Charlie."

"Listen, I used to tell Charlie all the time if I thought he was making a bad call," I explained. "Maybe it's you that's taking advantage of our friendship if you think I'm not going to do the same to you."

He pushed his notebook across the table. "I knew this wasn't going to work. It was a mistake to think . . ." Adrian's voice stopped midsentence when the conference room door opened.

Tristan walked in, and I almost yelled at him to get out. But something in his face stopped me.

"What is it?" Adrian barked.

I held my breath as Tristan met my eyes. He was looking at me with pity. "Erica, you're not answering your cell. So your mom called the main line. It . . ."

It was another heart attack. Welita died in the hospital with my abuela and my tía Andrea from Chicago at her side. It had been weeks since they'd placed a stent. There had been lots of complications, but she was improving. Selena and I had just visited her over the weekend, and she was able to talk to us for a few minutes. We'd convinced ourselves that she looked better. That she would be home soon.

Now, she was gone.

It only took me ten minutes to drive from the *News-Press* office to the hospital, but I still couldn't get there fast enough. Adrian didn't want me to drive at all, but I ignored him and flew out the door.

The waiting room was already filled with family. I guess that was the good thing about all of us living so close. When something bad happened, we could be there in a matter of minutes.

Some of my younger cousins were standing in the hallway, hugging each other and crying. I walked past them and straight to her room. My mother said the nurses had promised to let the family say our goodbyes before they did what had to be done next.

The small, private room was packed, yet there was no noise. The machines had stopped their beeping.

Someone, I didn't look to see who, grabbed my hand and led me to the bed. Welita's eyes were closed, and I noticed that all the tubes and the oxygen mask were gone. For the first time in weeks, I could finally see her entire face. I touched her arm. Her warmth was long gone too.

"I love you, Welita," I whispered as I bent to kiss her cheek. "Que Dios te bendiga."

"Mama, Mama, Mama!" My abuela's sobs pierced the silence. I realized then that she was the one holding my hand. Her other hand covered her own mouth, trying to stifle her grief. I pulled my abuela toward me so I could hold her up. And just when I thought I had her, her knees buckled. Hands came out of nowhere to grab her before she could fall.

The room filled with quiet sobs as my uncles took her away.

I turned around to look at my welita one last time before heading back to the waiting room to search for my parents.

But as I was about to leave, Gracie walked in. Our eyes met, and her face crumpled in grief. We crashed into each other and sobbed like we were little girls.

As we stood there, I felt my phone vibrate inside my purse.

I knew it was Adrian.

And for the first time in a long time, I didn't care.

Chapter Thirty-Nine

SELENA

I hadn't made it to the hospital in time to say my goodbye. Stupid LA traffic had taken that away from me.

So I'd ended up at my grandparents' house, along with everyone else. They trickled in throughout the afternoon and into the early evening. We were the walking wounded. Dazed, confused, and hurting like hell. The last few hours had left me with a painful thud in my head, swollen eyes, and a knot in my stomach.

I still couldn't believe that Welita was gone or that I would never get another chance to hear one of her stories or laugh at her attempts to tell a joke.

"Here. I opened another box," my sister tearfully said as she handed me yet another tissue.

We were sitting in my grandparents' patio—the same place where just a few months earlier we'd laughed and teased.

Welita was the first of my close relatives to die. My father's parents died when I was young, and I barely remembered them. I wondered if that's what would happen with my younger cousins. They were sad today, of course. But how long would it take before they forgot her smile or the way she smelled?

I felt sorry for them already.

Death sucked. And as you got older, the more it seemed that death came to take away those you loved.

I looked around the patio. It was filled with people I couldn't imagine my life without. I didn't want to think of ever not having my grandparents, my parents, my sisters, my cousins, or anyone else around. Where would I go on the weekends if my parents weren't around? Where would I spend Christmas, Thanksgiving, and Easter if my grandparents were gone? Who would I talk to about everything and anything if my sister wasn't just a phone call away?

My family included some of the nosiest, most frustrating, most meddling people around. But I loved every single one of them.

And I couldn't leave them. Not yet.

I walked outside and pulled out my phone and called Nathan. His voice mail answered instead. "Hey there. Um. Can you let Kane know that I'm no longer interested in the job? It's just not a good time right now. Okay, well. Oh, and my welita died. Call me when you can. Bye."

Wiping my tears away, I hung up and walked back to my family.

Chapter Forty
MARI

I couldn't believe my welita was dead.

After I'd hung up with Tía Marta, I just braced myself against the wall in my kitchen and slid to the floor. I couldn't move. I couldn't cry.

I was sitting there frozen for I don't know how long. I wanted to stand up and grab my purse and drive to Inland Valley so I could see my welita before the mortuary came to take her away. But I knew, even without traffic, I wouldn't make it in time.

You should be with your family.

I should've been. But my legs wouldn't move. It was Letty's day off. I was all alone in my big, empty house.

Tears wet my cheeks as I pulled my phone out of my pocket and called the first person I could think of—Chris. But he didn't answer, and I didn't leave a message.

So I sat there on the kitchen floor, alternating between numb and hysterical.

The light that had shown through the large window over the sink had dimmed to more of a haze by the time I heard the garage door open.

Esteban called out my name. I told him I was in the kitchen.

"Break out the champagne, cariño. The case went to the jury today and . . . ay, Dios! Oh my God! Did you fall? Are you hurt?" he yelled when he saw me on the floor. I lowered my head.

He bent down in front of me and cupped my chin with his fingers and lifted it so he could look me in the eyes. "Marisol, please tell me what is wrong," he pleaded.

I saw the gentle concern in his eyes, and that was all it took. The tears came, and I whispered, "My abuelita died." He didn't say a word, but sat next to me and pulled me to him. I grabbed his shirt and buried my head in his chest and sobbed.

I cried for Welita. I cried for my abuela. I cried for my cousins. And I cried because my marriage was broken and Esteban didn't want to see it.

"I'm so sorry, Marisol," he whispered into my hair. "I would do anything to take it away."

I looked up at him and searched his eyes. I knew he meant what he had said.

"Then take it away, Esteban," I whispered back. "Please, take it away."

He kissed my forehead first and then my left cheek. Slowly and softly, his lips brushed mine. He hesitated for a second and then kissed me softly again, this time full on the lips.

My whole body ached with grief. And I wanted something, anything, to make it stop.

"Let's go upstairs," I said breathlessly. He nodded and got up first. Then he pulled me up and kissed me some more. His cell phone rang.

"Leave it," I said between kisses.

"I . . . I . . . can't," he said after pulling away from my mouth. "It could be the clerk calling about the verdict. I'm sorry. I have to get it."

Regret darkened his eyes as he reached for the phone to answer. "This is Esteban Delgado . . ." His voice trailed off as he moved into the foyer.

With heavy steps, I made my way upstairs and into our bedroom. I didn't need to hear the rest of his conversation to know what was coming next. The apology because he had to leave. The promise he would make it up to me later. The defensiveness if I told him he didn't have to.

And then he'd leave anyway. Both of us mad at how the other had reacted. It was a never-ending cycle of blame and frustration.

I didn't have it in me to go through it again.

When he came home later, he found me sitting on the bed in the dark.

"I won," he said and flipped the light switch.

"Good for you," I said back.

He bristled at my words but didn't walk toward me. Instead, he loosened his tie. "I'm sorry I had to leave. But I'm here now."

And that's when it hit me. If things were good between us, I should've been glad he was home. But I wasn't. How sad was it that tonight of all nights I didn't even want to be around him?

When I didn't say anything, he started moving toward me.

"Stop," I said.

"What?"

"I want you to stop walking. I want you to stand right there and not talk either."

"Cariño, what are—"

"I said be quiet!"

My outburst surprised us both. It silenced him at least. I knew his words couldn't fix what was wrong in this house. And my words wouldn't bring back my welita.

Still, some words needed to be said. And I knew it was time to finally make him listen.

"Esteban, we're broken. We need help."

He opened his mouth, and I held up my hand. "I'm not happy. I haven't been for a long time. I almost left you tonight. I packed a suitcase and was writing you a note. Then I realized that wouldn't be fair to you. So, I threw away the note, unpacked, and waited for you to come home so we could finally have the conversation we've been avoiding for months. So, tell me now. Do you want to save this marriage?"

"What do you mean 'save'?" he accused. "We are fine."

"No. No, we're not."

"You're just sad right now. And that's okay. In a few days, everything will be back to the way it used to be."

I shook my head. "What if I don't want everything to go back to how it was before? I need . . ."

Esteban threw his hands up in the air. "What could you possibly need, Marisol? I've given you everything you've ever wanted."

"I'm not talking about material things. I need something that is just mine. I need a purpose."

"That's what a baby is for. I've been telling you that."

"I don't want a baby!"

He looked as though I'd slapped him. Guilt shamed me, and I tried to fix it. "I meant not right now."

I wasn't sure if he believed me. At least, he didn't press the issue. "So, now what?"

"I think we should go to counseling," I said.

He dragged his hand down his face in frustration. "¡Madre de Dios! I can't believe this. I just won a huge trial that's going to put my firm on the news for the next few days, and instead of celebrating, my wife wants me to see a goddamn shrink!"

I flinched at his tirade. But I wasn't going to back down. "We need this, Esteban. I need this."

"And if I don't agree?"

How could I answer his question when I wasn't ready to face the answer myself? Instead, I shrugged. "Then I don't know."

Esteban cursed in Spanish and then told me he was going out to clear his head and think about things. It was almost three in the morning when I finally got a text.

It was Chris.

Esteban showed up at my house drunk as a skunk. He's sleeping it off on my couch. He won't tell me what happened. Are you ok?

I texted back:

I'm fine. Thanks for taking care of him.

It was too late, or too early, to deal with Chris—or Esteban for that matter. My welita was gone. At that moment, it was all I could care about.

So, I turned off my phone, turned on my side, and cried into my pillow.

Chapter Forty-One
GRACIE

When I was a little girl, our mother took Selena and me to the circus.

I'd hated it, and we'd had to leave after fifteen minutes. "Cried the whole time," she told my grandparents and Welita when we'd gotten back. It was like she couldn't believe that a child could hate the circus.

To help calm me down, Welita warmed up some milk and poured it in a mug. Then she told me in her broken Spanglish that she didn't like the circus either.

It was her way of letting me know that I wasn't alone.

And although the logical part of my brain knew I wasn't alone now, it didn't register in my heart. So when Selena mentioned that she was going to go home to LA and then come back in the morning, I begged her to stay the night again.

"I don't have any clothes. Plus I need to stop by my office to pick up some files so I can do a little bit of work remotely. Don't worry, Gracie. I'll see you tomorrow."

But just like a kid, I followed her to her car and pleaded with her once again.

"Please, Selena. I need you to stay with me." I was bawling so bad that she pulled me into her car so no one in the family would hear me.

"What is wrong with you?" she asked. "I know you're sad, but this is not you. What's going on?"

She was right. This wasn't me. But I couldn't control the tidal wave of emotions rolling through my body. And it wasn't just today. I'd cried like a baby last night because Rachel drank the last can of Pepsi. Not only was I crying at the drop of a hat, I was exhausted. At first, I blamed the stress of the final preparations for the fiesta combined with coming back to school. I was a mess, and I needed to know why.

And so I confessed what I'd suspected for the last few weeks.

"I think I'm pregnant."

◆ ◆ ◆

"Geez, how long does it take to pee on a stick?" Selena yelled from the other side of the bathroom door.

"I already peed!" I yelled back. I closed the toilet lid and sat down. "You can come in now."

Selena opened the door to the bathroom slowly and walked inside. She glanced at the pregnancy test stick I had placed on top of a sheet of toilet paper on the black marble sink counter. She sat on the edge of the bathtub and put her hand over mine as it rested on my knee.

We'd left my grandparents' house and made a quick stop at the drugstore. My parents had said they'd be home in about an hour. We needed to do this on our own.

We sat there without talking until the alarm on my cell phone beeped to announce that three minutes had elapsed. It startled us both, and for a few seconds we just stared at the pregnancy stick on the counter. I moved to stand up, and Selena continued to hold my hand.

"Whatever happens, sis, we'll get through it together," she said.

I nodded and walked over to the stick. I squeezed my eyes shut and took a deep breath. I opened my eyes and looked down. Two dark-pink plus signs glared back at me.

I looked over at my sister, who was still sitting on the edge of the bathtub. When she saw my expression, she jumped up and came over to the sink. She picked up the stick and examined it.

"So, two plus signs means . . . ," she was going to ask.

"It means I'm going to have a baby," I answered before she could finish.

Chapter Forty-Two
ERICA

Breathe. Breathe. In and then out. In and then out.

I stood in my grandparents' backyard trying not to lose my shit on the day of my welita's funeral.

The Mass and the burial were over, and everyone had come back to my grandparents' house for a luncheon. But after a while, I'd needed a break from all the people and noise and had wandered into Welita's room.

In the days before the funeral, my grandmother had worked feverishly to clean out the room, much to the chagrin of the rest of the family. My mother told me it was her way of grieving. That leaving the room the way my welita had left it was just too much to bear. So she had begun packing up clothes and storing mementos until the room was almost empty. Today, as people came and went, she told them to go through the boxes and take whatever they wanted as a keepsake.

I didn't think I was ready to do it, but when I saw the familiar shoebox, I opened it. There were little trinkets inside like the snow globe from Canada that Gracie had brought back for her last year and assorted Mother's Day and birthday cards.

The walls of the room seemed to close in on me as I spotted the *Jersey Boys* CD on top of her dresser.

And then I remembered I would never be able to take her to see the show like I'd promised. So I ran out of that room, out of the house, and into the backyard, where I could breathe. Just breathe.

I was just starting to feel normal again when Mari opened the gate and walked toward me. I'd seen her at the church and cemetery, but neither of us had made an attempt to speak to each other until that moment.

"Erica, are you okay? Your mom asked me to come check on you." She looked uncomfortable; I could tell by the way she almost reached her hand out to touch my shoulder, only to pull it back.

"I'm fine, Mari. Tell my mom I'll come inside soon. You can go now."

She nodded her head but didn't move. Instead, she surveyed the backyard.

"Hey, what happened to the lemon tree?"

She stared at the back wall where our favorite lemon tree once stood. It was huge—well, at least when we were little, it had seemed huge to us. It was the most bountiful of all my grandmother's trees. She had an apricot one, a tangerine one, and a fig one. But the lemon tree was the grandest with its thick trunk and branches that seemed to reach the heavens. Underneath it, we held our picnics and played Barbies. During the summer, we'd gather all the lemons that had fallen to the ground and use them to make lemonade for our lemonade stand.

"The people who moved into the house on the other side of the wall kept complaining about the branches and lemons falling into their yard. Then the roots started cracking the wall, so Abuelo and my dad cut it down a few years ago."

She shrugged, still looking at the wall. "That's too bad. It was a good tree."

"Yeah, well, I guess that's what happens when you grow up. Nothing lasts forever, right?" There was a bitterness to my words, but I didn't care. Not anymore.

"What's that supposed to mean?" This time she turned to look at me. I noticed that she was skinny. I mean, really skinny—and not in a good way. Her black dress was most likely from a designer label, but it might as well have been a tablecloth, given the way it hung on her. Her boobs looked bigger, but I couldn't tell if that was because they were fake or because the rest of her was so small. Her dark-brown hair had blonde highlights, and it had grown past her shoulders in soft, wavy curls. Her makeup was immaculate, and so were her white, perfect teeth. She was a far cry from the Mari I had grown up with. Everything about her had changed. The saddest thing was that if we had run into each other somewhere else, away from the context of Welita's funeral and our grandparents' house, I probably wouldn't have recognized her. My cousin had become a stranger to me. And I was kind of pissed off about it.

I took a step closer to her and glared. "What do you think it means, Mari? Listen, just because you made time in your busy schedule to show up for Welita's funeral doesn't mean that I'm just going to forget everything and reminisce with you about a stupid lemon tree."

"Whatever, Erica. I didn't come here to be attacked," Marisol huffed and started to walk away.

Tears burned my eyes, and I could feel my body shaking with rage. I couldn't hold it back anymore. I opened my mouth and exploded. "That's right, Mari, walk away! You're good at walking away, aren't you? After all, you've been walking away from the family since you were sixteen! Jesus! I can't believe you turned into such a bitch."

Mari spun around on her six-inch black heels. "I'm a bitch? Please. The only reason you're acting like this is because you're jealous of me—you always have been."

"Jealous? Really? Wow, you really don't get it, do you? I couldn't fucking care less about your perfect life."

This time Mari walked up to me and looked me straight in the eyes. I had never seen her look so angry. "You don't know anything, so you better just shut your mouth."

I didn't care. I'd waited years to tell her how I felt, and I wasn't going to wait anymore.

"What don't I know, Mari? Please, by all means, enlighten me. Because all I see is a spoiled brat who couldn't handle her parents' divorce, and when she didn't get everything she wanted, she punished everyone in this family—including Welita!"

The slap was fast and hard. I should've seen it coming, but my eyes were swollen with tears. It burned for a second and then left a throbbing warmth. Mari looked as surprised as me. "Oh my God, Erica, oh my God, I'm sorry, I didn't . . ." She reached to touch my cheek with her finger, but I pushed her hand away and started to walk.

"Erica! I said I'm sorry. It's just you said all that stuff, and I was so mad. You have no idea what I've been through." Mari was crying and screaming at me, but I just kept walking. "How do you think it's been for me? I feel like a stranger in this family."

This time I stopped and turned around. "What do you expect, Mari? You did this to yourself."

"Me? So I'm the bad guy for not wanting to be around him after the way he treated me and my mom?"

For a second I didn't understand who she was talking about. But then I realized she meant her dad.

"What do you mean, Mari?" I asked. "All Tío Ricardo ever did was bend over backward whenever you came to visit. All of us did. And what did we get in return? Pouty looks, crossed arms, and exasperated sighs. But we put up with it because at least you were here. Then one day you weren't. And I don't just mean physically. I mean mentally and emotionally. You stopped being part of this family long before you stopped coming to visit."

Mari's tears also stopped. "Maybe it was you guys who stopped being my family, and that's why things changed. Maybe it was because I felt betrayed."

"Who betrayed you?"

Her hand swept across the air. "All of you. By siding with him, by letting him still be a part of this family even after he stopped being my dad. You're right. I did walk away. But in a way, you all pushed me."

"I have no fucking clue what you are saying," I said. "As usual, you're being the drama queen and making all kinds of shit up so you get the attention and so I can feel sorry for you. Well, guess what? We're not kids anymore, and I'm not playing your pathetic games."

By this time, Selena and Gracie had walked up behind Mari. I wasn't sure how much they'd heard, but it was enough to put shock on their faces.

"Guys, what's going on?" Gracie said, on the verge of tears. "Please don't fight. Please."

But Mari just stood there, looking at the ground and shaking her head.

"You know what's pathetic, Erica? A man who chooses alcohol over his own family," she said. "Even more pathetic is a man who lets his own daughter go hungry and without lights or electricity because he'd rather spend his money on tequila and beer."

Her words still didn't make sense. I couldn't believe she was talking about my tío Ricardo like that. I knew he had been a drinker, but not for once did I believe he had been a bad father. He had one daughter with my tía Espy, and little Araceli was his world. He was always taking her places and buying her things. And it had been the same with Mari. That's why I'd never understood why she hated him so much after the divorce.

"You're wrong, Mari." This time it was Selena who was yelling. "All your dad ever did was love you, and when you didn't love him back, it broke him. I saw it. Everyone saw it. He would've done anything for you. But you didn't let him."

Mari laughed, but it wasn't the kind of laugh that warmed you. In fact, it sent a shiver down my back.

"Well, maybe that's the picture he painted. I'm not surprised. He's always been a good liar. Promising me that things wouldn't change after the divorce—guess what? They did. He promised me that he would always take care of me—guess what? He didn't. Instead, he drank away those promises and left me and my mom to fend for ourselves. He didn't love me, Selena. You don't abandon people that you love."

"You did."

I didn't even recognize my own voice. It was high and wobbly as my throat tightened with emotion. And although my hand never left my side, Mari looked like I had slapped her. "Whatever you think your father did or didn't do had nothing to do with the rest of the family. Fine, you hated your dad, but what about me, or Gracie and Selena or Abuela or Welita? What did we do?"

"You're right. I should've visited Welita more. I will always regret that I didn't. She, along with Abuela and Abuelo, have always been there for me. That's why I'm here."

Mari's voice broke a little, and she looked away. When she gained her composure, she looked back at me and shrugged. "So now you know the whole ugly story."

"No, she doesn't. And neither do you."

We were all startled to see Tía Espy behind us.

"Excuse me?" Mari asked with a sneer. I could feel the hate in her words. Her tone was cold and bitter. Undeterred, Espy took a step forward.

"I said that wasn't the real story. Mari, your father never abandoned you. That was just the lie your mother told you so you would never know what really happened," she said. "This whole time, you've been angry at the wrong parent."

"What are you even talking about?" she said, placing her hands on her bony hips.

"You need to talk to your dad. It's his story to tell."

"Whatever. I'm so tired of everyone in this family making excuses for everyone else. Maybe I didn't pick up the phone as much as I should've. But my phone didn't ring either."

She turned to leave, and Gracie reached out to grab her wrist. "Please don't leave like this, Mari. Let's talk. Please. Welita wouldn't want us to be like this on today of all days."

"I know, Gracie. That's why I'm leaving."

Chapter Forty-Three
SELENA

I was never good at keeping secrets. Maybe it was because I always wanted to be the one to break news—and it didn't matter if it was my news to break. But my sister's pregnancy was a secret I swore that I would keep until she was ready to tell Tony and my parents. It was a promise I couldn't break.

I had to admit that it was hard, especially when I talked to Erica on the phone. Maybe it was her reporter's instinct, but she could tell something was up. I told her that I was just stressed out about work and still very confused about everything Mari had said after Welita's funeral. She didn't buy it and kept pressing me and pressing me.

Finally, just to get her to shut up, I told her about the job in New York and how I'd told Nathan to withdraw my name from the list of candidates. It came out of nowhere, and I actually surprised myself when I said it. Even more surprising was Erica's reaction.

"You should've taken it," she said matter-of-factly as we ate lunch at our favorite sushi place on the west side. We were both still on bereavement leave from our jobs, and I'd suggested we get out of Inland Valley for a few hours. Gracie had feigned more flu symptoms and stayed home. She wouldn't have been able to stomach all the smells anyway.

Plus she didn't trust herself with Erica and her nose for news. Gracie hated lying, especially to people's faces. I, however, had no issue with it if it meant giving my sister time to deal with her situation on her own terms. Little did I know, though, that lying to Erica about Gracie would open up a whole can of worms about me.

"It's a once-in-a-lifetime gig, Selena," she told me. "And it's not like you love the crap you're doing now—or the people you're doing it for. I'll never understand why you turned it down."

I popped a California roll in my mouth and shrugged my shoulders. "I don't know. It's just such a big step." That was true. Moving to New York would mean overhauling my entire life. I didn't know anyone in New York except for Nathan. Which meant it would be too easy to revolve everything I did around him. I couldn't risk that. Not again.

Erica just shook her head. "That's the point," she explained. "It's a step toward bigger and better things."

"I just couldn't leave the family; I couldn't leave Gracie, especially now." I kicked myself under the table for letting that last part slip. I waited for a reaction from Erica, but the comment seemed to go over her head. She just went on and on about how she'd always wanted to go to New York, and if I lived there, then she could stay with me. She talked about the museums, the Broadway shows, and the pizza.

"Selena, I heard there's like a pizza place on every corner," she stressed, apparently thinking that my love of pizza would be motivation enough to move across the country.

"Doesn't matter. It's too late now."

Later that night, I'd done everything I could to push thoughts of New York out of my head.

But then it called me. Literally.

"Hey," I said tentatively when I answered.

"Hey," Nathan said.

"Are you in town?" It was instinct to ask. I immediately wished I hadn't, though.

"No. No, I'm not."

"Oh."

"Listen, I think I know one of the reasons you changed your mind about the job, and I'm just calling to tell you that if you're worried about me—or rather, what I'm expecting—then I need you not to worry about it."

My heart raced. "What do you mean?"

"Selena, I've known you for over a year now. I know that you don't do real relationships. That's why we worked for so long. But I forgot that, okay? And that's on me, not you. So, just forget what I said before. The New York job doesn't come with any strings to me."

"What New York job, Nathan? I told you to tell them I wasn't interested. It's too late."

"It's not. I never told them. And the job is yours if you want it."

My heart stopped. "What?"

"Selena, you got the job."

"Are you serious right now?"

He chuckled. "Yes, I am. I knew I just had to get you in the door and you'd impress the hell out of them."

"Oh. So this is about your commission then?" I regretted the words as soon as I'd said them. He didn't deserve that. "I'm sorry. That was uncalled for."

"It was. You know I just want you to get your dream job. You deserve this."

My heart tightened. Nathan was such a good man. Maybe I deserved the job, but I sure as hell didn't deserve him.

"Okay, let me think about it."

"You have a week. They can't wait forever."

Why were people always telling me that now?

Chapter Forty-Four
MARI

For the fourth time that day, I dialed my dad's number.

And for the fourth time, I hung up before it even rang.

Espy's words at Welita's funeral still bothered me. But I wasn't ready to deal with that whole situation. Not when I didn't even know what was happening with my own marriage.

I put my phone back down on the counter and put on my oven mitts. Slowly, I pulled the lasagna out of the oven and then placed it on the stove. I inhaled wafts of garlic, tomato, and cheese, and my stomach rumbled with hunger. Skipping lunch wasn't the best idea, but I wanted to make sure to have an appetite since Esteban had promised he'd be home by six for dinner.

After telling me he wanted to work on our marriage on the day after Welita died, he'd made somewhat of an effort to spend more time with me. He'd even agreed to go to couples counseling. But that was days ago, and every time I'd tried to get him to nail down a day for our first appointment, he always had some excuse. I was determined to find a date tonight. The lasagna and a bottle of his favorite red wine were going to help me do just that.

My phone rang, and my heart sank, already expecting it would be Esteban telling me that he was going to be late. But it wasn't my husband. It was Chris.

I hesitated before answering. If I was going to try to fix things with Esteban, then I needed to put space between me and Chris. And there was no better time to do that than now.

"Hey," I said.

"Hey you," he replied, his voice soft and soothing. "How's it going?"

I walked into the dining room and took a seat. "Um, good. I actually just finished cooking dinner."

"Really? What did you make? Wait. Don't tell me. It will make me regret the bologna sandwich I just made."

I laughed. "Well, that's weird. I made a bologna sandwich too."

"Yeah, right. But I appreciate the effort to make me feel better about my pitiful dinner. But you know what would make me feel better?"

"What's that?"

"How about we meet for dinner sometime this week, you know, one night that Esteban has to meet a client?"

I didn't say anything right away. If I told him I couldn't, then he'd just ask again. I had to tell him the truth, and I had to do it face to face. It was the only way to make Chris understand.

The sound of the garage door opening made me jump.

"Actually, how about coffee on Sunday? Esteban is taking one of your clients to the country club for brunch."

"Sure. That sounds great. Should I pick you up?"

I heard a car door slam and knew I had to get off the phone. "No, I'll meet you there at eleven, okay? I have to go. Bye, Chris."

I didn't even wait for him to reply.

By the time Esteban was inside the house, I was already opening the wine. I heard him stop at his home office, and I carried the lasagna dish to the dining room table. A few minutes later, he joined me.

After a quick kiss on the cheek, he sat down and took a long sip of his wine.

"That bad, huh?"

He just sighed and began eating. I tried again.

"Everything okay?"

Esteban finally looked at me. "Everything is fine."

Of course I didn't believe him. I decided I'd let him decompress for a bit and started eating. We ate in silence for several minutes. I knew he was probably going to disappear into his office for the rest of the night, so I figured now was as good a time as any to nail down some possible dates for our first counseling session.

I took a huge gulp of my wine first. "So, did you get a chance to talk to Carla today and go over your calendar? I want to call the marriage counselor by Friday. Her sessions fill up pretty quickly."

He stabbed a piece of lasagna with his fork and shoved it into his mouth. "I had pretrial motions all morning and meetings all afternoon. This is the first time I'm eating today, so no, I didn't have time to go over my calendar."

Annoyance bubbled on the edge of my nerves like the mozzarella on the top of the lasagna. "God, sorry for asking. Why are you so irritated?"

Esteban finished off the last of his wine and poured himself some more. "I'm tired, Marisol. I don't want to have another fight with you."

I didn't want to fight either. I picked up my plate and glass and took them to the kitchen. I went back and picked up the lasagna dish.

"Did you try a new sauce?" he said before I turned to leave again.

"For the lasagna? No, it's the same sauce I always make."

"It tastes different," he said and pushed away his plate.

"Well, it's not."

He finally looked up at me. "Can't I be right about anything anymore?"

That was it.

I dropped the lasagna dish back onto the table. "What is going on with you tonight, Esteban? Por favor. Just tell me."

"I'm not going to counseling."

Of all the things I had expected him to say, that was not it. "What? You said you would."

He shrugged. "That was before."

"Before what?"

"Before I had time to think about things and I decided that if you're the one who isn't happy, then you're the one that needs help. I'm fine."

Fuming, I clenched my fists at my sides as if they could contain the screams I wanted to hurl at him. "You promised me. You told me you wanted to save this marriage."

"If you think you need counseling in order to stay married to me, then that's your issue. I'm working my ass off to give you everything you need or want. I'm doing my part."

I couldn't even look at him, so I focused on the lasagna dish. I'd lied to him earlier when I'd said it wasn't different. I had tried a new recipe, and I knew it was fucking delicious. But Esteban didn't like it only because it wasn't what he was used to. It wasn't what *he* wanted.

And that was the problem right there. He was never going to change. Deep down, I knew that. But I still needed to make sure.

"If you don't agree to come with me to at least one counseling session, then I don't think I can stay in this marriage anymore."

Esteban stood up, met my eyes briefly, and then walked out of the dining room.

He didn't say another word to me for the rest of the night.

And that was his answer.

Chapter Forty-Five
GRACIE

For the third time that day, I forced my eyes to stay open as I worked on my lesson plan for tomorrow.

My students had been gone for less than ten minutes, and I was already needing a nap. It didn't matter that I was sitting at my desk in the classroom. These days I could fall asleep anytime and anywhere.

Pregnancy had turned me into my dad.

It hadn't really been an issue when I was still on summer break. The heat was the perfect excuse to escape to my bedroom to rest. No one questioned why I'd doze off in the middle of watching TV on the couch because they were doing it too. It was harder now that I was back at school. It had only been ten days, and I'd never been so tired in all my life. And it was getting harder to hide that. My family and my coworkers had no idea I was so tired because I had a baby growing inside me.

Selena was still the only other person who knew what a doctor had confirmed a few days ago: I was about six weeks pregnant.

I still couldn't believe it. Normally, I would've asked God to help me accept it, but guilt wouldn't let me. Besides, what was done was done. And maybe it was denial, maybe it was because I was just a big old coward. But I wasn't ready to tell anyone else—not even Tony.

Or maybe I was just being selfish.

Even though we still weren't officially a couple, we were still doing everything we had been doing, and I didn't want that to change. I liked how things were between us. We saw each other every day at school, but tried not to make it obvious that we were also seeing each other at night. It was better that way for so many reasons. Not just because the gossip would be a distraction. Deep down I knew it was because Tony was still hoping he'd get the job in Texas. Selena, however, kept insisting that maybe telling Tony about the baby would bring us closer and make him want to stay in Inland Valley.

I knew better.

Another yawn escaped, and I shook my head in an effort to stop daydreaming and start focusing.

Dear God, help me finish my work so I can go home and take a nap. Making another human being is exhausting. Amen.

I stared at my planner for another minute or so. The words I'd already written were a blurry mess. My eyelids grew heavy, and I was just about to give up the fight when there was a knock on my classroom door.

"Come in," I yelled and sat up in my chair.

A tall, dark-haired man walked inside and gave me a little wave. "Hello. Mrs. Lopez?"

"Hello. How can I help you?" I said as he walked closer, ignoring the "Mrs." part.

"I'm Joshua Davila. I'm Celina's dad."

I smiled and stood up. "Oh, hello. It's nice to meet you."

We shook hands, and I couldn't help but notice that while his fingers and palms seemed rough, he held mine with such gentleness.

"I'm sorry to bother you," he said after we let go. "I just wanted to stop by to introduce myself. Celina talks about you all the time, you know."

That made me laugh. "Hopefully, it's all good."

He nodded. "Don't worry; it is. We just moved here from Bakersfield, and I was a little worried about her starting at a new school. But she really loves it, and I think that has a lot to do with you."

My cheeks heated with embarrassment. "I'm sure that's not true," I rushed out and then quickly regretted it. Why was it always so hard for me to accept a compliment? Or even believe it? "She's a sweet girl. You and your wife are doing a great job."

"It's just me and Celina, actually. But, thank you."

For some reason, I wasn't saddened by this news. And I should've been.

Dear God, I'm sorry. Please forgive me for being okay with the fact that poor Celina doesn't have a mom. I promise to say ten Hail Marys tonight before bed.

"Is everything okay, Mrs. Lopez?"

Mr. Davila's question brought me out of my quick prayer of regret. "Oh. Yes, sorry. And it's Ms. Lopez. Or Gracie. You can call me Gracie."

He smiled and nodded. "Okay. Please call me Joshua."

"Thank you." I had no idea why I thanked him. Fortunately, he didn't seem to question it.

"So, Gracie, how long have you been at St. Christopher's?"

"Well, I actually went to school here eons ago. But I've been a teacher now for almost six years," I answered.

"Wow, you went here? Let me guess. You were a straight-A student, right?"

I laughed at that way more than I should've. What was wrong with me? Is that what they called pregnancy brain?

"Not every year. I might have gotten a B or two in seventh grade."

A voice cleared behind us, and that's when I noticed Tony standing in the doorway. I hadn't even heard him come in. And why did he have that look on his face?

"Tony, um, I mean Mr. Bautista, this is Joshua—I mean Mr. Davila. He's Celina's dad."

My face heated again with embarrassment and some other feeling. Wait, was I feeling guilty about something?

Tony walked over and shook Joshua's hand. "Nice to meet you."

"Same," the other man responded.

The three of us looked at each other in an awkward silence. Finally, Joshua said he had to go and left Tony and me alone.

"I still need to pack up my things, and then I'll be ready to leave," I said and walked over to my desk.

"He seems like a nice guy," Tony said as I put my planner in my backpack.

"I guess. I just met him."

"And what does he think of you?"

That made me look at him. "What do you mean?"

"I don't know. I was just getting a vibe from him."

"What do you mean?"

Tony walked over and sat on the edge of my desk. "He was flirting with you."

Was he? Did that mean I was flirting back? That explained the guilt. But then again, what did I have to feel guilty about? Irritation bubbled up inside me.

Erica and Selena were definitely rubbing off on me. That was the only explanation for me to say what I was about to say.

"And?" I said, putting my hands on my hips. "Is it so hard to believe that some other man would find me attractive?"

Tony jumped off the desk, waving his hands. "What? No, of course not. That's not what I meant."

"Then what did you mean?"

"I guess I was just a little jealous," he said with a shrug.

"Of Joshua? Why?"

"Because you're my girl, Gracie."

If joy was helium, I would've floated to the ceiling. "I am?"

Tony wrapped his arms around my waist and pulled me against him. Then he kissed me softly. When we pulled apart, he smiled. "Of course you are."

Suddenly, I wasn't tired anymore.

Chapter Forty-Six
ERICA

Who knew that watching grown men fight over a little black-and-white ball would make me so happy?

Adrian knew.

He'd surprised me that morning with tickets to go see LAFC play against the Portland Timbers at the Banc of California Stadium in Los Angeles. Ever since the funeral, I'd become somewhat of a hermit. Although I'd seen him at work, I'd bowed out on going to dinner, going to the movies, and basically any activity that required me to change out of my sweatpants. But, I couldn't say no to soccer.

Especially professional soccer.

The game had been a nail-biter, and for ninety glorious minutes, I'd been able to not think about how sad I still was about Welita and how pissed off I still was about Mari.

After the game, we'd stopped to pick up dinner from a taco truck and sat down at one of the few nearby tables.

"Soccer, beer, and tacos really are the best combination," I said and took an enthusiastic bite of my carne asada taco.

Adrian laughed. "I know. You've told me this about a million times already."

"Still true, though."

He nodded. "I'm glad you're enjoying yourself."

I wiped my mouth and grinned from ear to ear. "Thank you, Adrian. I really needed this."

"You're welcome. I'm just happy to see that smile again."

Warmth bloomed inside me, filling me up with such light and happiness and . . .

Mierda.

I really was in love with Adrian. And it was his own damn fault.

Even though we'd had that blowup on the day that Welita died, he'd been there for me. I'd gone straight to his apartment after my fight with Mari and just bawled like a baby. He listened to everything and then made me tea.

Adrian had turned into the perfect nonboyfriend boyfriend. How on earth could I be expected to resist that?

Suddenly, I wasn't hungry anymore. I took a sip of my beer and tried very hard to not look like I was head over heels for the guy sitting across from me.

"I still can't believe you've never been to an LAFC game," he said, still oblivious to the tornado of shock and embarrassment currently wreaking havoc on my insides.

"My dad's been wanting to get tickets for a while, so I guess I was just waiting on him. It's kind of our thing."

Adrian put down his taco. "Oh, shit. I didn't know. I'm sorry."

I waved my hand at him. "No, it's fine. It's not like we can't go to another game. Actually, now that I think about it, I should just buy the tickets and surprise him too."

The more I thought about it, the more I liked the idea. What had I been waiting for? Why was I waiting to do anything anymore? If this crappy year had taught me anything, it was that I needed to take control of my life. In more ways than one.

Well, except when it came to Adrian.

He was my boss, and he was my best friend. Our relationship was already crossing the line into bad idea territory. I had no business throwing romantic feelings into the mix. I didn't want to risk this . . . what we had right now in this moment.

"Is there anything you and your dad like to do together?" I asked.

Adrian shrugged. "Golf, I guess. Well, I mean he likes to golf, and he likes it when I go with him. But I suck at it, so I really don't get why he keeps inviting me."

"He just wants to spend time with you, that's all. I bet he's really happy that you're back in town."

"I guess. Although, he's still trying to convince me to go work for him. And if we're golfing, I'm trapped in that little cart and have to listen to all the reasons why my life would be better if I worked at Mendes Market. Why is it that parents always think they know better than you?"

That made me laugh. "Right? But it's not just them. My tías, cousins, and even my abuela have an opinion when it comes to my life."

Adrian nodded and then polished off his last taco. "Speaking of your family, have you talked to that one cousin?"

"No," I said, shaking my head. "I'm still too mad."

"Erica."

"What? I get to be mad. She slapped me, remember?"

"Because of what you said."

Why had I told Adrian about what happened at Welita's funeral? He was just as shocked as I was about what Mari did. But, of course, now he was going to be logical and reasonable. I both hated and loved that about him.

"Fine. Maybe I was being a brat, but so was she. Gracie insists that something else is going on with her, and she thinks what happened between us is somehow because of whatever drama she has going on right now. But that's the thing with Mari—she is the OG Drama Queen. People get me mad every day. Doesn't mean I'm going around slapping their faces."

"Even though you want to," he added.

"Even though I want to," I confirmed.

"Fine. Erica, you have every right to be mad at her . . . for now. All I'm saying is that maybe Gracie is right. Maybe it's time to figure out why she did what she did."

"We'll see," I said and pushed my plate away. The subject of Mari really did make me lose my appetite. And I hated that it was because deep down I knew Adrian was right.

Dammit. Why couldn't he make it harder to love him?

Chapter Forty-Seven
SELENA

It was just after seven on a Friday night when I finally pulled into my driveway. It had been the day from hell, and all I wanted to do was soak in a hot bath and binge some mindless TV.

But the guy sitting on the bench on my porch obviously had other plans for me.

Nathan.

"Why aren't you in New York?" I said as soon as I climbed the steps to meet him.

"I've been in San Diego for the past two days and decided to drive up and see you before I fly back tomorrow."

I didn't have a response for that, so I unlocked my front door and let us both inside.

"I don't have any food," I said after dropping my keys and bag on my dining room table.

"I'm not hungry. I ate an energy bar while I was waiting for you."

That made me smile. Nathan hated energy bars. He also could eat every hour of every day. The man was always hungry—and not just for food.

X-rated thoughts ran through my mind, but I willed them to go away and take the ache between my legs with them. Nathan wasn't here for sex. He was here to convince me to move to New York.

I plopped on my couch and kicked off my shoes. "Let me guess—you want to know if I decided to take the job," I asked after he sat down next to me.

"I figured you haven't; otherwise you would've texted. But I haven't heard from you at all, Selena. And I wanted to know why."

"Because I don't have an answer yet."

"And that's the only reason you could have for talking to me? I thought we meant more to each other than some job," he said.

Guilt made me want to run to my room so I wouldn't have to have this conversation. It was true. I had been avoiding Nathan for this exact reason. Moving to New York was such a huge life-changing decision, and I couldn't risk making that decision for the wrong reasons. That meant New York and Nathan couldn't be connected in any way. I never wanted to be the type of woman who moved just to be with a man because I never wanted a man to have that kind of influence over me ever again. So, if I broke things off with Nathan, then I could trust that I was choosing New York for the right reasons.

"We did," I finally answered.

He flinched. "Did?"

"I'm sorry. But I have so much thinking to do, and I can't let anything or anyone be a distraction right now. I need to make sure that I'm doing what's right for my career."

"So, what are you saying? We're done?"

My throat tightened with such emotion that I honestly felt like I was choking. Tears I hadn't even expected showed up, threatening to spill and ruin my already cracking composure. I knew this moment was going to be hard. I didn't know it would hurt this bad.

"I'm sorry," I finally said. "I know you don't deserve this. You've been nothing short of amazing to me. God, Nathan, I owe you so much."

He put his hand up. "Stop. Just stop talking to me like I'm some pal or coworker. You and I both know that we were close to having something real together. But, for some reason, you still can't let me in. I've been patient, and I've tried to prove to you that I'm not going to hurt you, Selena. But, honestly, I'm tired of getting my hand slapped every time I try to make you see that we could be something great."

The tears were back, and this time I didn't care if they fell. "I'm sorry," I said again.

Nathan stood up and looked down at me. I didn't dare meet his eyes, though. "I'm sorry too. I really do hope you accept the job. Let me know either way by next week."

In the end, I didn't get my bath or mindless TV. I spent the night bawling my eyes out right there on the couch. Then, when I couldn't cry anymore, I called Erica.

"911," I said.

"What kind of emergency?" she replied. "Are we putting our hair up and taking off our hoop earrings, or is it something that can be cured with a tub of ice cream and Baileys?"

I let out a long sigh. "Somewhere in between."

"Phase 10?"

"Phase 10."

Chapter Forty-Eight
MARI

He'd moved into the spare bedroom on the first floor. He was gone before I woke up and home by the time I was asleep. Of course, I was never asleep. And now that he was basically living downstairs, I hadn't baked in days.

Letty was a mess as well. I caught her crying a few times, and then I'd cry and apologize for breaking up our family. I assured her that I would always be in her life.

Funny thing about losing the people you love—it makes you want to hold on to the ones you still have. So I'd made the decision to fix my relationship with my cousins, and I promised myself that I'd make the effort to spend more time with my grandparents.

And I was *considering* going to see my dad. I needed to finally get the truth.

It probably wasn't the best idea to do all this emotional reflecting when I also somehow needed to build a new life.

The doorbell rang, interrupting my thoughts. Had Letty forgotten her key *and* the garage remote? She'd gone to the dry cleaner's to pick up Esteban's suits. Or perhaps it was a salesman?

When I opened the door, though, it wasn't Letty or a stranger.

It was my mother-in-law, and she was holding a suitcase.

"What are you doing here?" she said as she pushed past me.

"I live here, Blanca. What are you doing here?"

I closed the door and followed her to the spare bedroom, the one she usually slept in but that was now being occupied by her son. A fact she quickly realized once she opened the door.

"I'm here to help Esteban, of course. I see you already kicked him out of his bedroom."

She put her suitcase on the bed and finally turned around to face me.

"Does Esteban know you're here?" I asked, putting my hands on my hips. She was an intimidating woman, especially now that she didn't have to hide her hate for me.

"I called him when I landed. He told me to call for a car and that he would meet me here after a meeting."

I hated that he hadn't given me the heads-up. Although, did he even owe me one at this point?

"Fine. I'll be upstairs if you need me."

"I knew you two wouldn't last. You were never good enough for my son."

"I'm sorry you felt that way, Blanca. I never meant for any of this to happen."

"Oh, but I think you did. I told Esteban after the first time I met you that you were nothing but a gold digger. I know you come from nothing. But you think my son is going to give you a beautiful life, and you tricked him into marrying you. I only thank God that you were too cold to ever give him children."

"Mama, that's enough."

We both jumped as Esteban entered the bedroom.

"Mijo, I'm so glad you're here. You see how this woman is now, yes? And now I'm here to take care of you."

He didn't look at me but grabbed the suitcase off the bed. "I told you on the phone that you shouldn't have come. Go wait in my car. I'm going to take you back to the airport."

"But Esteban! I traveled all this way. You cannot treat me like this."

"And you cannot treat Marisol that way either. I heard what you said, Mama. Our marriage is our business, and I don't need you in the middle of it anymore."

She covered her mouth in shock. I nearly did the same. I had never heard Esteban talk to her like that. Ever.

When Blanca left, he finally faced me. Something was different.

"Thank you for that. I know how hard that must have been for you."

He wouldn't meet my eyes. Instead, he turned to face the window. That's when I realized he couldn't even look at me. "When I come back, I want you gone too."

I was so surprised at what he said that I took a step back. "What? I thought we were going to both stay here until we met with the lawyers."

"That was before I knew you were leaving me for Chris."

My heart dropped into my stomach. "What are you talking about? I'm not leaving you for Chris."

He spun around and faced me at last. "Then why did he come into my office this afternoon and confess that he's been in love with you for months and that he's sorry for hurting me like this?"

The pain etched across Esteban's face strangled me, and I couldn't catch a breath. What was happening? My mind raced. I had never said anything to make him think that we were going to be together.

Esteban shook his head in disgust and left the room.

I chased after him. "Seriously? You're really just going to believe him and not even let me explain?"

He spun around, and the look he gave me chilled me to the bone. "Oh. So now you want to explain? You know, part of me thought you weren't serious about this divorce stuff. I thought maybe, in a week or two, you'd get over whatever it was that made you announce to me, out of the blue, that you didn't want to be married anymore. Because I honestly couldn't think of one reason why. Now it all becomes clear."

I reached out to grab his arm. "You have the wrong idea. I don't know why Chris told you those things, but I swear to God that I don't feel the same way about him. Esteban! You know me. I would never do that to you."

He shook off my hand. "Maybe not. But I also never thought you would leave me either."

"So, this is all my fault?"

"I'm not the one asking for a divorce."

I knew I'd hurt him deeply. He had every right to lash out. But I still wasn't going to take the blame for everything. Not anymore.

"There used to be two people in this marriage. If we both were happy, then this wouldn't be happening."

His face softened for a second, but then it was back to angry lines.

"You are free now to go find your happiness with Chris," he snapped.

I groaned and threw up my hands. "I'm not in love with Chris! You have to believe me!"

Esteban shook his head. "See, that's the thing, Marisol. I've realized that I don't *have* to do anything when it comes to you anymore. Well, except get the divorce proceedings started."

And then he walked out the front door, leaving me alone in the foyer of what was no longer my home.

I should've collapsed or let out a scream. But I didn't feel a thing.

I was numb.

Chapter Forty-Nine
GRACIE

I can't say exactly why I did what I did.

One minute I was going through my old photo albums and the next I was in my car on my way to Mari's house.

I could've blamed the photo that I'd found, but that didn't explain the sudden urge to drive to South Pasadena. Or why I didn't just text my cousin to let her know I was on the way. Instead, I pulled into her driveway unannounced on a Saturday afternoon.

But the second Mari opened the door, I knew why God had sent me there.

Mari looked horrible.

First of all, she had no makeup on. Her hair was hidden under a white bandana, and she wore a faded T-shirt, jeans, and tennis shoes. She looked just as surprised to see me.

"Gracie!" she announced. "What are you doing here?"

I had a little white lie ready and had already asked for forgiveness in the car. "Hi, Mari. Um, I was in the area and thought I'd stop by. I wanted to give you something."

She hesitated, and for a few seconds I thought she'd actually shut the door on me. But then she smiled and ushered me inside. I'd never been to Mari's house before, but I had her address since I always sent her and Esteban a Christmas card. Despite never having been inside, I still knew something was off. She led me through a maze of boxes that sat in the large foyer to a beautiful open kitchen. Drawers and cabinets were open, and more boxes sat on the counter.

"Are you guys moving?" I couldn't help but ask.

Sadness washed over her face, and I immediately felt bad for opening my mouth.

She cleared her throat and stuffed her hands into her pockets. "Yep. Well, I'm moving. Esteban and I are getting a divorce."

I had no poker face, so I'm sure my shock was as clear as the crystal glasses lining one of the open cabinet shelves. "Oh. I'm so sorry. I had no idea. Where are you moving to?"

She laughed, but I knew it was a hollow one. "Not quite sure yet. I'm staying at a hotel down the street for now. Eventually, I'll get my own place, I guess. We're going to sell the house soon. Good thing I decided to do some packing today while Esteban was at the office; otherwise you would have missed me."

"I'm pregnant, and the father of the baby wants nothing to do with me," I blurted out. I guess I thought sharing my drama would help lessen hers.

Mari's mouth dropped open. "Wow. I had no idea. Are you . . . ?"

Realization hit me slowly. "Oh! Yes, I'm keeping the baby."

She surprised me by coming over to give me a hug. "You're going to be a great mom, Gracie. I know it."

That was all it took. I hugged her back hard and didn't care that I was sobbing into her hair. "I've missed you, cousin. We all have."

She nodded, and judging by the dampness on my cheek, I knew she was crying.

We held each other for what seemed like forever. Eventually, our sobs quieted, and we untangled our arms. Then we looked at each other and laughed.

"So, you said you wanted to give me something?" Mari said after we'd regained our composure.

"Yes! I do!" I reached into my purse and pulled out the photograph I'd found that morning in my album. Then I handed it to her. "I thought you would want it."

Mari stared at the photo for a few seconds before meeting my eyes again. The sadness was back.

I hadn't meant to make her feel that way. In fact, it had been the opposite. I'd known something was going on with Mari after what had happened at the funeral. The photo was the excuse I'd needed to check on her. I had hoped it would make her happy. But she looked the complete opposite.

I wasn't exactly sure when it was taken, but Mari and Erica looked to be around eleven or twelve. They must have given Welita a makeover because she had on lots of eye shadow and red lipstick. All three of them had huge smiles on their faces.

"I'm sorry. I didn't mean to make you cry again," I rushed out as soon as Mari wiped away a tear.

"You didn't. It seems all I do is cry these days," she said with a sad shrug. "Thank you, Gracie. I love this picture."

"Good. I'm glad."

As she walked me to the door, I gave her another hug. "Call me, Mari. Anytime you need to talk, okay?"

She smiled. "Okay. Do you think . . ."

This time I knew exactly what she was about to say. "Yes, I know Erica would love to hear from you too."

Chapter Fifty
ERICA

For the first time in my life, I walked into a restaurant not hungry at all.

My stomach was doing the cha-cha, and putting food in it didn't seem like a very good idea.

"Can I help you?" the hostess asked.

"I'm meeting someone. Can I look around to see if she's here?"

The woman nodded, and I walked past her into the dining area. It didn't take me long to spot Mari. I told the hostess that I'd found her, walked to the table, and offered my cousin a quick wave as I took a seat.

"Thanks for meeting me," she said.

"Thanks for inviting me," I told her.

Gracie had told me that Mari was getting a divorce. When I'd heard that, it explained how she'd looked and acted at Welita's funeral. I couldn't stop thinking of her and whether she was okay. So I was shocked when she'd called earlier and invited me to lunch.

I picked up the menu, pretending to be interested in the lunch specials. I knew there was no way I would be able to eat anything other than water and crackers if we didn't start talking soon.

"They make their own potato chips here," I offered.

"Really?"

"Yes. They're pretty good."

I went back to studying the menu.

"I'm getting a divorce," she blurted.

Of course I already knew this, but I feigned surprise. "I'm sorry to hear that."

"No you're not." Her lips pressed into a firm line.

Her words surprised me, and I made sure she met my eyes. "Actually, I am."

She put down her menu and sighed. Her chin quivered.

Shit. I looked around the restaurant and took a sip of my water. I folded and then unfolded my napkin. After a few seconds, I forced myself to look at her again.

Her head was down, and I could see a few tears starting to spill onto the white linen tablecloth.

I shifted in my seat and cleared my throat. "I really am sorry that you're getting divorced. I never wanted that for you."

She finally looked up at me. I noticed that her face wasn't as gaunt as it was on the day of the funeral. Her makeup was minimal, and her hair was pulled up into a messy bun. For a second, I thought she looked like the Mari from before. My shoulders released their tense formation.

"I know. It's just that, I . . . I feel like maybe a little of you, just a little, wants to gloat."

"Why would you think that?" Old defenses kicked in.

"Because maybe it's what I deserve." Her voice cracked, and she hastily wiped her eyes with her fingers.

"No one deserves to have their heart hurt. Besides, what do I know about marriage? I can't even keep a boyfriend."

That made her stop crying. She even attempted a smile. It felt good. Familiar.

I became comfortable enough to ask the question I'd been wanting to ever since the funeral. "Have you talked to your dad?"

Her smile went away. "Not yet. I'm not ready."

"I saw him the other day. He asked if I'd talked to you."

"Really? I guess Espy told him about our, um, conversation that day. Speaking of, I want to apologize again for slapping you. I wasn't in a good place and that was uncalled for."

"And I was being a bitch."

Her eyes widened in surprise. But she was polite enough not to agree. That was the opening I needed.

"Listen, Mari. I just want you to know that we, I, never meant to make you feel like you weren't part of the family anymore. And we, I, really had no idea what was going on with you and your dad. I swear."

Mari offered me a small nod. "I think deep down I always knew that. I was so angry at my dad, and that made me angry at everyone else, too, I guess. I'm sure I made it hard for you to understand what I was going through. I know I wasn't the easiest to get along with back then."

It was my turn to be polite and not agree. "I'm sorry you had to deal with so much crap all on your own. And I'm sorry I gave up on you. I should've tried harder to be a part of your life."

She raised her hand to stop me. "No. I should've tried harder to be a part of yours. Can you forgive me?"

Tears clouded my vision, but I could still see how much Mari was still hurting. I didn't want to be one of the reasons why. Whatever had happened at Welita's funeral, or years ago, didn't matter anymore. So I said, "I'll forgive you if you forgive me."

"Deal," she said.

We smiled at each other for the first time in a long time. Then Mari picked up her menu and asked, "So, what are you going to order? Do you want appetizers, or do you want to just get an entrée?"

"Let's start with the potato chips and then go from there."

She nodded and smiled. "Sounds like a good plan to me."

Chapter Fifty-One
SELENA

It was time to do battle.

I walked into my abuela's patio and set down the reusable grocery bag on the table. One by one, I pulled out my weapons.

Bottle of tequila. Check.

Margarita mix. Check.

Salsa and cream cheese. Check.

Tortilla chips. Check.

Deck of Phase 10 playing cards. Check.

"Where are the sweets?" Tía Espy asked after checking the now-empty bag.

I pointed behind me just as Gracie walked inside carrying another bag. "This isn't our first rodeo, Tía. We have come prepared," I said and walked to the patio's freezer to get ice for the margaritas.

A few minutes later, Erica arrived with more drink options and something she called dessert nachos. When I'd told her over the phone that I'd needed a Phase 10 night, she'd insisted we needed to bring as much alcohol and carbs as possible. But not just any kind of alcohol. The older generation of Garcia women didn't do wine or beer. It was the hard stuff or nothing. And we were happy to oblige.

It was all very strategic.

Some families played poker. Others played bingo. Our family played Phase 10. Although *played* wasn't exactly the right word. Our tías and my mom were totally ruthless when it came to the card game. And they'd taught us well.

So, plying the older women in our family with booze and carbs was just another way to give us younger women an advantage. Especially since our game nights were known to last well into the early morning. You would think we played for money or something. Nope. It was just bragging rights.

"You should've brought piña colada mix too. You know my mom drinks those like fruit punch," Erica said as she blended the margaritas inside the kitchen.

I pulled some glasses down from the cabinet. "I forgot, dammit. How about you make her a Long Island iced tea?" I asked.

Erica stopped blending and looked at me. "With what? The strongest alcohol Abuela has is in the medicine cabinet."

"Should I run to the store?"

She went back to blending and shook her head. "I'll just make these really strong. Pour in some more tequila. How many are we making?"

I counted off on my fingers. "Your mom, my mom, Tía Espy, Tía Gloria, and us two makes six. Gracie and Abuela are going to drink water."

The blender turned off again. "What about Mari?"

"I don't know," I said with a shrug.

I'd called my cousin after confirming everyone else was free to meet up tonight. I hadn't talked to Mari since New York and was actually a little surprised when she picked up her phone. I'd heard about the divorce and that she was moving out from both Erica and Gracie. Part of me had been a little hurt that Mari hadn't told me herself. But the other part, the part that was still sad about how things had ended with Nathan, also understood. I couldn't imagine going through that with someone you thought you were going to spend the rest of your life with. No wonder she'd been so upset at Welita's funeral. So I couldn't blame her for not calling up every single person in the family just to tell us that her marriage was over.

Surprisingly, she'd sounded excited about coming tonight. But then she'd hesitated. "I really want to come, Selena. It's just that there's this apartment I've been trying to see in Pasadena, and I finally got an appointment at six p.m. With traffic, I don't know if I could make it to Inland Valley by seven p.m."

"That's okay if you're a little late," I'd said.

"But it's Phase 10. Won't it throw off the points if I start my phases later than everyone else?"

It would. But I wasn't going to give her an excuse to not come. In that moment, I realized what Erica had been saying all these years. We had made it easier for Mari to keep her distance because we always accepted her excuses.

Not anymore.

"Well, you're welcome to come. Late or on time," I told her, careful not to show the familiar frustration that had welled up in my gut. Gracie had insisted that it seemed like Mari was going to make more of an effort to hang out with us. Even Erica was convinced after having lunch with her the other day.

I checked my watch. It was already 7:15.

"Well," Erica said after filling the glasses I'd given her. "Let's pour her one, and if she doesn't show, then we'll give two to Espy. That lady can hold her liquor, so we're going to have to double up every round."

I'd half expected Erica to go off again about Mari being a possible no-show. The fact that it didn't even raise one of her eyebrows was a shocker. Come to think of it, Erica seemed to be in an especially good mood. My cousin intuition was tingling. Something was up with her, and I wanted to know what.

But before I could interrogate her, I heard screams of delight coming from the patio. Erica and I both looked at each other in confusion and walked toward the cacophony of excitement.

I nearly dropped my glass when I saw the reason for the ruckus.

There in the middle of the patio, surrounded by all the tías, stood my cousin Mari.

And, thanks be to the Phase 10 gods, she was holding a bottle of piña colada mix and what looked to be a pan of freshly baked brownies.

Chapter Fifty-Two
MARI

Whatever anxiety I'd been feeling in the car about game night with my cousins and tías disappeared as soon as I walked through the door.

Tía Marta was the first to see me. "Mari!" she yelled and ran over to give me a hug. The others were right behind her. Then my abuela took my hand and led me to the table. It was then that I noticed Espy. She waved from her seat in the corner, and I gave her a small smile. I figured she would be here and there was a good chance she'd try to bring up what she'd told me at the funeral. Still, I didn't let that scare me off from coming.

I had meant what I'd said to Gracie and Erica. I wanted to be a part of this family again. And I knew that meant I would have to face my dad sooner or later. I'd even canceled my appointment to see the Pasadena apartment just so I would have enough time to bake a batch of brownies (my abuela's favorite) and get here before they started playing. And I almost made it right on time, but I'd remembered that Selena had asked me to also bring some alcohol.

You would've thought I'd brought a hundred-dollar bottle of tequila instead of a $7.99 bottle of piña colada mix by the way she thanked me over and over again.

After everyone had their drinks and their dessert, it was finally time to start the game.

"Mari, do you need me to go over the rules?" Selena asked.

"No, I think I'm good. Thanks." I'd spent the afternoon refreshing myself on the rules, and slowly it had all come back to me.

"Mom? Do you need me to go over the rules? Because last time we played I kind of remember you not remembering all of them."

Everyone laughed. Selena and her mom bickered for a little before my abuela told them both to be quiet.

I couldn't help but smile. Things hadn't changed much since the last time I played Phase 10.

An hour later, we took our first break to refill our drinks and plates. I also walked inside to use the bathroom. That's when I ran into Espy.

"Hey, you're pretty good at this game," she told me. "I've been stuck on phase two forever."

I shrugged. "Yeah, I think most of it has to do with luck. I'm actually surprised that I'm keeping up. It's been a while."

"I'm glad you came tonight. I was worried that you wouldn't because of what happened at the funeral."

The anxiety I'd been feeling in the car came back. I hadn't had enough tequila to have this conversation. Not that I was planning to drink more than one margarita since I had a long drive back home.

"Well, I figured I needed a little fun."

Espy nodded. "I'm sure you did. Divorce is hard—believe me, I know. I was younger than you when my first marriage ended. I'm sorry you have to go through that."

I heard the sincerity in her words, and I wanted to accept them. But Espy was the last person in the world that I wanted to talk to about my failed marriage. Luckily, Erica came into the kitchen and told us we were going to start back up in five minutes.

I excused myself to go to the bathroom before Espy could see just how bothered I was. At that moment, it didn't matter if what she'd told me at the funeral was true or not. Because she wasn't the one I needed to hear from.

When I was ready, if I was ever ready, then I'd ask my dad all the questions I had.

Until then, I still didn't know who or what to believe.

Chapter Fifty-Three
GRACIE

St. Christopher's annual fall fiesta turned out to be quite the social event in town. There were carnival games, a handful of rides, and lots and lots of craft and food booths.

But the biggest draw so far had been the live bands.

Even though I was happy, I still couldn't wait for everything to be over.

I still hadn't told Tony anything. He'd gotten the job in Texas after all. And between all our last-minute preparations, I didn't want that hanging over our heads.

I'd tell him Sunday evening. One more day wouldn't hurt.

So I focused on walking from food booth to food booth to make sure all the volunteers had what they needed. Tony was checking in with the carnival games.

I greeted Sister Catherine at the fish fry table. "I'm so glad to see you. We've run out of change again."

"Didn't I leave an envelope of dollars and fives in your cash box an hour ago?" I asked.

"No. Perhaps you left it with a different booth?"

My brain seemed to be all over the place these days. I couldn't remember the simplest of things. In my head, I retraced my steps after leaving the office with the cash. I had stopped by the crafts booth to check out the beaded jewelry, but I hadn't bought anything because I didn't have my wallet on me. So I'd gone to get it from my backpack, which I'd stashed in my classroom's storage cabinet. I must have left the envelope inside my backpack.

"I think I know where it is," I told her and headed toward my classroom.

As soon as I unlocked the cabinet, I could see the envelope sticking out of the top of the backpack and reached to grab it.

"Did you find it?" Sister Catherine said over my shoulder.

I hadn't realized she'd followed me. I jumped at her voice and knocked my backpack onto the floor. Everything spilled out. The cash, my keys, a copy of *What to Expect When You're Expecting*, and a printout of an ultrasound with my name on it.

She picked up the book and the ultrasound.

"When were you going to tell us?" she said, looking at the paper. "I mean, I, we, didn't even know you had a boyfriend."

I tried to talk without breaking into tears. "I was going to announce it when I was ready." She looked at me with an expression of both disappointment and shock. I knew the questions weren't going to stop.

"Are you getting married?"

"No. I mean probably not. I don't know."

"What do you mean you don't know?" Sister Catherine sounded frustrated, and I wondered why she was taking such an interest in this at all. "Gracie, you are the most responsible woman I know. How could you get pregnant without knowing for sure that the baby's father was committed to . . . wait. Dear Lord, do you even know who the father is?"

My embarrassment quickly turned into anger. "Of course I know who the father of my baby is, Sister!"

"You're pregnant?" I froze at the sound of Tony's voice.

He was standing in the doorway holding a stuffed toy puppy. It was brown and beige and had a pink heart on its belly. It was adorable. Tony's expression, however, was not. As he walked toward us, his eyes never left mine.

Sister Catherine gave me what she was holding and picked up the cash and walked out.

"I won this for you." He held out the stuffed puppy. He wasn't smiling, and I couldn't stand to look at his face anymore. I turned to walk away, but he grabbed me by the chin and whispered, "Tell me, Gracie."

"Yes, I'm pregnant, and it's yours," I whispered back. He let go of my chin and ran his fingers through the sides of his hair.

I stood there holding the stuffed puppy, and my eyes followed him as he paced back and forth in the classroom. He stopped suddenly and came back toward me.

"And you're sure it's mine?" He looked different to me. Desperate, scared even. It wasn't a good look for him.

"How can you even ask me?" I almost cried. I wanted to tell him that he had been my first and only. But maybe he wouldn't believe that either.

"I'm sorry, but I had to. I mean, this is kind of a shock."

"No kidding."

He started pacing again, and again I just stood there until he was ready to start talking. It was another couple of minutes before he came back to me. "So what are you going to do?"

My heart sank that he'd said *you* and not *we*. Even though I had expected it, a tiny part of me had always wished he'd find out by accident and then he'd hold me in his arms and tell me how happy he was and that he wanted to marry me. It was obvious that he was anything but happy.

"I'm going to have the baby, and I'm going to raise it on my own," I told him.

"So, you're not expecting me to marry you or give you money. Because that's what some women think, and it's just that I'm not ready to . . ."

"I'm not some women, Tony. I didn't do this to trap you. Believe me, I was just as shocked as you. That said, this baby may not have been what I planned, but now I can't imagine not having it," I said. "And, no, I don't expect or want anything from you. Not money, not phone calls, nothing. Not even this."

I handed him the stuffed puppy and walked out.

◆ ◆ ◆

The house was quiet. The calm before the storm.

I sat down in my dad's blue recliner and waited for my parents to get home from the market. I had spent the night at Erica's. I was so upset and devastated after the fiesta that I knew I couldn't face my parents. One look at my face and they would've instantly known that something was wrong. I had stayed away on purpose.

At first, I drove around aimlessly. I had thought about calling Selena, but I knew if I did, then she would want to kill Tony. So instead, at about four p.m., I pulled into Erica's driveway.

"I'm pregnant," I'd said as soon as she opened the door. We spent the next couple of hours talking and crying. Eventually, we called Selena and told her the whole gory story. As I had thought, she'd immediately wanted to track down Tony and knock him out. She also had a few choice words for Sister Catherine. Erica asked why I hadn't told Tony when I found out. "Because, I didn't want him to stay because of the baby. I wanted him to stay because of me," I said.

We cried some more, and then all of us agreed that I had to tell my parents as soon as possible. There was a good chance the news about Goody Two-Shoes Gracie Lopez getting knocked up was already making its way through the church gossip pipeline.

I took a breath when I saw my parents' minivan pull into the driveway. My parents came inside a few minutes later carrying a few bags of groceries.

"Hija, help me put these things away," my mother told me after I followed behind them. I dutifully put away cans in the cupboard and perishables in the refrigerator.

"If you don't have to go back to the fiesta today, your dad is planning to cook your favorite—ribs in chile verde," my mother mentioned.

"I'm not going back to the fiesta today. But Mom, after we put everything away, I need to talk to you guys," I said.

"About what?" she asked me as she put boxes of cereal on top of the refrigerator. My dad wasn't even in the kitchen anymore. As soon as I'd started helping, he left for the living room to go watch a soccer game.

"I just need to talk to you. Um, where's Rachel?" The last thing I needed was Ms. Nosy hanging around when I talked to my parents.

"Oh, she ran into a friend last night at the fiesta, and we let her go over to the girl's house. I may need you to pick her up later."

I nodded and sat down at the table, watching my mom put away the rest of the groceries. Many people used to tell me that I looked a lot like Mom. I didn't see it, except that we had the same dark hair and dark eyes. She was a little taller than me and had always been a little heavier. Lately, though, she and my dad had started taking walks in the evening, and I could see she was losing weight. She once told me that she gained twenty pounds with every one of her pregnancies. I had a feeling I was going to do the same. The nausea had stopped about a week ago, and I was craving everything in sight.

Even now as I waited for my mom to finish, I was eating from the container of chocolate-covered raisins my parents had just bought.

When she was finally done, my mom sat down next to me at the kitchen table. "Okay, Gracie. What is it that you wanted to talk to me about?"

I told her to get my dad. By the look on her face, I knew she knew now that it was serious.

After some raised voices, again in Spanish, my dad turned off the television, and they both walked back into the kitchen.

My mom sat down. My dad stayed standing.

I couldn't even look at them. I could feel the tears welling up in my eyes and put my hand over my mouth to stifle the sobs or vomit that threatened to come up.

"Ay, Dios mío! Gracie, you're scaring me. What's wrong?" my mother pleaded and grabbed my other hand.

No matter how hard I tried, the words wouldn't come. I heaved with sobs, the kind where you can't catch your breath. All I could get out was "I . . . I . . . I . . . I."

My mother started crying too.

"I . . . I . . . I . . ."

"You're pregnant," my dad finally said, his face blank.

I nodded and just kept sobbing.

"What? Impossible! Impossible!" my mother kept yelling in Spanish.

"I'm sorry. I'm so sorry," I cried.

"Who's the father?" my dad asked. I didn't say anything. Again, he answered for me. "The PE teacher?" I nodded again. "And what does he say?"

This time I answered. "Nothing. He's moving to Texas for a job. He is not going to be around." I started crying again.

My dad walked over and pulled me up to face him. He grabbed my shoulders and said, "It's not terrible. Okay? I may not like it that you are not married, but you are older, and you have a good job. It's not like you are Rachel."

I nodded, but the tears wouldn't stop.

"Ay, chiquita." He called me by my childhood nickname. "Don't cry anymore."

Then he pulled my mother to him and put his arms around both of us. We stayed there, us three, for a while. Just holding each other and crying. Finally, when we broke apart, I looked at my mother and asked who was going to break the news to my grandmother.

Almost instantly we all said in unison, "Selena."

Chapter Fifty-Four
ERICA

They say there's a fine line between love and hate. What I wanted to know, though, was when exactly had my life turned into such a fucking cliché?

The writer in me was ashamed.

As I sat on my couch chewing angrily on a piece of salami, I thought of all the snarky things I was going to say to Adrian when he finally showed up to my place.

The Pinche Asshole was officially one hour late to our weekly viewing of our favorite Hulu series. Tonight was the season finale, the one where we were going to finally find out who the murderer was. I'd even spent money and time making a goddamn charcuterie board with his favorite meats and cheeses, and the bastard couldn't even text me a reason as to why he wasn't here yet.

I had called it, though. When he told me our usual Hulu night had to be pushed back a little later because it was Isela's mom's birthday and he and his parents were going to dinner with her family, I told him we could reschedule.

But no. He insisted he could still come over after dinner. I was doubtful, but I also wanted to see him. So, like a lovesick pendeja, I'd agreed to have some snacks ready and to wait for him so we could watch the episode together at nine.

This was my own damn fault. Still, I was pretty pissed that he hadn't answered my texts or called and it was already ten.

I'd eaten my way through all the chocolate and most of the cheese and finished off the wine when Adrian finally showed up at 10:15.

I waited a good five minutes before letting him inside.

"I know, I know," he rushed out as he walked to the couch. "I'm sorry. I left my phone at my house. There was a mix-up with the reservation, and we didn't even get our food until eight thirty, and it was just a big mess."

He was about to reach for a cracker when I slapped his hand away. I picked up the tray and said, "You don't deserve my charcuterie."

"It wasn't my fault. I really am sorry, Erica."

I hated that he looked so good in his button-down dress shirt and slacks. Dammit. I could feel myself relenting.

"You suck." It was the meanest thing I could come up with because by now I was just happy to see him.

Such. A. Pendeja.

I put the tray down, opened up another bottle of wine, and joined him on the couch. Thirty minutes later, the murderer had been revealed, and I was feeling pretty good. So much so that I'd ended up with my legs curled under me and my head against his shoulder.

It felt nice to be with him like this again. Between work and his many family commitments, our weekly Hulu nights had become the only time we could spend together out of the office. Now that the series had ended, what did that mean for us?

"What show should we watch next?" I asked after he'd turned off the TV. "It doesn't have to be on Hulu. We could have Netflix nights now, or Apple TV evenings."

He laughed and sighed deep. "Whatever you want. Except K-dramas. My brain is too tired after work to have to read a TV show."

I sat up to face him. "Don't use that as an excuse. I know the truth. You don't want to watch K-dramas because they're romances, and your cold, black heart refuses to watch anything having to do with l-o-v-e."

"I don't mind watching romantic movies or shows," he said after a yawn.

"Oh, really?"

"Really. I mean, most of them are ridiculous and predictable. But I'll watch one every once in a while."

I rolled my eyes and laughed. "You just made my point. You think they're too shallow for your very intelligent brain. You're such a snob."

"I'm not a snob. I just think the plots of some of these shows are simplistic or even unrealistic. Real romance doesn't work that way."

I scoffed. "Oh. Now you're an expert on romance too?"

"Not an expert. But, come on. Do you really expect a guy to do something out of the blue and out of character just to profess his love to you? Why not just have a conversation?"

My throat tightened, and my heart started beating way faster than I wanted it to. This conversation had turned from silly to dangerous. The wine had warmed me up and loosened my inhibitions. If I wasn't careful, I would confess something I had no right confessing. Especially because up to that point I had been debating kissing Adrian as a joke, just to make him shut up.

I should've changed the subject. Or at the very least, put some space between us.

But the wine, and my sorry-ass feelings for him, wouldn't let me.

"In case you haven't noticed, men don't like having the feelings conversation. So, yes, sometimes a guy has to do something big and bold to prove that he really loves you."

Adrian shook his head. "I don't know. I guess I just don't get it. When I wanted Isela to be my girlfriend, I just took her to get coffee and asked."

The mention of his ex stopped me cold.

"And how did that work out for you?" I snapped.

He shrugged. "Well, we did get engaged. So I guess okay."

Okay? What the fuck does that mean? Like okay that they're friends again or okay like they are getting back together?

Then it hit me. If Adrian wanted something more from me, he would just come right out and tell me. Part of me had been hoping that he did have romantic feelings for me but was holding back because of our working relationship and friendship.

I was starting to realize that maybe that wasn't the case at all. Maybe Adrian hadn't told me he loved me because he didn't. When was I ever going to learn my fucking lesson? It was Greg all over again. How many excuses had I made for him rather than accept the truth? I was never a priority for Greg. Just like I wasn't one for Adrian. At least, not anymore.

I wrestled to rein in my emotions so I didn't scream or burst into tears, and that resulted in the beginnings of a headache.

"Listen, I'm getting a little tired," I said and stood up. "I think I better go to bed."

Adrian looked at his watch. "Really? I thought we were going to hang out a little more. It seems like I never see you anymore outside of the office."

Irritation exploded in me, making my head pound even more. "Well, that's not my fault."

"What's that supposed to mean?"

I threw up my hands. "I'm here, Adrian. I'm here every fucking night. You're the one who always seems to have something better to do than hang out with me."

"That's not fair."

"You're right. It's not. It's not fair for you to expect me to wait around for your ass while you're out having dinner, golfing, going to the theater, or whatever else Isela decides you have to go do. Friendship is a two-way street, and right now I just feel like I'm the only person on the road."

"Erica, I—"

I cut him off. "I really don't feel good. Can you just go?"

He stood up and searched my eyes. "If that's what you want?"

"It is."

I called Selena as soon as he left.

"Take me with you to New York," I said as soon as she answered.

"If I go, definitely."

And just like that, Selena was making my bad mood go away. I could always count on her for that.

"Of course you're going to go," I told her. "I would."

"Maybe. I'm still deciding. But what's up with this sudden urge to uproot your life and go to New York?"

I let out a long sigh. "I need a change. I think I need a new job."

"Good for you. I always knew you could do better than the *News-Press*. What does Adrian say?"

"He doesn't know."

"Really. I thought you guys were pretty good friends. Don't you want to use him as a reference?"

"No. In fact, he's one of the main reasons why I want to leave."

"Oh no. What happened?"

I sighed again. "How much time have you got?"

Chapter Fifty-Five
SELENA

Erica was on my mind. I had no idea that she had fallen in love with Adrian.

And when I told Gracie about it, she was as shocked as I was.

"Poor Erica. She must really have it bad for this guy," I said.

"Why do you say that?"

"Because she hid it so well. You know Erica can't keep her mouth shut to save her life. We usually know she likes a guy before she does. I knew she was hanging out with her boss; I even teased her about it. But she never said a word."

"You're right," my sister admitted. "Well, I wonder if she's going to start looking for another job, then. It's not good for her if she has to see him every day."

I wondered if that was what she thought about Tony. I was about to ask when my abuela came back with the box of yarn we were at her house to pick up. My mom was going to crochet a tablecloth for my abuela's dining room table, and she wanted to use the scraps of yarn that Welita had kept in her room.

The box was full of different colors and different patterns.

"Didn't Welita used to be a seamstress?" I asked as I looked through the spools.

"Yes. It was one of her many jobs," my abuela answered. "When she first came to the United States after my father died, it was the only work she could find for several years."

"I still can't believe she came here with no husband and five kids. She must have been so scared," Gracie said.

"Maybe. But she had no choice. She had to do what was best for her family and for her. Sometimes, you find the strength to do what scares you most if you believe your life will be better because of it."

I thought about Welita and Erica and how much I wanted to be like them and go after a dream.

◆ ◆ ◆

"Gracie, can I tell you something?" I said on the drive back to our parents' house.

"Of course. Anything."

"I'm being offered a new job in New York."

"New York! With who? Nathan?"

"No, not Nathan. I mean, he helped get the interview, but it's with this huge advertising agency. I'd be handling clients from all over the country, even a few in Europe."

"Wow. That's . . . amazing. Are you going to take it?"

"I'm thinking about it. Erica wants me to go just so you guys can have an excuse to visit."

"Erica knows? Since when?"

"I just told her the other day. Actually, I had already turned it down and thought I'd lost it. Then Nathan called and told me the job was still mine if I wanted it. And I'm kinda thinking that I want it. I mean, is that totally crazy? To take a job in a city where I'd only know one person?"

Gracie stayed quiet for a few seconds. "Only you can answer that."

I hated when she was so rational. "That doesn't help me," I whined. "Tell me what you think I should do."

"I can't, Selena. But what I can say is that this is a major, major decision. You have to seriously think of all of the pros and cons."

We arrived at the house, and that was the end of the conversation. But my mind kept wandering to New York.

Later that night, I took out my laptop and googled images of the city. They were intimidating, but in an exciting kind of way. Then I spent the next ten minutes listing my pros and cons.

There was only one con, though, that mattered: leaving my family. A million thoughts rushed through my mind. I prayed and asked God to help me make the right decision.

I thought about Welita and how brave she had been. And, in my heart, I felt she would tell me to take the job.

Finally, just after eleven p.m., I pulled up Nathan's email. We hadn't spoken since that night he'd shown up at my place and I'd basically stepped all over his heart. Even after that, I had wanted so badly to pick up the phone. But Nathan deserved more than someone whose life was such a mess. Someone who didn't realize too late how lucky she was to have him in her life.

I told myself it was better this way. I was choosing New York for me and not anyone else.

I'll take the job, I typed. Thank you, Nathan.

Then I hit send.

Chapter Fifty-Six
MARI

I watched him, not quite sure what we were anymore to each other.

Could he still be my friend after all this? Did I want him to be?

"Thanks again for coming over," Chris said, then took a sip of the espresso he'd made just a few minutes earlier. I sat across from him on his couch holding my own cup. I met his eyes and smiled.

"Well, I figured I owed you a conversation. I'm sorry for not answering your texts or calls. I just needed some time to deal with, well, everything."

"You don't have to apologize. You needed your space. I understand that."

I put my cup down on the coffee table between us. "Honestly, I have to let you know that one of the reasons I didn't reach out is because I was angry at you, Chris. You had no right to tell Esteban about your feelings for me."

He hung his head. "I know. I'm sorry."

"What were you thinking?"

Chris put down his cup too. "Do you really want to know?"

I leaned back and folded my arms across my chest. "I do."

"I only said something because he pissed me off. That day Esteban kept going on and on about how you were going through some weird phase and that he was going to surprise you that night with some flowers and jewelry. He told me that you would never leave him because you had nowhere else to go. So, I got angry and told him that I loved you and that I would take care of you. And I will, Marisol. All you have to do is let me."

Although I was angry at Esteban for what he'd said about me, I was still irritated that Chris thought I needed to be taken care of. Neither of these men believed I was capable of doing anything without them.

"I can't, Chris."

"I'm sorry," he rushed out. "I'm so sorry. I know you're not ready."

It wasn't that at all.

"It's not that. You've been a good friend to me for so many years, but I don't love you like the way you love me. And I don't think I ever will."

I stood up and grabbed my purse. It had been a mistake to come here.

"You still love him, don't you?" he asked softly.

I ignored the question because I wasn't ready to face my feelings for Esteban. It made me too sad. "Our marriage hadn't been working for a while. The separation, the divorce was never about you. It was about me finally telling him that I didn't want to keep living a lie. And I still don't. I hope, eventually, you and I can be friends again. But we're never going to be more than that. I'm sorry."

Chris got up from his chair and walked over to me. "I guess I always knew that. But a guy can hope, right?"

I was about to turn to leave when a thought occurred to me. "How is he with you now?"

"We start proceedings next month to sever the business."

"Oh, Chris, I'm so sorry."

"You have nothing to be sorry about," he said with a shrug. "I did this to him. And even though you say the divorce isn't about me, I know I'm to blame for how he is with you, too, right now. I should've stayed out of it. I'm so sorry for ever saying anything. I wish I could do something to make things right."

"Thank you. Sadly, I don't think either of us can do anything. Esteban is too hurt right now to listen. He's going to believe the worst until he's ready to hear the truth."

"That's so sad," he said, shaking his head. "It's obvious you don't want things to be bad between you two. But how can either of you start over when he refuses to accept there were other reasons for doing what you did? Holding on to the past doesn't always help you in the future."

A realization struck me so hard that I gasped.

"I'm sorry, Chris. I have to go," I said and headed to the door.

"Where are you going?" I heard him ask.

"To start my future!" I yelled.

You could still leave. They haven't opened the door yet. Back away and jump in your car and go . . .

Except it was time to stop running away.

Esteban and I were getting a divorce, and I had finally drawn the line between Chris and me. It was time to start thinking of my new future. But to do that, I had to face my past.

Before coming to my dad's house, I'd called my mom. As soon as she'd heard I was divorcing Esteban, she'd started talking about alimony and asked how much money I'd get from selling the house. And when I tried to bring up what Espy had told me at the funeral, she told me to never believe a word that "whore" said.

Maybe she was right? This had been a mistake.

The door finally opened, and my half sister Araceli was holding it. I couldn't run away now.

"Is your dad home?" I asked.

Espy appeared and answered, "He is. Come inside."

For the first time, I noticed the gray hairs that framed her face and the deep lines that curved around her mouth. These days she looked more soccer mom than the evil home-wrecker I'd imagined her to be all these years.

Their house wasn't big, but it was a decent size. I knew she worked as a bank teller at the local credit union, and my dad still worked in a warehouse with my tío Carlos, Gracie and Selena's father. They were middle class all the way—not rich by any means, but still better off than I had been growing up.

I tried to swallow the bile of bitterness. I needed answers before I got the hell out of here.

Espy returned with my dad. He asked me to take a seat at their dining room table, and I did.

"Thank you for visiting," he began. "Espy says you want to ask me questions about, you know, before."

I willed my heart to stop beating so fast and tried to control the tone of my voice. "Yes, I do. I'm trying to make changes in my life, and I think it would help if I could finally get some closure. Obviously, we don't have a regular father-daughter relationship, which is fine, but I need to know what happened when you and Mom divorced."

He looked at Espy, who nodded. "Go ahead, Ricardo. Tell her the truth."

He sat down at the table across from me. "First, I need to say that this has nothing to do with your mom. This has to do with me and you, okay? I know now there are things you don't know. And, honestly, I never wanted you to know because you were just a kid back then. But things are different, and I'm hoping you can handle it."

"Just tell me what you want to tell me."

He began at the end—the end of my parents' marriage.

"After I lost my job, my drinking got worse. And I don't blame Vangie for wanting a divorce. I was so ashamed of what I'd turned into that I thought I was doing you a favor by not fighting for custody. Besides, you were a girl. I figured you were better off with her."

"I already know this."

"Right. Of course. Well, as soon as you guys moved away, I went into rehab. Your grandparents and my sisters confronted me one day and told me that if I didn't get help, I would lose you too. So I agreed."

My body froze. "What? How long were you in there?"

"I did the full ninety days."

"But that doesn't make sense," I said with a shake of my head. "I visited you at Abuela and Abuelo's on the weekends during the first few months."

He bowed his head. "You don't remember."

"Remember what?"

My dad looked at me again. "You didn't visit me those first thirty days. I called you and said I had to work weekends for a while, so I couldn't see you. Afterward, the treatment center let me go home on Fridays and come back Sunday nights. I didn't tell you because it was too embarrassing."

My fingers dug into my knees in an attempt to center myself. All this was almost too much already. "Fine. You got help. But what about the other stuff? Why didn't you send money or child support?"

"Mari, I was in rehab. I couldn't get a job for those three months. So during that time, Abuela sent money to your mom. And when I got out and started working again, I took over."

That made me jump to my feet. "You're lying. If you sent money, then why did we never have any? Why did our electricity always get turned off? Why did I go nights without any dinner?"

His face crumpled. "I had no idea that was happening, until it was too late. And I do blame myself for that."

"I still don't understand what you're talking about."

This time Espy answered. "Think about it, Mari. Do you really believe that your grandparents would let their granddaughter go without clothes or food or electricity? And if they were sending the money, then what happened to it?"

I shook my head. "I don't . . . this doesn't make sense."

I squeezed my eyes, and memories began to rush into my head. Like the time my mother had left me with a friend for the weekend because she was going on a business trip (even back then I thought it was strange that the grocery store where she worked as a cashier would send her to a training conference in Palm Springs). When she came back she was tanner and wearing clothes I had never seen on her before. I also remembered the time our electricity was turned off for the third or fourth time, and I pleaded with my mom to just go to my dad and demand that he give her some money. She became hysterical and said that I was accusing her of being a bad mom and that maybe I should just go live with my dad. The next day our electricity was back on, and when I asked her where she'd gotten the money from, she said she had borrowed it from a friend.

"As soon as we figured it out, we tried to help," my dad said. "Abuela brought groceries when you were at school, and I agreed to pay half of every utility bill."

It was all too incredible to believe. Yet, deep down I knew he was telling the truth. They were right. Things got better my senior year in high school. I had just thought it was because my mom had found a new job.

I dropped back onto the chair. "Why didn't you ever tell me this? And why are you telling me now?" I asked them.

My dad couldn't speak. Espy reached over and grabbed his hand.

"Because how you felt about him all these years—that he was a failure, a bad father, a bad husband—is how he felt about himself," she said, her voice thick with emotion. "He knew—he knows—that you hate him and that you would never believe him. He also knew Vangie would deny everything, and then he would be the bad guy all over again. So he let you hate him. Because he felt that he deserved it."

Her voice broke, and she quickly wiped the tears from her eyes. "And I'm telling you now because of your welita."

My head shot up, and my gut felt like someone had punched it. "What are you talking about?" I said, my face probably all scrunched up in confusion.

"The day before she died, me and your dad went to visit her. When he left the room to go get her some water, she asked me if we had talked to you recently. When I said that we hadn't, she told me that made her sad. She said that she knew there were problems between your dad and you. I lied and said things were getting better. She made me promise that I would help make things right. And this is me, keeping my promise."

I held my head in my hands because the weight of the revelation was too much for me to carry. The guilt of knowing that this was what Welita was worried about in her final days wrenched my gut into knots, coating my tongue in bitterness as bile built in my throat. "I can't deal with this right now." I jumped to my feet. "I'm sorry."

Then I ran out of the house. I'd driven maybe just a block or two when I pulled my car over and let the tears escape. Had I been wrong about everything this entire time? Had I broken Welita's heart all because I'd been too stubborn to demand answers—even though deep down I knew some things just didn't make sense? I didn't want to think about all the mean things I had ever said about my dad or all the times I'd canceled my weekend visits because I preferred to hang out with my friends or a boyfriend. I thought about my wedding day and how I hadn't even considered asking him to be there.

I gulped for air as I thought about all the lost moments between us. My heart knew they had told me the truth.

Now it was up to me to decide what to do with it.

Chapter Fifty-Seven
GRACIE

You wouldn't think it, but you can learn a lot of important life lessons from teaching seven-year-olds.

Lesson one: Never let your guard down. The second you think you're in control—bam! Chaos ensues.

Lesson two: Logic doesn't always win arguments. Sometimes you just have to accept that no matter what you say, you can't change minds.

Lesson three: It never hurts to ask for help. Especially from the Big Guy.

So just before I was to face a nun, a priest, and an ultraconservative school board president, I decided to prepare myself with a last-minute prayer.

Dear God, I don't know what is about to happen, but I put it in your hands. I trust that whatever happens will be part of your plan, and I just ask that you give me the strength and patience to get through this meeting without crying or calling someone a poopy head. Amen.

I had been summoned to the after-school meeting by Sister Catherine. She told me that we needed to discuss my "condition" and that Father Dominic, the school's head deacon, and the school board president, Agatha Warner, would be joining us.

After quick introductions, they got right down to the point.

"As you know, St. Christopher's has a very strict morality clause in our teacher contracts. And, while it doesn't specifically mention out-of-wedlock pregnancies, there could be an argument made that such a condition would go against the general spirit of the clause, which is to require teachers to honor our Catholic beliefs both professionally and personally."

Father Dominic cleared his throat and shifted in his chair. "What Sister Catherine is trying to say is that while we, of course, would never suggest that you violated the contract, others outside of this office could see it differently. This is a very complicated situation, and we want to make sure that we are all on the same page here."

"And what page is that, Father?"

Agatha threw her hands in the air. "Can we stop beating around the bush and just ask her?" The other two stayed quiet. "Fine. I'll be the bad guy. Ms. Lopez, we need to know two things—do you have plans to marry the father of your baby, and do you plan to keep teaching here? We're not trying to be nosy. But you need to understand the ramifications of having an unwed pregnant woman teaching first graders and then having to replace you midway through the school year, when we have no idea if you're going to even want to come back next fall."

I had to take a moment. How could I answer the question about the father of my baby? If they knew for sure it was Tony, they didn't let on. He wasn't on staff anymore since he was leaving in a few weeks. There was zero chance of us getting married, but I wasn't going to tell them that I hadn't talked to him since the day at the fiesta. I would start to dial his number but always hung up before the call went through.

"It would just be considerate of you, Gracie, to inform us of your plans since this situation affects everyone in the St. Christopher's family." I didn't miss the bitterness in Sister Catherine's voice.

She had hired me herself to take over the first grade—the class she had taught for fifteen years before finally being promoted to principal.

She had entrusted me with the privilege of caring for the youngest students at St. Christopher's. I was her protégé. And now she looked at me like I had betrayed her.

The guilt hit me hard. They were right. This pregnancy wasn't just going to turn my life upside down; it was going to affect my students in some way or another. It would be hard to explain to them why I was having a baby but wasn't married. Some of the more zealous parents might even stir things up with the school and threaten to take their children out.

My hand clutched the gold cross I was wearing on my neck as I silently prayed for God to tell me what to do. And then I remembered Welita. She'd given me the cross in high school when I told her that I'd decided not to become a nun after all. I thought she'd be disappointed. Instead, she said she was proud that I had the courage to do what I wanted and not what everyone expected.

Because even back then, I was the girl who'd usually acquiesce rather than confront. The girl who'd rather settle than challenge. The girl who was fine being in the background, quiet and complacent, because she was afraid of being noticed.

Welita, on the other hand, had fought to overcome so many obstacles in her life. She did what needed to be done and made sure her voice was always heard. She was a force to be reckoned with, a tsunami even. Meanwhile, I'd spent my life trying hard to not make any waves.

How had I become such a doormat? If I let them bully me or shame me now, then I didn't deserve her cross.

It was time to be a tsunami.

"While I appreciate your concern about my condition, quite frankly it's none of your business whether I plan to marry my baby's father or not. And if for some reason I don't, I also understand some people—but not any of you, of course—could use the morality clause to terminate my employment. I don't think that would fly, though, but I'm willing to hire a lawyer to challenge the clause if it ever comes to that."

Sister Catherine's jaw dropped, and Father Dominic cleared his throat again. "Gracie, I think you misunderstand—"

"No, I think I understand perfectly. That said, I'm a good teacher, and I care about my students. I would never do anything to take the focus away from their learning. It's never been an issue when a married teacher has had to take maternity leave in the middle of the school year, so that's not even an issue. You want us all to be on the same page, right? Well, here it is. I'm going to go on a paid leave starting January first. That way there will be no questions or rumors to deal with, and it gives you enough time to find a long-term substitute. Then I'll return next fall and teach a new class of first graders."

"The board will have to approve this arrangement, of course," Agatha said stiffly.

"Well, I'm sure you three will work hard to lobby on my behalf. Since, you know, this situation affects everyone in the St. Christopher's family."

How I managed to walk out of that meeting without pumping my fist in the air will always be a mystery.

Chapter Fifty-Eight
ERICA

I don't want this job.

I was sitting in the small lobby area of Above the Fold waiting for my appointment with the managing editor, and I tried to take my mind off the fact the building was in the heart of downtown Los Angeles.

Sure, it was beautiful with lots of restaurants and cool places to visit. But that didn't matter. Because I didn't want the job.

Nope, I didn't want it. Because if I did want it, then I'd be crushed when I didn't get it.

I had applied on a lark. It was one of those days at the *News-Press* when I was mad at Adrian for no particular reason.

Well, I guess there was one huge reason. I was mad because he'd made me fall in love with him, and there wasn't a damn thing I could do about it. That translated into a low threshold of annoyance when he was around. And if I was mad at him, then I couldn't be sad about him.

That day I applied had been one of the worst between us. We were supposed to go out with Deanna and Mark to the movies, but Isela had called and invited him to dinner with her parents and his parents. The thing with his dad had gotten better, and I knew he was trying to make the effort to see them more.

I'd told him I was fine if he wanted to cancel. But he didn't believe me and pulled me into the conference room.

"I know you're mad, and you're going to be mad all day if you don't get it out."

It made me even angrier that he was right.

"Yes, I'm pissed. What else is new? But you don't get to make me the witch that tells you to not go see your parents. And, honestly, the more we keep talking about this, the less I care. You don't owe me any explanation of what you do or where you go. Happy now?"

I stormed out, grabbed my purse, and headed for the elevator.

I heard him call my name as I got inside. The elevator started to close until Adrian stuck his foot between the doors, and they opened back up. He got inside with me and hit the button for the parking garage.

"What's wrong with you?" he shouted. "We were in the middle of a conversation. Why did you leave like that?"

"Because I told you I don't care anymore," I said. Too bad it couldn't have been the truth. The *P* button lit up, and the doors opened.

I started walking to my car, and he followed me. His legs were longer than mine, so he was able to pass me, and then he blocked my path. "Then why are you acting like I killed your dog?"

I couldn't answer him. Not without revealing the truth. The truth was I was in love with him. Desperately in love. But he was my boss and didn't feel the same way.

Maybe no pets had been harmed. Still didn't mean that I didn't get to be angry about it.

So I mustered every ounce of pride I could and looked him in the eye and lied my ass off. "I'm not. Everything is fine."

He put his hands in his pocket and said, "If you say so."

It wasn't until the elevators closed and I could trust he was well on his way back up to the newsroom that I allowed my knees to give from the weight of everything I'd been trying to keep inside.

The one thing that I refused to do, however, was think about how I was going to walk into that newsroom every day and pretend that my heart hadn't been broken in ways it had never been before.

And that's how I'd ended up in the lobby of Above the Fold.

It was a new online startup that had only been in business a few months. According to the company's website—which I'd read over and over again since scheduling the interview—the plan was to open up at least ten editions in the next year focusing on major regions or metropolitan areas. The editions would cover news, sports, and entertainment just like a print newspaper, except these articles would live only online.

They had already broken some of the biggest stories in the news. They were the next big thing in the publishing world, and it would be exciting to be a part of it.

Fuck. I so wanted this job.

"Erica, Natalie is ready to see you now."

The receptionist led me to a conference room at the end of a long hallway. The attractive woman seated at the table was the magazine's managing editor, Natalie Dagmire.

"So, Erica, why are you thinking about leaving the *News-Press*?" Natalie asked after we'd sat down.

Because I'm in love with my city editor, and now it's uncomfortable to be around him.

"Well, I've always been interested in the human side of the news. Frankly, after two years of covering education, it's starting to take its toll. I want—no, I need—to tell different kinds of stories." It was the honest truth. Sure, Adrian was one reason why it was time for me to move on. But it wasn't the only one.

The interview lasted forty-five minutes. At the end, we were chatting and laughing as if we'd known each other forever.

"Well, I think you have some great experience and would really fit in well with our company," Natalie said. "Let's have you come back for a writing test and then another round of interviews with our regional and assignment editors next week."

"Sounds great," I said and stood up. "Thank you so much."

As I walked out of the office and toward my car, I tried not to think about Adrian.

Which is probably why he decided to call me at that very second.

We hadn't spoken since the day we'd argued. We'd exchanged a few texts about work, but that was about it. I figured he was calling now because we were going to work together tomorrow, and he didn't want me to be mad.

"Where are you?" he asked after I answered.

"It's my day off."

"I know that. I wasn't asking as your editor."

My heart jumped despite my brain trying to remain impartial and unbothered. "I'm just running some errands."

"Want to grab some tacos later?"

I resisted the urge to ask if Isela was busy. "I could eat tacos," I said.

This was our mutual apology, I guess. It didn't fix things—at least not right now. But it was a start.

"Listen, Erica, I just want . . ."

I stopped him there because I wasn't ready for that conversation. "And I'm not talking those two-for-ninety-nine-cents tacos, either, Mr. Cheapskate," I said, interrupting. "I want the real deal, complete with rice and beans and margaritas."

He laughed. "Fine. I'll give you the real deal."

"Awesome. See you later."

I sat in my car for another thirty minutes or so thinking about the interview and whether I could make it through lunch without letting on what I was up to or what I was feeling.

The truth was, the only real thing I wanted from Adrian now had nothing to do with tacos and everything to do with his feelings for me.

Chapter Fifty-Nine
SELENA

I decided I wouldn't let Gracie ignore me any longer.

After my exit interview with the Umbridge brothers, I drove to St. Christopher's and parked across from the church. I knew school would be dismissed in less than ten minutes, so I waited outside the gates with the groups of parents there to pick up their children.

Once the gate opened, I made my way past the rush of kids and found Gracie's classroom. I waited outside until the last of her students had walked out. I could see her from the doorway. She was erasing the dry-erase board, and she looked tired and sad.

"Knock, knock," I said as I walked inside and shut the door behind me.

"Selena, what are you doing here? Did something happen?" she asked fearfully.

"No, no, everyone is fine. I just thought I'd stop by for a visit."

She raised her eyebrows and narrowed her stare. "Why? You've never done that before."

"Well, I've never needed to before," I said matter-of-factly. "I used to be able to get ahold of you when I needed to talk to you. What's going on? Why are you avoiding me?"

She looked away and walked back to her desk and started combing through a pile of papers. "I don't know what you're talking about."

She was always such a bad liar.

"Hey, I'm serious! I want to know. Tell me what I did or what I said to deserve the cold shoulder," I pleaded.

"I don't have time for this now. I have a lot of papers to grade and I'm supposed to be outside on traffic duty." She stood as if to walk out.

I moved forward and stood right in front of her so she couldn't leave. "Oh, my dear sister, we are totally going to do this now. What the hell is your problem?"

The look she gave me made my stomach churn. "You really don't know, do you? That is so like you. Oblivious to everyone and everything."

"Dammit, Graciela! Just freaking tell me already so I can apologize and we can get over this," I yelled.

Then Gracie did something I had never ever seen her do. She yelled back.

"You're leaving me! You're leaving us," she screamed.

"You mean the family?"

"I mean me and my baby! You're my sister. You were supposed to be here and help me through this. You were supposed to go to Lamaze classes with me. You were supposed to throw me a baby shower. You were supposed to do this with me. You promised me!"

She was really sobbing now.

"I can still do some of those things," I said and tried to give her a hug. She didn't hug me back.

"It won't be the same." She shook her head.

"What do you want me to say, Gracie?" We were facing each other again, and I searched her eyes for an answer. "I'm sorry. I didn't expect this to happen, just like you didn't expect to get pregnant."

"I knew it!" she screamed. "You don't want me to have this baby."

My heart broke at the accusation. I grabbed her shoulders to make sure she heard every word. “That’s not true, Gracie. You know that. I get that you’re hurt, but now you’re being mean. I love this baby. I love you.”

She slumped for a second but then stiffened in my grip. “Just forget it. It doesn’t matter anymore,” she said. Her words were cold, and I shivered at the chill that ran through me. I let go.

She walked back to the desk to sit down.

“It does matter. It matters to me,” I cried. “I didn’t do this to hurt you. I’m sorry that you feel like I’m abandoning you. I’m just so, so sorry.”

She covered her face with her hands and continued crying. Her words were muffled, but I could still understand them. “I’m just so scared. I don’t know how I’m going to do this all on my own.”

“But sweetie, that’s just it. You’re not alone.” I walked over and pulled her hands off her face. “You have Mom and Dad. Even Rachel can help. Then there’s all the tías. And, don’t forget, Erica and probably Mari too. And even though we may not see each other all the time, we can still talk on the phone and text. Heck, I’ll buy you the latest iPhone so we can video chat that way too.”

My voice started to break, and tears ran down my cheeks. I lowered my head so I could look directly in her eyes. “And, I will be there right by your side when you deliver this baby. Even if I have to get on a plane in an hour’s notice, I will be here. Nothing, and I mean nothing, is going to stop me from seeing the birth of my first niece or nephew.”

She sighed in resignation. “Whatever you say, Selena.”

It’s funny how you only come to appreciate things when it’s time to leave them behind. As I walked through the doors of the Inland Valley

International Airport, I couldn't believe how much it had changed and expanded over the last several years.

The last time I was here it was to say goodbye to Gracie before she left for Washington, DC, with her eighth-grade class from St. Christopher's. I remembered envying her, but also hating her at the same time.

It was the first time we would be apart for more than a day, and I cried and cried and begged my parents to let me go with her. To her credit, Gracie didn't hate the idea. Now I think it was because she was scared to go somewhere without me or my parents. If my parents had let her, Gracie would have taken her bratty kid sister all the way to Washington, DC.

Of course she survived the trip. I was mad at her for going and had refused to come with my parents to pick her up from the airport. I had planned on staying mad at her for the rest of my life, but as soon as I saw her getting out of the car in our driveway, I ran and hugged her. She hugged me back and gave me a snow globe from the Capitol.

It had taken many years for me to return to Inland Valley International. I usually only booked flights out of John Wayne in Orange County or LAX.

But it felt right to move to my new city from the city I'd grown up in. And it was convenient for my parents to come see me off, even if Gracie wouldn't.

"Do you need cash for the taxi when you get there?" my dad asked. He started to pull out his wallet.

"No, Daddy, remember? The agency is sending a car to pick me up."

"Is Nathan going to meet you?" This time it was Mom.

"I don't think so. But it's fine. I'm probably just going to go straight to the hotel and take a nap."

I hadn't told them that I hadn't heard from Nathan in weeks.

"Do you want us to wait with you until you have to go to the gate?" asked Erica, stifling a yawn.

"No, it's fine. I'm going to get some coffee and then just hang out and wait. I only have a couple of hours. Besides, you guys can't go upstairs to the boarding areas."

All of them nodded. When there was nothing left to say, I hugged each of them and tried hard not to cry. I looked one last time out the glass doors of the airport entrance.

"I'm sure she'll call you later," my mom offered.

I only nodded because my throat tightened with a sob. I took a deep breath, waved to my family, and started to walk to the escalator that would take me to Departures and on my way to my new life in New York.

"Selena! Wait! Selena!" My head whipped around to see my sister running up to me carrying a small purple gift bag.

She barreled into me, and I dropped my carry-on. She squeezed me hard, and I could hear her sobs against my shoulder.

"I'm . . . sorry. Please . . . don't . . . hate . . . me," she hiccupped.

I started sobbing just as hard. "It's . . . me . . . who's . . . sorry. I'm . . . such . . . a . . . bad . . . sister . . . leaving . . . you . . . when . . . you . . . need . . . me . . . the . . . most."

"Girls, girls." I heard my mother's voice. "People are starting to stare. What chillonas."

We both started laughing and wiped away our tears. I sighed, and for the first time in weeks, I felt light.

"I'm sorry if I made you feel bad for leaving," Gracie said after we'd both calmed down. "You know I just want you to be happy, right? And if moving to New York is going to make you happy, then I'm happy for you too."

I hugged her again. Then I bent down to her rounded belly and kissed it. "I'll see you soon, little baby."

I promise.

Chapter Sixty

MARI

"Happy Thanksgiving. I hope you enjoy."

As I spooned the stuffing onto the woman's plate, I noticed her eyes grow big.

"Are those real croutons?" she asked.

I smiled. "They sure are. I baked the sourdough bread myself."

She licked her lips in appreciation. "Thank you. And happy Thanksgiving to you and your family."

I shook off the twinge of sadness at the word *family* and went back to serving my homemade stuffing to the next person in line.

"Do you need another pan yet?" Gracie asked from behind me.

I still wasn't sure why I'd agreed to help her today. I'd been caught off guard when she'd called the day before to invite me to her church's annual Thanksgiving lunch for the homeless and other disadvantaged community members. But part of this whole effort to be a better Mari meant saying yes to chances to get to know my cousins again. Besides, hadn't I told Chris that day at lunch so long ago that I wanted my life to matter somehow?

The thought of Chris immediately led to Esteban. I hadn't spoken to him in over a month. My lawyer dealt with his lawyer and told me what I needed to know when it came to next steps and money stuff. Meanwhile, Letty was my source for all other intel on Esteban and his new life without me. A sad guilt had washed over me when she'd told me that instead of our annual Thanksgiving feast, Esteban was planning to spend the day golfing and then treating some of his associates to dinner at the country club.

Had I agreed to help Gracie to get rid of some of the guilt?

Definitely.

"Not yet," I told Gracie, grateful for the distraction. "Maybe in a few minutes. This line is getting longer and longer."

"Gotcha. I'll check back after I refill the green beans and mashed potatoes."

I smiled as she walked away. This might not have been how I'd imagined this holiday, but I was grateful that at least I wasn't alone.

Hours later, Gracie and I walked to my car in the church parking lot. My feet and my hands were killing me.

"I didn't think I could ever be this tired," I groaned and leaned against the driver's-side door. "I can't wait to go back to my hotel room and soak in a hot bath."

"You haven't found an apartment yet?" she asked.

I shook my head. "I'm still looking. Problem is, I have no idea where I want to live."

Gracie reached out and touched my arm. "I'm so sorry you're going through this. You know I'm here for you, right? We all are."

Her words brought up a new swell of emotions that spilled onto my cheeks. Even though I had lost my marriage, I had found my family again.

"I'm sorry. I didn't mean to make you cry," Gracie said.

"You didn't. It seems all I do is cry these days," I said with a sad shrug.

"Do you think you want to try to fix things between you guys?"

"I tried, but I think it's too late. Even though I was never unfaithful, I know I hurt Esteban and totally upended his life and his business."

I really did hope Esteban could forgive me one day. I knew from experience that holding grudges could be exhausting. I also knew that I couldn't worry about what other people thought about me. I could only control what I did and how I reacted. And right now I needed to focus on figuring out who I wanted to be.

Gracie reached out and squeezed my hand. "You're coming to dinner tonight, right?"

"Yes, I am."

What I didn't tell her was that I was a little nervous about being around the entire family again. There were a lot of them, and it could be overwhelming, even if I hadn't stayed away all these years. While my dad and I were working on our relationship slowly, I couldn't help but feel anxious about dinner at my abuela and abuelo's house. But I didn't tell Gracie that. I didn't want her to think I was having second thoughts.

"I'm so glad," she said, clapping her hands. "So, besides being exhausted, how was your first Thanksgiving feeding the homeless?"

"It was chaotic, but amazing. I never knew St. Christopher's did this for Thanksgiving."

"Not just Thanksgiving. We do it one Sunday a month. If we had more volunteers and money, we'd probably do it every week."

"I'd love to volunteer again. Do you think I could?"

"Of course! Helen, our food pantry director, is going to be so thrilled. I overheard her telling anyone who would listen how good your stuffing and homemade rolls were."

I laughed, remembering the woman who'd secretly asked her to put aside a cupful of stuffing and two rolls. This time it was my turn to reach out. "Thank you so much for inviting me. I needed this today."

We hugged again and said our goodbyes. But before she walked away, Gracie touched my arm. "Call me, Mari. Anytime you need to talk, okay?"

I smiled. "I will."

And I meant it.

Chapter Sixty-One
GRACIE

"It's from Texas."

Rachel and I stared at the envelope in her hand. I couldn't move. Didn't dare speak.

"Do you want me to open it for you?"

I shook my head and took the letter from her. I walked to my room and sat on my bed. Trembling, I tore it open from the side.

His letter was handwritten on yellow legal pad paper. The writing was neat and small. I took a deep breath and started to read:

> Dear Gracie,
>
> I don't know if you will ever read this letter, but I hope that you do. I need you to know that I never meant to hurt you. I never planned on being the kind of guy who leaves the woman pregnant with his child. I have no excuse, well, at least none that will take away your pain. If I didn't get this second chance, then maybe things would be different. I might have stayed at St. Christopher's and tried to be a part of the baby's life and be a part of yours. But I need to do this right

> now. I know I can't ask you to wait or even expect you to give us another chance. I want you to move on and find someone who will love you the way that you deserve. I promise to stay away, I don't want to hurt you any more than I have already. All I ask is that you take care of our baby and love him or her so he or she doesn't grow up to be a jerk like me.
>
> Take care of yourself,
>
> Tony

My tears spilled onto the paper, smearing the ink. I sat there on my bed crying and holding my stomach for a long time. I knew my sobs were loud, but I didn't care. I was tired of pretending that I was okay. I was tired of holding everything in. So for several minutes, maybe even hours, I let it all out.

Eventually I heard my door open, and I sensed someone walk over to me in the darkness. My wails had been reduced into sniffling hiccups. Without a word, the figure eased the letter from my grip and then gently pushed me down to the bed. I closed my eyes as the person lifted my legs and took off my socks and shoes. I felt a blanket being laid over me and a cool towel being slipped along my forehead.

I must have fallen asleep because the next time I opened my eyes, someone was brushing my hair. I turned to look at the figure behind me, and for a second I thought it was Selena.

It was Rachel.

"You have pretty hair," she said.

"Thanks," I whispered hoarsely.

"Do you want some water now? Do you want to try to eat?" I had never heard her talk so softly.

I nodded as tears slid sideways down my cheek. I felt her start to move off the bed. She hesitated for a second, and then I felt her kiss the top of my head.

The light from the hallway invaded my room as Rachel opened the door. I turned around then and called out her name.

"How did you . . . why?"

She shrugged. "Selena told me. I called her and asked her what I could do to help you. She said when she was sad you used to brush her hair, and it would make her feel better. So I thought if I did that to you, then maybe it would make you feel better too. Did it?"

I nodded and pulled a smile from my heart. "It did. Thank you."

Rachel stayed with me the rest of the night, and I realized that Selena had been right all along.

Maybe this baby wouldn't have a father, but it would have a family.

We would never be alone.

Chapter Sixty-Two
ERICA

The call I'd been waiting for came three days before Christmas.

I was going to be the new features reporter for Above the Fold. The first person I wanted to tell was Adrian. I'd decided that getting the job was permission for me to finally tell him how I felt as well.

If he laughed his ass off, then so be it. I'd be gone in two weeks anyway.

I was tired of the bullshit and needed to know, even if it broke me.

I waited until most of the staff had gone home for the day to tap his cubicle wall with my pen to get his attention. He was in the middle of editing my last article for the next day's issue.

"What's up?"

"So when you get a few minutes, or want to take a break, can I talk to you in the conference room?"

He narrowed his eyes. "Why?"

"Because I want to talk to you, duh?"

"Why can't you talk to me now? Honestly, I got a shit ton of stuff to do before I leave tonight."

Adrian was going to spend Christmas with his family in Big Bear. It would be the first time in years that he'd spent a holiday with them, and I couldn't help feeling some sense of proud responsibility. He was leaving tomorrow for two weeks.

The timing couldn't have been more perfect. It was an honest-to-goodness Christmas fucking miracle.

Well, it would be, if he ever stopped working long enough for me to tell him. "I realize that you're very busy, but it's very important."

His cell phone rang, and he put up his finger to let me know he'd be right back.

I sighed and went back to reading Twitter. But I stopped again when I noticed Isela walking into the newsroom.

"Where is he?" she said with a pout.

Annoyance bristled every nerve in my body. "He had to take a phone call. He'll be right back. How did you get in here? The lobby is locked at this time of night."

"The security guard recognized me from before. I told him my boyfriend was still working, and he let me in. Okay if I wait here?" She had already sat on his chair, so I nodded. Then she placed a shopping bag on his desk.

I stilled when I realized what she'd just said. Boyfriend? Since when?

"Did you bring him dinner from Bloomingdale's?" I joked, trying very hard not to freak out.

She laughed. "It's matching ski scarves. I bought them for our vacation. I want us to take a photo at the top of the mountain. That way we can use it for our Christmas cards next year."

My heart sank. "Wait. So you're going to Big Bear too?"

"I am. Me and my parents and Adrian and his parents. It's going to be just like the old days. Did he ever tell you that he proposed to me on Christmas Day in the very same cabin we're staying in? It's a sign. Don't you think? I predict we'll be snuggling by the fire by this time tomorrow night."

It was a sign, all right. A sign that I was a big old schmuck.

Adrian came back. "Isela. What are you doing here? How did you—"

"The security guard let her in," I answered for her.

"Surprise," she said and pulled out the scarves. She wrapped one around her neck and then the other one around his. But when she used it to pull him toward her, I decided I'd had enough. Of her. And him.

I stood up. "It's late. I'm going home. If you have any questions, just text me."

He pulled away from Isela. "Wait. I thought you needed to talk to me."

"It's not that important after all. Have a nice vacation. Bye, Isela."

I grabbed my things and moved as fast as I could out the door. As usual, I wasn't fast enough for Mr. Long Legs.

"Are you all right?"

I refused to look at him and stared at the elevator doors. "I'm fine. Just tired."

"So you're not even going to wish me a Merry Christmas? Some friend you are."

I knew he was joking. But I wasn't in the mood for his sarcasm. I lost it. "Yeah, well maybe I don't want to be your friend anymore." The words spilled out of my mouth, and there was nothing I could do to take them back. Especially when I finally looked at him and the expression of shock on his face.

He grabbed my arm. "What the fuck? Seriously? What. The. Fuck. Why are you acting this way?"

The doors opened, and I yanked my arm from his grasp and ran inside the waiting elevator. I pressed the button for the parking garage over and over again. And because I never pick the easy way out of anything, I glanced at Adrian one more time.

Every handsome feature was scrunched in confusion. The seconds seemed to tick by in excruciating torture, and eventually his expression morphed into something I'd never seen on him before.

Pain.

"Why don't you want us to be friends anymore?" he yelled as the doors began to finally move.

My watery eyes met his hurt ones.

"Because I'm in love with you, dummy."

Adrian's stunned face was the last thing I saw as the steel elevator doors closed between us.

The texts came fast and furious. But I turned off my phone as soon as I pulled out of the parking garage. And later, when I was in bed and heard him knocking on my front door, I put on my headphones and tried to go to sleep.

I'd said everything I'd wanted to say. And then some.

I couldn't second-guess my actions. Not anymore.

Because when it came down to it, it didn't matter if Adrian loved me or not. I had to do what was best for me and my career. Plus, when you confess your love to your boss, it's probably a good idea to go work for a new one.

And so the next day, while Adrian was snuggling in a cabin with Isela, I walked into Charlie's office and gave him my two weeks' notice.

Chapter Sixty-Three
SELENA

In a city filled with millions of people, why did I feel so alone?

I looked at my desk calendar and sighed. It had only been three weeks since I'd seen my family, yet I couldn't wait to see them again in just two days.

I was lucky that Kane closed its offices during the holidays. That meant I'd always be able to fly home for Christmas. But there was another reason why I was feeling so lonely. And he hadn't called or checked on me since I'd arrived.

Nathan, obviously, was still mad. Or hurt. Or both.

I'd sent him a text on my first day to let him know that everything had gone well. But he never responded. I tried calling once, and it went straight to voice mail.

In more ways than one, I'd gotten the message.

So I focused on building my new life in New York. I was still living out of a suitcase in the agency's hospitality suite at a nearby hotel. But I had some leads on apartments, and I'd even figured out the subway system in the neighborhood. I called my cousins and my family every other night. My mom told me that I talked to her more now than when I lived in Los Angeles.

In other words, I was getting used to life in the Big Apple.

My stomach grumbled, and I checked the time. It was already getting to be nine p.m., and I hadn't eaten dinner yet. I remembered seeing a Chinese place around the block, so I grabbed my thick coat and headed outside.

It was snowing. And so much colder than I had planned for. Still, I was determined to get food.

I walked the block, shivering every step. By the time I could spot the restaurant's sign, I was jogging. Anything to get out of the cold. This California girl couldn't hang with temps like these. I made a mental note to go shopping while I was home and stock up on leg warmers, mittens, and thick sweaters.

The restaurant was nearly empty when I finally crashed through the front doors. I'd never been so happy to see soup on the wall menu behind the counter and decided to eat it there so it could stay nice and hot. I was about to ask if they also had dumplings when I recognized a figure sitting by himself at the table in the back.

Nathan.

I froze, even though I was pretty frozen to begin with. He was looking down at his phone, so he hadn't seen me yet. That meant it was up to me as to how to handle it.

First, though, I ordered my soup, no dumplings. Nathan stood as I handed cash to the restaurant employee. I took the receipt with my order number and glanced over at him again. He finally looked up and caught me staring. For a moment, I thought he didn't recognize me. Or worse, was going to pretend he didn't recognize me.

He didn't, though. He continued walking and stopped at the counter.

"Hey there," he said with a small smile.

Suddenly, I ached to touch him and feel his arms around me. Why had I been such a fool? This man was gorgeous and smart and funny, and, most importantly, he had me all figured out. I would never find a man like him again.

"Hi, Nathan. Small world, huh?"

"Seems like. Sorry I never texted you back. I got busy and then forgot—you know how it is."

"Sure, of course. No biggie. I had just wanted to thank you again for helping me get this job. It's pretty great."

He nodded. "I'm glad it's working out for you."

We didn't say anything else and just stood there for a few seconds in silence.

"Ma'am?" the cashier said, and I'd never been more grateful for an interruption. "Your soup will be a few more minutes. I will bring it to you at your table." I smiled at him and then back at Nathan.

He cleared his throat and stuck his hands into his navy coat. "Well, I don't want to keep you from your dinner. I better get going. It was nice seeing you, Selena."

And just like that, he disappeared out the door.

A chill ran through my body, even though I was still inside the warmth of the restaurant. It was the emptiness of realizing I'd probably never see him again.

But then I did.

Nathan walked back into the restaurant and stopped in front of me. "I don't play games, Selena. You know that. And I've always told you the truth. So here it is. I miss you. And it kinda hurts when you text and call but won't let me be with you the way I want to be with you. So if you still don't want me, then please give me a break and leave me alone."

I was too stunned to say anything at first. He shook his head, and I think he called himself an idiot and turned toward the door.

He was going to disappear again, and I couldn't take the chance that he'd come back a second time. So I yelled, "No!"

"No?" he said as he walked back to me.

"No. I'm not going to leave you alone. I was an idiot, Nathan. I got scared and I pushed you away. You've never played games with me, and I should've just told you the truth."

"And what's the truth?"

"That I want to be with you. For real. Like dating and stuff."

He smiled finally and moved closer. "Dating and stuff, huh? That sounds fun."

"Oh, it is. So is that a yes?"

"It most certainly is," he said, and he leaned forward to kiss me.

Chapter Sixty-Four
MARI

I hated that I felt like an intruder in my own house.

But that's exactly what I was now.

I had called Letty to let me know when Esteban had left for the day so I could come by and pick up more of my things now that I'd moved into my own apartment back in Inland Valley. She'd texted that morning and said he would be gone by nine.

Although I wasn't technically breaking in, since I still had a key, I didn't like having to go behind Esteban's back. But I had no choice. Through our lawyers, we'd agreed to put the house on the market in January. I had requested numerous times to talk to him in person because he wouldn't return my phone calls or texts. I didn't blame him. He thought I'd betrayed him, and in some ways I had.

If he never talked to me again, I wouldn't have blamed him.

The house was empty. It made me sad not to see a Christmas tree in the foyer or garland around the staircase. Letty had told me that Esteban had forbidden her from putting up any decorations. And if my heart wasn't already broken, it surely wouldn't have survived hearing that.

But I couldn't dwell. I ran upstairs and started grabbing clothes from the drawers and stuffing them in the bag I'd brought with me.

It took me less than ten minutes to get what I needed. The rest could wait for another day.

As I headed down the stairs, I heard motion in the kitchen. Thinking Letty had returned early from her shopping trip, I put down my bags by the front door and walked over to give her a long-overdue hug.

I stopped when I saw Esteban standing over the sink.

"Oh," I said. "It's you."

"What are you doing here?" he replied.

"I needed to get a few things. You wouldn't answer my texts, so I asked Letty if I could come by while you were out. I'm done now, so I'll be leaving."

His face was blank. "She told me I had to come home right away because the sink was flooding the kitchen."

"That's strange. I didn't think she was even here."

He dragged his hand over his face. That's when I noticed how tired he looked. "She's not here. I think she was trying to make us talk."

My heart pounded in my chest. I thought I was ready to see him and talk to him face to face. But I wasn't.

"Oh. Well, I'm sorry she did that. I know you're busy and don't have time to leave the office for things like this. Like I said, I'll go so you can get back to work."

"Are you staying with him?"

I knew who he meant. "No, I'm not. Did he tell you that?"

"No."

"I found an apartment in Inland Valley," I explained.

He raised his eyebrows. "Really?"

"Really. It's a long story."

We stood there staring at each other. I wasn't sure anymore if he wanted me to go.

He folded his arms against his chest. "Chris didn't say you were staying with him. In fact, he denied it too. I just thought he was lying. I always think he's lying now."

My heart sank. "He's not lying. And I'm not lying, Esteban. Chris is not the reason why our marriage wasn't working. I swear. Nothing happened between us."

"Then why?"

And that's when I realized Esteban still didn't understand.

"Because I've been unhappy for a very long time."

"You never said anything."

"I did. Well, I tried. You were never around long enough to listen."

He threw up his hands and walked around the counter. "So this is my fault? I am such a bad husband that I worked long hours to provide you with this beautiful life."

I walked farther into the kitchen. "That so-called beautiful life was both of ours. And I worked just as hard, if not more, to build it."

"How?"

"By becoming the pretty, perfect wife you could show off to your friends and clients. And in the process, I lost the real me."

Esteban's face turned red. He shook his finger at me. "You told me when we first got together that your biggest fear in the world was having to live like you did when you were younger. Everything I've done, Marisol, was to make you feel safe. To show you that I wasn't your father, that you could trust me to always take care of you. I thought that's what you wanted."

His words killed me. Because they were true. "I thought that's what I wanted too."

"When did you change?" His question was an accusation.

I shrugged and noticed how heavy my shoulders were. "I don't know. But I've been trying to tell you, Esteban. I've been trying to tell you that I need to be someone other than just your wife. I need something of my very own . . . and I don't mean a baby."

"But you said . . ."

"No. *You* said. You never asked me. You just assumed. You always assumed, or expected, that I wanted the same thing you did. Or, that you knew better."

He flinched. "I've always asked for your opinion."

"Yes, but then you ignore it if it's not the same as yours."

"That's not fair," Esteban replied.

"What about the fountain?"

"What about it? It's the one you wanted . . . wasn't it?"

The look on my face must have answered his question because his entire body sagged.

It was time to admit it all. It was now or never. "I told you when we first met that I always felt like I wasn't good enough for my dad or smart enough to run my own business. You promised me you would never make me feel like that. Except . . . you did."

The pain that washed over his face killed me a second time. "I did?"

A tear dropped onto my cheek as I sadly nodded.

"You have to know that I didn't mean to ever make you feel that way."

I nodded again.

He took a step closer. "Do you still love me?"

I didn't hesitate. "I do. But sometimes I forget that I need to love me too."

"So that's it? We're over?"

"I don't know." I covered my face in my hands and cried.

Arms encircled my shoulders, and Esteban pulled me against him. "Shh, don't cry. Perdóname. Please, cariño."

He moved my hands and cradled my face with his. "I'm sorry too. I'm sorry that I didn't see how unhappy you've been. Or maybe I did, but I just figured the more things I could give you, the better you would feel. But I was wrong. I know that now."

Esteban pleaded with me with his eyes, and I could see the reflection of regret and sadness. And I hated that it was there because of me. In that moment, the only thing that mattered was that I make that disappear.

My hands came up and cradled his face like he was doing to mine. Then my lips covered his. I kept my eyes open to see his reaction. He did the same. We kissed again and again and again. Soon he was devouring my mouth, while his hands grabbed my ass and lifted me onto the counter.

"I've missed you so much," he panted.

My tears continued to fall as he kissed my mouth, my neck, my chin. This was what I'd wanted. To be wanted by my husband. Not by Chris. Not by any other man ever. I still loved Esteban. Maybe I always would.

"Please," I whispered as he rolled his hips against me. "Please. I need you inside me."

With a groan, he pulled my shirt over my head and unbuckled my jeans. After I wiggled my legs free, he pulled his own pants off. Then he picked me up and carried me to the couch in the family room. I barely had time to take off my panties. Within seconds, he was naked and pulled me on top of him as he sat down on the couch. He reached around to unclasp my bra and quickly latched on to one breast.

"Now, Marisol," he said with a grunt.

I moved until he was inside me, and we became one body, one heart all over again.

Shudders of relief racked my body as my orgasm washed over me. The heaviness I'd been feeling for months disappeared with each wave of pleasure.

Afterward, Esteban held me in his arms a little longer. Even then, I knew things would never be the same between us after this. I was different now. I wanted my life to be different too.

And I had no idea in that moment if that life would include him.

Chapter Sixty-Five
GRACIE

Closing my eyes, I took a breath and prepared myself to do battle.

I entered the Target store, and the craziness of shopping two days before Christmas hit me. There were no shopping carts, and the register lines stretched in every direction. But I couldn't turn back now. So I grabbed a hand basket from a rack in the corner and walked the crowded aisles in search of slippers for my abuela and a specific brand of makeup brushes for Rachel.

A half hour later, I'd found my items and also picked up another roll of tape and gift tags. Then I remembered I had also wanted to get a book for Erica. But as I made my way over to that area, I passed the baby department. Was it my imagination, or did it actually smell different than the rest of the store?

Before I knew it, I was looking at pajama sets, crib sheets, and the tiniest pairs of sneakers I'd ever seen. I hadn't bought anything for the baby except for the book that Sister Catherine had seen. Part of it was that I really hadn't had the time.

"Ms. Lopez?"

I turned around to see the mom of one of my former first graders. Her name was Sarah Dawson, and she looked very, very pregnant.

"Hello, Mrs. Dawson. How are you? Is Annabelle running around nearby somewhere?"

"I'm good. And no Annabelle today. I had to pick up some Santa gifts for her stocking, so she's back at home with her dad."

I offered her a warm smile. "Totally understand. Please wish her a Merry Christmas from me. I really do miss having her in my class. And, it looks like I should also say congratulations." We both looked at her rounded belly. She rubbed the top of it with her palm.

"Thank you. Less than two weeks to go. By the way, I bought those frog pajamas last week," she said, pointing at the one-piece I was holding. "Is that for a baby shower gift or Christmas gift? Because they also have the matching blanket on the other side if you want to spend a little more."

At first, I didn't know how to explain. Or if I should even try.

When I first found out I was pregnant, I did everything I could to hide it.

When it wasn't a secret anymore, it became a challenge. Something I had to overcome in order to survive, almost.

It was time to think of this pregnancy in the only way I should—I was going to have a baby.

"Actually, I'm thinking of buying it for myself. Well, for my baby. I'm due in June."

Mrs. Dawson clapped and gave me a hug. "I'm so happy for you. Have you done your registry yet? Oh, because you definitely want to put the new Graco swing on there."

"What's a Graco?" I asked.

She laughed. "Come with me. I'm about to give you a quick and dirty lesson on everything you will ever need for a baby."

An hour later, I walked out of Target with my Christmas gifts and another bag filled with my first baby purchases.

Chapter Sixty-Six
ERICA

I woke up shivering.

Even underneath my down comforter, I couldn't stop shaking. I looked at the clock and cursed out loud when I saw that it was only four a.m. I had to be up in less than two hours, and I was still so sleepy. I closed my eyes and tried to think of things to make me feel warm—chicken soup, a fireplace, the beach in August. I pulled up my knees and tried to get the comforter snug against me. I knew the heater was on, so I couldn't figure out why I felt so cold. I closed my eyes again and tried to fall asleep.

The shivering eventually went away.

This time I woke up to the buzzing of my cell phone. My eyes opened, and I wondered why there was so much light outside already. I grabbed my phone and said a groggy hello.

"Where are you?" I heard my mother's voice. "Are you just waking up?"

"No, I've been awake. But then I fell asleep. What time is it?"

"It's almost eight."

"What? Oh, my alarm didn't go off. I'll be right there, Mom," I said and hung up without letting her tell me goodbye.

I got dressed in a record two minutes and was out my door in another two. By the time I arrived at my grandparents', the driveway was full of cars. I parked at the end, near the sidewalk, even though I knew I'd eventually have to move when people started leaving later.

I walked in and expected to see everyone in the patio chattering away while they worked. Instead, there were only a few of my younger cousins sitting around looking at their cell phones. From inside, I heard the sound of voices and laughter.

"Erica!" Tía Espy screamed as I walked through the kitchen door. "You made it, sleepyhead."

My tías and cousins were sitting around my abuela's large dining table eating pan dulce and drinking coffee. I walked over and started saying my hellos and kissing everyone on the cheek. Even Mari. She looked surprised and then gave me a hug.

We had started texting and calling each other a few weeks ago. She and Esteban still weren't living together, and Mari had needed someone to talk to. After all, I was the expert on breakups. I could tell she still loved him, and I hoped they could find their way back to each other one day. In the meantime, she was looking for a job at a restaurant until she could start her own catering business.

"Please tell me you brought the buñuelos?"

"Sí, cómo no. I even packed you your own batch to take home."

I gave her another hug just for that. Then I walked over to my mom, who was filling up the teakettle with water. "Mom, why haven't you started yet? It's late."

"Well, I couldn't get up this morning. I was just so cold. So I stayed in bed longer than I usually do. By the time I got here, your abuela was barely getting dressed. Then your tías and cousins only showed up about a half hour ago. Turns out everyone decided to sleep in a little this morning."

"But the tamales? Usually by now, we're already making the second batch to cook. Are we going to have enough time to cook all of them?"

"Well, we cut down a little this year. Abuela said she didn't want to end up with so many in her freezer. So since we're making less, it will take less time."

"Is the masa ready?"

She smiled. "It will be."

I believed that what truly made my family's tamales stand out from all the rest was the light and tasty masa that held all the fillings inside. Made from corn, the masa required lots of attention and love in order to get it to the perfect consistency and flavor that I began to crave in the months and weeks leading up to Christmas Eve.

I'd had many tamales in my lifetime—both homemade and at restaurants. It never mattered how they were wrapped or what was inside; if the masa was crap to start with, then so was the entire tamale. It didn't escape me that our masa was what it was because of Welita.

An hour later, our tamale assembly line was in full production mode. I had started to spoon pieces of shredded chicken and slivers of green chiles onto a corn husk when I realized there was no jack cheese to put on top. I looked around the table and inside every bowl. I walked inside the house and found my abuela pulling a box of raisins out of the cupboard.

"Abuela, there's no jack cheese outside. Do you have it in here?"

My abuela stopped and put her hand to her forehead. "Ay, el queso! No, mija, I forget the cheese. Marta! Marta!"

My mom came running in and asked what was wrong. In Spanish, my grandmother explained that she forgot to buy the cheese for the chicken tamales and asked her to take her to the store at once.

"Mama Garcia, it's okay. We don't need it."

"Yes, we do," I said. My mom turned to me and raised her eyebrows.

Her voice was slow and determined. "No, we don't, Erica. Abuela is busy, and so is everyone else. We can go without it this one year."

Once my mom raised those eyebrows of hers, it usually meant that was the end of the conversation. But this time I wasn't done talking.

"No, we can't, Mom. We always have cheese in the chicken tamales. I'll go to the store," I insisted.

I turned to walk away, but my mom grabbed my wrist. She told my abuela to go to the patio because one of my tías needed her. After she left, my mother let go of my wrist.

"Erica, I already said we didn't need the cheese. Why are you arguing with me?"

And for no good reason, I just started blubbering like a two-year-old right there in the middle of my abuela's kitchen.

"Because we do need it! It will be different if we don't have the cheese. And it's already different, Mom. Don't you see? Doesn't anyone care? This year is already different because she's not here!"

With that I stormed out of the kitchen, past all my tías and cousins, and into my abuela's backyard.

I stood there in the middle of the tangerine and fig trees and wept into my hands.

"Were they mean to you too?"

I looked down and realized I wasn't the only one crying underneath the trees. Araceli—my tío Ricardo's daughter—walked out from the shadows of the branches. I could see her brown eyes were wet and shiny, and her nose matched her pink pouty lips.

"Who?"

Araceli pointed to my other cousins who were running around the backyard. "Were they mean to you like they were mean to me?"

"No. No one was mean to me, sweetie."

She nodded sadly. "They told me I'm too little to play with them. But I'm not. I'm seven now."

I smiled through my tears. "They're just being silly. Why don't you go inside and get some hot chocolate, okay?"

That seemed to cheer her up, and she went inside the patio just as my mom walked out. I wiped my tears away and folded my arms across my chest.

"What's going on with you, Erica?" She stood in front of me and clasped her hands over mine. "I know this can't just be about the cheese."

I didn't answer because I was afraid I'd start blubbering again.

"Look, this is a hard day for everyone. Especially your abuela. She's worked day and night for the past week trying to get everything ready for the tamales. She called me at one a.m. this morning to remind me for the tenth time to bring more foil pans." My mother's voice broke. "She's been so worried about making the tamales perfect this year, but we all know she's really just distracting herself so she won't think about Welita. And reminding her that she forgot something like buying the cheese, well, she didn't really need to hear it at that moment. Do you understand?"

I nodded. "I just miss her so much, Mom."

She hugged me. "I know, mija. I know."

We stood there for a while just crying and holding each other. My body was shaking, and it had nothing to do with the December cold. Eventually, she let go and dug a Kleenex out from the front pocket of her apron. She wiped her eyes and then mine. Even though my tears were gone, my heart was still heavy.

"Mom, I know you think it's silly that I wanted the cheese so badly. But I'm afraid if we start changing things, then they won't be her tamales anymore, and we'll lose a part of her."

My mom smiled a little. "Erica, what makes them Welita's tamales—is the masa. It is and will always be her recipe."

Evidently satisfied that I wasn't going to break down again, my mom hugged me one more time and told me to come back inside. I told her to give me a few minutes and I'd be right in. As she walked away, I felt like there was one more thing I needed to know.

"Mom," I called, and she turned around. "Do you think we're going to be okay?"

She didn't hesitate. "Of course, mija. Welita taught us well."

We both knew we weren't talking about the tamales anymore.

Through the windows of my abuela's enclosed patio, I saw the faces of the people I loved most in this world. I smiled at the sound of their laughter and their voices each trying to talk over one another. It had been a long, rough year for everyone, and there were still some challenges ahead. But today was Christmas Eve, and all that mattered was being together.

I realized then that Welita's legacy wasn't the recipes she had left behind on those yellowed and frayed index cards.

It was all of us. It was family.

I walked inside my abuela's patio, and even though I could feel everyone's eyes on me, I ignored them and went straight to Araceli, who was sitting next to her mom. I grabbed her hand and led her back outside to where the other girls were playing.

I instructed them all to sit in a circle on the grass and told them to listen to me because I had something very important to say. When they were finally quiet, I tried to think of the words Welita had once told me.

"All of you are family," I began. "That is never going to change. Just because someone makes you mad or doesn't share her toys doesn't mean that she doesn't love you. Why? Because you're family, that's why. One day, you girls are going to grow up and move away from each other—"

"Not me," interrupted Jaycee, my tío David's daughter.

"Me either. I'm always going to live with Jaycee," her sister Jenny insisted.

Sophia, my tía Gloria's youngest, raised her hand.

"Yes, Sophia?" I asked softly.

"When I grow up, I want to live here in Abuelo and Abuela's house."

"I think that would be amazing," I said. "But what I want you to remember is that wherever you live, you always need to find a way to stay close with your cousins. Friends will come and go. But your family, tu familia, is forever."

The girls nodded and then got up to go finish playing, even Araceli. I watched them for a bit, and for the first time since Welita passed away, I felt some peace.

It was time to get back to the tamales. I rubbed my eyes one last time and walked back inside to the biggest surprise of my life.

Adrian was standing in the middle of my abuela's patio.

When our eyes met, he didn't smile or nod. He just yelled out, "Why did you quit?"

"You quit?" My mom, who had been sitting at a table next to my tía Espy, shot up from her chair. "Why, Erica? What were you thinking?"

I ignored her and the rest of the questioning looks I could feel being thrown in my direction. But I didn't look at anyone. Only Adrian.

"What are you doing here?" I asked instead.

"Because I need to know why you quit."

"Why aren't you in Big Bear?" The questions in my head wouldn't stop because there was no way this was really happening right now.

"I drove back this morning. I needed to talk to you."

"So, wait, do they work together?" I heard my tía Espy whisper behind me.

Selena whispered back, "I think that's her boss."

"Why does her boss, or her *former* boss, need to talk to her on Christmas Eve? I'm so confused right now."

She wasn't the only one. "Why couldn't this wait until after your vacation?"

"I'll tell you if you tell me why you quit."

"I . . ." The words wouldn't come out. Couldn't.

I finally looked around the patio, and the first eyes I met belonged to Mari. Without saying a word, I pleaded with her to help me. She nodded in understanding.

"These tamales aren't going to make themselves. Come on, everyone, back to work. Erica, why don't you take your friend outside to the front?"

I nodded.

Adrian followed behind me as I walked outside to my abuela's driveway. Cars were packed in like sardines. I stopped walking once I got to my mom's SUV.

"How did you know I was here?" I asked when he joined me.

"I tried calling your cell a couple of times, but you didn't answer," he explained.

"My phone is charging inside the house."

He looked away. "Anyway, your personnel file has your parents' phone listed as an emergency contact. Your dad told me where you were."

"You talked to my dad?" I couldn't grasp anything he was saying.

His quick nod turned into a furious shaking. "Look, I'm sorry for just barging into your Christmas Eve like this. But I don't understand what's going on. And I really need to. Were you already planning to quit before . . ."

"Before I told you that I was in love with you?" The calmness in my voice surprised me. "Yes. I got a job as a features reporter with Above the Fold. I'm going to be working out of their LA office."

Adrian's eyes widened. "Holy shit, Erica. That's amazing. Congratulations."

The sound of genuine enthusiasm, and even pride, in his words warmed my insides despite the cool weather. "Thank you. Now your turn. Why couldn't this wait until you came back from Big Bear?"

"Actually, you still didn't answer my first question. Why did you quit?"

"I told you already. I got another job with Above the Fold."

"But why did you even apply? Am I that horrible of a boss?"

"Yes, of course," I deadpanned. "But that's not why."

"Then why?"

"Honestly, at first, it was because of you. There was a part of me that thought maybe if I didn't work at the *News-Press* anymore, then you'd let yourself see me as more than just your friend and your employee. I thought maybe something more could happen between us."

"Erica, I—"

"Let me finish. That was why I applied, but it's not why I took the job. I took the job because it's time for me to move on. For the longest time, I was comfortable with settling for what was easy. It was why I stayed with Greg for so long. It was why I stayed at the *News-Press*. But when I went to interview, I realized something. I really wanted to work there. Even though I was afraid of what would happen if they turned me down or, especially, if they hired me. Either way, I realized how much I'd been missing out on by not trying for something better. And that's the real reason why I quit."

I was on the verge of tears, and I was so tired of letting him see me cry. Since when had I turned into Gracie?

He came closer. "I came back from Big Bear because Charlie texted me that you had quit. And it made me realize what a coward I'd been."

My heart sped up, and I dug my nails into my palms to keep from hoping. "What do you mean?"

"I mean that I love you, Erica." He took another step toward me and reached out to cup my face. "I think I've been in love with you ever since you danced like a fool to no music at the Scoreboard. But I didn't want to admit it. I told myself my feelings weren't real, that I was confusing them with friendship. And then I screwed up by not making it clear to you that Isela and I weren't back together. We're not. Because even though I convinced myself I couldn't have you, I still didn't want anyone else."

The tears were back, and I didn't care anymore if he saw them. I still couldn't quite believe what was happening. "You love me too?"

He nodded and leaned in. "Yes, you ridiculous woman. I love you so fucking much."

I smiled, and in an instant his lips were on mine. Although I'd imagined it a thousand times, nothing could have prepared me for what it felt like to have Adrian Mendes kiss me. There was nothing timid or unsure about it. Like everything he did in life, there was a purpose. And that purpose was to make me forget the world existed.

When we finally stopped tasting and licking, he hugged me close, and I laid my head against his chest. "And to think this all started because I took a raspberry streusel bar from you," I told him.

He chuckled. "That's right. And come to think of it, you still owe me big-time for that."

"What do you want then?"

Adrian squeezed me tight and then lifted my chin with one finger so he could look into my eyes. "All I want is you, Erica," he whispered. Then he grinned. "Well, you and maybe some of your family's tamales."

Later that afternoon, my cousins and I gathered at the cemetery in front of Welita's marble headstone. We held hands, said a Hail Mary, and then each laid a red rose at her grave. Then we did a group hug.

It had been a tough year. Maybe the toughest of our lives.

But I knew now that we could get through anything as long as we always remembered what she'd taught us—family is the most important thing in the world.

"Merry Christmas, Welita," the four of us said in unison. "Que Dios te bendiga."

Epilogue
GRACIE

"I'm here! I'm here! You can start now," Selena yelled as she came crashing through the hospital room door.

"Did you hear that, baby? Your tía Selena says you can come now," I spat out sarcastically, then immediately regretted it.

Dear God, I'm very sorry for . . . well, for everything that I'm going to say and think until this baby is out of me. Amen.

I had heard labor could bring out the worst in a woman, but I didn't want sarcasm to be the first thing my baby girl heard from her mommy as she entered this world.

After all, that's what she had her tía Erica for.

"Sorry, Selena. I didn't mean it. I'm glad you're . . . oh dear, oh dear, oh dear!" The pain tore through my pelvis like a blazing knife, and I felt like I was going to die. I screamed and cried until the contraction started to subside. Erica and Mari started rubbing my feet again in an effort to soothe some of my anguish. They were standing on either side of the hospital bed, getting ready to bend my legs all the way up to my ears as the nurse had instructed them to just before Selena arrived.

My sister threw down her tote bag and rushed to hold my hand. "There, there now. You're okay, sweetie. Just squeeze my hand and concentrate on my face. Hey, I know what will make you feel better. After this is over, I say we splurge on In-N-Out. I'm starving! Nurse, she can eat a burger after having a baby, can't she?"

The nurse raised her eyebrows and then shook her head. By the look on her face I could tell she was glad the hospital had a limit of only three people in the delivery room. She probably couldn't handle having any more of my family in here for this.

They had been coming in all day. When they weren't arguing with her about why I couldn't eat a sandwich, they were sharing their own labor horror stories. Tía Espy and Tía Marta scared me so much that I asked for a second epidural just a few minutes after the first one just to make sure it wouldn't wear off before the real pain began. Then my mom kept asking the nurse questions about every beep, buzz, and alarm coming from the monitors, and my abuela wanted to bring in Father Benedicto while my catheter was being inserted.

Now they were all waiting in a room down the hall with the rest of the family. I wouldn't have been surprised if the nurse had cornered Father Benedicto and asked him to say a quick prayer for the delivery to go smoothly, just so that the small army could finally go home.

"Holy shit, Selena," Erica yelled. "What's that on your hand?"

"Erica! Please do not cuss—" I stopped as I noticed the giant diamond on my sister's finger. "Jesus Christ, Selena! Did you get engaged?"

A huge smile exploded on her face, and she started jumping up and down. "I did!"

"When?" Mari asked.

Selena's glow matched the bling on her finger. "Last night. He did this big setup with a violinist at our favorite restaurant. I had just said yes when my mom called to tell me that Gracie was in labor."

Everyone started talking at once. Then another contraction hit, and I screamed, "Excuse me! Can I have this baby first before we start discussing centerpieces?"

For the first time in my life, I had silenced a room.

Mari and Erica returned to their positions, and Selena grabbed my hand again. The nurse took another look between my legs and then met my eyes. "Okay, Gracie, it's time to push. Are you ready?"

I panicked for a second and wanted to scream "No!" But then I looked at my cousins and my sister's smiling but tear-streaked face. Deep down in my heart I knew that I wasn't going to do this parenthood thing alone. The three of them, and everyone down the hall, were going on this adventure with me.

I squeezed my sister's hand, took a deep breath, and said, "I'm ready."

AUTHOR'S NOTE

Dear Reader,

Thank you so much for taking the time to read my book. I hope you enjoyed meeting the Garcia cousins and the rest of the family. I can't even put into words just how much this book means to me. It was the first book I ever attempted to write once I decided to finally pursue my dream of becoming a published author. There were certain scenes I couldn't get out of my head, and one night I got out of bed, turned on my laptop, and just started typing. That was in 2012. Over the years, other writing projects became a priority. But every once in a while, I'd open up this book and add words. The book evolved, character names changed, and plot points came and went. But the core story about four Mexican American cousins and their relationship with each other and their great-grandmother stayed the same. In 2017, I heard about a writing contest and decided I would finally try to finish this book so I could enter. I didn't make the cut, but I got so much positive feedback that I was more determined than ever to get it published. A dozen rejections by agents and editors later, I finally got the one yes I needed, and the rest, as they say, is history.

The Garcia family is fictional, but they are definitely inspired by my own large and loud extended family. We also called my maternal great-grandmother Welita, and we were blessed that she lived to be one hundred years old. She taught us that faith and family were the two most important things in life, and I try to remember that lesson every single day. Sadly, when I was in the middle of editing this book, my maternal grandmother passed away at the age of ninety-five. My grandma Rosario, also known as Grandma Chayo, was the second oldest of Welita's children and my immediate family's matriarch. Every family event was centered around her—especially the making of tamales on Christmas Eve morning. Even as I write this, I can't imagine not having her around to tell my cousin Valentine how much salt to add to the masa or triple-check that I'm counting every batch correctly. As in the book, she, too, never said goodbye. Instead, it was always, "Que Dios te bendiga." It would be the last words she ever said to me.

I was blessed to have had these two amazing women in my life for so long. And I am blessed to have so many strong, smart, and independent women in my life still. This book is because of—and for—all of them.

Rosario "Grandma Chayo" Graciano, left, and Eudocia "Welita" Ramirez.

ACKNOWLEDGMENTS

This book has been a journey. And I know I never would've gotten here without the love, support, and efforts of so many.

First, I want to thank my amazing agent, Sarah Younger. You believed in this book from the very beginning and made a dream come true. I feel so lucky to be on #TeamSarah.

Thank you also to Maria Gomez at Montlake for the second yes that changed my life. Your sincere reaction and thoughtful comments touched my heart, and I love that you love each cousin as much as I do. Special thanks to editor extraordinaire Holly Ingraham for your insightful feedback and for helping me find ways to better tell this story. And a shout-out to the rest of the amazing team at Montlake, who worked hard to make sure this version of the book was the best version.

While I might have written the words you just read, there was a very special group of people who held my hand through it all.

To Marie Loggia-Kee and Nichelle Scott-Williams, thank you for your enduring friendship and love. Our writing weekends aren't just productive; they lift my spirit and fill my well.

To Alexis Daria, Priscilla Oliveras, and Mia Sosa, you three are the best writer friends a chica could ever ask for. You have been my inspiration to keep writing, and I'm so thankful for our friendship. And to my Latinx Romance Retreat queridas amigas—Adriana Herrera, Diana Muñoz Stewart, and Zoraida Cordova—thank you for your continued support, cheerleading, and fun Zoom chats. I'm so proud to belong to this community.

To my mom, Rosa; sister, Yolanda; sisters-in-law, Susana and Annie; mother-in-law, Lupe; and all my aunties and cousins, you teach me every day what it means to be a strong, independent Latina who isn't afraid to do things on her own but also knows she can ask for help if she needs it. Thank you for being excited about this book, even though you were a little nervous about what and who I was writing about. I love that you are my family.

And, finally, thank you to my husband, Patrick, and my kids. I couldn't have done this without you. I wouldn't ever want to. I love you all.

ABOUT THE AUTHOR

Photo © 2021 Sabrina Kay Vasquez

Annette Chavez Macias writes stories about love, family, and following your dreams. She is proud of her Mexican American heritage, culture, and traditions, all of which can be found within the pages of her books. For readers wanting even more love stories and guaranteed happily ever afters, Annette also writes romance novels under the pen name Sabrina Sol. A Southern California native, Annette lives just outside Los Angeles with her husband, three children, and four dogs.